The Fifth Form at Saint Dominic's
A School Story

By Talbot Baines Reed

Preface.

The Fifth Form at Saint Dominic's is a story of public-school life, and was written for the *Boy's Own Paper*, in the Fourth Volume of which it appeared. The numbers containing it are now either entirely out of print or difficult to obtain; and many and urgent have been the requests—from boys themselves, as well as from parents, head masters, and others—for its re-issue as a book.

Of the story itself little need be said. It deals in a bright and vigorous style with the kaleidoscopic, throbbing life of a great public school—that world in miniature which, in its daily opportunities and temptations, ambitions and failures, has so often afforded superabundant material for narratives powerful to enchain the attention and sway the emotions, whether to smiles or tears. This will take its place, amongst the best of them.

Though the story is one of school life, its interest is by no means limited to school or college walls. Boys of all sorts and conditions—ay, and their parents too—will follow its fortunes with unflagging zest from the first page to the last; and it is difficult to conceive of any reader, be he young or old, who would not be the better for its vivid portraiture and bracing atmosphere. There is a breeziness about it calculated to stir the better life in the most sluggish; and without pretence or affectation it rings out its warnings, no less than its notes of cheer, clear and rousing as trumpet blasts.

"Do right, and thou hast nought to fear,
   Right hath a power that makes thee strong;
The night is dark, but light is near,
   The grief is short, the joy is long."

Without the most distant approach to that fatal kind of sermonising which all but inevitably repels those whom it is meant to benefit, the story forcefully illustrates how rapidly they may sink who once tamper, for seeming present advantage, with truth, and how surely, sooner or later, a noble character comes to vindication and honour; and in all such respects it is eminently true to life. These boys of Saint Dominic's, even the best of them, are very human—neither angels nor monstrosities, but, for the most part, ardent, impulsive, out-and-out, work-a-day lads; with the faults and failings of inexperience and impetuosity, no doubt, but also with that moral grit and downright honesty of purpose that are still, we believe, the distinguishing mark of the true British public-school boy. Hence one is impelled to take from the outset a most genuine interest in them and their affairs, and to feel quite as though one had known many of them personally for years, and been distinctly the better, too, for that knowledge. Such boys stand at the antipodes alike of the unreal abstractions of an effeminate sentimentalism—the paragons who prate platitudes and die young—and of the morbid specimens of youthful infamy only too frequently paraded by the equally unreal sensationalism of to-day to meet the cravings of a vitiated taste.

The Fifth Form at Saint Dominic's is the kind of book we should place with confidence in the hands of our own boys when leaving the home shelter, whether for school or the sterner after-battle; and we cannot conceive of the parent who, having read it with care and pleasure, as we have done, and knowing at the same time anything of the stress and strain of daily life, would not, with gratitude to the author, gladly do the same. With all their faults, Oliver Greenfield and Wraysford are splendid boys, of just the fibre that the Church needs, and the world cannot afford to do without; and yet their school career proves by no means a bed of roses. To drift with the current is proverbially easy; to seek to stem it manfully, and steer by the stars, may, and often does, lay one open to misapprehension or envy, and all the ills that follow in their train; yet—

"God is God, and right is right,
   And truth the day must win;

To doubt would be disloyalty,
  To falter would be sin."

Our heroes had their full share of trouble—what real hero has not?—but they come out of the ordeal purified and strengthened, with nobler aspirations after duty, and tenderer thoughts of helpfulness towards those needing, if far from seeking, their succouring arm.

How all this comes about it is not for us to tell. Readers will find that out for themselves, and thank us for allowing them, unaided, to do so. The school cricket match, the grand football struggle, the ever-memorable prize-day—these are matters that no alien pen may touch. Our prayer is that God may abundantly bless the book to the building up in our schools and families of strong Christian characters, who in the after days shall do valiant service for Christ and humanity.

G.A. Hutchison.

Chapter One.
The Notice Board.

The four o'clock bell was sounding up the staircase and down the passages of Saint Dominic's school. It was a minute behind its time, and had old Roach, the school janitor, guessed at half the abuse privately aimed at his devoted head for this piece of negligence, he might have pulled the rope with a good deal more vivacity than he at present displayed.

At the signal there was a general shuffling of feet and uproar of voices—twelve doors swung open almost simultaneously, and next moment five hundred boys poured out, flooding the staircases and passages, shouting, scuffling, and laughing, and throwing off by one easy effort the restraint and gravity of the last six hours.

The usual rush and scramble ensued. Some boys, taking off their coats and tucking up their sleeves as they ran, made headlong for the playground. Some, with books under their arms, scuttled off to their studies. The heroes of the Sixth stalked majestically to their quarters. The day boarders hurried away to catch the train at Maltby. A few slunk sulkily to answer to their names in the detention-room, and others, with the air of men to whom time is no object and exertion no temptation, lounged about in the corridors with hands in pockets, regarding listlessly the general stampede of their fellows, and apparently not knowing exactly what to do with themselves.

Among these last happened to be Bullinger of the Fifth and his particular friend Ricketts, who, neither of them having any more tempting occupation, were comfortably leaning up against the door of the Fourth junior class-room, thereby making prisoners of some twenty or thirty youngsters, whose infuriated yells and howls from within appeared to afford the two gentlemen a certain languid satisfaction.

"Open the door! do you hear?" shrieked one little treble voice.

"All right!" piped another. "I know who you are, you cads. See if I don't tell Dr Senior!"

"Oh, please, I say, I shall lose my train!" whimpered a third.

"Wait till I get out; see if I don't kick your shins!" howled a fourth.

It was no use. In vain these bantams stormed and raved, and entreated and blubbered. The handle would not turn, and the door would not yield. Mr Bullinger and his friend vouchsafed no reply, either to their threats or their supplications, and how long the blockade might have lasted it is impossible to say, had not a fresh dissension called the beleaguerers away. A cluster of boys at a corner of the big corridor near the main entrance attracted their curiosity, and suggested a possibility of even more entertainment than the goading into fury of a parcel of little boys, so, taking advantage of a moment when the besieged had combined, shoulder to shoulder, to make one magnificent and desperate onslaught on to the obdurate door, they quietly "raised the siege," and quitting their hold, left the phalanx of small heroes to topple head over heels and one over another on to the stone floor of the passage, while they sauntered off arm-in-arm to the scene of the new excitement.

The object which had attracted the knot of boys whom they now joined was the School Notice Board, on which, from time to time, were posted notices of general and particular interest to the school. On this particular afternoon (the first Friday of the Summer term) it was, as usual, crowded with announcements, each interesting in its way.

The first was in the handwriting of Dr Senior's secretary, and ran as follows:—

"A Nightingale Scholarship, value 50 pounds a year for three years, will fall vacant at Michaelmas. Boys under seventeen are eligible. Particulars and subject of examination can be had any evening next week in the secretary's room."

"Fifty-pounds a year *for* three years!" exclaimed a small boy, with a half whistle. "I wouldn't mind getting that!"

"Well, why don't you, you avaricious young Jew? You're under seventeen, I suppose?" retorted the amiable Mr Bullinger, thereby raising a laugh at the expense of this little boy of eleven, who retired from the scene extinguished.

The next notice was in the classical handwriting of the secretary of the Sixth Form Literary Society, and ran as follows:—

"This Society will meet on Tuesday. Subject for debate, 'That the present age is degenerate,' moved by A.E. Callander, opposed by T. Winter. Boys from the Senior Fifth are invited as auditors."

This notice, even with the patronising postscript, would have passed without comment, as Sixth Form notices usually did, had not some audacious hand ventured to alter a word and make the subject of debate, instead of "That the present age is degenerate," read "That the present Sixth is degenerate." Who the perpetrator of this outrage might be was a mystery, but the alteration was quite enough to render the notice very amusing to many of the readers, especially the Fifth Form boys, and very terrible to others, especially the small boys, who looked nervous and guilty, and did not dare by the slightest sign to join in the mirth of their irreverent seniors. Most of the assembly agreed that "there would be a row about it," with which assurance they passed on to the next notice.

"Wanted, a Smart Fag. No Tadpoles or Guinea-pigs need apply. Horace Wraysford, Fifth Form."

"Bravo, Horatius!" said Ricketts. "A lucky young cub it will be that he takes on," added he, turning to a group of the small boys near. "He'll do your sums and look over your exercises for you like one o'clock. Ugh! though, I suppose every man Jack of you is a Tadpole or a Pig?"

Tadpoles and Guinea-pigs, I should say, were the names given to two combinations or clubs in the clannish Junior School, the mysteries of which were known only to their members, but which were not regarded with favour by the older boys.

As no one answered this charge, Ricketts indulged in a few general threats, and a few not very complimentary comments on the clubs in question, and then returned to the notice board, which contained two more announcements.

"Cricket Notices. To-morrow will be a final big practice, when the elevens for the 'A to M *versus* N to Z' match on the 25th will be chosen. 'Sixth *versus* School' will be played on the 1st proxo. The School Eleven will be selected from among players in the two above matches."

"A private meeting of the Fifth will be held this afternoon at 4.30 to discuss an important matter."

"Hullo!" said Bullinger, looking up at the clock, "it's half-past now! Come along, Rick."

And the two demagogues disappeared arm-in-arm down the passage, followed by the admiring glances of the juniors, who spent the next half-hour in wondering what could be the important matter under consideration at the private meeting of the Fifth. The universal conclusion was that it had reference to the suppression of the Tadpoles and Guinea-pigs—a proceeding the very suggestion of which made those small animals tremble with mingled rage and fear, and sent them off wriggling to their own quarters, there to deliberate on the means of defence necessary to protect themselves from the common enemy.

The meeting in the Fifth, however, was to consider a far more important subject than the rebellious clubs of the Junior School.

The reader will doubtless have inferred, from what has already been said, that the young gentlemen of the Fifth Form at Saint Dominic's entertained, among other emotions, a sentiment something like jealousy of their seniors and superiors in the sixth. Perhaps Saint Dominic's is not the only school in which such a feeling has existed; but, at any rate during the particular period to which I am referring, it was pretty strong there. Not that the two Forms were at war, or that there was any fear of actual hostilities. It was not so bad as all that. But the Fifth were too near the heroes of the top Form to consent to submit to their authority. They would be Sixth men themselves soon, and then of course they would expect the whole school to reverence them. But till that time they resented the idea of bowing before these future comrades; and not only that, they took every opportunity of asserting their authority among the juniors, and claiming the allegiance for themselves they refused to render to others. And they succeeded in this very well, for they took pains to make themselves popular in the school, and to appear as the champions quite as much as the bullies of the small fry. The consequence was that while Tadpoles and Guinea-pigs quaked and blushed in the presence of the majestic Sixth, they quaked and smirked in the presence of the Fifth, and took their thrashings meekly, in the hope of getting a Latin exercise looked over or a minor tyrant punished later on.

Just at the present time, too, the Fifth was made up of a set of fellows well able to maintain the peculiar traditions of their fellowship. They numbered one or two of the cleverest boys (for their age) in Saint Dominic's; and, more important still in the estimation of many, they numbered not a few of the best cricketers, boxers, football-players, and runners in the school. With these advantages their popularity as a body was very great—and it is only due to them to say that they bore their honours magnanimously, and distributed their kicks and favours with the strictest impartiality.

Such was the company which assembled on this afternoon in their own class-room, with closed doors, to deliberate on "private and important business." About twenty boys were present, and the reader must let me introduce a few of them, before his curiosity as to the occasion of their assembling themselves together can be satisfied.

That handsome, jovial-looking boy of sixteen who is sitting there astride of a chair, in the middle of the floor, biting the end of a quill pen, is the redoubtable Horace Wraysford, the gentleman, it will be remembered, who is in want of a fag. Wraysford is one of the best "all-round men" in the Fifth, or indeed in the school. He is certain to be in the School Eleven against the County, certain to win the mile race and the "hurdles" at the Athletic Sports, and is not at all unlikely to carry off the Nightingale Scholarship next autumn, even though one of the Sixth is in for it too. Indeed, it is said he would be quite certain of this honour, were it not that his friend and rival Oliver Greenfield, who is standing there against the wall, with his head resting on a map of Greece, is also in for it. Greenfield does not strike one as nearly so brilliant a fellow as his friend. He is quieter and more lazy, and more solemn. Some say he has a temper, and others that he is selfish; and generally he is not the most popular boy in Saint Dominic's. Wraysford, however, sticks to him through thick and thin, and declares that, so far from being ill-tempered and selfish, he is one of the best fellows in the school, and one of the cleverest. And Mr Wraysford is prepared to maintain his allegation at the point of the—knuckle! That hulking, ugly youth is Braddy, the bully, the terror of the Guinea-pigs, and the laughing-stock of his own class-mates. The boy who is fastening a chalk duster on to the collar of Braddy's coat is Tom Senior, the Doctor's eldest son, who, one would have imagined, might have learned better manners. Last, not least (for we need not re-introduce Messrs Ricketts or Bullinger, or go out of our way to present Simon, the donkey of the Form, to the reader), is Master Anthony Pembury, the boy now mounting up onto a chair with the aid of two friends. Anthony is lame, and one of the most dreaded boys in Saint Dominic's. His father is editor of the *Great Britain*, and the son seems to have inherited his talent for saying sharp things. Woe betide the Dominican who raises Tony's dander! He cannot box, he cannot pursue; but he can *talk*, and he can ridicule, as his victims all the school over know.

He it is who has, of his own sweet will, summoned together the present meeting, and the business he is now about to explain.

"The fact is, you fellows," he begins, "I wanted to ask your opinion about a little idea of my own. You know the *Sixth Form Magazine*?"

"Rather," says Ricketts; "awful rubbish too! Papers a mile long in it about Greek roots; and poetry about the death of Seneca, and all that sort of thing."

"That's just it," continued Pembury; "it's rubbish, and unreadable; and though they condescend to let us see it, I don't suppose two fellows in the Form ever wade through it."

"I know *I don't*, for one," says Wraysford, laughing; "I *did* make a start at that ode on the birth of Senior junior in the last, which began with—

"'Hark, 'tis the wail of an infant that wakes the still echoes of
lofty Olympus,'

"but I got no farther."

"Yes," says Tom Senior, "Wren wrote that. I felt it my duty to challenge him for insulting the family, you know. But he said it was meant as a compliment, and that the Doctor was greatly pleased with it."

"Well," resumed Pembury, laughing, "they won't allow any of us to contribute. I suggested it to the editor, and he said (you know his stuck-up way), 'They saw no reason for opening their columns to any but Sixth Form fellows.' So what I propose is, that we get up a paper of our own!"

"Upon my word, it's a splendid idea!" exclaimed Wraysford, jumping up in raptures. And every one else applauded Pembury's proposition.

"We've as good a right, you know," he continued, "as they have, and ought to be able to turn out quite as respectable a paper."

"Rather," says Ricketts, "if you'll only get the fellows to write."

"Oh, I'll manage that," said Anthony.

"Of course you'll have to be editor, Tony," says Bullinger.

"If you like," says the bashful Tony, who had no notion of *not* being editor.

"Well, I call that a splendid idea," says Braddy. "Won't they be in a fury? (Look here, Senior, I wish you wouldn't stick your pins into my neck, do you hear?)"

"What shall we call it?" some one asks.

"Ah, yes," says Pembury, "we ought to give it a good name."

"Call it the *Senior Wrangler*," suggested Ricketts.

"Sounds too like a family concern," cried Tom Senior.

"Suppose we call it the *Fifth Form War Whoop*," proposed Wraysford, amid much laughter.

"Or the *Anti-Sixth*," says Braddy, who always professes an implacable enmity towards the Sixth when none of them are near to hear him.

"Not at all," says Greenfield, speaking now for the first time. "What's the use of making fools of ourselves? Call it the *Dominican*, and let it be a paper for the whole school."

"Greenfield is right," adds Pembury. "If we can make it a regular school paper it will be a far better slap at the Sixth than if we did nothing but pitch into them. Look here, you fellows, leave it to me to get out the first number. We'll astonish the lives out of them—you see!"

Every one is far too confident of Tony's capacity to raise an objection to this proposal; and after a good deal more talk, in which the idea of the *Dominican* excites quite an enthusiasm among these amiable young gentlemen, the meeting breaks up.

That evening, as the fellows passed down the corridor to prayers, a new notice appeared on the board:

"The first number of the *Dominican* will appear on the 24th inst."

"What does it mean?" asked Raleigh of the Sixth, the school captain, of his companion, as they stopped to examine this mysterious announcement; "there's no name to it."

"I suppose it's another prank of the Fifth. By the way, do you see how one of them has altered this debating society notice?"

"Upon my word," said Raleigh reading it, and smiling in spite of himself, "they are getting far too impudent. I must send a monitor to complain of this."

And so the two grandees walked on.

Later in the evening Greenfield and Wraysford sat together in the study of the former.

"Well, I see the Nightingale is vacant at last. Of course you are going in, old man?" said Wraysford.

"Yes, I suppose so; and you?" asked the other.

"Oh, yes. I'll have a shot, and do my best."

"I don't mean to let you have it, though," said Greenfield, "for the money would be valuable to me if I ever go up to Oxford."

"Just the reason I want to get it," said Wraysford, laughing. "By the way, when is your young brother coming?"

"This week, I expect."

"I wonder if he'll fag for me?" asked Wraysford, mindful of his destitute condition.

Greenfield laughed. "You'd better ask the captain about that. I can't answer for him. But I must be off now. Good-night."

And an hour after that Saint Dominic's was as still and silent as, during the day, it had been bustling and noisy.

Chapter Two.

A New Boy.

"Good-Bye, my boy; God bless you! and don't forget to tell the housekeeper about airing your flannel vests."

With this final benediction ringing in his ears, the train which was to carry Master Stephen Greenfield from London to Saint Dominic's steamed slowly out of the station, leaving his widowed mother to return lonely and sorrowful to the home from which, before this day, her youngest son had never wandered far without her.

Stephen, if the truth must be told, was hardly as affected by the parting as his poor mother. Not that he was not sorry to leave home, or that he did not love her he left behind; but with all the world before him, he was at present far too excited to think of anything rationally. Besides, that last remark about the flannel vests had greatly disturbed him. The carriage was full of people, who must have heard it, and would be sure to set him down as no end of a milksop and mollycoddle.

He blushed to the roots of his hair as he pulled up the window and sat down in his corner, feeling quite certain every one of his fellow-travellers must be secretly smiling at his expense. He wished his mother would have whispered that last sentence. It wasn't fair to him. In short, Stephen felt a trifle aggrieved; and, with a view to manifesting his hardihood, and dispelling all false impressions caused by the maternal injunction, he let down the window and put his bare head out of it for about a quarter of an hour, until a speck of dust settled in his eye and drove him back to his seat.

It is decidedly awkward to get dust in your eye when you want to figure as a hero, for the eyes will water, and must be wiped, and that looks particularly like weeping. Stephen refrained from using his handkerchief as long as he could; but it was no use; he must wipe his eye in the presence of his fellow-passengers. However, if he whistled a tune while doing so, no one could suspect him of real tears; so he struck up, "Glide along, my bonny boat," as cheerfully as he could, and mopped his smarting eye at the same time. Alas! the dust only got farther in, and the music, after half an hour's heroic perseverance, flagged altogether. It was no use trying to appear heroic any longer, so, what with pain and a dawning sense of loneliness and home-sickness, Stephen shed a *few* real tears into his handkerchief, an indulgence which did him good in every way, for it not only relieved his drooping spirits, but washed that wretched piece of dust fairly out of its hiding-place.

This relief, with the aid of a bun and a bottle of ginger-beer at one of the stations, set him, so to speak, on his feet again, and he was able to occupy the rest of his journey very pleasantly in drumming his heels on the floor, and imagining to himself all the marvellous exploits which were to mark his career at Saint Dominic's. He was to be a prodigy in his new school from the very first; in a few terms he was to be captain of the cricket club, and meanwhile was to gain the favour of the Sixth by helping them regularly in their lessons, and fighting any one against whom a special champion should be requisite. He was, indeed, just being invited to dinner with the Doctor, who was about to consult him concerning some points of school management, when the train suddenly pulled up at Maltby, and his brother Oliver's head looked in at the window with a "Hullo! here you are! Tumble out!"

Oliver and Stephen were Mrs Greenfield's only children. Their father had died twelve years ago, when Stephen was a baby, and the two boys had been left in charge of an uncle, who had carefully watched over their education, and persuaded his sister to allow her elder boy to go to a public school. Mrs Greenfield had consented, with many tremblings, and Oliver had, four years ago, been sent to Saint Dominic's, where he was now one of the head boys in the Fifth Form. Only a *few* weeks before the opening of this story the boys' uncle had died, leaving in his will a provision for sending Stephen to the same school as his brother, or any other his mother might select. The poor widow, loth to give up her boy, yet fain to accept the offer held out, chose to send Stephen to Saint Dominic's too, and this was the reason of that young gentleman's present appearance on the stage at that centre of learning.

"I'll send up your traps by the carter; we can walk," said Oliver, taking his young brother into charge.

Stephen was only too glad, as it gave him time to breathe before plunging at once into the scene of his future exploits. "Is it far?" he asked.

"Only a mile," said Oliver; "come on. Hullo, Rick, where have you been to?"

This was addressed to Ricketts, whom they met just outside the station.

"Oh! to Sherren's about my togs. I wanted them for the match to-morrow, you know. I've told him if he doesn't send them up in time we'll all get our things made in London, so I guess he'll hurry himself for once. Oh, look here! did you get a paper with the result of the American match? Bother! Here, you kid, what's your name, cut back to the station and get a daily. Look sharp! Bring it to me in my room. Come on, Greenfield."

Master Stephen looked so astonished at this cool request from a total stranger that both the elder boys laughed.

"This is my young brother, Rick, just come—"

"Oh, I beg your pardon," said Mr Ricketts, blushing, "I'll go—"

"No, I'll go," said Stephen, darting off, and expending a penny of his own to get this magnifico of the Fifth his paper.

This little incident served to break the ice for the new boy, who felt highly honoured when Ricketts said he was "much obliged to him."

"By the way," said Oliver, suddenly, "I ought to get my togs up too. Bother that Sherren! I say, Rick, see my young brother up to the school, will you? while I cut back; he can wait in my study."

Stephen felt very desolate to be left thus alone the moment after his arrival, and it did not add to his pleasure to observe that Ricketts by no means appeared to look upon the task of seeing him to Saint Dominic's as a privilege. They walked on in silence for about half a mile, and then encountered several groups of boys strolling out along the road. Ricketts stopped to talk to several of them, and was very nearly going off with one of the party, when he suddenly remembered his charge. It was rather humiliating this, for Stephen; and already his triumphal entry into Saint Dominic's was beginning to be shorn of some of its glory. No one noticed him; and the only one that paid him the least attention appeared to look upon him as a nuisance.

"Here, Tony," suddenly shouted Ricketts to Pembury, who was jogging along on his crutches a little way ahead, towards the school; "do you mind showing this kid the way up? I have to go back with Wren. There's a good fellow."

"Well, that's cool," replied Master Pembury; "I'm not a kid-conductor! Come on, youngster; I suppose you haven't got a name, have you?"

"Yes, Stephen Greenfield."

"Oh, brother of our dear friend Oliver; I hope you'll turn out a better boy than him, he's a shocking character."

Stephen looked concerned. "I'm sure he doesn't mean to do what's wrong," began he, apologetically.

"That's just it, my boy. If he doesn't mean to do it, why on earth does he do it? I shall be sorry if he's expelled, very sorry. But come on; don't mind if I walk too fast," added he, hobbling along by Stephen's side.

Stephen did not know what to think. If Ricketts had not addressed his companion as "Tony" he would have fancied he was one of the masters, he spoke with such an air of condescension. Stephen felt very uncomfortable, too, to hear what had been told him about Oliver. If he had not been told, he could not have believed his brother was anything but perfection.

"I'm lame, you see," said Pembury, presently. "You are quite sure you see? Look at my left leg."

"I see," said Stephen, blushing; "I—I hope it doesn't hurt."

"Only when I wash my face. But never mind that Vulcan was lame too, but then he never washed. You know who Vulcan was, of course?"

"No, I don't think so," faltered Stephen, beginning to feel very uneasy and ignorant.

"Not know Vulcan! My eye! where have you been brought up? Then of course you don't know anything about the Tenth Fiji War? No? I thought not. Dreadful! We shall have to see what you do know. Come on."

Stephen entered Saint Dominic's thoroughly crestfallen, and fully convinced he was the most ignorant boy that ever entered a public school. The crowds of boys in the playground frightened him, and even the little boys inspired him with awe. *They*, at any rate, had heard of Vulcan, and knew about the Tenth Fiji War!

"Here," said Anthony, "is your brother's study. Sit here till he returns, and make the most of your time, for you'll have to put your best foot foremost to-morrow in the Doctor's examination."

So saying, he left abruptly, and the poor lad found himself alone, in about as miserable a frame of mind as a new boy would wish to be in.

He looked about the study; there were some shelves with books on them. There was a little bed let into the wall on one side; there was an easy-chair, and what professed to be a sofa; and there was a pile of miscellanies, consisting of bats and boots and collars and papers, heaped up in the corner, which appeared to be the most abundantly furnished portion of the little room. Stephen sat there, very dismal, and wishing himself home again once more, when the door suddenly opened and a small boy of his own age appeared.

"Hullo! What do you want?" demanded this hero.

"I'm waiting for my brother."

"Who's your brother?"

"Oliver Greenfield."

"Oh, all right! you can get his tea as well as I can; you'll find all the things in the cupboard there. And look here, tell him Bullinger wants to know if he can lend him some jam—about half a pint, tell him."

Poor Stephen! even the small boys ordered him about, and regarded him as nobody. He would fain have inquired of this young gentleman something about Vulcan, and have had the advantage of his experience in the preparation of his brother's tea; but the youth seemed pressed for time, and vanished.

As well as he could, Stephen extricated the paraphernalia of his brother's tea-table from the cupboard, and set it out in order on the table, making the tea as well as profound inexperience of the mystery and a kettle full of lukewarm water would permit. Then he sat and waited.

Before Oliver arrived, four visitors broke in upon Stephen's vigil. The first came "to borrow" some tea, and helped himself coolly to two teaspoonfuls out of Oliver's canister. Stephen stood by aghast and speechless.

"Tell him I'll *owe* it him," calmly remarked the young gentleman, as he departed with his booty, whistling a cheerful ditty.

Then a fag came in and took a spoon, and after him another fag, with a mug, into which he poured half of the contents of Oliver's milk-jug; and finally a big fellow rushed in in a desperate hurry and snatched up a chair and made off with it.

Stephen wondered the roof of Saint Dominic's did not fall in upon these shameless marauders, and was just contemplating putting the stores all back again into the cupboard to prevent further piracy, when the welcome sound of Oliver's voice in the passage put an end to further suspense.

"Well, here you are," said Oliver, entering with a friend. "Wray, this is my young brother, just turned up."

"How are you?" said Wraysford, in a voice which won over Stephen at once; "I heard you were coming. Have you—"

"Oh!" suddenly ejaculated Oliver, lifting up the lid of his teapot. "If that young wretch Paul hasn't been and made my tea with coal-dust and cold water! I'd like to scrag him! And—upon my word—oh, this is too much!—just look, Wray, how he's laid the table out! Those Guinea-pigs are beyond all patience. Where *is* the beggar?"

"Oh!" exclaimed Stephen, starting up, very red in the face, as his brother went to the door; "it wasn't him. I made the tea. The boy told me to, and I didn't know the way. I had to guess."

Oliver and Wraysford both burst out laughing.

"A pretty good guess, too, youngster," said Wraysford. "When you come and fag for me I'll give you a few lessons to begin with."

"Oh! by the way, Wray," said Oliver, "that's all knocked on the head. Loman makes out the captain promised him the first new boy that came. I'm awfully sorry."

"Just like Loman's cheek. I believe he did it on purpose to spite me or you. I say, Greenfield, I'd kick-up a row about it if I were you."

"What's the use, if the captain says so?" answered Oliver. "Besides, Loman's a monitor, bad luck to him!"

"Loman's a fellow I don't take a great fancy to," said Wraysford. "I wouldn't care for a young brother of mine to fag to him."

"You are prejudiced, old man," said Oliver. "But I wish all the same Stephen was to fag for you. It's a pity, but it can't be helped."

"I'll speak to the captain, anyhow," growled Wraysford, sitting down to his tea.

All this was not very pleasant for Stephen, who gathered that he was destined to serve a not very desirable personage in the capacity of fag, instead of, as he would have liked, his brother's friend Wraysford.

However, he did justice to the tea, bad as it was, and the sardines Oliver had brought from Maltby. He was relieved, too, to find that his brother was not greatly exasperated on hearing of the various raids which had been made on his provisions, or greatly disconcerted at Mr Bullinger's modest request for half a pint of jam.

Then, as the talk fell upon home, and cricket, and other cheerful topics, the small boy gradually forgot his troubles, even down to the Fiji War, and finished up his first evening at Saint Dominic's in a good deal more cheerful frame of mind than that in which he had begun it.

Chapter Three.
A Morning with a Tadpole.

It so happened that on the day following Stephen Greenfield's arrival at Saint Dominic's, the head master, Dr Senior, was absent.

This circumstance gave great satisfaction to the new boy when his brother told him of it, as it put off for another twenty-four hours the awful moment when he would be forced to expose his ignorance before that terrible personage.

"You'd better stick about in my room while I'm in school," said Oliver, "and then you can come down to the cricket-field and see the practice. By the way, some of the fellows may be in to bag my ink; they always run short on Friday; but don't let them take it, for I shall want it to-night. Ta, ta; give my love to the *mater* if you're writing home. I'll be back for you after the twelve bell."

And off he went, leaving Stephen to follow his own sweet devices for three hours.

That young gentleman was at no loss how to occupy part of the time. He must write home. So after much searching he unearthed a crumpled sheet of note-paper from one of the drawers, and set himself to his task. As he wrote, and his thoughts flew back to the home and the mother he had left only yesterday, his spirits fell, and the home-sickness came over him worse than ever. What would he not give to change places with this very letter, and go back home!

Here, no one cared for him, every one seemed to despise him. He wasn't used to those rough public schools, and would never get on at Saint Dominic's. Ah! that wretched Tenth Fiji War. What *would* become of him to-morrow when the Doctor would be back? There was no one to help him. Even Oliver seemed determined to let him fight his own battles.

Poor boy! He sat back in his chair and let his mind wander once more back to the snug little home he had left. And, as he did so, his eyes unconsciously filled with tears, and he felt as if he would give anything to escape from Saint Dominic's.

At this moment the door opened and a small boy entered.

He did not seem to expect to find any one in the room, for he uttered a hurried "Hullo!" as he caught sight of Stephen.

Stephen quickly dashed away a tear and looked up.

"Where's Greenfield?" demanded the small boy.

"He's in school," replied Stephen.

"Hullo! what are you blubbering at?" cried the small boy, growing very bold and patronising all of a sudden, "eh?"

Stephen did not answer this home question.

"I suppose you are a new kid, just left your mammy?" observed the other, with the air of a man of forty; "what's your name, young 'un?"

"Stephen Greenfield."

"Oh, my! is it? What form are you in?"

"I don't know yet."

"Haven't you been examined?"

"No, not yet."

"Oh, of course; old Senior's away. Never mind, you'll catch it to-morrow, blub-baby!"

This last epithet was thrown in in such a very gratuitous and offensive way, that Stephen did not exactly like it.

The small youth, however, finding himself in a bantering mood, pursued his questions with increasing venom.

"I suppose they call you Steenie at home?" he observed, with a sneer that was meant to be quite annihilating.

"No, they don't," replied Stephen; "mother calls me Steevie."

"Oh, Steevie, does she? Well, Steevie, were you ever licked over the knuckles with a ruler?"

"No," replied Stephen; "why?"

"Because you will be—I know who'll do it, too, and kick you on the shins, too, if you're cheeky!"

Stephen was quite at a loss whether to receive this piece of news in the light of information or a threat. He was inclined to believe it the latter; and as he was a rash youth, he somewhat tartly replied, "*You* won't!"

The small boy looked astounded—not that he ever contemplated attempting the chastisement about which he had talked; but the idea of a new boy defying *him*, one of the chosen leaders of the Tadpoles, who had been at Saint Dominic's two years, was amazing. He glared at the rash Stephen for half a minute, and then broke out, "Won't I? that's all! you see, you pretty little blubber boy! Yow-ow-ow! little sneak! why don't you cut behind your mammy's skirt, if you're afraid? I would cry if I were you. Where's his bottle? Poor infant! Yow-ow-boo-boo!"

This tornado, delivered with increasing vehemence and offensiveness, quite overpowered Stephen, who stared at the boy as if he had been a talking frog.

That youth evidently seemed to expect that his speech would produce a far deeper impression than it did, for he looked quite angry when Stephen made no reply.

"Wretched little sneak!" the amiable one continued; "I suppose he'll go peaching to his big brother. Never mind, *we'll* pay you out, see if we don't! Go and kiss your mammy, and tell your big brother what they did to little duckie Steevie, did they then? they shouldn't! Give him a suck of his bottle! oh, my!" and he finished up with a most withering laugh. Then, suddenly remembering his errand, he walked up to the table, and said, "I want that inkpot!"

Now was Stephen's time. He was just in the humour for an argument with this young Philistine.

"What for?"

"What's that to you? give it up!"

"I shan't give it up; Oliver said it was not to be taken."

"What do you say?" yelled the small boy, almost beside himself with rage and astonishment. "It's my brother's ink, and I'm not to give it up," said Stephen, shutting the top and keeping his hand on it.

It was enough! The patriarch of the Tadpoles knew his strong point was in words rather than action; but this could not be endured. At whatever risk, the dignity of his order must be maintained, and this insolent, mad new boy must be—kicked.

"I'll kick you on the legs if you don't give it up," said the Tadpole, in a suppressed white heat.

Stephen said nothing, but kept his hand on the pot, and awaited what was to follow.

The hero stepped back a pace or two, to allow of a run worthy of the coming kick; and what might have happened no one knows. At that moment the door opened, and Pembury entered on his crutches.

At sight of this Fifth Form celebrity the Tadpole cringed and cowered, and tried to sneak out of the study unobserved. But Anthony was too quick for him. Gently hooking him by the coat-collar with the end of a crutch, he brought him back.

"What are you doing here?"

"Nothing."

"Yes, he is," shouted Stephen; "he's been trying to take, away Oliver's ink."

"Silence, young gentleman, pray!" said Pembury, very grandly. Then, turning to the Tadpole, he added, "Oh, so you've been trying to bag some ink, have you?"

"Well, I only wanted a little; and this—"

"Silence! how much ink did you want?"

"Only half a potful."

"You shall have half a potful!" said Pembury. "Come here."

The Tadpole obeyed, and glared triumphantly at Stephen.

"Now, Master Greenfield," said Pembury, addressing Stephen; "have the kindness to hand me the ink."

Stephen hesitated; he felt *sure* Anthony was a master; and yet Oliver's directions had been explicit.

"Do you hear?" thundered Anthony.

"Do you hear?" squeaked the Tadpole, delighted to have the tables turned on his adversary.

"Oliver said I wasn't to let it go," faltered Stephen.

"Do you hear me, sir?" again demanded Anthony.

"Do you hear? give it up!" again squeaked the Tadpole.

Stephen sighed, and surrendered the inkpot. There was an air of authority about Pembury which he dared not defy.

"Now, Master Tadpole, here's your ink; half a pot you said? Put your hands behind you, and stir if you dare!" and Pembury looked so awful as he spoke that the wretched boy was quite petrified.

The Fifth Form boy then solemnly emptied half the inkpot on to the top of the young gentleman's head, who ventured neither by word nor gesture to protest.

"Now you can go, sir!" and without another word he led the small youth, down whose face trickled a dozen tiny streams of black, making it look very like a gridiron, to the door, and there gently but firmly handed him into the passage. The wretched youth flew off to proclaim his sorrows to his confederates, and vow vengeance all over Tadpole and Guinea-pig-land against his tormentor and the new boy, who was the author of all his humiliation.

Pembury meanwhile returned to Stephen. That young gentleman had felt his belief in Pembury's authority somewhat shaken by this unusual mode of punishment, but the Fifth Form boy soon reassumed his ascendency. He produced from his pocket a paper, and thus addressed Stephen: "Dr Senior regrets that he should be absent at such an important time in the history of Saint Dominic's as the day of your arrival, Master Greenfield, but he will be back to-morrow. Meanwhile, you are to occupy yourself with answering the questions on this paper, and take the answers to the head master's study at ten to-morrow. Of course you will not be so dishonourable as to show the questions to any one, not even your brother, or attempt to get the slightest help in answering them. Good-bye, my boy. Don't trouble to stare at my left leg, if it *is* shorter than the other. Good-bye."

Poor Stephen felt so confused by the whole of this oration, particularly the last sentence, which made him blush scarlet with shame, that for some time after the lame boy had hobbled off he could not bring himself to look at the paper. At last, however, he took it up.

This, then, was the awful examination paper which was to determine his position at Saint Dominic's, or else expose his ignorance to the scorn of his masters. How he wished he was on the other side of it, and that the ordeal was over!

"Question 1. Grammar. Parse the sentence, 'Oh, ah!' and state the gender of the following substantives: 'and,' 'look,' 'here.'"

Stephen scratched his head and rubbed his eyes. This was not like anything he had learned at home. They must learn out of quite different books at Saint Dominic's.

"Question 2. History—"

"Hullo," thought Stephen, "they don't give many questions in grammar; that's a good job."

"Question 2. History. Whose daughter was Stephen the Second, and why was he nicknamed the 'Green?'"

Stephen laughed. He had found out a mistake in his examiners. "'Daughter,' the paper said, should be 'son' of course. Funny for Dr Senior to make such a slip," thought he.

"Question 3. History and Geography. Who built England? and state the latitude and longitude of Saint Dominic's, and the boundaries of Gusset Weir."

"*However* am I to know?" murmured Stephen, in despair. "I was never here before in my life. Oh, dear, I shall *never* pass!"

"Question 4. Compound Theology. Give a sketch of the rise and history of the Dominicans from the time of Herod the Conqueror to the death of Titmus."

"Whew!" was Stephen's despairing ejaculation. "I never heard of Titmus; it sounds like a Latin name."

"Question 5. Pure Theology. Who was Mr Finis? Give a list of the works bearing his signature, with a short abstract of their contents. What is he particularly celebrated for?"

"Mr Finis?" groaned Stephen. "How can they expect a boy like me to know who he was? And yet I seem to know the name. Oh dear me!"

"Question 6, and last but one," ("That's a comfort," sighed Stephen). "Mathematics. What is a minus? Describe its shape, and say how many are left when the whole is divided by seven. Reduce your answer to vulgar decimals."

"I'm certain I can never do that. Minus? Minus? I know the name, too. But here's the last."

"Question 7. Miscellaneous. Give a brief history of your own life from the earliest times, being particular to state your vicious deeds in chronological order."

Stephen sighed a sigh of relief. "I can answer that, after a fashion," he said; "but I can't even then be sure of all the dates. As for the others—" and he dashed the paper down on the table with an air of bewildered despair.

"What am I to do? They are all too hard for me. Oh! I wish I might just show them to Oliver. If I was only at home, mother could help me. Oh, dear! I wish I had never come here!"

And he gave himself over to the extreme of misery, and sat staring at the wall until the twelve bell rang, and Oliver and Wraysford broke in on his solitude.

"Hullo, young 'un; in the dumps? Never mind; you'll be used to it in a day or two, won't he, Wray?"

"Of course you will," said Wraysford, cheerily; "it's hard lines at first. Keep your pecker up, young 'un."

The young 'un, despite this friendly advice, felt very far from keeping up his pecker. But he did his best, and worked his face into a melancholy sort of a smile.

"Fish us my spike shoes out of that cupboard, Stee, there's a good fellow," said Oliver, "and come along to the cricket-field. There's a big practice on this afternoon."

Stephen hesitated.

"I've got to do my exam before ten to-morrow. Some one brought me up the paper and said so. Perhaps I'd better stop here and do it?"

"I thought you weren't to be had up till the Doctor came back. Who brought you the paper? I suppose it was Jellicott, the second master?"

"I suppose so," said Stephen, who had never heard of Mr Jellicott in his life before.

"Let's have a look at it," said the elder brother.

"I promised I wouldn't."

"Oh, all serene; I only wanted to see the questions. It's a new dodge giving papers, isn't it, Wray? We were examined *viva voce* in the Doctor's study. Well, come on, old man, or we shall be late. You'll have lots of time for that this evening."

And off they went, the wretched Stephen wrestling mentally with his problems all the while.

Of course, profound reader, you have made the brilliant discovery by this time that Master Stephen Greenfield was a very green boy. So were you and I at his age; and so, after all, we are now. For the more we think we know, the greener we shall find we are; that's a fact!

Chapter Four.
Fagging.

There is a queer elasticity about boys which no one, least of all themselves, can account for. A quarter of an hour after the big practice had begun Stephen had forgotten all about his examination, and could think of nothing but cricket.

As he sat cross-legged on the grass among half a dozen youngsters like himself, he even began to forget that he was a new boy, and was surprised to find himself holding familiar converse with one and another of his companions.

"Well bowled, sir!" shouted Master Paul, as a very swift ball from Ricketts took Bullinger's middle stump clean out of the ground—"rattling well bowled! I say," he added, turning round; "if Ricketts bowls like that to-day week, the others will be nowhere."

"Oh," said Stephen, to whom this remark seemed to be addressed.

Master Paul looked sharply round.

"Hullo, young 'un, is that you? Jolly good play, isn't it? Who are you for, A or Z?"

"What do you mean?"

"Mean? Do you back the A's or the Z's? that's what I mean. Oh, I suppose you don't twig, though. A to M, you know, against N to Z."

"Oh," said Stephen, "I back the A to M's, of course; my brother is in that half."

"So he is—isn't that him going in now? Yes; you see if Ricketts doesn't get him out in the first over!"

Stephen watched most eagerly and anxiously. They were not playing a regular game, only standing up to be bowled at in front of the nets, or fielding at fixed places; but each ball, and each hit, and each piece of fielding, was watched and applauded as if a victory depended on it, for out of those playing to-day the two elevens for the Alphabet match were to be chosen; and out of those two elevens, as every one knew, the School eleven, which would play the County in June, was to be selected. Oliver, despite Paul's prophecy, stood out several overs of Rickett's, and Loman's, and the school captain's, one after the other, cutting some of their balls very hard, and keeping a very steady guard over his wicket. At last a ball of Loman's got past him and snicked off his bails.

Stephen looked inquiringly round at Paul, and then at the small knot of Sixth fellows who were making notes of each candidate's play.

"He's all right," said Paul; "I guess Raleigh," (that was the school captain) "didn't fancy his balls being licked about like that. Never mind—there goes Braddy in."

And so the practice went on, each candidate for the honour of a place in the eleven submitting to the ordeal, and being applauded or despised according as he acquitted himself. Wraysford, of course, came out of the trial well, as he always did.

"I declare, the Fifth could lick the Sixth this year, Tom," said Pembury to Tom Senior, as they sat together looking on.

"I'm sure they could; I hope we challenge them."

Just then a Sixth Form fellow strolled up to where the speakers were standing.

"I say, Loman," said Pembury, "we were just saying our men could lick yours all to fits. Don't you think so yourself?"

"Can't say I do; but you are such a wonderful lot of heroes, you Fifth, that there's no saying what you couldn't do if you tried," replied Loman, with a sneer.

"But you take such precious good care we shall not try, that's just it," said Pembury, winking at his companion. "Never mind, we'll astonish you some day," growled the editor of the *Dominican* as he hobbled away.

Loman strolled up to where the small boys were sitting.

"Which of you is young Greenfield?" he said.

"I am," said Stephen, promptly.

"Run with this letter to the post, then, and bring me back some stamps while you are there, and get tea ready for two in my study by half-past six—do you hear?"

And off he went, leaving Stephen gaping at the letter in his hand, and quite bewildered as to the orders about tea.

Master Paul enjoyed his perplexity.

"I suppose you thought you were going to get off fagging. I say, you'll have to take that letter sharp, or you'll be late."

"Where's the post-office?"

"About a mile down Maltby Road. Look here, as you are going there, get me a pound of raisins, will you?—there's a good chap. We'll square up to-night."

Stephen got up and started on his errands in great disgust.

He didn't see why he was to be ordered about and sent jobs for the other boys, just at a time, too, when he was enjoying himself. However, it couldn't be helped.

Three or four fellows stopped him as he walked with the letter in his hand to the gates.

"Oh, are you going to the post? Look here, young 'un, just call in at Splicer's about my bat, will you? thanks awfully!" said one.

Another wanted him to buy a sixpenny novel at the library; a third commissioned him to invest threepence in "mixed sweets, chiefly peppermint;" and a fourth to call at Grounding, the naturalist's, with a dead white mouse which the owner wanted stuffed.

After this, Stephen—already becoming a little more knowing—stuffed the letter in his pocket, and took care, if ever he passed any one, not to look as if he was going anywhere, for fear of being entrusted with a further mission.

He discharged all his errands to the best of his ability, including that relating to the dead mouse, which he had great difficulty in rescuing from the clutches of a hungry dog on the way down, and then returned with Paul's raisins in one pocket, the mixed sweets in another, the book in another, and the other boy's bat over his shoulder.

Paul was awaiting him at the gate of Saint Dominic's.

"Got them?" he shouted out, when Stephen was still twenty yards off.

Stephen nodded.

"How much?" inquired Paul.

"Eighteenpence."

"You duffer! I didn't mean them—pudding raisins I meant, about sixpence. I say, you'd better take them back, hadn't you?"

This was gratitude! "I can't now," said Stephen.

"I've got to get somebody's tea ready—I say, where's his study?"

"Whose? Loman's? Oh, it's about the eighth on the right in the third passage; next to the one with the kicks on it. What a young muff you are to get this kind of raisin! I say, you'd have plenty of time to change them."

"I really wouldn't," said Stephen, hurrying off, and perhaps guessing that before he met Mr Paul again the raisins would be past changing.

The boy to whom belonged the mixed sweets was no more grateful than Paul had been.

"You've chosen the very ones I hate," he said, surveying the selection with a look of disgust.

"You said peppermint," said Stephen.

"But I didn't say green, beastly things!" grumbled the other. "Here, you can have one of them, it's sure to make you sick!"

Stephen said "Thank you," and went off to deliver up the bat.

"What a time you've been!" was all the thanks he got in that quarter. "Why couldn't you come straight back with it?"

This was gratifying. Stephen was learning at least one lesson that afternoon—that a fag, if he ever expects to be thanked for anything he does, is greatly mistaken. He went off in a highly injured frame of mind to Loman's study.

Master Paul's directions might have been more explicit—"The eighth door on the right; next to the one with the kicks." Now, as it happened, the door with the kicks on it was itself the eighth door on the right, with a study on either side of it, and which of these two was Loman's Stephen could not by the unaided light of nature determine. He peeped into Number 7; it was empty.

"Perhaps he's cut his name on the door," thought Stephen.

He might have done so, but as there were about fifty different letters cut on the door, he was not much wiser for that.

"I'd better look and see if his name is on his collars," Stephen next reflected, remembering with what care his mother had marked his own linen.

He opened a drawer; it was full of jam-pots. At that moment the door opened behind him, and the next thing Stephen was conscious of was that he was half-stunned with a terrific box on the ears.

"Take that, you young thief!" said the indignant owner of the study; "I'll teach you to stick your finger in my jam. What do you mean by it?" and a cuff served as a comma between each sentence.

"I really didn't—I only wanted—I was looking for—"

"That'll do; don't tell lies as well as steal; get away."

"I never stole anything!" began Stephen, whose confusion was being rapidly followed by indignation at this unjust suspicion.

"That'll do. A little boy like you shouldn't practise cheating. Off you go! If I catch you again I'll take you to the Doctor."

In vain Stephen, now utterly indignant, and burning with a sense of injustice, protested his innocence. He could not get a hearing, and presently found himself out in the passage, the most miserable boy in all Saint Dominic's.

He wandered disconsolately along the corridor, trying hard to keep down his tears, and determined to beg and beseech his brother to let him return home that very evening, when Loman and a friend confronted him.

"Hullo, I say, is tea ready?" demanded the former.

"No," said Stephen, half choking.

"Why ever not, when I told you?"

Stephen looked at him, and tried to speak, and then finally burst into tears.

"Here's an oddity for you! Why, what's the row, youngster?"

"Nothing," stammered Stephen.

"That's a queer thing to howl at. If you were weeping because you hadn't made my tea, I could understand it. Come along, I'll show you how to do it this time, young greenhorn."

Stephen accompanied him mechanically, and was ushered into the study on the other side of the door with the kicks to that in which he had been so grievously wronged.

He watched Loman prepare the meal, and was then allowed to depart, with orders to be in the way, in case he should be wanted.

Poor Stephen! Things were going from bad to worse, and life was already a burden to him. And besides—that exam paper! It now suddenly dawned upon him. Here it was nearly seven o'clock, and by ten to-morrow he was to deliver it up to Dr Senior!

How *ever* was he to get through it? He darted off to Oliver's study. It was empty, and he sat down, and drawing out the paper, made a dash at the first question.

The answer *wouldn't* come! Parse "Oh, ah!"

"Oh" is an interjection agreeing with "ah."

"Ah" is an interjection agreeing with "oh." It wouldn't do. He must try again.

"Why," cried the voice of Wraysford, half an hour later, "here's a picture of industry for you, Greenfield. That young brother of yours is beginning well!"

Stephen hurriedly caught up his papers for fear any one should catch a glimpse of the hopeless attempts at answers which he had written. He was greatly tempted to ask Oliver about "Mr Finis," only he had promised not to get any help.

"Let's have a look at the questions," again demanded Oliver, but at that moment Loman's voice sounded down the passage.

"Greenfield junior, where are you?"

Stephen, quite glad of this excuse for again refusing to show that wretched paper, jumped up, and saying, "There's Loman wants his tea cleared away," vanished out of the room.

Poor Stephen! There was little chance of another turn at his paper that night. By the time Loman's wants had been attended to, and his directions for future fagging delivered, the prayer-bell rang, and for the half-hour following prayers the new boy was hauled away by Master Paul into the land of the Guinea-pigs, there to make the acquaintance of some of his future class-fellows, and to take part in a monster indignation meeting against the monitors for forbidding single wicket cricket in the passage, with a door for the wicket, an old inkpot for the ball, and a ruler for the bat. Stephen quite boiled with rage to hear of this act of tyranny, and vowed vengeance along with all the rest twenty times over, and almost became reconciled with his enemy of the morning (but not quite) in the sympathy of emotion which this demonstration evoked.

Then, just as the memory of that awful paper rushed back into his mind, and he was meditating sneaking off to his brother's study, the first bed-bell sounded.

"Come on," said Paul, "or they'll bag our blankets."

Stephen, wondering, and shivering at the bare idea, raced along the passage and up the staircase with his youthful ally to the dormitory. There they found they had been anticipated by the blanket-snatchers; and as they entered, one of these, the hero of the inky head, was deliberately abstracting one of those articles of comfort from Stephen's own bed.

"There's young Bramble got your blanket, Greenfield," cried Paul, "pitch into him!"

Stephen, nothing loth, marched up to Master Bramble and demanded his blanket. A general engagement ensued, some of the inhabitants of the dormitory siding with Stephen, and some with Bramble, until it seemed as if the coveted blanket would have parted in twain. In the midst of the confusion a sentry at the door suddenly put his head in and shouted "Nix!" The signal had a magical effect on all but the uninitiated Stephen, who, profiting by his adversaries' surprise, made one desperate tug at his blanket, which he triumphantly rescued.

"Look sharp," said Paul, "here comes Rastle." Mr Rastle was the small boys' tutor and governor. Stephen took the hint, and was very soon curled up, with his brave blanket round him, in bed, where, despite the despairing thought of his paper, the cruel injustice of the owner of the jam-pots, and the general hardness of his lot, he could not help feeling he was a good deal more at home at Saint Dominic's than he had ever yet found himself.

Of one thing he was determined. He would be up at six next morning, and make one last desperate dash at his exam paper.

Chapter Five.
Shaking down to Work.

"Master Greenfield, junior, is to go to the head master's study at half-past nine," called out Mr Roach, the school porter, putting his head into the dormitory, at seven o'clock next morning.

Stephen had been up an hour, making fearful and wonderful shots of answers to his awful questions, half of which he had already ticked off as done for better or worse. "If I write *something* down to each," thought he to himself, "I might happen to get one thing right; it'll be better than putting down no answer at all."

"Half-past nine!" said he to Paul, on hearing this announcement; "*ten* was the time I was told."

"Who told you?"

"The gentleman who gave me my paper."

"What paper? you don't have papers. It's *viva voce*."

"I've got a paper, anyhow," said Stephen, "and a precious hard one, too, and I've only half done it."

"Well, you'll have to go at half-past nine, or you'll catch it," said Paul. "I say, there's Loman calling you."

Stephen, who, since the indignation meeting last night, had felt himself grow very rebellious against the monitors, did not choose to hear the call in question, and tried his hardest to make another shot at his paper. But he could not keep deaf when Loman himself opened the door, and pulling his ear inquired what he meant by not coming when he was told? The new boy then had to submit, and sulkily followed his lord to his study, there to toast some bread at a smoky fire, and look for about half an hour for a stud that Loman said had rolled under the chest of drawers, but which really had fallen into one of that gentleman's boots.

By the time these labours were over, and Stephen had secured a mouthful of breakfast in his brother's study, it was time to go down to prayers; and after prayers he had but just time to wonder what excuse he should make for only answering half his questions, when the clock pointed to the half-hour, and he had to scuttle off as hard as he could to the Doctor's study.

Dr Senior was a tall, bald man, with small, sharp eyes, and with a face as solemn as an owl's. He looked up as Stephen entered.

"Come in, my man. Let me see; Greenfield? Oh, yes. You got here on Tuesday. How old are you?"

"Nearly eleven, sir," said Stephen, with the paper burning in his pocket.

"Just so; and I dare say your brother has shown you over the school, and helped to make you feel at home. Now suppose we just run through what you have learned at home."

Now was the time. With a sigh as deep as the pocket from which he pulled it, Stephen produced that miserable paper.

"I'm very sorry, sir," he began, "I've not had time—"

"Tut, tut!" said the Doctor; "put that away, and let us get on."

Stephen stared. "It's the paper you gave me!" he said.

The Doctor frowned. "I hope you are not a silly boy," he said, rather crossly.

"I'm afraid they are all wrong," said Stephen; "the questions were—were—rather hard."

"What questions?" exclaimed the Doctor, a trifle impatient, and a trifle puzzled.

"These you sent me," said Stephen, humbly handing in the paper.

"Hum! some mistake; let's see, perhaps Jellicott—ah!" and he put on his glasses and unfolded the paper.

"Question 1. Grammar!" and then a cloud of amazement fell over the Doctor's face. He looked sharply out from under his spectacles at Stephen, who stood anxiously and nervously before him. Then he glanced again at the paper, and his mouth twitched now and then as he read the string of questions, and the boy's desperate attempts to answer them.

"Humph!" he said, when the operation was over, "I'm afraid, Greenfield, you are not a very clever boy—"

"I know I'm not, sir," said Stephen, quite relieved that the Doctor did not at once order him to quit Saint Dominic's.

"Or you would have seen that this paper was a practical joke." Then it burst all of a sudden on Stephen. And all this about "Mr Finis," "Oh, ah," and the rest of it had been a cruel hoax, and no more!

"Come, now, let us waste no more time. I'm not surprised," said the Doctor, suppressing a smile by a very hard twitch; "I'm not surprised you found these questions hard. How far have you got in arithmetic?"

And then the Doctor launched Stephen into a *viva voce* examination, in which that young prodigy of learning acquitted himself far more favourably than could have been imagined, and at the end of which he heard that he would be placed in the fourth junior class, where it would be his duty to strain every nerve to advance, and make the best use of his time at Saint Dominic's. Then the Doctor rang his bell.

"Tell Mr Rastle kindly to step here," said he to the porter.

Mr Rastle appeared, and to his charge, after solemnly shaking hands and promising to be a paragon of industry and good conduct, Stephen was consigned by the head master.

"By the way," said the Doctor, as Stephen was leaving, "will you tell the boy who gave you this paper I wish to see him?"

Stephen, who had been too much elated by the result of the real examination to recollect for the moment the trickery of the sham one, now blushed very red as he remembered what a goose he had been, and undertook to obey the Doctor's order. And this it was very easy to do. For as he opened the study-door he saw Pembury just outside, leaning against the wall with his eyes on the clock as it struck ten.

As he caught sight of Stephen emerging from the head master's study, his countenance fell, and he said eagerly and half-anxiously, "Didn't I tell you ten o'clock, Greenfield?"

"Yes, but the Doctor said half-past nine. And you are a cad to make a fool of me," added Stephen, rising with indignation, "and—and—and—" and here he choked.

"Calm yourself, my young friend," said Pembury. "It's such a hard thing to make a fool of you that, you know, and—and—and—!"

"I shall not speak to you," stammered Stephen.

"Oh, don't apologise," laughed Pembury. "Perhaps it would comfort you to kick me. Please choose my right leg, as the other is off the ground, eh?"

"The Doctor wants to speak to you, he says," said Stephen.

Pembury's face fell again. "Do you mean to say he saw the paper, and you told him?" he said, angrily.

"I showed him the paper, because I thought he had sent it; but I didn't tell him who gave it to me."

"Then why does he want me?"

"He wants the boy who gave me the paper, that's all he said," answered Stephen, walking off sulkily to his quarters, and leaving Anthony to receive the rebukes of Dr Senior, and make his apologies for his evil deeds as best he could.

The offence after all was not a very terrible one, and Pembury got off with a mild reprimand on the evils of practical joking, at the end of which he found himself in his usual amiable frame of mind, and harbouring no malice against his innocent victim.

"Greenfield," said he, when shortly afterwards he met Oliver, "I owe your young brother an apology."

"What on earth for?"

"I set him an examination paper to answer, which I'm afraid caused him some labour. Never mind, it was all for the best."

"What, did that paper he was groaning over come from you? What a shame, Tony, to take advantage of a little beggar like him!"

"I'm awfully sorry, tell him; but I say, Greenfield, it'll make a splendid paragraph for the *Dominican*. By the way, are you going to let me have that poem you promised on the Guinea-pigs?"

"I can't get on with it at all," said Oliver. "I'm stuck for a rhyme in the second line."

"Oh, stick down anything. How does it begin?"

"'Oh, dwellers in the land of dim perpetual,'" began Oliver.

"Very good; let's see; how would this do?—

"'I hate the day when first I met you all,
And this I undertake to bet you all,
One day I'll into trouble get you all,
And down the playground steps upset you all,

21

And with a garden hose I'll wet you all,
And then—'"

"Oh, look here," said Oliver, "that'll do. You may as well finish the thing right out at that rate."

"Not at all, my dear fellow. It was just a sudden inspiration, you know. Don't mention it, and you may like to get off that rhyme into another. But I say, Greenfield, we shall have a stunning paper for the first one. Tom Senior has written no end of a report of the last meeting of the Sixth Form Debating Society, quite in the parliamentary style; and Bullinger is writing a history of Saint Dominic's, 'gathered from the earliest sources,' as he says, in which he's taking off most of the Sixth. Simon is writing a love-ballad, which is sure to be fun; and Ricketts is writing a review of Liddell and Scott's *Lexicon*; and Wraysford is engaged on 'The Diary of the Sixth Form Mouse.'"

"Good!" said Oliver, "and what are *you* writing?"

"Oh, the leading article, you know, and the personal notes, and 'Squeaks from Guineapigland and Tadpoleopolis,' and some of the advertisements. Come up to my study, you and Wray, this evening after prayers, I say, and we'll go through it."

And off hobbled the editor of the *Dominican*, leaving Oliver greatly impressed with his literary talents, especially in the matter of finding rhymes for "perpetual."

By the time he and Wraysford went in the evening to read over what had been sent in, the poem on the Guinea-pigs was complete.

They found Pembury busy over a huge sheet of paper, the size of his table.

"What on earth have you got there?" cried Wraysford.

"The *Dominican*, to be sure," said Anthony, gravely.

"Nonsense! you are not going to get it out in that shape?"

"I am, though. Look here, you fellows," said Anthony, "I'll show you the dodge of the thing. The different articles will either be copied or pasted into this big sheet. You see each of these columns is just the width of a sheet of school paper. Well, here's a margin all round—do you twig?—so that when the whole thing's made up it'll be ready for framing."

"Framing!" exclaimed Greenfield and his friend.

"To be sure. I'm getting a big frame, with glass, made for it, with the title of the paper in big letters painted on the wood. So the way we shall publish it will be to hang it outside our class-room, and then every one can come and read it who likes—much better than passing it round to one fellow at a time."

"Upon my word, Tony, it's a capital notion," exclaimed Wraysford, clapping the lame boy on the back; "it does you credit, my boy."

"Don't mention it," said Tony; "and don't whack me like that again, or I'll refuse to insert your 'Diary of the Sixth Form Mouse.'"

"But, I say," said Greenfield, "are you sure they'll allow it to hang out there? It may get knocked about."

"I dare say we may have a row with the monitors about it; but we must square them somehow. We shall have to keep a fag posted beside it, though, to protect it."

"And to say 'Move on!' like the policemen," added Wraysford. "Well, it's evident you don't want any help, Tony, so I'll go."

"Good-bye; don't ask me to your study for supper, please."

"I'm awfully sorry, I promised Bullinger. I know he has a dozen sausages in his cupboard. Come along there. Are you coming, Greenfield?"

And the worthy friends separated for a season.

Meanwhile, Stephen had made his *début* in the Fourth Junior. He was put to sit at the bottom desk of the class, which happened to be next to the desk owned by Master Bramble, the inky-headed blanket-snatcher. This young gentleman, bearing in mind his double humiliation, seemed by no means gratified to find who his new neighbour was.

"Horrid young blub-baby!" was his affectionate greeting, "I don't want you next to me."

"I can't help it," said Stephen. "I was put here."

"Oh, yes, because you're such an ignorant young sneak; that's why."

"I suppose that's why you were at the bottom before I came—oh!"

The last exclamation was uttered aloud, being evoked by a dig from the amiable Master Bramble's inky pen into Stephen's leg.

"Who was that?" said Mr Rastle, looking up from his desk.

"Now then," whispered Bramble, "sneak away—tell tales, and get me into a row—I'll pay you!"

Stephen, feeling himself called upon, stood up.

"It was me," he said.

"It was I, would be better grammar," said Mr Rastle, quietly.

Mr Rastle was a ruddy young man, with a very good-humoured face, and a sly smile constantly playing at the corners of his mouth. He no doubt guessed the cause of the disturbance, for he asked, "Was any one pinching you?"

"Go it," growled Bramble, in a savage whisper. "Say it was me, you sneak."

Stephen said, No, no one had pinched him; but finished up his sentence with another "Oh!" as the gentle Bramble gave him a sharp side-kick on the ankle as he stood.

Mr Rastle's face darkened as he perceived this last piece of by-play.

"Bramble," said he, "oblige me by standing on the form for half an hour. I should be sorry to think you were as objectionable as your name implies. Sit down, Greenfield."

And then the class resumed, with Master Bramble perched like a statue of the sulky deity on his form, muttering threats against Greenfield all the while, and the most scathing denunciations against all who might be even remotely connected with big brothers, and mammies, and blub-babies.

Stephen, who was beginning to feel himself much more at home at Saint Dominic's, betrayed no visible terror at these menaces, and only once took any notice of his exalted enemy, when the latter attempted not only to stand on the form, but upon a tail of Stephen's jacket, and a bit of the flesh of his leg at the same time. Then he gave the offending foot a knock with his fist and an admonitory push.

"Please, sir," squeaked the lordly Bramble, "Greenfield junior is trying to knock me over."

"I was not," shouted Stephen; "he was squashing me with his foot, and I moved it away."

"Really, Bramble," said Mr Rastle, "you are either very unfortunate or very badly behaved. Come and stand on this empty form beside my desk. There will be no danger here of 'squashing' any one's leg or of being knocked over. Come at once."

So Mr Bramble took no advantage by his last motion, and served the rest of his term of penal servitude, in the face of the entire class, under the immediate eye of Mr Rastle.

Directly class was over, Stephen had to go and wait upon Loman for a particular purpose, which the reader must hear of in due time.

Chapter Six.
Mr Cripps the younger.

Loman was a comparatively new boy at Saint Dominic's. He had entered eighteen months ago, in the Fifth Form, having come direct from another school. He was what many persons would call an agreeable boy, although for some reason or other he was never very popular. What that something was, no one could exactly define. He was clever, and good-tempered, and inoffensive. He rarely quarrelled or interfered with any one, and he had been known to do more than one good-natured act. But whether it was that he was conceited, or selfish, or not quite straight, or a little bit of all three, he never made any very great friends at Saint Dominic's, and since he had got into the Sixth and been made a monitor, he had quite lost the favour of his old comrades in the Fifth.

As far as Wraysford and Greenfield were concerned, this absence of goodwill had ripened into something like soreness, by the way in which Loman had made use of his own position as a monitor, on a casual reference by Oliver to the probable coming of Stephen to Saint Dominic's, to secure that young gentleman as his fag, although he quite well knew that Wraysford was counting on having him. Though of course the captain's word was final, the two friends felt that they had not been quite fairly dealt with in the matter. They took no trouble to conceal what they thought from Loman himself, who seemed to derive considerable satisfaction from the fact, and to determine to keep his hand on the new boy quite as much for the sake of "scoring off" his rivals as on the fag's own account.

Loman, Wraysford, and Greenfield *were* rivals in more matters than one. They were all three candidates for a place in the school eleven, and all three candidates for the Nightingale Scholarship next autumn; and besides this, they each of them aspired to control the Junior Dominicans; and it was a sore mortification to Loman to find that, though a monitor, his influence among the small fry was by no means as great as that of the two Fifth Form boys, who were notoriously popular, and thought much of by their juniors.

For these and other reasons, the relations between the two friends and Loman were at the present time a little "strained."

To Stephen, however, Loman was all civility. He helped him in his lessons, and gave him the reversion of his feasts, and exercised his monitorial authority against Master Bramble in a way that quite charmed the new boy, and made him consider himself fortunate to have fallen into the hands of so considerate a lord.

When he entered Loman's study after his first morning's work in class, he found that youth in a highly amiable frame of mind, and delighted to see him.

"Hullo, Greenfield!" he said; "how are you? and how are you getting on? I hear you are in the Fourth Junior; all among the Guinea-pigs and Tadpoles, eh? Which do you belong to?"

"I don't know," said Stephen; "they are going to draw lots for me to-morrow."

"That's a nice way of being elected! I say, have you any classes this afternoon?"

"No; Mr Rastle has given us a half-holiday."

"That's just the thing. I'm going to scull up the river a bit after dinner, and if you'd like you can come and steer for me."

Stephen was delighted. Of all things he liked boating. They lived near a river at home, he said, and he always used to steer for Oliver there.

So, as soon as dinner was over, the two went down to the boathouse and embarked.

"Which way shall you row?" asked Stephen, as he made himself comfortable in the stern of the boat, and took charge of the rudder-lines.

"Oh, up stream. Keep close in to the bank, out of the current."

It was a beautiful afternoon, and Loman paddled lazily and luxuriously up, giving ample time to Stephen, if so inclined, to admire the wooded banks and picturesque windings of the Shar. Gusset Lock was reached in due time, and here Loman suggested that Stephen should get out and go round and look at the weir, while he went on and took the boat through. Stephen acceded and landed, and Loman paddled on to the lock.

"Hello, maister," called down a feeble old voice, as he got up to the gate.

"Hullo, Jeff, is Cripps about?" replied Loman.

"Yas; he be inside or somewheres, maister," replied the old lock-keeper.

"All right! take the boat up; I want to see Cripps."

Cripps was the son of the old man whom Loman had addressed as Jeff. He was not exactly a gentleman, for he kept the Cockchafer public-house at Maltby, and often served behind the bar in his own person. Neither was he altogether a reputable person, for he frequently helped himself to an overdose of his own beverages, besides being a sharp hand at billiards, and possessing several packs of cards with extra aces in them. Neither was he a particularly refined personage, for his choice of words was often more expressive than romantic, and his ordinary conversation was frequently the reverse of edifying; it mainly had to do with details of the stable or the card-room, and the anecdotes with which he enlivened it were often "broader than they were long," to put it mildly. In short, Cripps was a blackguard by practice, whatever he was by profession. He had, however, one redeeming virtue; he was very partial to young gentlemen, and would go a good bit out of his way to meet one. He always managed to know of something that young gentlemen had a fancy for. He could put them into the way of getting a thoroughbred bull-dog dirt-cheap; he could put them up to all the tips at billiards and "Nap," and he could make up a book for them on the Derby or any other race, that was bound to win. And he did it all in such a pleasant, frank way that the young gentlemen quite fell in love with him, and entrusted their cash to him with as much confidence as if he were the Bank of England.

Of all the young gentlemen whose privilege it had been to make the acquaintance of Mr Cripps—and there were a good many—he professed the greatest esteem and admiration for Loman, of Saint Dominic's school, to whom he had been only recently introduced. The two had met at the lock-keeper's house a week ago, when Loman was detained there an hour or two by stress of weather, and, getting into conversation, as gentlemen naturally would, Loman chanced to mention that he wanted to come across a really good fishing-rod.

By a most curious coincidence, Mr Cripps had only the other day been asked by a particular friend of his, who was removing from the country to London—"where," said Mr Cripps, "there ain't over much use for a rod,"—if he knew of any one in want of a really good fishing-rod. It was none of your ordinary ones, made out of green wood with pewter joints, but a regular first-class article, and would do for trout or perch or jack, or any mortal fish you could think of. Cripps had seen it, and flattered himself he knew something about rods, but had never seen one to beat this. Reel and all, too, and a book of flies into the bargain, if he liked. He had been strongly tempted to get it for himself—it seemed a downright sin to let such a beauty go—and would have it if he had not already got a rod, but of a far inferior sort, of his own. And he believed his friend would part with it cheap.

"I tell you what, young gentleman," said he, "I'll bring it up with me next time I come, and you shall have a look at it. Of course, you can take it or not, as you like, but if my advice is worth anything—well, never mind, I suppose you are sure to be up stream in the course of the next week or so."

"Oh, yes," said Loman, who in the presence of this universal genius was quite deferential; "when can you bring it?"

"Well, my time ain't so very valuable, and I'd like to oblige you over this little affair. Suppose we say to-day week. I'll have the rod here, and you can try him."

"Thank you—have you—that is—about what—"

"You mean, about what figure will he want for it? Well, I don't know exactly. They run so very various, do good rods. You could get what they call a rod for ten bob, I dare say. But *you* wouldn't hardly fancy that style of thing."

"Oh no; if it was a really good one," said Loman, "I wouldn't mind giving a good price. I don't want a rotten one."

"That's just it. This one I'm telling you of is as sound as a bell, and as strong as iron. And *you* know, as well as I do, these things are always all the better after a little use. My friend has only used this twice. But I'll find out about the price, and drop you a line, you know. May be 2 pounds or 3 pounds, or so."

"I suppose that's about what a really good rod ought to cost?" said Loman, who liked to appear to know what was what, but secretly rather taken aback by this estimate.

"So it is. It's just a guess of mine though; but I know for *me* he'll put it as low as he can."

"I'm sure I shall be very much obliged to you," said Loman, "if you can manage it for me."

"Not at all, young gentleman. I always like to oblige where I can; besides, you would do as much for me, I'll wager. Well, good-day, Mr—what's your name?"

"Loman—at Saint Dominic's. You'll send me a line, then about the price?"

"Yes, sir. Good-day, sir."

But Mr Cripps had forgotten to send the line, and to-day, when Loman, according to arrangement, came up to the lock-keeper's to receive the rod, the keeper of the Cockchafer was most profuse in his apologies. He was most sorry, but his friend had been ill and not able to attend to business. He had been a *trifle* afraid from what he heard that he was not quite as anxious to part with that rod as formerly. But Cripps had gone over on purpose and seen him, and got his promise that he should have it to-morrow certain, and if Mr Loman would call or send up, it should be ready for him, without fail.

At this stage, Stephen, having explored the weir, rejoined his schoolfellow, and the two, after partaking of a bottle of ginger-beer at Mr Cripps's urgent request, returned with the stream to Saint Dominic's.

The result of this delay was to make Loman doubly anxious to secure this famous fishing-rod, on which his heart was set. Next day, however, he had classes all the afternoon, and could not go himself. He therefore determined to send Stephen.

"I want you to run up to Gusset Weir," said he to his fag, "to fetch me a rod the keeper's son is getting for me. Be quick back, will you? and ask him what the price is."

So off Stephen trotted, as soon as school was over, in spite of the counter attraction of a Guinea-pig cricket match. When he reached the lock, Cripps had not arrived.

"He warn't be long, young maister," said old Jeff, who was one of the snivelling order. "Take a seat, do 'ee. Nice to be a young gemm'un, I says—us poor coves as works wery 'ard, we'd like to be young gemm'un too, with lots o' money, and all so comfortable off. Why, young maister, you don't know now what it is to be in want of a shillun. I do!"

Stephen promptly pulled out one of his five shillings of pocket-money in answer to this appeal, and felt rather ashamed to appear "comfortable off" in the presence of this patriarch.

"Not that I complains o' my lot, young gemm'un," continued old Cripps, pulling his forelock with one hand and pocketing the shilling with the other. "No, I says, the honest working man don't do no good a-grumblin', but when he's got his famerly to feed," (old Cripps was a widower, and his family consisted of the landlord of the Cockchafer), "and on'y this here shillin' to do it with—"

Stephen was *very* green. He almost cried at the sight of this destitute, tottering, honest old man, and before the latter could get farther in his lament another shilling was in his palsied old hand, and the grey old forelock was enduring another tug.

It was well for Stephen that Mr Cripps junior turned up at this juncture, or the entire five shillings might have made its way into the old man's pouch.

Mr Cripps junior had the rod. He had had a rare job, he said, to get it, for his friend had only yesterday had an offer of 3 pounds 15 shillings, and was all but taking it. However, here it was, and for only 3 pounds 10 shillings tell Mr Loman; such a bargain as he wouldn't often make in his life, and he could get him the fly-book for a sovereign if he liked. And Mr Cripps would charge him nothing for his trouble.

After this Mr Cripps junior and the boy got quite friendly. The former was greatly interested in hearing about Saint Dominic's, especially when he understood Stephen was a new boy. Cripps could remember the day when *he* was a new boy, and had to fight three boys in three hours the first afternoon. He was awfully fond of cricket when he was a boy. Was Stephen?

"Oh, yes," said Stephen; "I like it more than anything."

"Ah, you should have seen the way we played. Bless me! I'd a bat, my boy, that could tip the balls clean over the school-house. You've got a bat, of course, or else—"

"No, I haven't," said Stephen. "I shall get one as soon as I can."

"Well, that *is* lucky! Look here, young gentleman," continued Cripps confidentially; "I've taken a fancy to you. It's best to be plain and speak out. I've taken a fancy to you, and you shall have that bat. It's just your size, and the finest bit of willow you ever set eyes on. I'll wager you'll make top score every time you use it. You shall have it. Never mind about the stumpy—"

"Stumpy!" ejaculated Stephen; "I don't want stumps, only a bat."

"What I meant to say was, never mind about the price. You can give me what you like for it. I wish I could make you a present of it. My eye, it's a prime bat! Spliced! Yes. Treble-cane, as I'm a poor man. I'll send it up to you, see if I don't, and you can pay when you like."

And so he chattered on, in a way which quite charmed Stephen, and made him rejoice in his new friend, and still more at the prospect of the bat.

"If it's awfully dear," he said, at parting, with a sort of sigh, "I couldn't afford it. My pocket-money's nearly all gone."

He did not say how.

"Oh, never mind, not if you don't pay at all," replied the genial Cripps. "You'll be having more tin soon, I bet."

"Not till June," said Stephen.

"Well, leave it till June—no matter. But you may as well have the use of the bat now. Good-day, Master Green—"

"Greenfield, Stephen Greenfield," said Stephen.

"Good-day, and give my respects to Mr Loman, and I hope I shall see you both again."

Stephen hoped so too, and went off, highly elated, with Loman's rod under his arm.

Loman pulled rather a long face at hearing the price, and pulled a still longer face when Stephen told him about the bat. He read his fag a long lecture about getting into debt and pledging his pocket-money in advance.

That evening Stephen was solemnly tossed up for by the Guinea-pigs and Tadpoles. "Heads, Guinea-pigs; tails, Tadpoles." It turned up heads, and from that time forward Greenfield junior was a Guinea-pig.

Chapter Seven.
The "Dominican," Number One.

The eventful day had come at last. Anthony and his confederates had worked hard, evening after evening, in the secrecy of their studies, and the first number of the *Dominican* was ready for publication. The big frame had been smuggled in, and the big sheet was now safely lodged behind the glass, with its eight broad columns of clearly-written manuscript all ready to astonish Saint Dominic's. Two nails had surreptitiously been driven into the wall outside the Fifth Form room, on which the precious document was to be suspended, and Tony only waited for "lights out" to creep down and, with the aid of Ricketts and Bullinger, fix it in position. Everything succeeded well. The secret had been kept most carefully, and when, next morning, Saint Dominic's woke up and swarmed down the passage past the Fifth Form class-room, the sight of a huge frame, with the words *The Dominican* staring out from it, and several yards of writing underneath, fairly startled them. Master Paul, the fag who had been deputed to the no easy task of preserving the structure from injury, had a hard time of it, there was such a hustling and crowding in front of it whenever classes were not going on. The little boys squeezed in front; the bigger boys read over their heads; the Sixth examined it from the back of the crowd, and the Fifth Form from various positions watched with complacency the effect of this venture.

At first it was looked upon as a curiosity, then as a joke; then gradually it dawned on Saint Dominic's that it was a Fifth Form production, and finally it appeared in its true light as a school newspaper.

Loman, attracted by the crowd of boys, strolled down the passage to the place and joined the group, just as a small boy was reading aloud the following descriptive extract from:—

"Our Special Correspondent in Guinea-pig Land.

"Last night the ceremony of admitting a new member into the ancient and honourable craft of Guinea-pigs was celebrated with the usual mysteries. The event took place in the fourth junior class-room. The Guinea-pigs assembled in force, with blackened faces and false whiskers. The lights being put out, Brother Bilke proposed, and Brother Smudge seconded, the election of the new aspirant, and the motion being put to the Guinea-pigs, was received with a unanimous grunt. The Guinea-pig elect was then admitted. He was classically attired in a pair of slippers and a collar, and the ceremony of initiation at once commenced. The candidate was stretched across the lowest desk, face downwards, and in this position greeted with the flat side of a cricket-bat by the junior brother present. He was then advanced to the next desk, where a similar compliment was paid by the next youngest; and so on to the senior brother present. Half way through the ceremony the new member expressed a desire to withdraw his candidature, but this motion was negatived by a large majority. When our reporter left, the ceremony was being repeated with the round side of the bat. We understand the new Guinea-pig is keeping his bed to-day after the exciting ceremony of initiation."

This was capital fun, and greatly appreciated by all—even by Stephen, who knew it was intended to represent his own experience, which, mercifully, had not been nearly so sore as pictured.

But the next extract was not quite as pleasing.

"Cricket Notice.

"The Alphabet Match will be played on Saturday. The following are the two elevens (and here the list followed). Of these twenty-two players, it is worthy of mention that fourteen are from the Fifth, and only eight from the Sixth. What is our Sixth coming to?"

This was not at all gratifying to the Sixth Form fellows present. It was unfortunately true, but they did not at all fancy such prominence being given to the fact. The next extract was still more pointed.

"Sixth Form Debating Society.

"The usual meeting of the Sixth Form Debating Society was held last week, the Doctor in the chair. A sprinkling of lads from the Fifth, in their Sunday coats and collars, was present, by kind permission. The subject for discussion was, 'That the present Sixth is degenerate.' In the absence of any member of the Sixth to open the discussion, Master Bramble, captain of the Tadpoles, kindly undertook the task. He had no hesitation in asserting that the Sixth were degenerate. They had fallen off in cricket since he could remember, and in intellect, he was sorry to say, the falling off was still worse. If they would take his advice, they would avoid the playground during the present season, and by all means withdraw their candidate for the Nightingale Scholarship, as he was certain to be beaten by boys in a lower form. As to behaviour, he could point to virtuous behaviour among the Tadpoles, quite equal to that of the monitors. He didn't wish to ask questions, but would like to know what they all found so attractive in Maltby. Then, too, they all oiled their hair. No previous Sixth had ever been guilty of this effeminacy, or of wearing lavender kid gloves on Sundays. He repeated, 'What were we coming to?'"

"Mr R-g-h opened in the negative. He denied all the charges made by the young gentleman who had last spoken. He undertook to get up an eleven to beat any eleven the Tadpoles could put into the field; and as to intellect, why, didn't the Tadpoles, some of them, get their sums done by the Sixth? Besides, even if their intellect was weak, couldn't they use cribs? He didn't use them himself, but he knew one or two who did. He didn't understand the objection to the hair-oil; he used it to make the hair sit down on his head. (Raleigh, it should be said, had a most irrepressible bunch of curls on his head.) He wore kid gloves on Sunday because he had had a pair given him by his great-aunt Jane Ann. He maintained the Sixth was not degenerate.

"Mr L-m-n followed on the same side. He thought it the greatest liberty of any one to discuss the Sixth. He was a Sixth Form fellow, and a monitor, and if he wasn't looked up to he ought to be, and he intended to be. He was in the cricket eleven, and he was intellectual—very, very much so. He was going in for the Nightingale Scholarship, and had no doubt in his own mind as to the result. He hardly understood his friend's reference to Maltby. Why shouldn't he go there and take his fag too if he chose? He didn't see what right the Fifth had to fags at all. He had a fag, but then he was in the Sixth. His fag admired him, and he never told him not to. The Sixth *could not* be degenerate so long as *he* was in it."

"Other speakers followed, including Mr W-r-n, who maintained that Michael Angelo was a greater musician than Queen Anne. He was here called to order, and reminded that Michael Angelo had nothing to do with the degeneracy of the Sixth. He begged leave to explain—

"At this point our reporter fell asleep."

The laughter which greeted the reading of this extract was by no means shared by the Sixth Form boys present, who, had the next selection been in a similar strain, would have quitted the scene and taken their chance of satisfying their curiosity as to the rest of the contents of the paper at a more convenient season.

But the next lucubration was the unfortunate Stephen's examination paper, with the answers thereto embellished, and in many cases bodily supplied, by the fertile Anthony. The luckless Stephen, who was wedged up in the front row of readers, could have sunk into the earth on meeting once more that hateful paper face to face, and feeling himself an object of ridicule to the whole school. For the wonderful answers which now appeared were hardly any of them his own composition, and he did not even get credit for the few correct things he had said. Shouts of laughter greeted the reading, during which he dared not lift his eyes from the ground. But the answer to Question 6, "What is a minus?" was more than human flesh and blood could endure.

"What is a Minus?"

"'Minus' is derived from two English words, 'my,' meaning my, and 'nus,' which is the London way of pronouncing 'nurse.' My nurse is a dear creature; I love her still, especially now she doesn't wash my face. I hated having my face washed. My nurse's name is Mrs Blake, but I always call her my own Noodle-oodle-oo. I do love her so! How I would like to hug her! She sewed the strings of my little flannel vest on in front just before I came here because she knew I couldn't tie them behind by myself—"

"She didn't!" shouted Stephen, in a voice trembling with indignation.

Poor boy! The laughter which greeted this simple exclamation was enough to finish up any one, and, with a bursting heart, and a face crimson with confusion, he struggled out of the crowd and ran as fast as his legs would take him to his own class-room.

But if he imagined in his misery that the whole school was going to spend the entire day jeering at him, and him alone, he was greatly mistaken, for once out of sight Stephen soon passed out of mind in presence of the next elegant extract read out for the benefit of the assembled audience. This was no other than Simon's "Love-Ballad."

Simon, it should be known, was one of the dullest boys in Saint Dominic's, and it was a standing marvel how he ever came to be in the Fifth, for he was both a dunce and an idiot. But he had one ambition and one idea, which was that he could write poetry; and the following touching ballad from his pen he offered to the *Dominican*, and the *Dominican* showed its appreciation of real talent by inserting it:—

"A Love-Ballad.

"I wish I was a buttercup,
Upon the mountain top,
That you might sweetly pick me up,
And sweetly let me drop.
I wish I was a little worm,
All rigling in the sun,
That I myself towards thee might turn
When thou along didst come.
Oh, I wish I was a doormat, sweet,
All prostrate on the floor,
If only thou wouldst wipe thy feet,
On me, what could I want more?"

("Rigling" is possibly "wriggling".)

Simon, who, with true poet's instinct, was standing among the crowd listening to his own poem, was somewhat perplexed by the manner in which his masterpiece was received. That every one was delighted there could be no doubt. But he had an impression he had meant the ballad to be pathetic. Saint Dominic's, however, had taken it up another way, and appeared to regard it as facetious. At any rate his fame was made, and looking as if a laurel wreath already encircled his brow, he modestly retired, feeling no further interest, now his own piece was ended.

Oliver's poem on the Tadpoles, with its marvellous rhymes, fell comparatively flat after this; and Bullinger's first chapter of the History of Saint Dominic's failed to rivet the attention of the audience, which, however, became suddenly and painfully absorbed in the "Diary of the Sixth Form Mouse," from the pen of Wraysford. We must inflict a few passages from this document on the reader, as the paper was the cause of some trouble hereafter.

"Diary of the Sixth Form Mouse.

"Monday.—Up early and took a good breakfast in one of the desks where there was a jam sandwich and several toffee-drops. The Sixth seem to like jam sandwiches and toffee-drops, there are some of them in nearly every desk. The desk I was in had a packet of cigarettes in one corner. They were labelled 'Mild.' I wonder why the Sixth like their cigarettes mild. In the same desk were one or two books written by a man called Bohn; they seemed queer books, for they had Latin and Greek names outside, but all the reading inside was English. It is sad to see the quarrelling that goes on in this room. You would not suppose, to see these monitors walking grandly up and down the passages striking terror into the hearts of all the small boys, that they could possibly condescend to quarrel over the possession of an inkpot or the ownership of an acid-drop found among the cinders. Alas! it is very sad. They don't seem anything like the Sixth of old days. I shall emigrate if this goes on.

"Wednesday.—A great row to-day when the Doctor was out of the room. The two senior monitors engaged in a game of marbles—knuckle down—in the course of which one player accused the other of cheating. There was nearly a fight, only neither seemed exactly to like to begin, and both appeared relieved when the Doctor came in and confiscated the marbles."

And so the diary went on, in a strain highly offensive to the Sixth and equally delighting to the lower forms. After this the Sixth withdrew, not caring to face further taunts of the kind, and leaving a free field to the rest of Saint Dominic's, who perused this wonderful broadside to the end with unflagging interest. Some of the advertisements with which Tony had filled up the gaps caused considerable mirth—such as this: "A gentleman about to clear out his desk, begs to give notice that he will Sell by Auction to-morrow after 'Lights out,' all those rare and valuable articles, to wit:—one and a half gross best cherry-stones, last year's, in excellent condition. About twelve assorted bread crusts, warranted dry and hard—one with a covering of fossilised sardine. Six quires of valuable manuscript notes on various subjects, comprising Latin, Greek, Mathematics, French, and Crambo. One apple, well seasoned, and embellished with a brilliant green fur of two years' growth. And many other miscellaneous treasures, such as slate pencils, nutshells, an antique necktie, several defunct silkworms, a noble three-bladed knife (deficient of the blades), and half a pound of putty. No reserve price. Must be cleared out at whatever sacrifice."

And this was another:—

"This is to give notice, that whereas certain parties calling themselves Guinea-pigs have infringed on our patent rights, we, the Tadpoles of Saint Dominic's, have been and are from time immemorial entitled to the exclusive privilege of appearing in public with dirty faces, uncombed hair, and inky fingers. We have also the sole right of making beasts of ourselves on every possible occasion; and we hereby declare that it is our intention to institute proceedings against all parties, of whatever name, who shall hereafter trespass on these our inalienable rights. By order, B. Smudgeface and T. Blacknose, Secretaries."

This final onslaught broke up the party. The aggrieved Tadpoles rushed to their quarters and fumed and raged themselves into a state bordering on, madness; and vowed revenge till they were hoarse.

It was a curious fact, nevertheless, that at prayers that evening there were more clean faces among the Tadpoles than had been seen there since the formation of that ancient and honourable fraternity.

Chapter Eight.
A Quarrel and a Cricket Match.

The first number of the *Dominican* had undoubtedly caused a sensation; and it would have created far more sensation but for the fact that the Alphabet Match was to be played on the following day. But even this counter-attraction could not wholly divert the mind of Saint Dominic's from this new literary marvel; and a skirmish took place on the very afternoon of its appearance.

Pembury and his friends had quite expected that the Sixth would attempt a high-handed blow at their paper, and they were not disappointed. For no sooner had Loman and his peers stalked away from the scene of their indignation, and found themselves in the retirement of their own room, than they fell to talking in terms the reverse of pleasant about the event of the morning. The least important of their number was specially wroth.

"There's a great row out in the passage to-day," said Raleigh, who was blissfully ignorant of the whole matter; "why can't some of you monitors keep a little better order? The Doctor will be wanting to know what it's all about!"

"All very well," said Raikes, one of the monitors; "but if the Fifth will stick their tomfoolery out in the passage, there's sure to be a row."

"What tomfoolery? Some of you are for ever grumbling at the Fifth."

"And so would you if you saw the complimentary remarks they make about you in this precious newspaper of theirs."

"Oh, the *Dominican*? I must have a look at it by and by; but meanwhile something had better be done to stop that row, or we shall catch it ourselves."

And so saying, the captain left these injured youths to their own counsels, which it is to be feared were moved more by dislike for the *Dominican* than by a burning desire for the good order of the school.

However, they must do something; and there would be nothing inconsistent with their dignity in demanding the withdrawal of the obnoxious broadside on account of the noise it caused. This would be a safe move, and might be checkmate. Loman was deputed to wait upon the Fifth with the demand of the monitors, and lost no time in carrying out this welcome task. Class was just over, and the Fifth were just about to clear out of their room when Loman entered. It was not often that a Sixth Form fellow penetrated into their camp, and had they not guessed his mission they might have resented the intrusion.

"Oh, you fellows," began Loman, feeling not quite so confident now as he had felt five minutes ago, "we can't have that thing of yours hanging out in the passage like that. It makes a crowd—too much row. Whose is it?"

"Not mine," said Wraysford, laughing; "ask Bully—perhaps it's his."

"Not a bit of it," said Bullinger; "it's yours, isn't it, Simon?"

"Only part," said the poet of the "Love-Ballad," "and I presented that to the paper."

"Suppose it was mine?" said Oliver, with a drawl.

"Then," said Loman, losing his temper, "all I can say is, the sooner you clear it away the better."

"Oh! all right; only it's not mine."

"Look here," said Loman, "I'm not going to fool about with you. You may think it all very funny, but I'll report it to the Doctor, and then you'll look foolish."

"How nice! So pleasant it will be to look for once like what you look always," observed Pembury, gnawing the top of his crutch.

At that moment there was a loud shout of laughter in the passage outside, confirming the monitor's complaint. Wraysford walked hastily to the door.

"The next time there's a row like that outside our door," called he to the group outside, "we'll—what do you mean by it, you young blackguard?"

So saying, he caught Master Bramble, who happened to be the nearest offender within reach, by the collar of his coat, and lugged him bodily into the class-room.

"There, now! Do you know this gentleman? He's a monitor. Have a good look at him. He's been complaining of the row you are making, and quite rightly. Take that, and tell all the little Pigs outside that if they don't hold their noise they will find themselves, every man jack of them, *mentioned by name* in the next number!"

So saying, with a gentle cuff he handed the ill-starred Master Bramble out again to his fellows, and from that time there was scarcely a sound audible from the passage.

"Good-bye," said Pembury, kissing his hand to Loman, who all this time had been standing in the middle of the room, in a white heat, and perplexed what to do or say next.

"You aren't going to live here, are you?" asked Bullinger.

"Any one got a toffee-drop?" drily inquired Oliver. To his surprise, and to the surprise of every one, Loman wheeled round towards the last speaker, and without a word struck him a blow on the mouth with his hand.

He saw he had made a mistake, and looked ashamed the moment the deed was done. All eyes turned to Oliver, whose face was crimson with a sudden flush of pain and anger. He sprang to his feet, and Braddy, the bully, was already beginning to gloat over the prospect of a fight, when, to every one's amazement, Oliver coolly put his hands back into his pockets, and walking up to Loman said, quietly, "Hadn't you better go?"

Loman stared at him in astonishment. He had at least expected to be knocked down, and this behaviour was quite incomprehensible.

He turned on his heel and quitted the room without a word; and somehow or other from that time the Fifth heard no more protests from the monitors on the subject of the *Dominican*.

But Oliver's conduct, much as it had astonished the person chiefly concerned, had astonished the Fifth still more. For the first time in the history of their class, as far as they could recollect, a blow struck had not been returned, and they could not tell what to make of it.

The blow had been a cowardly one, and certainly unmerited, and by all schoolboy tradition one fairly demanding a return. Could it be possible their man was lacking in courage? The idea was a shock to most present, who, although Oliver was never very popular among them, as has been said, had never before suspected his pluck. In fact, it was an awkward moment for all, and it was quite a relief when Simon broke silence by asking Oliver, "Why didn't you knock him down, I say?"

"Because I did not choose, if you want to know," replied Oliver, shortly.

"Oh! I beg your pardon," replied Simon, rather taken aback by this brusque answer.

This was not satisfactory. Had the offender been a Guinea-pig, one could have understood the thing; but when it was a Sixth Form fellow—a good match in every respect, as well as a rival—the Fifth were offended at their man for drawing back as he had done.

"I suppose you *will* fight him?" said Ricketts, in a voice which implied that there was no doubt about it.

"Do you?" replied Oliver, briefly.

The boy's manner was certainly not winsome, and, when once put out, it was evident he took no trouble to conceal the fact. He refused to answer any further questions on the subject, and presently quitted the room, leaving more than half his class-fellows convinced that, after all, he *was* a coward.

An angry discussion followed his departure.

"He ought to be made to fight, whether he likes or not," said Braddy the bully.

"Some one ought to pay Loman out," suggested Ricketts, "if Greenfield doesn't."

"A nice name we shall get, all of us," said Bullinger, "when it gets abroad all over the school."

"It's a shame, because one fellow funks, for the whole Form to be disgraced; that's what I say," said some one else.

There were, however, two boys who did not join in this general cry of indignation against Oliver, and they were Wraysford and Pembury. The latter was always whimsical in his opinions, and no one was surprised to see him come out on the wrong side. As for Wraysford, he always backed his friend up, whether others thought him right or wrong. These two scouted the idea of Oliver being a coward; the one with his usual weapon of ridicule, the other with all the warmth of friendship.

"Who calls him a coward?" exclaimed Wraysford, glaring at the last speaker.

Wraysford was not a coward, and looked so ready to avenge his friend by hard knocks, that the boy who had insinuated that Greenfield was afraid withdrew his charge as mildly as he could. "I only meant, it looks as if he didn't like to fight," he said.

"And what business of yours is it what it looks like?" demanded Wraysford.

"Come, old man," said Pembury; "don't eat him up! I fancy Greenfield might screw up courage to pull *his* nose, whoever else he lets off, eh? It's my private opinion, though, Oliver knew what he was about."

"Of course he did," sneered Braddy; "he knew jolly well what he was about."

"Dear me! Is that you, Mr Braddy? I had not noticed you here, or I should not have ventured to speak on a matter having to do with pluck and heroism. I'm glad you agree with me, though, although I didn't say he knew *jolly* well what he was about. That is an expression of your own."

Braddy, who as usual felt and looked extinguished when Pembury made fun of him, retired sulkily, and the editor of the *Dominican* thereupon turned his attack on another quarter. And so the dispute went on, neither party being convinced, and all satisfied only on one point—that a cloud had arisen to mar the hitherto peaceful horizon of Fifth Form existence.

The cricket match of the following day, however, served to divert the thoughts of all parties for a time.

As it was only the prelude to a much more important match shortly to follow, I shall not attempt to describe it fully here, as the reader will probably be far more interested in the incidents of Sixth versus School Match when it comes off.

The Alphabet Match was, to tell the truth, not nearly as interesting an affair as it promised to be, for from the very first the N's to Z's had the best of it. Stephen, who with a company of fellow-Tadpoles and Guinea-pigs was perched on the palings, looking on, felt his heart sink within him as first one and then another of his brother's side lost their wickets without runs. For once he and Bramble were in sympathy, and he and Paul were at difference. The row these small boys kicked up, by the way, was one of the most notable features of the whole match. Every one of them yelled for his own side. There had, indeed, been a question whether every Guinea-pig, whatever his private initial, ought not to yell for the G's, and every Tadpole for the T's; but it was eventually decided that each should yell "on his own hook," and the effect was certainly far more diverting.

The first four men of the A to M went out for two runs between them, and Stephen and Bramble sat in gloomy despair. The next man in knocked down his wicket before he had played a single ball. It was frightful, and the jeers of the Z's were hateful to hear.

But Stephen brightened as he perceived that the next batsman was his brother. "Now they'll pick up!" said he.

"No they won't! Greenfield senior skies his balls too much for my taste," cheeringly replied the small Bramble.

But Stephen was right. For the first time that afternoon the A's made a stand. Oliver's partner at the wickets was Callonby, of the Sixth, a steady, plodding player, who hardly ever hit out, and got all his runs (if he got any) from the slips. This afternoon he hardly scored at all, but kept his wicket carefully while Oliver did the hitting.

Things were looking up. The telegraph went up from 2 to 20. Wraysford, who had hitherto been bowling with Ricketts against his friend, gave up the ball to Raikes, and the field generally woke up to the importance of getting rid of this daring player.

Stephen's throat was too hoarse to roar any more, so he resigned that duty to Bramble, and looked on in delighted silence. The score crept up, till suddenly Callonby tipped a ball into cover-slip's hand and was caught, to the great delight of the Z's, who guessed that, once a separation had been effected, the survivor would soon be disposed of.

The next man in was Loman. He was better as a bowler than a batsman; but he followed Callonby's tactics and played a steady block, leaving the boy he had struck yesterday to do the hitting.

Oliver was certainly playing in fine form, and for a moment his class-fellows forgot their resentment against him in applauding his play. The score was at 35, and the new coalition promised to be as formidable as the last, when Oliver cut a ball past point.

"Run! no! yes, run!" he shouted. Loman started, then hesitated, then started again—but it was too late. Before he could get across, the ball was up and he was run out. He was furious, and it certainly was hard lines for him, although there would have been time enough for the run had he not pulled up in the middle. Forgetful of all the rules of cricket, he turned round to Oliver and shouted, "You are a fool!" as he left the wicket.

Stephen luckily was too much engrossed in watching the telegraph to hear or notice this remark; which, however, was not lost on the Fifth generally, who experienced a return of their former discontent when they observed that Oliver (though he must have heard it) took not the slightest notice of the offensive expression.

The match passed off without further incident. The Z's won in the end by two wickets, after a closer match than it had promised to be at first, and Stephen was comforted for the reverse by feeling sure that his brother at any rate had played his best, and would certainly get his place in the School Eleven.

Chapter Nine.
A Rod in Pickle.

Loman, who had arrived at the same conclusion respecting Oliver's bravery as the majority in the Fifth, did not allow his conscience to trouble him as to his share of the morning's business. He never had liked Oliver, and lately especially he had come to dislike him. He was therefore glad to have made him smart; and now, since the blunder in the cricket match, he felt greatly inclined to repeat the blow, particularly as there did not seem much to fear if he did so.

He was quick, too, to see that Oliver had lost favour with his comrades, and had no hesitation in availing himself of every opportunity of widening the breach. He affected to be sorry for the poor fellow, and to feel that he had been too hard on him, and so on, in a manner which, while it offended the Fifth, as applied to one of their set, exasperated them all the more against Oliver. And so matters went on, getting more and more unsatisfactory.

Loman, however, had other things to think of than his rival's cowardice, and foremost among these was his new fishing-rod—or rather, the rod which he coveted for his own. Until the day after the Alphabet Match he had not even had time to examine his treasure. Three pounds ten was an appalling figure to pay for a rod; "But then," thought Loman, "if it's really a good one, and worth half as much again, it would be a pity to miss such a bargain;" and every one knew the Crippses, father and son, were authorities on all matters pertaining to the piscatorial art. Loman, too, was never badly off for pocket-money, and could easily raise the amount, he felt sure, when he represented the case at home. So he took the rod out of its canvas bag, and began to put it together.

Now, a boy's study is hardly the place in which to flourish a fishing-rod, and Loman found that with the butt down in one bottom corner of the room, the top joint would have to be put on up in the opposite top corner. When this complicated operation was over, there was no room to move it from its position, still less to judge of its weight and spring, or attach the winch and line. Happy thought! the window! He would have any amount of scope there. So, taking it to pieces, and putting it together again in this new direction, he had the satisfaction of testing it at its full length. He was pleased with the rod, on the whole. He attached the line, with a fly at the end, in order to give it a thorough trial, and gave a scientific "cast" into an imaginary pool. It was a splendid rod, just right for him; how he wished he was up above Gusset Weir at that moment! Why, he could—

Here he attempted to draw up the rod. There was an ugly tug and a crack as he did so, and he found, to his disgust, that the hook, having nothing else to catch, had caught the ivy on the wall, and, what was worse, that the top joint of the rod had either snapped or cracked in its inability to bring this weighty catch to shore. It was a long time before Loman was able to disengage his line, and bring the rod in again at the window. The top joint was cracked. It looked all right as he held it, but when he tried to bend it it had lost its spring, and the crack showed only too plainly. Another misfortune still was in store. The reel in winding up suddenly stuck. Loman, fancying it had only caught temporarily, tried to force it, and in so doing the spring broke, and the handle turned uselessly round and round in his hand. This *was* a streak of bad luck, and no mistake! The rod was not his, and what was worse, it was (so Cripps said) a rod of extraordinary excellence and value. Loman had his doubts now about this. A first-rate top-piece would bend nearly double and then not break, and a reel that broke at the least pressure could hardly be of the best kind. Still, Cripps thought a lot of it, and Loman had undoubtedly himself alone to blame for the accidents which had occurred. As it was, the rod was now useless. He knew there was no place in Maltby where he could get it repaired, and it was hardly to be expected that Cripps would take it back.

What was to be done? Either he must pay 3 pounds 10 shillings for a rod of no value, or—

He slowly took the rod to pieces and put it back into the canvas bag. The top joint after all did not look amiss; and, yes, there was a *little* bit of elasticity in it. Perhaps the crack was only his fancy; or perhaps the crack was there when he got it. As to the reel, it looked as if it *ought* to work, and perhaps it would if he only knew the way. Ah! suppose he just sent the rod back to Cripps with a message that he found he did not require it? He would not say he had not used it, but if Cripps chose to imagine he received it back just as he sent it, well, what harm? Cripps would be sure to sell it to some one else, or else put it by (he had said he possessed a rod of his own). If he, Loman, had felt quite certain that he had damaged the rod himself, of course he would not think of such a thing; but he was not at all certain the thing was not defective to begin with. In any case it was an inferior rod—that he had no doubt about—and Cripps was not acting honestly by trying to pass it off on him as one of the best make. Yes, it would serve Cripps right, and be a lesson to him, and he was sure, yes, quite sure now, it had been damaged to begin with.

And so the boy argued with himself and coquetted with the tempter. Before the afternoon was over he felt (as he imagined) quite comfortable in his own mind over the affair. The rod was tied up again in its bag exactly as it had been before, and only wanted an opportunity to be returned to Mr Cripps.

After that Loman settled down to an evening's study. But things were against him again. Comfortable as his conscience was, that top joint would not let him alone. It seemed to get into his hand in place of the pen, and to point out the words in the lexicon in place of his finger. He tried not to mind it, but it annoyed him, and, what was worse, interfered with his work. So, shutting up his books, and imagining a change of air might be beneficial, he went off to Callonby's study, there to gossip for an hour or two, and finally rid himself of his tormentor.

Stephen, meanwhile, had had Mr Cripps on his mind too, for that afternoon his bat had come home. It was addressed to "Mr Greenfield, Saint Dominic's," and of course taken to Oliver, who wondered much to receive a small size cricket-bat in a parcel. Master Paul, however, who was in attendance, was able to clear up the mystery.

"Oh! that's your young brother's, I expect; he said he had got a bat coming."

"All I can say is, he must be more flush of cash than I am, to go in for a thing like this. Send him here, Paul."

So Paul vanished, and presently Stephen put in an appearance, blushing, and anxious-looking.

"Is this yours?" asked the elder brother.

"Yes; did Mr Cripps send it?"

"Mr Cripps the lock-keeper?"

"No, his son. He said he would get it for me. I say, is that a good bat, Oliver?"

"Nothing out of the way. But, I say, young 'un, how much have you given for it?"

"Not anything yet. Mr Cripps said I could pay in June, when I get my next pocket-money."

"What on earth has he to do with when you get your pocket-money?" demanded Oliver. "Who is this young Cripps? He's a cad, isn't he?"

"He seemed a very nice man," said Stephen.

"Well, look here! the less you have to do with men like him the better. What is the price of the bat?"

"I don't know; it's one Mr Cripps had himself when he was a boy. He says it's a beauty! I say, it looks as good as new, Oliver."

"You young muff!" said the elder brother; "I expect the fellow's swindling you. Find out what he wants for it at once, and pay him; I'm not going to let you run into debt."

"But I can't; I've only two shillings left," said Stephen, dejectedly.

"Why, whatever have you done with the five shillings you had last week?"

Stephen blushed, and then faltered, "I spent sixpence on stamps and sixpence on— on brandy-balls!"

"I thought so. And what did you do with the rest?"

"Oh! I—I—that is—I—gave them away."

"Gave them away! Who to—to Bramble?"

"No," said Stephen, laughing at the idea; "I gave them to a poor old man!"

"Where?—when? Upon my word, Stephen, you *are* a jackass—who to?"

And then Stephen confessed, and the elder brother rated him soundly for his folly, till the little fellow felt quite miserable and ashamed of himself. In the end, Oliver insisted on Stephen finding out at once what the price of the bat was, and promised he would lend his brother the money for it. In return for this, Stephen promised to make no more purchases of this kind without first consulting Oliver, and at this juncture Wraysford turned up, and Stephen beat a retreat with his bat over his shoulder.

The two friends had not been alone together since *the fracas* in the Fifth two days before, and both now appeared glad of an opportunity of talking over that and subsequent events.

"I suppose you know a lot of the fellows are very sore at you for not thrashing Loman?" said Wraysford.

"I guessed they would be. Are you riled, too, Wray?"

"Not I! I know what *I* should have done myself, but I suppose you know your own business best."

"I was greatly tempted to let out," said Oliver, "but the fact is—I know you'll jeer, Wray—the fact is, I've been trying feebly to turn over a new leaf this term."

Wraysford said "Oh!" and looked uncomfortable.

"And one of the things I wanted to keep out of was losing my temper, which you know is not a good one."

"Not at all," said Wraysford, meaning quite the opposite to what he said.

"Well, if you'll believe me, I've lost my temper oftener in trying to keep this resolution than I ever remember to have done before. But on Friday it came over me just as I was going to thrash Loman. That's why I didn't."

Wraysford looked greatly relieved when this confession was over. "You are a rum fellow, Noll," said he, after a pause, "and of course it is all right; but the fellows don't know your reason, and think you showed the white feather."

"Let them think!" shouted Oliver, in a voice so loud and angry that Master Paul came to the door and asked what he wanted.

"What do I care what they think?" continued Oliver, forgetting all about his temper; "they can think what they like, but they had better let me alone. I'd like to knock all their heads together! so I would!"

"Steady, old man!" said Wraysford, good-humouredly; "I quite agree with you. But I say, Noll, I think it's a pity you don't put yourself right with them and the school generally, somehow. Everybody heard Loman call you a fool yesterday, and you know our fellows are so clannish that they think, for the credit of the Fifth, something ought to be done."

"Let them send Braddy to thrash him, then; I don't intend to fight to please *them*!"

"Oh! that's all right. And if they all knew what you've told me they would understand it; but as it is, they don't."

"They'll find out some day, most likely," growled Oliver; "I'm not going to bother any more about it. I say, Wray, do you know anything of Cripps's son?"

"Yes. Don't you know he keeps a dirty public-house in Maltby?—a regular cad, they say. The fishing-fellows have seen him up at the Weir now and then."

"I don't know how he came across him, but my young brother has just been buying a bat from him, and I don't much fancy it."

"No, the youngster won't get any good with that fellow; you had better tell him," said Wraysford.

"So I have, and he won't do it again."

Shortly after this Pembury hobbled in on his way to bed.

"You're a pretty fellow," said he to Oliver; "not one of our fellows cares a rush about the *Dominican* since you made yourself into the latest sensation."

"Oh, don't let us have that up again," implored Oliver.

"All very well, but what is to become of the *Dominican*?"

"Oh, have a special extra number about me. Call me a coward, and a fool, and a Tadpole, any mortal thing you like, only shut up about the affair now!"

Pembury looked concerned.

"Allow me to feel your pulse," said he to Oliver.

"Feel away," said Oliver, glad of any diversion.

"Hum! As I feared—feverish. Oliver, my boy, you are not well. Wandering a bit in your mind, too; get to bed. Be better soon. Able to talk like an ordinary rational animal then, and not like an animated tom-cat. Good-bye!"

And so saying he departed, leaving the friends too much amused to be angry at his rudeness.

The two friends did a steady evening's work after this, and the thought of the Nightingale Scholarship drove away for the time all less pleasant recollections.

They slept, after it all, far more soundly than Loman, whose dreams were disturbed by that everlasting top joint all the night long.

The reader will no doubt have already decided in his own mind whether Oliver Greenfield did rightly or wrongly in putting his hands into his pockets instead of using them to knock down Loman. It certainly did not seem to have done him much good at the time. He had lost the esteem of his comrades, he had lost the very temper he had been trying to keep—twenty times since the event—and no one gave him credit for anything but "the better part of valour" in the whole affair.

And yet that one effort of self-restraint was not altogether an unmanly act. At least, so thought Wraysford that night, as he lay meditating upon his friend's troubles, and found himself liking him none the less for this latest singular piece of eccentricity.

Chapter Ten.
The Fourth Junior at home.

Stephen, before he had been a fortnight in the school, found himself very much at home at Saint Dominic's. He was not one of those exuberant, irrepressible boys who take their class-fellows by storm, and rise to the top of the tree almost as soon as they touch the bottom. Stephen, as the reader knows, was not a very clever boy, or a very dashing boy, and yet he somehow managed to get his footing among his comrades in the Fourth Junior, and particularly among his fellow Guinea-pigs.

He had fought Master Bramble six times in three days during his second week, and was engaged to fight him again every Tuesday, Thursday, and Friday during the term. He had also taken the chair at one indignation meeting against the monitors, and spoken in favour of a resolution at another. He had distributed brandy-balls in a most handsome manner to his particular adherents, and he had been the means of carrying away no less than two blankets from the next dormitory. This was pretty good for a fortnight. Add to this that he had remained steadily at the bottom of his class during the entire period, and that once he had received an "impot" (or imposition) from Mr Rastle, and it will easily be understood that he soon gained favour among his fellows.

This last cause of celebrity, however, was one which did not please Stephen. He had come to Saint Dominic's with a great quantity of good resolutions, the chief of which was that he would work hard and keep out of mischief, and it grieved him much to find that in neither aim was he succeeding.

The first evening or two he had worked very diligently at preparation. He had taken pains with his fractions, and looked out every word in his Caesar. He had got Oliver to look over his French, and Loman had volunteered to correct the spelling of his "theme;" and yet he stuck at the bottom of the class. Other boys went up and down. Some openly boasted that they had had their lessons done for them, and others that they had not done them at all. A merry time they had of it; but Stephen, down at the bottom, was in dismal dumps. He could not get up, and he could not get down, and all his honest hard work went for nothing.

And so, not content to give that system a longer trial, he grew more lax in his work. He filched the answers to his sums out of the "Key," and copied his Caesar out of the "crib." It was much easier, and the result was the same. He did not get up, and he could not get down.

Oliver catechised him now and then as to his progress, and received vague answers in reply, and Loman never remembered a fag that pestered him less with lessons. Stephen was, in fact, settling down into the slough of idleness, and would have become an accomplished dunce in time, had not Mr Rastle come to the rescue. That gentleman caught the new boy in an idle mood, wandering aimlessly down the passage one afternoon.

"Ah, Greenfield, is that you? Nothing to do, eh? Come and have tea with me, will you, in my room?"

Stephen, who had bounded as if shot on hearing the master's unexpected voice behind him, turned round and blushed very red, and said "Thank you," and then looked like a criminal just summoned to the gallows.

"That's right, come along;" and the master took the lad by the arm and marched him off to his room.

Here the sight of muffins and red-currant jam, in addition to the ordinary attractions of a tea-table, somewhat revived Stephen's drooping spirits.

"Make yourself comfortable, my boy, while the tea is brewing," said Mr Rastle, cheerily. "Have you been playing any cricket since you came?"

"Only a little, sir," said Stephen.

"Well, if you only turn out as good a bat as your brother—how well he played in the Alphabet Match!"

Stephen was reviving fast now, and embarked on a lively chat about his favourite sport, by the end of which the tea was brewed, and he and Mr Rastle sitting "cheek by jowl" at the table, with the muffins and jam between them.

Presently Mr Rastle steered the talk round to Stephen's home, a topic even more delightful than cricket. The boy launched out into a full account of the old house and his mother, till the tears very nearly stood in his eyes and the muffins very nearly stuck in his throat. Mr Rastle listened to it all with a sympathetic smile, throwing in questions now and then which it charmed the boy to answer.

"And how do you like Saint Dominic's?" presently inquired the master. "I suppose you've made plenty of friends by this time?"

"Oh yes, sir. It's not as slow as it was at first."

"That's right. You'll soon get to feel at home. And how do you think you are getting on in class?"

Stephen was astonished at this question. If any one knew how he was getting on in class Mr Rastle did, and, alas! Mr Rastle must know well enough that Stephen was getting on badly.

"Not very well, I'm afraid, sir, thank you," replied the boy, not feeling exactly comfortable.

"Not? That's a pity. Are the lessons too hard for you?" kindly inquired Mr Rastle.

"No, I don't think so—that is—no, they're not, sir."

"Ah, your Latin exercise I thought was very fair in parts to-day."

Stephen stared at his master, and the master looked very pleasantly at Stephen.

"I copied it off Raddleston," said the boy, in a trembling voice, and mentally resigning himself to his fate.

"Ah!" said Mr Rastle, laughing; "it's a funny thing, now, Greenfield, I knew that myself. No two boys could possibly have translated 'nobody' into '*nullus corpus*' without making common cause!"

Stephen was desperately perplexed. He had expected a regular row on the head of his confession, and here was his master cracking jokes about the affair!

"I'm very sorry I did it. I won't do it again," said he. "That's right, my boy; Raddleston isn't infallible. Much better do it yourself. I venture to say, now, you can tell me what the Latin for 'nobody' is without a dictionary."

"*Nemo*," promptly replied Stephen.

"Of course! and therefore if you had done the exercise yourself you wouldn't have made that horrid—that fearful mistake!"

Stephen said, "Yes, sir," and meditated.

"Come now," said Mr Rastle, cheerily, "I'm not going to scold you. But if you take my advice you will try and do the next exercise by yourself. Of course you can't expect to be perfect all at once, but if you always copy off Raddleston, do you see, you'll *never* get on at all."

"I'll try, sir," said Stephen, meaning what he said.

"I know you will, my boy. It's not easy work to begin with, but it's easier far in the long run. Try, and if you have difficulties, as you are sure to have, come to me. I'm always here in the evenings, and we'll hammer it out between us. School will not be without its temptations, and you will find it hard always to do your duty. Yet you have, I hope, learnt the power of prayer; and surely the Saviour is able not only to forgive us our sins, but also to keep us from falling. At school, my boy, as elsewhere, it is a safe rule, whenever one is in doubt, to avoid everything, no matter who may be the tempter, of which one cannot fearlessly speak to one's father or mother, and above all to our Heavenly Father. Don't be afraid of Him—He will always be ready to help you and to guide you with His Holy Spirit. Have another cup of tea?"

This little talk, much as he missed at the time its deeper meaning, saved Stephen from becoming a dunce. He still blundered and boggled over his lessons, and still kept pretty near to the bottom form in his class, but he felt that his master had an interest in him, and that acted like magic to his soul. He declined Master Raddleston's professional assistance for the future, and did the best he could by himself. He now and then, though hesitatingly, availed himself of Mr Rastle's offer, and took his difficulties to head-quarters; and he always, when he did so, found the master ready and glad to help, and not only that, but to explain as he went along, and clear the way of future obstacles of the same sort.

And so things looked up with Stephen. He wrote jubilant letters home; he experienced all the joys of an easy conscience, and he felt that he had a friend at court.

But as long as he was a member of the honourable fraternity of Guinea-pigs, Stephen Greenfield was not likely to be dull at Saint Dominic's.

The politics of the lower school were rather intricate. The Guinea-pigs were not exactly the enemies of the Tadpoles, but the rivals. They were always jangling among themselves, it was true; and when Stephen, for the second time in one week, had hit Bramble in the eye, there was such jubilation among the Guinea-pigs that any one might have supposed the two clans were at daggers drawn. But it was not so—at least, not always—for though they fell out among themselves, they united their forces against the common enemy—the monitors!

Monitors, in the opinion of these young republicans, were an invention of the Evil One, invented for the sole purpose of interfering with them. But for the monitors they could carry out their long-cherished scheme of a pitched battle on the big staircase, for asserting their right to go down the left side, when they chose, and up on the right. As it was, the monitors insisted that they should go up on the left and come down on the right. It was intolerable tyranny! And but for the monitors their comb-and-paper musical society might give daily recitals in the top corridor and so delight all Saint Dominic's. What right had the monitors to forbid the performance and confiscate the combs? Was it to be endured? And but for the monitors, once more, they might perfect themselves in the art of pea-shooting. Was such a thing ever heard of, as that fellows should be compelled to shoot peas at the wall in the privacy of their own studies, instead of at one another in the passages? It was a shame—it was a scandal—it was a crime!

On burning questions such as these, Guinea-pigs and Tadpoles sunk all petty differences, and thought and felt as one man; and not the least ardent among them was Stephen.

"Come on, quick! Greenfield junior," squeaked the voice of Bramble, one afternoon, as he and Stephen met on the staircase.

Stephen had fought Bramble yesterday at four o'clock, and was to fight him again to-morrow at half-past twelve, but at the call of common danger he forgot the feud and tore up the stairs, two steps at a time, beside his chronic enemy.

"What's the row?" he gasped, as they flew along.

"Row? Why, what do you think? Young Bellerby has been doctored for tying a string across the passage!"

"Had up before the Doctor? My eye, Bramble!"

"It is your eye indeed! One of the monitors tripped over it, and got in a rage, and there's Bellerby now catching it in the Black Hole. Come on to the meeting; quick!"

The two rushed on, joined by one and another of their fellows who had heard the terrible news. The party rushed pellmell into the Fourth Junior class-room, where were already assembled a score or more youths, shouting, and stamping, and howling like madmen. At the sight of Bramble, the acknowledged leader of all malcontents, they quieted down for a moment to hear what he had to say.

"Here's a go!" classically began that hero.

At this the clamour, swelled twofold by the new additions, rose louder than ever. It *was* a go!

"I wish it had been *me*!" again yelled Bramble; "I have let them know."

Once more the shouts rose high and loud in approval of this noble sentiment.

"*I'd* have kicked their legs!" once more howled Bramble, as soon as he could make himself heard.

"So would we; kicked their legs!"

"They ought to be hanged!" screamed Bramble.

"*I'll* not fag any more for Wren!" bellowed Bramble.

"I'll not fag any more for Greenfield senior!" thundered Paul.

"I'll not fag any more for Loman!" shrieked Stephen.

"Why don't some of you put poison in their teas?" cried one.

"Or blow them up when they're in bed with gunpowder?"

"Or flay them alive?"

"Or boil them in tar?"

"Or throw them into the lions' den?"

"Those who say we won't stand it any longer," shouted Bramble, jumping up on to a form, "hold up your hands!"

A perfect forest of inky hands arose, and a shout with them that almost shook the ceiling.

At that moment the door opened, and Wren appeared. The effect was magical; every one became suddenly quiet, and looked another way.

"The next time there's a noise like that," said the monitor, "the whole class will be detained one hour," and, so saying, departed.

After that the indignation meeting was kept up in whispers. Now and then the feelings of the assembly broke out into words, but the noise was instantly checked.

"If young Bellerby has been flogged," said Bramble, in a most sepulchral undertone, "I've a good mind to fight every one of them!"

"Yes, every one of them," whispered the multitude.

"They're all as bad as each other!" gasped Bramble.

"*We'll* let them know," muttered the audience.

"I'll tell you what I've a good mind to—to—ur—ur—I've a good mind to—ugh!"

Again the door opened. This time it was Callonby.

"Where's young Raddleston?—What *are* you young beggars up to?—is Raddleston here?"

"Yes," mildly answered the voice of Master Raddleston, who a moment ago had nearly broken a blood-vessel in his endeavours to scream in a whisper.

"Come here, then."

The fag meekly obeyed.

"Oh, and Greenfield junior," said Callonby, as he was turning to depart, "Loman wants to know when you are going to get his tea; you're to go at once, he says."

Stephen obeyed, and was very humble in explaining to Loman that he had forgotten (which was the case) the time. The meeting in the Fourth class-room lasted most of the afternoon; but as oratory in whispers is tedious, and constant repetition of the same sentiments, however patriotic, is monotonous, it flagged considerably in spirit towards the end, and degenerated into one of the usual wrangles between Guinea-pigs and Tadpoles, in the midst of which Master Bramble left the chair, and went off in the meekest manner possible to get Wren to help him with his sums for next day.

Stephen meanwhile was engaged in doing a little piece of business for Loman, of which more must be said in a following chapter.

Chapter Eleven.
In the Toils.

The afternoon of the famous "indignation meeting" in the Fourth Junior was the afternoon of the week which Mr Cripps the younger, putting aside for a season the anxieties and responsibilities of his "public" duties in Maltby, usually devoted to the pursuit of the "gentle craft," at his worthy father's cottage by Gusset Weir. Loman, who was aware of this circumstance, and on whose spirit that restless top joint had continued to prey ever since the evening of the misadventure a week ago, determined to avail himself of the opportunity of returning the unlucky fishing-rod into the hands from which he had received it.

He therefore instructed Stephen to take it up to the lock-house with a note to the effect that having changed his mind in the matter since speaking to Cripps, he found he should not require the rod, and therefore returned it, with many thanks for Mr Cripps's trouble.

Stephen, little suspecting the questionable nature of his errand, undertook the commission, and duly delivered both rod and letter into the hands of Mr Cripps, who greatly astonished him by swearing very violently at the contents of the letter. "Well," said he, when he had exhausted his vocabulary (not a small one) of expletives—"well, of all the grinning jackanapeses, this is the coolest go! Do you take me for a fool?"

Stephen, to whom this question appeared to be directly applied, disclaimed any idea of the kind, and added, "I don't know what you mean."

"Don't you, my young master? All right! Tell Mr Loman I'll wait upon him one fine day, see if I don't! Here's me, given up a whole blessed day to serve him, and a pot of money out of my pocket, and here he goes! not a penny for my pains! Chucks the thing back on my 'ands as cool as a coocumber, all because he's changed his mind. I'll let him have a bit of my mind, tell him, Mr Gentleman Schoolboy, see if I don't. I ain't a-going to be robbed, no! not by all the blessed monkeys that ever wrote on slates! *I'll* wait upon him, see if I don't!"

Stephen, to whom the whole of this oration, which was garnished with words that we can hardly set down in print, or degrade ourselves by suggesting, was about as intelligible as if it had been Hebrew, thought it better to make no reply, and sorrowed inwardly to find that such a nice man as Mr Cripps should possess so short a temper. But the landlord of the Cockchafer soon recovered from his temporary annoyance, and even proceeded to apologise to Stephen for the warmth of his language.

"You'll excuse me, young gentleman," said he, "but I'm a plain-spoken man, and I was—there, I won't deny it—I was a bit put out about this here rod first go off. You'll excuse me—of course I don't mean no offence to you or Mister Loman neither, who's one of the nicest young gentlemen I ever met. Of course if you'd a' paid seventy bob out of your own pocket it would give *you* a turn; leastways, if you was a struggling, honest working man, like me."

"That's it," snivelled, old Mr Cripps, who had entered during this last speech; "that's it, Benny, my boy, honest Partisans, that's what we is, who knows what it are to be in want of a shillin' to buy a clo' or two for the little childer."

What particular little "childer" Mr Cripps senior and his son were specially interested in no one knew, for neither of them was blessed with any. However, it was one of old Mr Cripps's heart-moving phrases, and no one was rude enough to ask questions.

Stephen did not, on the present occasion, feel moved to respond to the old man's lament, and Cripps junior, with more adroitness than filial affection, hustled the old gentleman out of the door.

"Never mind him," said he to Stephen. "He's a silly old man, and always pretends he's starvin'. If you believe me, he's a thousand pounds stowed away somewheres. I on'y wish," added he, with a sigh, "he'd give me a taste of it, for its 'ard, up-'ill work makin' ends meet, particular when a man's deceived by parties. No matter. I'll pull through; you see!"

Stephen once more did not feel called upon to pursue this line of conversation, and therefore changed the subject.

"Oh, Mr Cripps, how much is that bat?"

"Bat! Bless me if I hadn't nearly forgot all about it. Ain't it a beauty, now?"

"Yes, pretty well," said Stephen, whose friends had one and all abused the bat, and who was himself a little disappointed in his expectations.

"Pretty well! I like that. You must be a funny cricketer, young gentleman, to call that bat only pretty well. I suppose you want me to take *that* back, too?" and here Mr Cripps looked very fierce.

"Oh, no," said Stephen, hurriedly. "I only want to know what I am to pay for it."

"Oh, come now, we needn't mind about that. That'll keep, you know. As if I wanted the money. Ha, ha!"

Even a green boy like Stephen could not fail to wonder why, if Mr Cripps was as hard up as he had just described himself, he should now be so anxious to represent himself as not in want of money.

"Please, I want to know the price."

"As if I was a-going to name prices to a young gentleman like you! Please yourself about it. I shall not be disappointed if you gives me only eighteenpence, and if *you* thinks twelve bob is handsome, well, let it be. *I* can struggle on somehow."

This was uncomfortable for Stephen, who, too green, fortunately, to comprehend the drift of Mr Cripps's gentle hints, again asked that he would name a price.

This time Mr Cripps answered more precisely.

"Well, that there bat is worth a guinea, if you want to know, but I'll say a sovereign for cash down."

Stephen whistled a long-drawn whistle of dismay.

"A sovereign! I can't pay all that! I thought it would be about seven shillings!"

"Did you? You may think what you like, but that's my price, and you are lucky to get it at that."

"I shall have to send it back. I can't afford so much," said Stephen, despondingly.

"Not if I know it! I'll have none of your second-hand bats, if I know it. Come, young gentleman, I may be a poor man, but I'm not a fool, and you'll find it out if I've any of your nonsense. Do you suppose I've nothing to do but wait on jackanapeses like you and your mates? No error! There you are. That'll do, and if you don't like it—well, the governor shall know about it!"

Stephen was dreadfully uncomfortable. Though, to his knowledge, he had done nothing wrong, he felt terribly guilty at the bare notion of the Doctor being informed of his transactions with Mr Cripps, besides greatly in awe of the vague threats held out by that gentleman. He did not venture on further argument, but, bidding a hasty farewell, returned as fast as he could to Saint Dominic's, wondering whatever Oliver would say, and sorely repenting the day when first he was tempted to think of the unlucky bat.

He made a clean breast of it to his brother that evening, who, of course, called him an ass, and everything else complimentary, and was deservedly angry. However, Stephen had reason to consider himself lucky to possess an elder brother at the school who had a little more shrewdness than himself. Oliver was determined the debt should be paid at once, without even waiting to write home, and by borrowing ten shillings from Wraysford, and adding to it the residue of his own pocket-money, the sovereign was raised and dispatched that very night to Mr Cripps; after which Oliver commanded his brother to sit down and write a full confession of his folly home, and ask for the money, promising never to make such a fool of himself again. This task the small boy, with much shame and trembling at heart, accomplished; and in due time an answer came from his mother which not only relieved his mind but paid off his debts to Oliver and Wraysford, and once for all closed the business of the treble-cane splice bat.

It would have been well for Loman if he could have got out of his difficulties as easily and as satisfactorily.

Ever since he had gathered from Stephen Mr Cripps's wrath on receiving the returned rod, he had been haunted by a dread lest the landlord of the Cockchafer should march up to Saint Dominic's, and possibly make an exposure of the unhappy business before the Doctor and the whole school. He therefore, after long hesitation and misgiving, determined himself to call at the Cockchafer, and try in some way to settle matters. One thing reassured him. If Cripps had discovered the crack or the fracture in the rod, he would have heard of it long before now; and if he had not, then the longer the time the less chance was there of the damage being laid at his door. So he let three weeks elapse, and then went to Maltby. The Cockchafer was a small, unpretentious tavern, frequented chiefly by carriers and tradesmen, and, I regret to say, not wholly unknown to some of the boys of Saint Dominic's, who were foolish enough to persuade themselves that skittles, and billiards, and beer were luxuries worth the risk incurred by breaking one of the rules of the school. No boy was permitted to enter any place of refreshment except a confectioner's in Maltby under the penalty of a severe punishment, which might, in a bad case, mean expulsion. Loman, therefore, a monitor and a Sixth Form boy, had to take more than ordinary precautions to reach the Cockchafer unobserved, which he succeeded in doing, and to his satisfaction—as well as to his trepidation—found Mr Cripps the younger at home.

"Ho, he! my young shaver," was that worthy's greeting, "here you are at last."

This was not encouraging to begin with. It sounded very much as if Mr Cripps had been looking forward to this visit. However, Loman put as bold a face as he could on to it, and replied, "Hullo, Cripps, how are you? It's a long time since I saw you; jolly day, isn't it?"

"Jolly!" replied Mr Cripps, looking very gloomy, and drawing a glass of beer for the young gentleman before he ordered it. Loman did not like it at all. There was something about Cripps's manner that made him feel very uncomfortable.

"Oh, Cripps," he presently began, in as off-hand a manner as he could assume under the depressing circumstances—"Oh, Cripps, about that rod, by the way. I hope you didn't mind my sending it back. The fact is," (and here followed a lie which till that moment had not been in the speaker's mind to tell)—"the fact is, I find I'm to get a present of a rod this summer at home, or else of course I would have kept it."

Mr Cripps said nothing, but began polishing up a pewter pot with a napkin.

"I hope you got it back all right," continued Loman, who felt as if he must say something. "They are such fragile things, you know. I thought I'd just leave it in the bag and not touch it, but send it straight back, for fear it should be damaged."

There was a queer smile about Mr Cripps's mouth as he asked, "Then you didn't have a look at it even?"

"Well, no, I thought I would—I thought I wouldn't run any risk."

Loman was amazed at himself. He had suddenly made up his mind to tell one lie, but here they were following one after another, as if he had told nothing but lies all his life! Alas, there was no drawing back either!

"The fact is," he began again, speaking for the sake of speaking, and not even knowing what he was going to say—"the fact is—" Here the street door opened, and there entered hurriedly a boy whom Loman, to his confusion and consternation, recognised as Simon of the Fifth, the author of the "Love-Ballad." What could the monitor say for himself to explain his presence in this prohibited house?

"Hullo, Loman, I say, is that you?" remarked Simon.

"Oh, Simon, how are you?" faltered the wretched Loman; "I've just popped in to speak to Cripps about a fishing-rod. You'd better not come in; you might get into trouble."

"Oh, never mind. You won't tell of me, and I won't tell of you. Glass of the usual, please, Cripps. I say, Loman, was that the fishing-rod you were switching about out of your window that afternoon three weeks ago?"

Loman turned red and white by turns, and wished the earth would swallow him! And to think of this fellow, the biggest donkey in Saint Dominic's, blurting out the very thing which of all things he had striven to keep concealed!

Mr Cripps's mouth worked up into a still more ugly smile.

"I was below in the garden, you know, and could not make out what you were up to. You nearly had my eye out with that hook. I say, what a smash you gave it when it caught in the ivy. Was it broken right off, or only cracked, eh? Cripps will mend it for you, won't you, Cripps?"

Neither Mr Cripps nor Loman spoke a word. The latter saw that concealment was no longer possible; and bitterly he rued the day when first he heard the name of Cripps.

That worthy, seeing the game to have come beautifully into his own hands, was not slow to take advantage of it. He beckoned Loman into the inner parlour, whither the boy tremblingly followed, leaving Simon to finish his glass of "the usual" undisturbed.

I need not repeat the painful conversation that ensued between the sharper and the wretched boy. It was no use for the latter to deny or explain. He was at the mercy of the man, and poor mercy it was. Cripps, with many oaths and threats, explained to Loman that he could, if he chose, have him up before a magistrate for fraud, and that he would do so for a very little. Loman might choose for himself between a complete exposure, involving his disgrace for life, or paying the price of the rod down and 20 besides, and he might consider himself lucky more was not demanded.

The boy, driven to desperation between terror and shame, implored mercy, and protested with tears in his eyes that he would do anything, if only Cripps did not expose him.

"You know what it is, then," replied Cripps.

"But how am I to get the 20 pounds? I daren't ask for it at home, and there's no one here will lend it me. Oh, Cripps, what shall I do?" and the boy actually caught Mr Cripps's hand in his own as he put the question.

"Well, look here," said Mr Cripps, unbending a little, "that 20 pounds I must have, there's no mistake about it; but I don't want to be too hard on you, and I can put you up to raising the wind."

"Oh, can you?" gasped Loman, eager to clutch at the faintest straw of hope. "I'll do anything."

"Very good; then it's just this: I've just got a straight tip about the Derby that I know for certain no one else has got—that is, that Sir Patrick won't win, favourite and all as he is. Now there's a friend of mine I can introduce you to, who's just wanting to put a twenty on the horse, if he can find any one to take it. It wouldn't do for me to make the wager, or he'd smell a rat; but if you put your money *against* the horse, you're bound to win, and all safe. What do you say?"

"I don't know anything about betting," groaned Loman. "Are you quite sure I'd win?"

"Certain. If you lose I'll only ask 10 pounds of you, there! that's as good as giving you 10 pounds myself on the horse, eh?"

"Well," said Loman, "I suppose I must. Where is he?"

"Wait here a minute, and I'll bring him round."

Loman waited, racked by a sense of ignominy and terror. Yet this seemed his only hope. Could he but get this 20 pounds and pay off Cripps he would be happy. Oh, how he repented listening to that first temptation to deceive!

In due time Mr Cripps returned with his friend, who was very civil on hearing Loman's desire to bet against Sir Patrick.

"Make it a 50 pounds note while you are about it," said he.

"No, 20 pounds is all I want to go for," replied Loman.

"Twenty then, all serene, sir," said the gentleman, booking the bet. "What'll you take to drink?"

"Nothing, thank you," said Loman, hurriedly rising to leave.

"Good-day, sir," said Cripps, holding out his hand.

Loman looked at the hand and then at Mr Cripps's face. There was the same ugly leer about the latter, into which a spark of anger was infused as the boy still held back from the proffered hand.

With an inward groan Loman gave the hand a spiritless grasp, and then hurried back miserable and conscience-stricken to Saint Dominic's.

Chapter Twelve.
The "Dominican" again.

The circumstances which had attended the publication of the first number of the *Dominican* had been such as to throw a damper over the future success of that valuable paper. It was most uncomfortably connected in the minds of the Fifth with the cowardice of Oliver Greenfield, and with the stigma which his conduct had cast upon the whole Form, and they one and all experienced a great diminution of interest in its future.

The Fifth were far more intent on vindicating their reputation with the Sixth—and, indeed, with the rest of the school. They sought every opportunity of bringing on a collision with the monitors. One or two of their number went, so far as to pick quarrels with members of the rival class, in hopes of a fight. But in this they were not successful. The Sixth chose to look upon this display of feeling among their juniors as a temporary aberration of mind, and were by no means to be tempted into hostilities. They asserted their authority wherever they could enforce it, and sacrificed it whenever it seemed more discreet to do so. Only one thing evoked a temporary display of vexation from them, and that was when Ricketts and Braddy appeared one day, arm-in-arm, in the passages with *tall hats* on their heads. Now, tall hats on week-days were the exclusive privilege of the Sixth at Saint Dominic's, and, worn by them during school hours, served as the badge of monitorship. This action on the part of the Fifth, therefore, was as good as a usurpation of monitorial rights, and that the Sixth were not disposed to stand. However, Raleigh, the captain, when appealed to, pooh-poohed the matter. "Let them be," said he; "what do you want to make a row about it for? If the boys do mistake them for monitors, so much the less row in the passages."

Raleigh was always a man of peace—though it was rumoured he could, if he chose, thrash any two Dominicans going—and the monitors were much disgusted to find that he did not authorise them to interfere with the Fifth in the matter. But the Fifth *were* interfered with in another quarter, and in a way which caused them to drop their chimney-pots completely. One afternoon the entire Fourth Junior appeared in the corridors in their Sunday tiles! In their Sunday tiles they slid down the banisters; in their Sunday tiles they played leapfrog; in their Sunday tiles they executed a monster tug-of-war in the bottom corridor! Stephen and Bramble fought their usual battle in top hats, and Master Paul insisted on wearing the same decoration while washing up Oliver's tea-things. It was a splendid hit, and for once in a way Guinea-pigs and Tadpoles scored one, for the Fifth appeared next day in their ordinary "boilers," and the dignity of the monitors was vindicated.

But the blood was up between Fifth and Sixth, and each Form looked forward to the match, Sixth *versus* School, with redoubled interest.

"Were not these boys fools?" some one asks.

To be sure they were, sir. But what of that? they were none the less boys, and most of them fine young fellows, too, with all their nonsense.

However, as has been said, all this came out of the circumstances which attended the bringing out of the first number of the *Dominican*, and there seemed but a poor look-out for Number 2, which was now nearly due, in consequence.

"What on earth am I to do?" asked Pembury of Tom Senior one day; "I've not got a single contribution yet. There's you making out you're too busy, and Rick the same. It's all humbug, I know! What are you busy at I'd like to know? I never saw you busy yet."

"Upon my word, old man," said Tom, "I'm awfully sorry, but I've got a tremendous lot to do. I'm going to try for the French prize; I am, really."

"And you'll get it, too; rather! Wasn't it you who translated 'I know the way to write' into '*Je non le chemin a writer*' eh? Oh, stick to French by all means, Tom; it's in your line! But you might just as well write for Number 2."

"I really can't this time," said Tom.

Ricketts had an excuse very similar. Bullinger had hurt his foot, he said, and could not possibly write; and Braddy had begun to study fossils, he said, and was bound to devote all his spare time to them. To all of whom Master Pembury gave a piece of his mind.

"Wray, old man," said he, that evening, "you and Noll and I shall have to do the whole thing between us, that's all about it."

"Awfully sorry!" said Wraysford; "you'll have to let me off this time. I'm working like nails for the Nightingale."

"Bother the Nightingale, I say! What is it to the *Dominican*? Come, I say, old man, that won't do! you aren't going to leave me in the lurch like all the rest?"

But Wraysford was; he would gladly have helped if he could, but he really must not this time; perhaps he would for the next.

Oliver was as bad; he declared the things he had written before—even with Pembury's assistance—had taken him such ages to do, that he wasn't going in for the next number. He was very sorry to disappoint, and all that; but if Tony was in for a scholarship next Michaelmas he would understand the reason. Why not let the thing drop this month?

This, however, by no means met Tony's views. A pretty figure he would cut if it were to be said he couldn't keep up a paper for two numbers running! No! his mind was made up. Number 2 *should* come out, even if he wrote every word of it himself! And with that determination he hobbled off to his study. Here he met Simon waiting for him.

"Oh," said the poet; "I only brought this, if you'll put it in. I think it's not bad. I could make it longer if you like. I find poetry comes so easily, you know!"

Tony glanced over the paper and grinned. "Thanks, awfully! This will do capitally; it would spoil it to make it any longer. You're a brick, Simon! I wish *I* could write poetry."

"Oh, never mind. I could do some more bits about other things, you know, if you like."

Pembury said he didn't think he should require any more "bits," but was awfully obliged by this one, which was first-rate, a recommendation which sent Simon away happy to his study, there immediately to compose the opening stanza of his famous epic, "The Sole's Allegery—a sacred Poem."

With one contribution in hand, Tony locked his door and sat down to write. There was something out of the common about Pembury. With the body of a cripple he had the heart of a lion, and difficulties only made it more dauntless. Any one else would have thought twice, indeed, before undertaking the task he was now setting himself to do, and ninety-nine out of every hundred would have abandoned it before it was half done. But Tony was indomitable. Every night that week he locked his study-door, and threats and kicks and entreaties would not open it even to his dearest friends. And slowly the huge white sheet before him showed the signs of his diligence. The great long columns, one after another, filled up; paragraph followed paragraph, and article article. He coolly continued the "History of Saint Dominic's" begun last month by Bullinger, and the "Reports of the Sixth Form Debates" commenced by Tom Senior. And the "Diary of the Sixth Form Mouse" went on just as if Wraysford had never abandoned it; and the poem on the Guinea-pigs, promised in Number 1, by the author of "To a Tadpole," duly appeared also. Besides this, there were the continuations of Tony's own articles, and his "Personal Notes," and "Squeaks from Tadpoleopolis," and advertisements just as usual; until, in due time, the last column was filled up, the sheet triumphantly fixed in its frame, and as triumphantly hung up on its own particular nails on the wall outside the Fifth Form door.

It was a feat to be proud of, and Tony was justly and pardonably proud. It was at least a gratification next morning to see not only that the school generally took unabated interest in the *Dominican*, but that he had fairly astonished his own class-fellows. Their admiration of the editor was unbounded and undisguised. Their consciences had all, more or less, reproached them for backing out of their responsibilities in the way they had; and now it quite touched them to see how, notwithstanding, Anthony had by his own labour made up for their defect, and sustained the reputation of the Fifth before all the school.

The crush outside the door was greater than ever this time, and Master Paul, who again acted as policeman, was obliged to summon Stephen to his assistance in watching to see that no damage came to the precious document.

The account of the Alphabet Match was very graphic, and written quite in the usual absurd "sporting style," greatly to the amusement of most of those who had taken part in it. Here is a specimen:—

"At 4.30, sharp, the leather was taken into custody by 'Gamey' Raikes, at the washhouse end, who tried what his artful 'yorkers' could do in the way of dissolving partnership. But Teddy Loman kept his willow straight up, and said 'Not at home' to every poser, leaving Noll to do all the smacking. This pretty business might have gone on till to-morrow week had the men's upper stories been as 'O.K.' as their timbers, but they messed about over a pretty snick of Noll's, and, after popping the question three times, Teddy got home just in time to see his two bails tumble out of their groove. Teddy didn't like this, and bowled his partner a wide compliment, which Noll, like a sensible man, didn't walk out to, and Teddy was astonished to find his party could get on without him;" and so on.

This version of the incident was by no means pleasant to Loman, but to every one else it was highly diverting, and it actually made one or two of the Fifth think that Oliver, after all, had not done such a very discreditable thing in taking that angry word in silence. If only he had shown more spirit about the blow, they could have forgiven the rest.

Then followed more from the "Sixth Form Mouse":—

"The Sixth held a Cabinet Council to-day to discuss who should go out for nuts. The choice fell on Callonby. I wonder why the Sixth are so fond of nuts. Why, monkeys eat nuts. Perhaps that is the reason. What a popular writer Mr Bohn is with the Sixth! they even read him at lesson time! I was quite sorry when the Doctor had to bone Wren's Bohn. I wonder, by the way, why that bird found it so hard to translate the simplest sentence without his Bohn! The Doctor really shouldn't—I hope he will restore to Wren his backbone by giving him back his Bohn. Hum! I heard some one smiling. I'll go."

The Sixth, a good many of them, were imprudent enough to look very guilty at the reading of this extract, a circumstance which appeared to afford keenest delight to the Fifth. But as Simon's poem followed, they had other food for thought at the moment. The poem was entitled—

A Revverie.

I.

I walked me in the garden, all in the garden fair,
And mused upon my hindmost sole all in the open air.
When lo! I heard above my head a sound all like a wisk,
I stepped me aside thereat out of the way so brisk.

(Hindmost sole, possibly "inmost soul"; wisk, possibly "whisk.")

II.

I looked me up, and there behold! and lo! a window broad,
And out thereof I did dizzern a gallant fishing-rod,
All sporting in the breaze untill the hook in ivy caught,
And then the little lad he tried to pull it harder than he ought.

III.

It broke, alas! and so messeems fades life's perplecksing dreems,
And vanish like that fishing-rod all in the dark messeems.
I wonder if my perplecksing dreems will vanish like the rod in the dark,

And I shall rise and rise and rise and rise all like a lark.

                IV.

Oh wood I was a lark, a lark all lofty in the sky,
I do not know what I should do to quench my blazing eye.
I'd look me down on Dominic's, and think of the days when I was young,
Or would I was an infant meek all sucking of my thumb.

    Again Simon, who had watched with intense interest the reception of his poem, was perplexed to notice the amusement it had caused. Even Pembury had mistaken its "inmost soul," for he had placed it in the column devoted to "Facetiae." Nor could Simon understand why, for the next week, every one he met had his thumb in his mouth. It was very queer—one of life's mysteries—and he had thoughts of embodying the fact in his "Sole's Allegery," which was now rapidly approaching completion.

    After this bubbling up of pure verse there followed a few remarks about Guinea-pigs and Tadpoles, which had the effect of highly incensing those young gentlemen. The paragraph was entitled—

    "Market Intelligence.

    "Half a dozen mixed Guinea-pigs and Tadpoles were offered for sale by auction on the centre landing yesterday. There was only a small attendance. The auctioneer said he couldn't honestly recommend the lot, but they must be got rid of at any cost. He had scrubbed their faces and combed their hair for the occasion, but couldn't guarantee that state of things to last. But they might turn out to be of use as substitutes in case worms should become scarce; and, any way, by boiling down their fingers and collars, many gallons of valuable ink could be obtained. The first bid was a farthing, which seemed to be far beyond the expectation of the salesman, who at once knocked the lot down. The sale was such a success that it is proposed to knock down several more lots in a like manner."

    The rage of the Fourth Junior on reading this paragraph was something awful to witness. Bramble, feeling he must kick somebody on the legs, kicked Stephen, who, forgetting that he was on police duty, seized Bramble by the hair of his head and rushed off with him to the "meeting," closely followed by Paul and the whole swarm. That meeting lasted from three to five. What awful threats were uttered, and what awful vows taken, no one knew. At five o'clock Stephen's fight with Bramble came off as usual, and all that evening Guinea-pigs and Tadpoles did nothing but make paper darts. It was certain a crisis had come in their history. The "dogs of war" were let loose! They would be revenged on somebody! So they at once began to be revenged on one another, till it should be possible to unite their forces against the common foe.

    But the remainder of the crowd stayed on to read one more extract from the *Dominican*. Under the title of "Reviews of Books," Anthony had reviewed in style the last number of the *Sixth Form Magazine* as follows:—

    "This book appears to be the praiseworthy attempt of some ambitious little boys to enter the field of letters. We are always pleased to encourage juvenile talent, but we would suggest that our young friends might have done better had they kept to their picture-books a little longer before launching out into literature on their own account. In the words of the poet we might say—

    "Babies, wait a little longer,
Till the little wings are stronger,
Then you'll fly away."

"Nevertherless, we would refer to one or two of these interesting attempts. Take, for example, the essay on the 'Character of Julius Caesar,' by one who signs himself Raleigh. This is very well written. Pains have been taken about the formation of the letters, and some of the capitals are specially worthy of praise. For one so young, we rarely saw the capital D so well done. Dr Smith, were he alive, would be pleased to see his remarks on Caesar so well and accurately copied out. Master Wren gives us some verse— a translation out of Horace. We wonder if Mr Wren is any relation to the late Jenny Wren who married Mr Cock Robin. We should imagine from these verses that Mr Wren must be well acquainted with *Robbin*. Take one more, Master Loman's 'A Funny Story.' We are sorry to find Master Loman tells stories. Boys shouldn't tell stories; it's not right. But Master Loman unfortunately does tell stories, and this is one. He calls it 'A Funny Story.' That is a story to begin with, for it is not funny. We don't know what Master Loman thinks funny; perhaps he calls being run out at cricket funny, or hitting another boy in the mouth when he's looking another way. In any case, we can't make out why he calls this story funny. The only funny thing about it is its title, and his spelling 'attach' 'attatch.' The last is really funny. It shows how partial Mr Loman is to *tea*. If this funny story is the result of his partiality to tea, we are afraid it was very weak stuff."

Loman, who had already been made dreadfully uncomfortable by Simon's poem, made no secret of his rage over this number of the *Dominican*. He was one of those vain fellows who cannot see a jest where it is levelled at themselves. The rest of the Sixth had the sense, whatever they felt, to laugh at Anthony's hard hits. But not so Loman; he lost his temper completely. He ordered the *Dominican* to be taken down; he threatened to report the whole Fifth to the Doctor. He would not allow the junior boys to stand and read it. In short, he made a regular ass of himself.

Undoubtedly Anthony had put a great deal of venom into his pen. Still, by taking all the poison and none of the humour to himself Loman made a great mistake, and displayed a most unfortunate amount of weakness.

He shut himself up in his study in a fume; he boxed Stephen's ears for nothing at all, and would see no one for the rest of the evening. He knew well he could not have given his enemies a greater crow over him than such conduct, and yet he could not command his vanity to act otherwise.

But that evening, just before tea-time, something happened which gave Loman more to think about than the *Dominican*. A letter marked "Immediate" came to him by the post. It was from Cripps, to say that, after all, Sir Patrick *had* won the Derby!

Chapter Thirteen.
Company at the Cockchafer.

Cripps's letter was as follows:

"Hon. Sir,—This comes hoping you are well. You may like to know Sir Patrick won. The tip was all out. Honourable Sir,—My friend would like his ten pounds sharp, as he's a poor man. Please call in on Saturday afternoon. Your very humble servant, Ben Cripps."

This letter was startling enough to drive fifty *Dominicans* out of Loman's head, and for a long time he could hardly realise how bad the news it contained was.

He had reckoned to a dead certainty on winning the bet which Cripps had advised him to make with his friend. Not that Loman knew anything about racing matters, but Cripps had been so confident, and it seemed so safe to bet against this one particular horse, that the idea of events turning out otherwise had never once entered his head.

He went to the door and shouted for Stephen, who presently appeared with a paper dart in his hand.

"Greenfield," said Loman, "cut down at once to Maltby and bring me a newspaper."

Stephen stared.

"I've got my lessons to do," he said.

"Leave them here, I'll do them," replied Loman; "look sharp."

Still Stephen hesitated.

"We aren't allowed out after seven without leave," he faltered, longing to get back to the war preparations in the Fourth Junior.

"I know that, and I give you leave—there!" said Loman, with all the monitorial dignity he could assume. This quite disarmed Stephen. Of course a monitor could do no wrong, and it was no use objecting on that score.

Still he was fain to find some other excuse.

"I say, will it do in the morning?" he began.

Loman's only reply was a book shied at his fag's head—quite explicit enough for all practical purposes. So Stephen hauled down his colours and prepared to start.

"Look sharp back," said Loman, "and don't let any one see you going out. Look here, you can get yourself some brandy-balls with this."

Stephen was not philosopher enough to argue with himself why, if he had leave to go out, he ought to avoid being seen going out. He pocketed Loman's extra penny complacently, and giving one last longing look in the direction of the Fourth Junior, slipped quietly out of the school and made the best of his way down to Maltby.

It was not easy at that time of day to get a paper. Stephen tried half a dozen stationers' shops, but they were all sold out. They were evidently more sought after than brandy-balls, of which he had no difficulty in securing a pennyworth at an early stage of his pilgrimage. The man in the sweet-shop told him his only chance of getting a paper was at the railway station.

So to the station he strolled, with a brandy-ball in each cheek. Alas! the stall was closed for the day.

Stephen did not like to be beaten, but there was nothing for it now but to give up this "paper-chase," and return to Loman with a report of his ill-success.

As he trotted back up High Street, looking about everywhere but in the direction in which he was going (as is the habit of small boys), and wondering in his heart whether his funds could possibly stand the strain of another pennyworth of brandy-balls, he suddenly found himself in sharp collision with a man who expressed himself on the subject of clumsy boys generally in no very measured terms.

Stephen looked up and saw Mr Cripps the younger standing before him.

"Why!" exclaimed that worthy, giving over his irascible expletives, and adopting an air of unfeigned pleasure, "why, if it ain't young Master Greenhorn. Ha, ha! How do, my young bantam? Pretty bobbish, eh?"

Stephen did not know exactly what was meant by "bobbish," but replied that he was quite well, and sorry he had trodden on Mr Cripps's toes.

"Never mind," said Mr Cripps, magnanimously, "you're a light weight. And so you're taking a dander down town, are you? looking for lollipops, eh?"

Stephen blushed very red at this. However had Mr Cripps guessed about the brandy-balls?

"I came to get a paper for Loman," he said, "but they're all sold out."

"No, are they? I wonder what Mr Loman wants with a paper, now?"

"He said it was very important, and I was to be sure to get one of to-day's," said Stephen. "Do you know where I can get one?"

"Of course. Come along with me; I've got one at home you can have. And so he said it was very important, did he? That's queer. There's nothing in to-day's paper at all. Only something about a low horse-race. He don't want it for that, I guess; eh?"

"Oh, no, I shouldn't think," said Stephen, trotting along beside his amiable acquaintance.

Mr Cripps was certainly a very friendly man, and as he conducted Stephen to the Cockchafer, Stephen felt quite a liking for him, and couldn't understand why Oliver and Wraysford both ran him down.

True, Mr Cripps did use some words which didn't seem exactly proper, but that Stephen put down to the habit of men in that part. The man seemed to take such an interest in boys generally, and in Stephen in particular, and was so interested and amused to hear all about the Guinea-pigs, and the *Dominican*, and the Sixth*versus* School, that Stephen felt quite drawn out to him. And then he told Stephen such a lot of funny stories, and treated him with such evident consideration, that the small boy felt quite flattered and delighted.

So they reached the Cockchafer. Here Stephen, whose former visits had all been to the lock-house, pulled up.

"I say," said he, "is this a public-house?"

"Getting on that way," said Mr Cripps.

"We aren't allowed to go in public-houses," said Stephen, "it's one of the rules."

"Ah, quite right too; not a good thing for boys at all. We'll go in by the private door into my house," said Mr Cripps.

Stephen was not quite comfortable at this evasion, but followed Mr Cripps by the side door into his bar parlour.

"You won't forget the paper," he said, "please. I've got to be back in school directly."

"I'll have a look for it. Now, I guess you like ginger-beer, don't you?"

Stephen was particularly partial to ginger-beer, as it happened, and said so.

"That's the style," said Mr Cripps, producing a bottle. "Walk into that while I go and get the paper."

Stephen did walk into it with great relish, and began to think Mr Cripps quite a gentleman. He was certain, even if that bat had been a poor one, it was quite worth the money paid for it, and Oliver was unjust in calling Cripps hard names.

The landlord very soon returned with the paper.

"Here you are, young governor. Now don't hurry away. It's lonely here all by myself, and I like a young gentleman like you to talk to. I knew a nice little boy once, just your age, that used to come and see me regular once a week and play bagatelle with me. He was a good player at it too!"

"Could he get clear-board twice running with two balls?" asked Stephen, half jealous of the fame of this unknown rival.

"Eh!—no, scarcely that. He wasn't quite such a dab as that."

"I can do it," said Stephen with a superior smile.

"You? Not a bit of you!" said Mr Cripps, incredulously.

"Yes, I can," reiterated Stephen, delighted to have astonished his host.

"I must see it before I can believe that," said Mr Cripps. "Suppose you show me on my board."

Stephen promptly accepted the challenge, and forgetting in his excitement all about school rules or Loman's orders accompanied Cripps to the bagatelle-room, with its sanded floor, smelling of stale tobacco and beer-dregs. His first attempt, greatly to Mr Cripps's glee, was unsuccessful.

"I knew you couldn't," exclaimed that worthy.

"I know I can do it," said Stephen, excitedly. "Let's try again."

After a few more trials he made the two clear-boards, and Mr Cripps was duly astonished and impressed.

"That's what I call smart play," said he. "Now, if I was a betting man, I'd wager a sixpence you couldn't do it again."

"Yes, I can, but I won't bet," said Stephen. He did do it again, and Mr Cripps said it was a good job for him the young swell didn't bet, or he would have lost his sixpence. Stephen was triumphant.

How long he would have gone on showing off his prowess to the admiring landlord of the Cockchafer, and how far he might have advanced in the art of public-house bagatelle, I cannot say, but the sudden striking of a clock and the entry of visitors into the room reminded him where he was.

"I must go back now," he said, hurriedly.

"Must you? Well, come again soon. I've a great fancy to learn that there stoke. I'm a born fool at bagatelle. What do you say to another ginger-beer before you go?"

Stephen said "Thank you," and then taking the newspaper in his hand bade Cripps good-bye.

"Good-bye, my fine young fellow. You're one of the right sort, you are. No stuck-up nonsense about you. That's why I fancy you. Bye-bye. My love to Mr Loman."

Stephen hurried back to Saint Dominic's as fast as his legs would carry him. He was not quite comfortable about his evening's proceedings, although he was not aware of having done anything wicked. Loman, a monitor, had given him leave to go down to Maltby, so that was hardly a crime; and as to the Cockchafer—well, he had only been in the private part of the house, and not the public bar, and surely there had been no harm in drinking ginger-beer and playing bagatelle, especially when he had distinctly refused to bet on the latter. But, explain it as he would, Stephen felt uncomfortable enough to determine him to say as little as possible about his expedition.

He found Loman impatiently awaiting him.

"Wherever have you been to all this time?" he demanded.

"The papers were all sold out," said Stephen. "I tried seven places."

Loman had eagerly caught up and opened the paper while Stephen nervously made this explanation, and he took no further heed of his fag, who presently, seeing he was no longer wanted, and relieved to get out of reach of questions, prudently retired.

A glance sufficed to confirm the bad news about the Derby. Sir Patrick had won, and it was a fact therefore that Loman owed Cripps and his friend between them thirty pounds, without the least possibility of paying them.

One thing was certain. He must see Cripps on Saturday, and trust to his luck (though that of late had not been very trustworthy) to pull him through, somehow.

Alas! what a spirit this, in which to meet difficulties! Loman had yet to learn that it is one thing to regret, and another thing to repent; that it is one thing to call one's self a fool, and another thing, quite, to cease to be one.

But, as he said to himself, he must go through with it now, and the first step took him deeper than ever into the mire.

For the coming Saturday was the day of the great cricket match, Sixth versus School, from which a Dominican would as soon think of deserting as of emigrating.

But Loman must desert if he was to keep his appointment, and he managed the proceeding with his now characteristic untruthfulness; a practice he would have scorned only a few months ago. How easy the first wrong step! What a long weary road when one, with aching heart, attempts to retrace the way! And at present Loman had made no serious effort in that direction.

On the Friday morning, greatly to the astonishment of all his class-fellows, he appeared in his place with his arm in a sling.

"Hullo, Loman!" said Wren, the first whom he encountered, "what's the row with you?"

"Sprained my wrist," said Loman, to whom, alas!—so easy is the downward path when once entered on—a lie had become an easy thing to utter.

"How did you manage that?" exclaimed Callonby. "Mind you get it right by to-morrow, or we *shall* be in a fix."

This little piece of flattery pleased Loman, who said, "I'm afraid I shan't be able to play."

"What! Who's that won't be able to play?" said Raleigh, coming up in unwonted excitement.

"Loman; he's sprained his wrist."

"Have you shown it to Dr Splints?" said Raleigh.

"No," said Loman, beginning to feel uncomfortable. "It's hardly bad enough for that."

"Then it's hardly bad enough to prevent your playing," said Raleigh, drily.

Loman did not like this. He and Raleigh never got on well together, and it was evident the captain was more angry than sympathetic now.

"Whatever shall we do for bowlers?" said some one.

"I'm awfully sorry," said Loman, wishing he was anywhere but where he was; "but how am I to help?"

"Whatever induced you to sprain your wrist?" said Wren. "You might just as well have put it off till Monday."

"Just fancy how foolish we shall look if those young beggars beat us, as they are almost sure to do," said Winter.

Loman was quickly losing his temper, for all this was, or seemed to be, addressed pointedly to him.

"What's the use of talking like that?" he retorted. "You ass, you! as if I could help."

"Shouldn't wonder if you could help," replied Winter.

"Perhaps," suggested some one, "it was the *Dominican* put him out of joint. It certainly did give him a rap over the knuckles."

"What do you mean?" exclaimed Loman, angrily, and half drawing his supposed sprained hand out of the sling.

"Shut up, you fellows," interposed Raleigh, authoritatively. "Baynes will play in the eleven to-morrow instead of Loman, so there's an end of the matter."

Loman was sorely mortified. He had expected his defection would create quite a sensation, and that his class-fellows would be inconsolable at his accident. Instead of that, he had only contrived to quarrel with nearly all of them, alienating their sympathy; and in the end he was to be quietly superseded by Baynes, and the match was to go on as if he had never been heard of at Saint Dominic's.

"Never mind; I'm bound to go and see Cripps. Besides," said he to himself, "they'll miss me to-morrow, whatever they say to-day."

Next day, just when the great match was beginning, and the entire school was hanging breathless on the issue of every ball, Loman quietly slipped out of Saint Dominic's, and walked rapidly and nervously down to the Cockchafer in Maltby.

"What *shall* I say to Cripps?" was the wild question he kept asking himself as he went along; and the answer had not come by the time he found himself standing within that worthy's respectable premises.

Mr Cripps was in his usual good humour.

"Why, it's Mr Loman! so it is!" he exclaimed, in a rapture. "Now who *would* have thought of seeing *you* here?"

Loman was perplexed.

"Why, you told me to come this afternoon," said he.

"Did I? Ah, I dare say! Never mind. Very kind of a young gentleman like you to come and see the likes of me. What'll you take?"

Loman did not know what to make of this at all.

"I came to see you about that—that horse you told me to bet against," he said.

"I remember. What's his name? Sir Patrick, wasn't it? My friend told me that he'd had the best of that. What was it? Ten bob?"

This affected ignorance of the whole matter in hand was utterly bewildering to Loman, who had fully expected that, instead of having to explain himself, he would have the matter pretty plainly explained to him by his sportive acquaintance.

"No, ten pounds. That was what I was to pay if the horse won; and, Cripps, I can't pay it, or the twenty pounds either, to you."

Cripps whistled.

"That's a go and no mistake!" he said. "Afraid it won't do, mister."

"You told me Sir Patrick was sure not to win," said Loman.

"Ah, there was several of us took in over that there horse," coolly said Mr Cripps. "I lost a shilling myself over him. Nice to be you, flush of cash, and able to pay straight down."

"I can't pay," said Loman.

"Ah, but the governor can, I'll wager," insinuated Cripps.

"He would never do it! It's no use asking him," said Loman.

Cripps whistled again.

"That's awkward. And my friend wants his money, too, and so do I."

"I really can't pay," said Loman. "I say, Cripps, let us off that twenty pounds. I really didn't mean about that rod."

Mr Cripps fired up in righteous indignation.

"Ah, I dare say, mister. You'll come and snivel now, will you? But you were ready enough to cheat a honest man when you saw a chance. No, I'll have my twenty or else there'll be a rumpus. Make no mistake of that!"

The bare idea of a "rumpus" cowed Loman at once. Anything but that.

"Come, now," said Cripps, encouragingly, "I'll wager you can raise the wind somewheres."

"I wish I knew how. I see no chance whatever, unless—" and here a brilliant idea suddenly struck him—"unless I get the Nightingale. Of course; I say, Cripps, will you wait till September?"

"What! Three months! And how do you suppose I'm to find bread to eat till then?" exclaimed Mr Cripps.

"Oh, do!" said Loman. "I'm certain to be able to pay then. I forgot all about the Nightingale."

"The Nightingale? It must be an uncommon spicy bird to fetch in thirty pound!"

"It's not a bird," said Loman, laughing; "it's a scholarship."

"A what?"

"A scholarship. I'm in for an exam, you know, and whoever's first gets fifty-pounds a year for three years."

"But suppose you ain't first? what then?"

"Oh, but I'm *sure* to be. I've only got Fifth Form fellows against me, and I'm certain to beat them!"

"Well," said Mr Cripps, "I don't so much care about your nightingales and cocksparrows and scholarships, and all them traps, but I'd like to oblige you."

"Oh, thank you!" cried Loman, delighted, and feeling already as if the debt was paid. "And you'll get your friend to wait too, won't you?"

"Can't do that. I shall have to square up with him and look to you for the lot, and most likely drop into the workhouse for my pains."

"Oh, no. You can be quite certain of getting the money."

"Well, blessed if I ain't a easy-going cove," said Mr Cripps, with a grin. "It ain't every one as 'ud wait three months on your poll-parrot scholarships, or whatever you call 'em. Come, business is business. Give us your promise on a piece of paper—if you must impose upon me." Loman, only too delighted, wrote at Mr Cripps's dictation a promise to pay the thirty pounds, together with five pounds interest, in September, and quitted the Cockchafer with as light a heart as if he had actually paid off every penny of the debt.

"Of course I'm safe to get it! Why ever didn't I think of that before? Won't I just work the rest of the term! Nothing like having an object when you're grinding."

With this philosophical reflection he re-entered Saint Dominic's, and unobserved rejoined the spectators in the cricket-field, just in time to witness a very exciting finish to a fiercely contested encounter.

Chapter Fourteen.
Sixth versus School.

Never had a Sixth versus School Match been looked forward to with more excitement at Saint Dominic's than the present one. Party feeling had been running high all the term, intensified on the one hand by the unpopularity of some of the monitors, and on the other by the defiant attitude of the Fifth and the tone of their organ, the *Dominican*.

The lower school naturally looked on with interest at this rivalry between the two head forms, the result of which, as might have been expected, was the reverse of beneficial for the discipline of the school generally. If the big boys set a bad example and disregard rules, what can one expect of the little ones?

So far, anything like conflict had been avoided. The Fifth had "cheeked" the Sixth, and the Sixth had snubbed the Fifth; but with the exception of Loman's assault on Oliver, which had not led to a fight, the war had been strictly one of words. Now, however, the opposing forces were to be ranged face to face at cricket; and to the junior school the opportunity seemed a grand one for a display of partisanship one side or the other.

The School Eleven, on this occasion, moreover, consisted exclusively of Fifth Form boys—a most unusual circumstance, and one which seemed to be the result quite as much of management as of accident. At least so said the disappointed heroes of the Fourth.

The match was, in fact—whatever it was formally styled—a match between the Sixth and the Fifth, and the partisans of either side looked upon it as a decisive event in the respective glories of the two top forms.

And now the day had come. All Saint Dominic's trooped out to the meadows, and there was a rush of small boys as usual for the front benches. Stephen found himself along with his trusty ally, Paul, and his equally trusty enemy, Bramble, and some ten other Guinea-pigs and Tadpoles, wedged like sardines upon a form that would comfortably hold six, eagerly canvassing the prospects of the struggle.

"The Sixth are going to win in a single innings, if you fellows want to know," announced Bramble, with all the authority of one who knows.

"Not a bit of it," replied Paul. "The Fifth are safe to win, I tell you."

"But they've got no decent bowlers," said Raddleston.

"Never mind," said Stephen. "Loman's not going to play for the Sixth. He's sprained his wrist."

"Hip, hip, hurrah?" yelled Paul, "that *is* jolly! They are sure to be licked now. Are you sure he's out of it?"

"Yes. Look at him there with his arm in a sling."

And Stephen pointed to where Loman stood in his ordinary clothes talking to some of his fellows.

"Well, that *is* a piece of luck!" said Paul. "Who's to take his place?"

"Baynes, they say. He's no use, though."

"Don't you be too cock-sure, you two," growled Bramble. "I say we shall beat you even if Loman don't play. Got any brandy-balls left, Greenfield?"

Similar speculations and hopes were being exchanged all round the field, and when at last the Fifth went out to field, and Callonby and Wren went in to bat for the Sixth, you might have heard a cat sneeze, so breathless was the excitement.

Amid solemn silence the first few balls were bowled. The third ball of the first over came straight on to Wren's bat, who played it neatly back to the bowler. It was not a run, only a simple block; but it was the first play of the match, and so quite enough to loosen the tongues of all the small boys, who yelled, and howled, and cheered as frantically as if a six had been run or a wicket taken. And the ice once broken, every ball and every hit were marked and applauded as if empires depended on them.

It was in the midst of this gradually rising excitement that Loman slipped quietly and unobserved from the scene, and betook himself to the errand on which we accompanied him in the preceding chapter.

The two Sixth men went quickly to work, and at the end of the second over had scored eight. Then Callonby, in stepping back to "draw" one of Wraysford's balls, knocked down his wicket.

How the small boys yelled at this!

But the sight of Raleigh going in second soon silenced them.

"They mean hard work by sending in the captain now," said Paul. "I don't like that!"

"No more do I," said Stephen. "He always knocks Oliver's bowling about."

"Oh, bother; is your brother bowling?" said Master Paul, quite unconscious of wounding any one's feelings. "It's a pity they've got no one better."

Stephen coloured up at this, and wondered what made Paul such a horrid boy.

"Better look-out for your eyes," said Bramble, cheerily. "The captain always knocks up this way, over square-leg's head."

There was a general buzz of youngsters round the field, as the hero of the school walked up to the wicket, and coolly turned to face Oliver's bowling.

The scorer in the tent hurriedly sharpened his pencil. The big fellows, who had been standing up to watch the opening overs, sat down on the grass and made themselves

60

comfortable. Something was going to happen, evidently. The captain was in, and meant business.

Oliver gripped the ball hard in his hand, and walked back to the end of his run. "Play!" cried the umpire, and amid dead silence the ball shot from the bowler's hand.

Next moment there rose a shout loud enough to deafen all Saint Dominic's. The ball was flying fifty feet up in the air, and Raleigh was slowly walking, bat in hand, back to the tent he had only a moment ago quitted!

The captain had been clean bowled, first ball!

Who shall describe the excitement, the yelling, the cheering, the consternation that followed? Paul got up and danced a hornpipe on the bench; Bramble kicked the boy nearest to him. "Well bowled, sir!" shouted some. "Hard lines!" screamed others. "Hurrah for the Fifth!"

"You'll beat them yet, Sixth!" such were a few of the shouts audible above the general clamour.

As for Stephen, he was wild with joy. He was a staunch partisan of the Fifth in any case, but that was nothing to the fact that it was *his* brother, his own brother and nobody else's, who had bowled that eventful ball, and who was at that moment the hero of Saint Dominic's. Stephen felt as proud and elated as if he had bowled the ball himself, and could afford to be absolutely patronising to those around him, on the head of this achievement.

"That wasn't a bad ball of Oliver's," he said to Paul. "He can bowl very well when he tries."

"It was a beastly fluke!" roared Bramble, determined to see no merit in the exploit.

"Shut up and don't make a row," said Stephen, with a bland smile of forgiveness.

Bramble promised his adversary to shut *him* up, and after a little more discussion and altercation and jubilation, the excitement subsided, and another man went in. All this while the Fifth were in ecstasies. They controlled their feelings, however, contenting themselves with clapping Oliver on the back till he was nearly dead, and speculating on the chances of beating their adversaries in a single innings.

But they had not won the match yet.

Winter was next man in, and he and Wren fell to work very speedily in a decidedly business-like way. No big hits were made, but the score crawled up by ones and twos steadily, and the longer they were at it the steadier they played. Loud cheers announced the posting of thirty on the signal-board, but still the score went on. Now it was a slip, now a bye, now a quiet cut.

"Bravo! well played!" cried Raleigh and his men frequently. The captain, by the way, was in excellent spirits, despite his misfortune.

Thirty-five, forty! The Fifth began to look hot and puzzled. The batsmen were evidently far too much at home with the bowling. A change must be made, even though it be to put on only a second-rate bowler.

Tom Senior was put on. He was nothing like as good a bowler as either Wraysford, or Oliver, or Ricketts. He bowled a very ordinary slow lob, without either twist or shoot, and was usually knocked about plentifully; and this appeared likely to be his fate now, for Wren got hold of his first ball, and knocked it right over into the scorer's tent for five. The Fifth groaned, and could have torn the wretched Tom to pieces. But the next ball was more lucky; Winter hit it, indeed, but he hit it up, sky-high, over the bowler's head, and before it reached the ground Bullinger was safe underneath it. It was with a sigh of relief that the Fifth saw this awkward partnership broken up. The score was at forty-eight for three wickets; quite enough too!

After this the innings progressed more evenly. Men came in and went out more as usual, each contributing his three or four, and one or two their ten or twelve. Among the latter was Baynes, who, at the last moment, it will be remembered, had been put into the eleven to replace Loman. By careful play he managed to put together ten, greatly to his own delight, and not a little to the surprise of his friends.

In due time the last wicket of the Sixth fell, to a total of eighty-four runs.

The small boys on the bench had had leisure to abate their ardour by this time. Bramble had recovered his spirits, and Paul and Stephen looked a little blue as they saw the total signalled.

"Eighty-four's a lot," said Stephen.

Paul nodded glumly.

"Ya, ha! How do you like it, Guinea-pigs?" jeered Bramble. "I hope *you'll* get half as much. *I* knew how it would be."

The two friends listened to these taunts in silent sorrow, and wished the next innings would begin.

It did presently, and not very brilliantly either. The Fifth only managed to score fifty-one, and to this total Wraysford was the only player who made anything like good scoring. Oliver got out for six, Ricketts for nine, and Tom Senior and Braddy both for a "duck's-egg." Altogether it was a meagre performance, and things looked very gloomy for the Fifth when, for a second time, their adversaries took the wickets.

Things never turn out at cricket as one expects, however, and the second innings of the Sixth was no exception to the rule. They only made thirty-six runs. Stephen and Paul were hoarse with yelling, as first one wicket, then another, went down for scarcely a run. Raleigh and Baynes seemed the only two who could stand up at all to the bowling of Oliver and Wraysford, but even their efforts could not keep the wickets up for long.

Every one saw now that the final innings would be a desperate struggle. The Fifth wanted sixty-nine to be equal and seventy to win, and the question was, Would they do it in time?

Stephen and his confederate felt the weight of this question so oppressive that they left the irritating company of Mr Bramble, and walked off and joined themselves to a group of Fourth Form fellows, who were watching the match with sulky interest, evidently sore that they had none of their men in the School Eleven.

"They'll never do it, and serve them right!" said one. "Why didn't they put Mansfield in the eleven, or Banks? They're far more use than Fisher or Braddy."

"For all that, it'll be a sell if the Sixth lick," said another.

"I wouldn't much care. If we are going to be sat upon by those Fifth snobs every time an eleven is made up, it's quite time we did go in with the Sixth."

"Jolly for the Sixth!" retorted the other; whereupon Stephen laughed, and had his ears boxed for being cheeky. The Fourth Senior could not stand "cheek."

But Saint Dominic's generally was "sweet" on the Fifth, and hoped they would win. When, therefore, Tom Senior and Bullinger went in first and began to score there was great rejoicing.

But the Fourth Form fellows, among whom Stephen now was, refused to cheer for any one; criticism was more in their line.

"Did you ever see a fellow hit across wickets more horribly than Senior?" said one.

"Just look at that!" cried another. "That Bullinger's a downright muff not to get that last ball to leg! I could have got it easily."

"Well, with that bowling, it's a disgrace if they *don't* score; that's all I can say," remarked a third.

And so these Fourth Form grandees went on, much to Stephen's wrath, who, when Oliver went in, removed somewhere else, so as to be out of ear-shot of any offensive remarks.

Oliver, however, played so well that even the Fourth Form critics could hardly run him down. He survived all the other wickets of his side, and, though not making a brilliant score, did what was almost as useful—played steadily, and gradually demoralised the bowling of the enemy.

As the game went on the excitement increased rapidly; and when at length the ninth wicket went down for sixty-one, and the last man in appeared, with nine to win, the eagerness on both sides scarcely knew bounds. Every ball, every piece of fielding, was cheered by one side, and every hit and every piece of play was as vehemently cheered by the other. If Raleigh and Wren had been nervous bowlers, they would undoubtedly have been disconcerted by the dead silence, followed by terrific applause, amid which every ball—even a wide—was delivered. But happily they were not.

It was at this critical juncture that Loman reappeared on the scene, much consoled to have the interview with Cripps over, and quite ready now to hear every one lament his absence from the match.

The last man in was Webster, a small Fifth boy, who in the last innings had signalised himself by making a duck's-egg. The Fifth scarcely dared hope he would stay in long enough for the nine runs required to be made, and looked on now almost pale with anxiety.

"Now," said Pembury, near whom Loman, as well as our two Guinea-pigs, found themselves, "it all depends on Oliver, and I back Oliver to do it, don't you, Loamy?"

Loman, who since the last *Dominican* had not been on speaking terms with Pembury, did not vouchsafe a reply, "I do!" said Stephen, boldly.

"Do you, really?" replied Pembury, looking round at the boy. "Perhaps you back yourself to talk when you're not spoken to, eh, Mr Greenhorn?"

"Bravo! bravo! Well run, sir! Bravo, Fifth!" was the cry as Oliver, following up the first ball of the over, pilfered a bye from the long-stop.

"Didn't I tell you!" exclaimed Pembury, delighted; "he'll save us; he's got down to that end on purpose to take the bowling. Do you twig, Loamy? And he'll stick to that end till the last ball of the over, and then he'll run an odd number, and get up to the other end. Do you comprehend?"

"You seem to know all about it," growled Loman, who saw the force of Pembury's observations, but greatly disliked it all the same.

"Do I, really?" replied the lame boy; "how odd that is, now—particularly without a crib!"

Loman was fast losing patience—a fact which seemed to have anything but a damping effect on the editor of the *Dominican*. But another hit or two by Oliver created a momentary diversion. It was quite clear that Pembury's version of Oliver's tactics was a correct one. He could easily have run three, but preferred to sacrifice a run rather than leave the incompetent and flurried Webster to face the bowling.

"Six to win!" cried Stephen; "I'm *certain* Oliver will do it!"

"Yes, Oliver was always a plodding old blockhead!" drily observed Pembury, who seemed to enjoy the small boy's indignation whenever any one spoke disrespectfully of his big brother.

"He's not a blockhead!" retorted Stephen, fiercely.

"Go it! Come and kick my legs, young 'un; there's no one near but Loamy, and he can't hurt."

"Look here, you lame little wretch!" exclaimed Loman, in a passion; "if I have any more of your impudence I'll box your ears!"

"I thought your wrist was sprained?" artlessly observed Pembury. "Here, young Paul, let's get behind you, there's a good fellow, I *am* in such a funk!"

Whether Loman would have carried out his threat or not is doubtful, but at that moment a terrific shout greeted another hit by Oliver—the best he had made during the match—for which he ran four. One to tie, two to win! will they do it?

It was a critical moment for Saint Dominic's. Had the two batsmen been playing for their lives they could not have been more anxiously watched; even Pembury became silent.

And now the last ball of the over is bowled in dead silence. Onlookers can even hear the whizz with which it leaves Wren's hand.

It is almost wide, but Oliver steps out to it and just touches it. Webster is half across the wickets already—ready for a bye. Oliver calls to him to come on, and runs. It is a desperate shave—too desperate for good play. But who cares for that when that run has pulled the two sides level, and when, best of all, Oliver has got up to the proper end for the next over?

Equal! What a shout greets the announcement! But it dies away suddenly, and a new anxious silence ensues. The game is saved, but not won; another run is wanted.

No one says a word, but the Fifth everywhere look on with a confidence which is far more eloquent than words.

Raleigh is the bowler from the lower end, and the Sixth send out their hearts to him. He may save them yet!

He runs, in his usual unconcerned manner, up to the wicket and delivers the ball. It is one which there is but one way of playing—among the slips.

Oliver understands it evidently, and, to the joy of the Fifth, plays it. But why does their cheer drop suddenly, and why in a moment is it drowned, over and over and over again, by the cheers of the Sixth and their partisans, as the crowd suddenly breaks into the field, and the ball shoots high up in the air?

A catch! Baynes, the odd man, had missed a chance a few overs back from standing too deep. This time he had crept in close, and saved the Sixth by one of the neatest low-catches that had ever been seen in a Dominican match.

Chapter Fifteen.
A Lower School Festival.

"I tell you what, Wray," said Oliver one evening about a week after the match, "I heartily wish this term was over."

"Why, that's just what I heard your young brother say. He is going to learn the bicycle, he says, in the holidays."

"Oh, it's not the holidays I want," said Oliver. "But somehow things have gone all wrong. I've been off my luck completely this term."

"Off your luck!—You great discontented, ungrateful bear. Haven't you got the English prize? Aren't you in the School Eleven? and didn't you make top score in the match with the Sixth last Saturday? Whatever do you mean by 'off your luck'?"

"Oh, it's not that, you know," said Oliver, pulling a quill pen to bits. "What I mean is—oh, bother!—a fellow can't explain it."

"So it seems," laughed Wraysford; "but I wish a fellow could, for I've not a notion what you're driving at."

"Well, I mean I'm not doing much good. There's that young brother of mine, for instance. What good have I been to him? There have I let him go and do just what he likes, and not looked after him a bit ever since he came here."

"And I wager he's got on all the better for not being tied up to your apron strings. He's a fine honest little chap, is young Greenfield."

"Oh, I dare say; but somehow I don't seem to know as much of him now as I used to do before he came here."

"That's Loman's fault, I bet you anything," exclaimed Wraysford. "I'm sure he won't do the kid any good. But Rastle was saying only yesterday how well Stephen was getting on in class."

"Was he? It's little thanks to me if he is," said Oliver, gloomily.

"And what else have you got to grumble about?" asked his friend.

"Why, you know how I'm out with the Fifth over that affair with Loman. They all set me down as a coward, and I'm not that."

"Of course you aren't," warmly replied the other. "But, Noll, you told me a little while ago you didn't care a snap what they thought."

"No more I do, in a way. But it's very uncomfortable."

"Why don't you tell them straight out why you didn't let out at Loman? They are sure to respect your motive."

"Yes, and set me down as posing as a martyr or a saint! No! I'd sooner pass as a coward than set up as a saint when I'm not one. Why, Wray, if you'll believe me, I've been a worse Christian since I began to try to be one, than I ever was before. I'm for ever losing my temper, and—"

"Shut up that tune, now," interposed Wraysford, hurriedly. "If you are beginning at that again, I'll go. As if you didn't know you were the best fellow in the school!"

"I'm not the best, *or* anything like," said Oliver, warmly; "I hate your saying so—I wish almost I had never told you anything about it."

"Well, I don't know," said Wraysford, walking to the window and looking out. "Ever since you told me of it, I've been trying myself in a mild way to go straight. But it's desperate hard work."

"Desperate hard work even if you try in more than a mild way," said Oliver.

Both were silent for a little, and then Oliver, hurriedly changing the subject, said, "And then, to proceed with my growl, I'm certain to come a howler over the Nightingale."

Wraysford turned from the window with a laugh.

"I suppose you expect me to sympathise with you about that, eh? The bigger the howler the better for me! I only wish you were a true prophet, Noll, in that particular."

"Why, of course you'll beat me—and if you don't Loman will. I hear he's grinding away like nuts."

"Is he, though?" said Wraysford.

"Yes, and he's going to get a 'coach' in the holidays too."

"More likely a dog-cart. Anyhow, I dare say he will run us close. But he's such a shifty fellow, there's no knowing whether he will stay out."

Just at that moment a terrific row came up from below.

"Whatever's up down there?"

"Only the Guinea-pigs and Tadpoles. By the way," said Wraysford, "they've got a grand 'supper,' as they call it, on to-night to celebrate their cricket match. Suppose we go and see the fun?"

"All right!" said Oliver. "Who won the match?"

"Why, what a question! Do you suppose a match between Guinea-pigs and Tadpoles *ever* came to an end? They had a free fight at the end of the first innings. The Tadpole umpire gave one of his own men 'not out' when he hit his wicket, and they made a personal question of it, and fell out. Your young brother, I hear, greatly distinguished himself in the argument."

"Well, it doesn't seem to interfere with their spirits now, to judge of the row they are making. Just listen!"

By this time they had reached the door of the Fourth Junior room, whence proceeded a noise such as one often hears in a certain popular department of the Zoological Gardens. Amid the tumult and hubbub the two friends had not much difficulty in slipping in unobserved and seating themselves comfortably in an obscure corner of the festive apartment, behind a pyramid of piled-up chairs and forms.

The Junior "cricket feast" was an institution in Saint Dominic's, and was an occasion when any one who had nerves to be excruciated or ear-drums to be broken took care to keep out of the way. In place of the usual desks and forms, a long table ran down the room, round which some fifty or sixty urchins sat, regaling themselves with what was left of a vast spread of plum-cake, buns, and ginger-beer. How these banquets were provided was always a mystery to outsiders. Some said a levy of threepence a head was made; others, that every boy was bound in honour to contribute something eatable to the feast; and others averred that every boy had to bring his own bag and bottle, and no more. Be that as it might, the Guinea-pigs and Tadpoles at present assembled looked uncommonly tight about the jackets after it all, and not one had the appearance of actual starvation written on his lineaments.

The animal part of the feast, however, was now over, and the intellectual was beginning. The tremendous noise which had brought Oliver and Wraysford on to the scene had indeed been but the applause which followed the chairman's opening song—a musical effort which was imperatively encored by a large and enthusiastic audience.

The chairman, by the way, was no other than our friend Bramble, who by reason of seniority—he had been two years in the Fourth Junior, and showed no signs of rising higher all his life—claimed to preside on all such occasions. He sat up at the top end in stately glory, higher than the rest by the thickness of a Liddell and Scott, which was placed on his chair to lift him up to the required elevation, blushingly receiving the applause with which his song was greeted, and modestly volunteering to sing it again if the fellows liked.

The fellows did like. Mr Bramble mounted once more on to the seat of his chair, and saying, "Look-out for the chorus!" began one of the time-honoured Dominican cricket songs. It consisted of about twelve verses altogether, but three will be quite enough for the reader.

"There was a little lad,
 (Well bowled!)
And a little bat he had;
 (Well bowled!)
He skipped up to the wicket,
And thought he'd play some cricket,
But he didn't, for he was—
 Well bowled!

"He thought he'd make a score
 (So bold),
And lead-off with a four

(So bold);
So he walked out to a twister,
But somehow sort of missed her,
And she bailed him, for he was
    Too bold.

"Now all ye little boys
    (So bold),
Who like to make a noise
    (So bold),
Take warning by young Walker,
Keep your bat down to a yorker,
Or, don't you see? you'll be—
    Well bowled!"

The virtue of the pathetic ballad was in the chorus, which was usually not sung, but spoken, and so presented a noble opportunity for variety of tone and expression, which was greedily seized upon by the riotous young gentlemen into whose mouths it was entrusted. By the time the sad adventures of Master Walker had been rehearsed in all their twelve verses, the meeting was so hoarse that to the two elder boys it seemed as if the proceedings must necessarily come abruptly to a close for want of voice.

But no! If the meeting was for the moment incapable of song, speech was yet possible and behold there arose Master Paul in his place to propose a toast.

Now Master Paul was a Guinea-pig, and accounted a mighty man in his tribe. Any one might have supposed that the purpose for which he had now risen was to propose in complimentary terms the health of his gallant opponents the Tadpoles. This, however, was far from his intention. His modesty had another theme. "Ladies and gentlemen," he began. There were no ladies present, but that didn't matter. Tremendous cheers greeted this opening. "You all know me; I am one of yourselves." Paul had borrowed this expression from the speech of a Radical orator, which had appeared recently in the papers. Every one knew it was borrowed, for he had asked about twenty of his friends during the last week whether that wouldn't be "a showy lead-off for his cricket feast jaw?"

The quotation was, however, now greeted as vociferously as if it had been strictly original, and shouts of "So you are!"

"Bravo, Paul!" for a while drowned the orator's voice. When silence was restored his eloquence took a new and unexpected departure. "Jemmy Welch, I'll punch your head when we get outside, see if I don't!" Jemmy Welch was a Guinea-pig who had just made a particularly good shot at the speaker's nose with a piece of plum-cake. "Now, ladies and gentlemen, I shall not detain you with a speech (loud cheers from all, and 'Jolly good job!' from Bramble). I shall go on speaking just as long as I choose, Bramble, so now! (Cheers.) I've as much right to speak as you have. (Applause.) You're only a stuck-up duffer. (Terrific cheers, and a fight down at the end of the table.) I beg to drink the health of the Guinea-pigs. (Loud Guinea-pig cheers.) We licked the old Tadpoles in the match. ('No you didn't!' 'That's a cram!' and groans from the Tadpoles.) I say we did! Your umpire was a cheat—they always are! We beat you hollow, didn't we, Stee Greenfield?"

"Yes, rather!" shouted Stephen, snatching a piece of cake away from a Tadpole and shying it to a Guinea-pig.

"That's eight matches we've won," proceeded Paul; "and—all right, Spicer! I saw you do it this time! See if I don't pay you for it!" whereat the speaker hurriedly quitted his seat and, amid howls and yells, proceeded to "pay out" Spicer.

Meanwhile Stephen heard his name suddenly called upon for a song, an invitation he promptly obeyed. But as the clamour was at the time deafening, and the attention of the audience was wholly monopolised by the commercial transactions taking place between Paul and Spicer, the effect of the performance was somewhat lost. Oliver certainly did see his young brother mount up on the table, turn very red in the face, open his mouth and shut it, smile in one part, look sorrowful in another, and wave his hand above his head in another. But that was the only intimation he had of a musical performance proceeding. Words and tune were utterly inaudible by any one except the singer himself—even if *he* heard them.

This was getting monotonous, and the two visitors were thinking of withdrawing, when the door suddenly opened, and a dead silence prevailed. The new-comer was the dirtiest and most ferocious-looking of all the boys in the lower school, who rushed into the room breathless, and in what would have been a white heat had his face been clean enough to show it. "What do you think?" he gasped, catching hold of the back of a chair for support; "Tony Pembury's kept me all this while brushing his clothes! I told him it was cricket feast, but he didn't care! What do you think of that? Of course, you've finished all the grub; I knew you would!"

This last plaintive wail of disappointment was drowned in the clamour of execration which greeted the boy's announcement. Lesser feuds were instantly forgotten in presence of this great insult. The most sacred traditions of Guinea-pigs and Tadpoles were being trampled upon by the tyrants of the upper school! Not even on cricket feast night was a fag to be let off fagging!

It was enough! The last straw breaks the camel's back, and the young Dominicans had now reached the point of desperation.

It was long before silence enough could be restored, and then the redoubtable Spicer yelled out, "Let's strike!"

The cry was taken up with yells of enthusiasm—"Strike! No more fagging!"

"Any boy who fags after this," screamed Bramble, "will be cut dead! Those who promise hold up your hands—mind, it's a promise!"

There was no mistaking the temper of the meeting, every hand in the room was held up.

"Mind now, no giving in!" cried Paul. "Let's stick all together. Greenfield senior shall *kill* me before I do anything more for him!"

"Poor fellow!" whispered Oliver, laughing; "what a lot of martyrdoms he'll have to put up with!"

"And Pembury shall kill me," squealed the last comer, who had comforted himself with several crusts of plum-cakes and the dregs of about a dozen bottles of ginger-beer. And every one protested their willingness to die in the good cause.

At this stage Oliver and Wraysford withdrew unobserved. "I'm afraid we've been eavesdropping," said Oliver. "Anyhow, I don't mean to take advantage of what I've heard."

"What a young ruffian your brother is!" said Wraysford; "he looked tremendously in earnest!"

"Yes, he always is. You'll find he'll keep his word far better than most of them."

"If he does, I'm afraid Loman will make it unpleasant for him," said Wraysford.

"Very likely."

"Then you'll have to interfere."

"Why, what a bloodthirsty chap you are, Wray! You are longing for me to quarrel with Loman. I'll wait till young Stephen asks me to."

"Do you think he will? He's a proud little chap."

Oliver laughed. "It'll serve him right if he does get a lesson. Did ever you see such a lot of young cannibals as those youngsters? Are you coming to have supper with me?"

The nine o'clock bell soon rang, and, as usual, Oliver went to his door and shouted for Paul.

No Paul came.

He shouted again and again, but the fag did not appear. "They mean business," he said. "What shall I do? Paul!"

This time there came a reply down the passage—"Shan't come!"

"Ho, he!" said Oliver; "this is serious; they are sticking to their strike with a vengeance! I suppose I must go and look for my fag, eh, Wray? Discipline must be maintained."

So saying, Oliver stepped out into the passage and strolled off in the direction from which the rebel's voice had proceeded. The passages were empty; only in the Fourth Junior room was there a sound of clamour.

Oliver went to the door; it was shut. He pushed; it was fortified. He kicked on it; a defiant howl greeted him from the inside. He called aloud on his fag; another "Shan't come!" was his only answer.

It was getting past a joke, and Oliver's temper was, as we have seen not of the longest. He kicked again, angrily, and ordered Paul to appear.

The same answer was given, accompanied with the same yell, and Oliver's temper went faster than ever. He forgot he was making himself ridiculous; he forgot he was only affording a triumph to those whom he desired to punish; he forgot the good resolutions which had held him back on a former occasion, and, giving way to sudden rage, kicked desperately at the door once more.

This time his forcible appeal had some effect. The lower panel of the door gave way before the blow and crashed inwards, leaving a breach large enough to admit a football.

It was an unlucky piece of success for Oliver, for next moment he felt his foot grabbed by half a dozen small hands within and held firmly, rendering him unable to stir from his ridiculous position. In vain he struggled and raged; he was a tight prisoner, at the mercy of his captors.

It was all he could do to stand on his one foot, clinging wildly to the handle of the door. In this dignified attitude Wraysford presently found his friend, and in such a state of passion and fury as he had never before seen him.

To rap the array of inky knuckles inside with a ruler, and so disengage the captive foot, was the work of a minute. Oliver stood for a moment facing the door and trembling with anger, but Wraysford, taking him gently by the arm, said, "Come along, old boy!"

There was something in his voice and look which brought a sudden flush into the pale face of the angry Oliver. Without a word, he turned from the door and accompanied his friend back to the study. There were no long talks, no lectures, no remorseful confessions that evening. The two talked perhaps less than usual, and when they did it was about ordinary school topics.

No reference was made either then or for a long while afterwards to the events of the evening. And yet Oliver and Wraysford, somehow, seemed more than ever drawn together, and to understand one another better after this than had ever been the case before.

Chapter Sixteen.
Guinea-Pigs and Tadpoles on Strike.

If anything had been required to make the "strike" of the Guinea-pigs and Tadpoles a serious matter, the "affair of Greenfield senior's right foot" undoubtedly had that effect. The *éclat* which that heroic exploit lent to the mutiny was simply marvellous. The story was told with fifty exaggerations all over the school. One report said that the whole body of the monitors had besieged the Fourth Junior door, and had been repulsed with heavy slaughter. Another declared that Oliver had been captured by the fags, and branded on the soles of his feet with a G and a T, to commemorate the emancipation of the Guinea-pigs and Tadpoles; and a third veracious narrative went so far as to say that the Upper Fifth and several members of the Sixth had humbly come and begged forgiveness for their past misdeeds, and were henceforth to become the fags of their late victims.

True or untrue as these stories were, any amount of glory accompanied the beginning of the strike, and there was sufficient sense of common danger to unite the youngsters in very close bonds. You rarely caught a Guinea-pig or a Tadpole alone now; they walked about in dozens, and were very wide awake. They assembled on every possible occasion in their room, and fortified their door with chairs and desks, and their zeal with fiery orations and excited conjurations. One wretched youth who the first evening had been weak enough to poke his master's fire, was expelled ignominiously from the community, and for a week afterwards lived the life of an outcast in Saint Dominic's. The youngsters were in earnest, and no mistake. Stephen Greenfield, as was only natural, did not altogether find cause for exultation over the event which led to the strike. For a whole day he was very angry on his brother's account, and threatened to stand aloof from the revolution altogether; but when it was explained to him this would lead to a general "smash-up" of the strike, and when it was further explained that the fellows who caught hold of his big brother's right foot couldn't possibly be expected to know to whom that foot belonged, he relented, and entered as enthusiastically as any one into the business. Indeed, if all the rebels had been like Stephen, the fags at Saint Dominic's would be on strike to this day. He contemplated martyrdom with the utmost equanimity, and the Inquisition itself never saw a more determined victim.

The morning after the famous "cricket feast" gave him his first opportunity of sacrificing himself for the good of his country. Loman met him in the passage after first-class.

"Why didn't you turn up and get my breakfast, you idle young vagabond?" inquired the Sixth Form boy, half good-humouredly, and little guessing what was in the wind. "I'm not idle," said Stephen.

"Then what do you mean by not doing your work?"

"It's not my work."

Loman opened his eyes in amazement, and stared at this bold young hero as if he had dropped from the clouds. "What!" he cried; "what do you say?"

"It's not my work," repeated Stephen, blushing, but very determined.

"Look here, young fellow," said Loman, when he was sure that he had really heard correctly, "don't you play any of your little games with me, or you'll be sorry for it."

Stephen said nothing, and waited with a tremor for what was to follow.

Loman was hardly a bully naturally. It was always easier for him to be civil than to be angry, especially with small boys, but this cool defiance on the part of his fag was too much for any one's civility, and Loman began to be angry.

"What do you mean by it?" he said, catching the boy by the arm.

Stephen wrenched away his arm and stood dogged and silent.

Nothing could have irritated Loman more. To be defied and resisted by a youngster like this was an experience quite new to him.

"Just come to my room," said he, gripping his fag angrily by the shoulder. "We'll see who's master of us two!"

Stephen was forced to submit, and allowed himself to be dragged to the study.

"Now!" said Loman shutting the door.

"Now!" said Stephen, as boldly as he could, and wondering what on earth was to become of him.

"Are you going to do what you're told, or not?" demanded Loman.

"Not what *you* tell me," replied Stephen, promptly, but not exactly cheerfully.

"Oh!" said Loman, his face becoming crimson, "you're quite sure?"

"Yes," said Stephen.

"Then take that!" said Loman.

It was a sharp box on the ears, suddenly administered. Stephen recoiled a moment, but only a moment. He had expected something a good deal worse. If that was all, he would brave it out yet.

"Don't you hit me!" he said, defiantly.

Loman could not stand to be defied. His vanity was his weak point, and nothing offended his vanity so much as to find any one as determined as himself.

He took up a ruler, and in his passion flung it at the luckless Stephen's head. It struck him hard on the cheek. The blood flushed to the boy's face as he stood a moment half-stunned and smarting with the pain, confronting his adversary. Then he rushed blindly in and flung himself upon the bully.

Of course it was no match. The small boy was at the mercy of the big one. The latter was indeed taken aback for a moment at the fury of his young assailant, impotent as it was, but that was all. He might have defended himself with a single hand; he might have carried the boy under one arm out into the passage. But the evil spirit had been roused within him, and that spirit knew no mercy. He struck out and fought his little foeman as if he had been one of his own size and strength. For every wild, feeble blow Stephen aimed, Loman aimed a hard and straight blow back. If Stephen wavered, Loman followed in as he would in a professional boxing match, and when at last the small boy gave up, exhausted, bleeding, and scarcely able to stand, his foe administered a parting blow, which, if he had struck no other, would have stamped him as a coward for ever.

"Now!" exclaimed Loman, looking down on his victim, "will you do what you're told now, eh?"

It was a critical moment for poor Stephen. After all, was the "strike" worth all this hardship? A single word would have saved him; whereas if he again defied his enemy, it was all up with him.

He did waver a moment; and lucky for him he did. For just then the door opened, and Simon entered. Stephen saw his chance. Slipping to the open door, he mustered up energy to cry as loud as he could, "No, I won't;" and with that made good his escape into the passage, as done up as a small boy well could be without being quite floored.

A dozen eager friends were at hand to aid in stopping the bleeding of their hero's nose, and to apply raw steak to his black eye. The story of his desperate encounter flew on the wings of fame all over the school, and the glory and pride of the youngsters reached its climax when, that afternoon, Stephen with his face all on one side, his eye a bright green and yellow, and his under lip about twice its ordinary thickness, took his accustomed place in the arithmetic class of the Fourth Junior.

"Why, Greenfield," exclaimed Mr Rastle, when in due time the young hero's turn came to stand up and answer a question, "what have you been doing to yourself?"

"Nothing, sir," remarked Stephen, mildly.

"How did you come by that black eye?" asked the master.

"Fighting, sir," said Stephen, rather pompously.

"Ah! what did you say forty-eight sixths was equal to?"

This was Mr Rastle's way. He very rarely hauled a boy over the coals before the whole class.

But after the lesson he beckoned Stephen into his study.

"I'm afraid you got the worst of that fight," he said.

Stephen, who by this time knew Mr Rastle too well to be afraid of him, and too well, also, not to be quite frank with him, answered meekly, "The fellow was bigger than me."

"I should guess that by the state of your face. Now, I don't want to know what the fight was about, though I dare say you'd like to tell me (Stephen was boiling to tell him). You small boys have such peculiar reasons for fighting, you know, no one can understand them."

"But this was because—"

"Hush! Didn't I tell you I won't hear what it was about, sir!" said Mr Rastle, sharply. "Did you shake hands afterwards?"

"No, I didn't, *and I won't!*" exclaimed Stephen, forgetting, in his indignation, to whom he was speaking.

"Then," said Mr Rastle, quietly, "write me out one hundred lines of Caesar, Greenfield; and when you have recollected how to behave yourself, we will talk more about this. You can go."

Mr Rastle *was* a queer man; he never took things as one expected. When Stephen expected him to be furious he was as mild as a lamb. There was no making him out.

But this was certain: Stephen left his room a good deal more crestfallen than he entered it. He had hoped to win Mr Rastle's sympathy and admiration by an account of his grievances, and, instead of that, he was sent off in disgrace, with an imposition for being rude, and feeling anything but a hero.

Even the applause of his friends failed to console him quite. Besides, his head ached badly, and the bruise on his cheek, which he had scarcely felt among his other wounds, now began to swell and grow painful. Altogether, he was in the wars.

He was groaning over his imposition late that evening in the class-room, feeling in dreadful dumps, and wishing he had never come to Saint Dominic's, when a hand laid on his shoulder made him start. He looked up and saw Mr Rastle.

"Greenfield," said the master, kindly, "how much of your imposition have you done?"

"Seventy lines, sir."

"Hum! That will do this time. You had better get to bed."

"Oh, sir!" exclaimed Stephen, moved far more by Mr Rastle's kind tone than by his letting him off thirty lines of the Caesar, "I'm so sorry I was rude to you."

"Well, I was sorry, too; so we'll say no more about that. Why, what a crack you must have got on your cheek!"

"Yes, sir; that was the ruler did that."

"The ruler! Then it wasn't a fair fight? Now don't begin telling me all about it. I dare say you were very heroic, and stood up against terrible odds. But you've a very black eye and a very sore cheek now, so you had better get to bed as fast as you can."

And certainly the pale, bruised, upturned face of the boy did not look very bright at that moment.

Stephen Greenfield went off to bed that night in a perturbed state of mind and body. He had stuck loyally to his promise not to fag, and he had earned the universal admiration of his comrades. But, on the other hand, he had been awfully knocked about, and, almost as bad, he had been effectively snubbed by Mr Rastle. He did not exactly know what to think of it all. Had he done a fine deed or a foolish one? and what ought he to do to-morrow?

Like a sensible little man, he went sound asleep over these questions, and forgot all about them till the morrow.

When he woke Stephen was like a giant refreshed. His eye was certainly a rather more brilliant yellow than the day before, and his cheek still wore a dull red flush. But somehow he felt none of the misgivings and dumps that had oppressed him the night before. He was full of hope again and full of courage. The Guinea-pigs should never charge *him* with treachery and desertion, and what he had gone through already in the "good cause" he would go through again.

With this determination he dressed and went down to school. Loman, whose summons he expected every moment to hear, did not put him to the necessity of a renewed struggle. From all quarters, too, encouraging reports came in from the various insurgents. Paul announced that Greenfield senior took it "like a lamb"; Bramble recounted how his "nigger-driver," as he was pleased to call Wren, had chased him twice round the playground and over the top of the cricket-shed without being able to capture him; and most of the others had exploits equally heroic to boast of. Things were looking up in the Fourth Junior.

They spent a merry morning, these young rebels, wondering in whispers over their lessons what this and that Sixth or Fifth Form fellow had done without them. With great glee they imagined Raleigh blacking his own boots and Pembury boiling his own eggs, and the very idea of such wonders quite frightened them. At that rate Saint Dominic's would come to a standstill altogether.

"Serve 'em right!" said Bramble; "they want a lesson. I wish I'd two fellows to strike against instead of one!"

"One's enough if he strikes you back," said Stephen, with a rueful grin.

Master Bramble evinced his sympathy by laughing aloud. "I say, you look just like a clown; doesn't he, Padger, with his eye all sorts of colours and his cheek like a house on fire?"

"All very well," said Stephen; "I wish you'd got my cheek."

"Bramby's got cheek enough of his own, I guess," put in Paul; whereat Master Bramble fired up, and a quarrel became imminent.

However, Stephen prevented it by calling back attention to his own picturesque countenance. "I don't mind the eye, that don't hurt; but I can tell you, you fellows, my cheek's awful!"

"I always said you'd got an awful cheek of your own, young Greenfield," said Bramble, laughing, as if *he* was the inventor of the joke. Stephen glowered at him.

"Well, you said so yourself," put in Bramble, a little mildly, for since Stephen's exploit yesterday that young hero had advanced a good deal in the respect of his fellows. "But, I say, why don't you stick some lotion or something on it? It'll never get right if you don't, will it, Padger?"

Padger suggested that young Greenfield might possibly have to have his cheek cut off if he didn't look-out, and Paul said the sooner he "stashed his cheek" the better.

The result of this friendly and witty conference was that Stephen took it into his head to cure his cheek, and to that end applied for leave from Mr Rastle to go down that afternoon to Maltby to get something from the chemist.

Mr Rastle gave him leave, and told him the best sort of lotion to ask for, and so, as soon as afternoon school was over, our young champion sallied boldly forth on his errand. He felt very self-satisfied and forgiving to all the world as he walked along. There was no doubt about it, he was a hero. Every one seemed to take an interest in his black eye and sore cheek, from Mr Rastle downwards. Very likely that fight of his with Loman yesterday would be recorded as long as Saint Dominic's remained, as the event which saved the lower school from the tyranny of the upper!

His way to the chemist's lay past the turning up to the Cockchafer, and the idea occurred to him to turn in on the way back and talk over the event of the hour with Mr Cripps, whom he had not seen since the bagatelle-lesson a week ago. He was sure that good gentleman would sympathise with him, and most likely praise him; and in any case it would be only civil, after promising to come and see him sometimes, to look in.

The only thing was that the Cockchafer, whatever one might say about it, was a public-house. The private door at the side hardly sufficed to satisfy Stephen that he was not breaking rules by going in. He would not have entered by the public door for worlds, and the thought did occur to him, Was there very much difference after all between one door and the other? However, he had not answered the question before he found himself inside, shaking hands with Mr Cripps.

That gentleman was of course delighted, and profuse in his gratitude to the "young swell" for looking him up. He listened with profound interest and sympathy to his story, and made some very fierce remarks about what he would do to "that there" Loman if he got hold of him. Then the subject of bagatelle happened to come up, and presently Stephen was again delighting and astonishing the good gentleman by his skill in that game. Then in due time it came out that the boy's mother had bought him a bicycle, and he was going to learn in the holidays, a resolution Mr Cripps highly approved of, and was certain a clever young fellow like him would learn in no time, which greatly pleased Stephen.

Before parting, Mr Cripps insisted on lending his young friend a lantern for his bicycle, when he rode it in the dark. It was a specially good one, he said, and the young gentleman could easily return it to him after the holidays, and so on.

Altogether it was a delightful visit, and Stephen wondered more than ever how some of the fellows could think ill of Mr Cripps.

"Oh, I say," said the boy, at parting; "don't do what you said you would to Loman. I'm not afraid of him, you know."

"I'd like to knock his ugly head off for him!" cried Mr Cripps, indignantly.

"No, don't; please don't! I'd rather not. I dare say he's sorry for it."

"I'll see he is!" growled Mr Cripps.

"Besides, I've forgiven him," said Stephen, "and oughtn't to have told tales of him; so mind you don't do it, Mr Cripps, will you?"

"I'll see," said Mr Cripps. "Good-bye for the present, young gentleman, and come again soon."

And so, at peace with all the world, and particularly with himself, Stephen strolled back to Saint Dominic's, whistling merrily.

Chapter Seventeen.
The Doctor among the Guinea-Pigs.

The *Dominican* appeared once more before the holidays, and, as might have been expected (besides its usual articles at the expense of the Sixth Form), made itself particularly merry over the rebellion of the Guinea-pigs and Tadpoles.

Pembury was not the fellow to give quarter in his own particular line of attack; and it must be confessed he had the proud satisfaction of making his unfortunate young victims smart.

The "leading article" of the present number bore the suggestive title, "Thank Goodness!" and began as follows:

"Thank goodness, we are at last rid of the pest which has made Saint Dominic's hideous for months past! At a single blow, with a single clap of the hands, we have sent Guinea-pigs and Tadpoles packing, and can now breathe pure air. No longer shall we have to put up with the plague. We are to be spared the disgust of seeing them, much more of talking to them or hearing their hideous voices. No longer will our morning milk be burned; no longer will our herrings be grilled to cinders; no longer will our jam be purloined; no longer will our books and door-handles be made abominable by contact with their filthy hands! Thank goodness! The Doctor never did a more patriotic deed than this! The small animals are in future to be kept to their own quarters, and will be forbidden the liberty they have so long abused of mixing with their betters. It is as well for all parties; and if any event could have brightened the last days of this term, it is this—" and so on.

Before this manifesto, a swarm of youngsters puzzled on the day of publication with no little bewilderment and fury. They had refused to allow any of their number to act as policeman, and had secretly been making merry over the embarrassment of their late persecutors, and wondering whatever they would be able to say for their humiliated selves in the *Dominican*—and lo! here was an article which, if it meant anything, meant that the heroic rebellion of the juniors was regarded not with dismay, but with positive triumph, by the very fellows it had been intended to "squash!"

"What does it mean, Padger?" asked Bramble, who, never much of a scholar, was quite unable to master the meaning of this.

"It's all a pack of crams," replied Padger, not quite sure of the sense himself.

"It means," said Stephen, "the fellows say they are jolly glad to get rid of us."

"Eh?" yelled Bramble; "oh, I say, you fellows, come to the meeting! Jolly glad! They aren't a bit glad."

"They say so," said Paul. "Hold hard, Bramble, let's read the rest."

It was all his friends could do to restrain the ardent Bramble from summoning a meeting on the spot to denounce the *Dominican* and all its "crams." But they managed to hold him steady while they read on.

"The Doctor never did a more—pat—pat—ri—what do you call it?—patriotic deed than this!"

"Hullo, I say, look here!" cried Stephen, turning quite yellow; "the Doctor's in it, they say, Bramble. 'The small animals'—that's you and Padger—'are to be kept in their own quarters.' Whew! there's a go."

"What!" shrieked Bramble, "who says so? The Doctor never said so. I shall do what I choose. He never said so. Bother the Doctor! Who's coming to the meeting, eh?"

But at that moment the grave form of Doctor Senior appeared in the midst of the group, just in time to hear Master Bramble's last complimentary shout.

The head master was in the most favourable times an object of terror to the "guilty-conscienced youth" of the Fourth Junior, and the sight even of his back often sufficed to quell their tumults. But here he stood face to face with his unhappy victims, one of whom had just cried, "Bother the Doctor!" and all of whom had by word and gesture approved of the sentiment. Why would not the pavement yawn and swallow them? And which of them would not at that moment have given a thousand pounds (if he had it) to be standing anywhere but where he was?

"Go to your class-room," said the Doctor, sternly, eyeing the culprits one by one, "and wait there for me."

They slunk off meekly in obedience to this order, and waited the hour of vengeance in blank dismay.

Dr Senior did not keep them long in suspense, however. His slow, firm step sounded presently down the corridor, and at the sound each wretched culprit quaked with horror.

Mr Rastle was in the room, and rose as usual to greet his chief; the boys also, as by custom bound, rose in their places. "Good morning, Mr Rastle," said the Doctor. "Are your boys all here?"

"Yes, sir, we have just called over."

"Ah! And what class comes on first?"

"English literature, sir."

"Well, Mr Rastle, I will take the class this morning, please—instead of you."

A groan of horror passed through the ranks of the unhappy Guinea-pigs and Tadpoles at these words. Bramble looked wildly about him, if haply he might escape by a window or lie hid in a desk; while Stephen, Paul, Padger, and the other ringleaders, gave themselves up for lost, and mentally bade farewell to joy for ever.

"What have the boys been reading?" inquired Dr Senior of Mr Rastle.

"Grey's *Elegy*, sir. We have just got through it."

"Oh! Grey's *Elegy*!" said the Doctor; and then, as if forgetting where he was, he began repeating to himself,—

"The curfew tolls the knell of parting day,
The lowing herds wind slowly o'er the lea."

"The first boy,—what can you tell me about the curfew?" The first boy was well up in the curfew, and rattled off a "full, true, and particular account" of that fine old English institution, much to everybody's satisfaction. The Doctor went on repeating two or three verses till he came to the line,—

"The rude Forefathers of the hamlet sleep."

"What does that line mean?" he asked of a boy on the second desk.

The boy scarcely knew what it meant, but the boy below him did, and was quite eager for the question to be passed on. It was passed on, and the genius answered promptly, "Four old men."

"Four rude old men," shouted the next, seeing a chance.

"Four rude old men who used to sleep in church," cried another, ready to cap all the rest.

The Doctor passed the question on no further; but gravely explained the meaning of the line, and then proceeded with his repetition in rather a sadder voice.

Now and again he stopped short and demanded an explanation of some obscure phrase, the answers to which were now correct, now hazy, now brilliantly original. On the whole it was not satisfactory; and when for a change the Doctor gave up reciting, and made the boys read, the effect was still worse. One boy, quite a master of elocution, spoilt the whole beauty of the lines,—

"Nor Grandeur hear with a disdainful smile
The short and simple annals of the Poor,—"

by reading "animals" instead of "annals"; while another, of an equally zoological turn of mind, announced that—

"On some fond *beast* the parting soul relies,—"

instead of "breast."

But the climax of this "animal mania" was reached when the wretched Bramble, finally pitched upon to go on, in spite of all his efforts to hide, rendered the passage:—

"Haply some hoary-headed swain may say,

Oft have we seen him at the peep of dawn," etcetera, as—

"Happy some hairy-headed swine may say."

This was a little too much.

"That will do, sir," said the Doctor, sternly. "That will do. What is your name, sir?"

"Bramble, please, sir."

"Well, Bramble, how long have you been in this class?"

"Two years, sir."

"And have you been all the while on the bottom desk?"

"Yes, please, sir."

"Sir, it displeases me. You are a dunce, sir."

And then, to Bramble's utter despair and to the terror of all the other unprofitable members of the class, the Doctor proceeded to catechise sharply the unhappy youth on his general knowledge of the subjects taught during the term.

As might be expected, the exhibition was a miserable one; Bramble was found wanting in every particular. The simplest questions could hardly coax a correct answer out of him, whereas an ordinary inquiry was hopelessly beyond his powers. He mixed up William the Conqueror and William of Orange; he subtracted what ought to be multiplied, and floundered about between conjunctions and prepositions in a sickening way. The Doctor did not spare him. He went ruthlessly on—exposing the boy's ignorance, first in one thing, then another. Bramble stood and trembled and perspired before him, and wished he was dead, but the questions still came on. If he had answered a single thing correctly it would have been a different matter, but he knew nothing. I believe he did know what twice two was, but that was the one question the Doctor did not ask him. As to French, Latin, Grammar, and Euclid, the clock on the wall knew as much of them as Bramble. It came to an end at last.

"Come here, Bramble," said the Doctor, gravely; "and come here, you, and you, and you," added he, pointing to Stephen and Paul and four or five others of the party who had been reading the *Dominican* that morning.

The luckless youngsters obeyed, and when they stood in a row before the dreaded Doctor, the bottom form and half of the bottom form but one were empty.

"Now, you boys," began the head master, very gravely, "I hadn't intended to examine you to-day; but, from something I heard one of you say, I felt rather anxious to know how some of you are doing in your studies. These half-dozen boys I was particularly anxious to know of, because I heard them talking to-day as if they were the most important boys in the whole school. They *are* the most important; for they are the most ignorant, and require, and in future will receive, the closest looking after. You, little boys," said the Doctor, turning to the row of abashed culprits, "take a word of warning from me. Do not be silly as well as dunces. Do not think, as long as you know least of any one in the school you can pretend to rule the school. I hope some of you have been led to see to-day you are not as clever as you would like to be. If you try, and work hard, and stick like men to your lessons, you will know more than you do now; and when you do know more you will see that the best way for little boys to get on is not by giving themselves ridiculous airs, but by doing their duty steadily in class, and living at peace with one another, and submitting quietly to the discipline of the school. Don't let me hear any more of this recent nonsense. You'll be going off in a day or two for the holidays. Take my advice, and think over what I have said; and next term let me see you in your right minds, determined to work hard and do your part honestly for the credit of the good old school. Go to your places, boys."

And so the Doctor's visitation came to an end. It made a very deep impression on the youthful members of the Fourth Junior. Most of them felt very much ashamed of themselves; and nearly every one felt his veneration and admiration for the Doctor greatly heightened. Only a few incorrigibles like Bramble professed to make light of the scene through which they had just passed, and even he, it was evident, was considerably chastened by his experience.

That evening, after the first bed-bell, Dr Senior requested some of the masters to meet with him for a few minutes in his study.

"Do any of you know," asked the head master, "anything about this newspaper, the *Dominican*, which I see hanging outside the Fifth door?"

"I hear a great many boys talking about it," said Mr Jellicott of the Fifth. "It is the joint production of several of the boys in my form."

"Indeed! A Fifth form paper!" said the Doctor. "Has any one perused it?"

"I have," said Mr Rastle. "It seems to me to be cleverly managed, though perhaps a little personal."

"Ah, only natural with schoolboys," said the Doctor. "I should like to see it. Can you fetch it, Rastle?"

"It is nailed to the wall," said Mr Rastle, smiling, "like Luther's manifesto; but I can get one of the boys, I dare say, to unfasten it for you."

"No, do not do that," said the Doctor. "If the mountain will not come to Mahomet, you know, Mahomet and his disciples must go to the mountain, eh, Mr Harrison? I think we might venture out and peruse it where it hangs." So half-stealthily, when the whole school was falling asleep, Dr Senior and his colleagues stepped out into the passage, and by the aid of a candle satisfied their curiosity as to the mysterious *Dominican*.

A good deal of its humour was, of course, lost upon them, as they could hardly be expected to understand the force of all the allusions it contained. But they saw quite enough to enable them to gather the general tenor of the paper; it amused and it concerned them.

"It shows considerable ability on the part of its editor," said the Doctor, after the masters had returned to his study, "but I rather fear its tone may give offence to some of the boys—in the Sixth for instance."

"I fancy there is a considerable amount of rivalry between the two head forms," said Mr Harrison.

"If there is," said Mr Jellicott, "this newspaper is hardly likely to diminish it."

"And it seems equally severe on the juniors," said Mr Rastle.

"Ah," said the Doctor, smiling, "about that 'strike.' I can't understand that. Really the politics of your little world, Rastle, are too intricate for any ordinary mortal. But I gather the small boys have a grievance against the big ones?"

"Yes, on the question of fagging, I believe."

"Oh!" said the Doctor. "I hope that is not coming up. You know I'm heretic enough to believe that a certain amount of fagging does not do harm in a school like ours."

"Certainly not," said Mr Jellicott. "But these small boys are really very amusing. They appear to be regularly organised, and some of them have quite a martyr spirit about them."

"As I can testify," said Mr Rastle, proceeding to recount the case of Stephen Greenfield and his sore cheek. The Doctor listened to it all, half gravely, half amused, and presently said:

"Well, it is as well the holidays are coming. Things are sure to calm down in them; and next term I dare say we shall be all the wiser for the lessons of this. Meanwhile I should like to see the editor of this paper to-morrow. Who is he, Jellicott?"

"I believe it is Pembury."

"Very well. Send him to me, will you, to-morrow at ten? Good-night. Thank you for your advice!"

Next morning the Doctor talked to Pembury about the *Dominican*. He praised the paper generally, and congratulated him on the success of his efforts. But he took exception to its personal tone.

"As long as you can keep on the broad round of humour and pure fun, nothing can please us more than to see you improving your time in a manner like this. But you must be very careful to avoid what will give pain or offence to any section of your schoolfellows. I was sorry to see in the present number a good deal that might have been well omitted of that kind. Remember this, Pembury, I want all you boys, instead of separating off one set from another, and making divisions between class and class, to try to make common cause over the whole school, and unite all the boys in common cause for the good of Saint Dominic's. Now your paper could help not a little in this direction. Indeed, if it does not help, it had better not be issued. There! I shall not refer to the matter again unless you give me cause. I do not want to discourage you in your undertaking, for it's really an excellent idea, and capitally carried out. And *verbum sap*, you know, is quite sufficient."

Anthony, with rather a long face, retired from the Doctor's presence.

A few days later the school broke up for the summer holidays.

Chapter Eighteen.
A Holiday Adventure.

When a big school like Saint Dominic's is gathered together within the comparatively narrow compass of four walls, there *is* some possibility of ascertaining how it prospers, and what events are interesting it. But when the same school is scattered to the four winds of heaven during the holidays, it would require a hundred eyes and more to follow its movements.

It would be impossible, for instance, at one and the same time to accompany Raleigh and his sisters up Snowdon, and look on at Bramble catching crabs on the rocks at Broadstairs; nor, while we follow Dr Senior among the peaks and passes of Switzerland (and remark, by the way, what a nice quiet boy Tom Senior is, when he has only his father and his mother to tempt him into mischief) can we possibly expect to regard very attentively the doings of Simon, as he gapes about before the London shop-windows, and jerks off a score or more stanzas of his "Hart's Earnings," which is now about a quarter done.

So the reader must imagine how most of the boys spent their holidays, how they enjoyed them, and how they behaved themselves during the period, and be content to be told only about two groups of holiday-makers, about whom, as they are destined to figure pretty conspicuously in next term's doings at Saint Dominic's, it will be interesting to hear rather more particularly now.

And the first group—if we can call a single person a "group"—is Loman.

Loman began his holidays in anything but cheerful spirits. No one had seemed particularly sorry to say good-bye to him at Saint Dominic's, and a good many had been unmistakably glad. And he had quite enough on his mind, apart from this, to make his home-coming far less joyous than it might have been. It ought to have been the happiest event possible, for he was coming home to parents who loved him, friends who were glad to see him, and a home where every comfort and pleasure was within his reach. Few boys, indeed, were more blessed than Loman with all the advantages of a Christian and happy home; and few boys could have failed to return to such a home after a long absence without delight. But to Loman, these holidays, the surroundings of home afforded very little pleasure. His mind was ill at ease. The burden of debt was upon him, and the burden of suspense. He had tried hard to assure himself that all would come right—that he would certainly win the scholarship, and so wipe off the debt; but his confidence became less and less comfortable as time went on.

He dared not tell his troubles to his father, for he feared his upbraiding; and he would not confess them to his mother, for she, he knew, would tell all to his father. He still clung to the hope that all would come right in the end; and then what would have been gained by telling his parents all about it?

The one thing was hard work—and Loman came home determined to work. His parents saw him out of spirits, and were concerned. They did what they could to cheer him, but without much success.

"Come, Edward, put away your books to-day," his mother would say; "I want you to drive me over to Falkham in the pony-chaise."

"I really can't, mother; I must work for the scholarship."

"Nonsense, boy; what is a scholarship compared with your health? Besides, you'll work all the better if you take some exercise."

But for a week nothing could tempt him out. Then, instead of accompanying his father or mother, he would take long solitary rides on his own pony, brooding all the while over his troubles.

One day, when in the course of one of these expeditions he had taken the direction of Maltby—which was only fifteen miles distant from his home—he became suddenly aware of an approaching dog-cart in the road before him, and a familiar voice crying, "Why, if it ain't young Squire Loman, riding a bit of very tidy horseflesh too, as I'm a Dutchman!"

It was Cripps. What evil spirit could have brought him on the scene now?

"Well, I never reckoned to see you now," said he, in his usual jaunty manner. "Fact is, I was just trotting over to see *you*. I wanted to try what this here cob was made of, and, thinks I, I may as well kill two birds with one stone, and look up my young squire while I'm about it."

"Coming to see me!" exclaimed Loman, horrified. "I say, Cripps, you mustn't do that. My father would be very angry, you know."

"Nice, that is! As if I wasn't as good company as any one else!"

"Oh! it's not that," said Loman, fearing he had given offence. "What I mean is—"

"Oh, I know—about that there rod. Bless me! I won't let out on you, my beauty—leastways, if you come up to scratch. He'd like to hear the story, though, the old gentleman, I fancy. Wouldn't he now?"

"I wouldn't have him know it for worlds. It'll be all right, Cripps, indeed it will about the money."

Mr Cripps looked very benignant.

"All right, young swell, I hope it will. Funny I feel such an interest in you, 'specially since that young greeny friend of yours put in a word for you. He's a real nice sort, he is—he owes you one, and no mistake."

"What!" said Loman, in surprise; "who do you mean? Young Greenfield?"

"To be sure. Regular young chum of mine, he is. I know all about you, my master, and no mistake!"

"What—the young sneak? What has he been saying about me?"

"Eh!—what ain't he been saying! In course you didn't half murder him, eh? In course you ain't a good hand at cheatin' all round up at the school! What? In course you ain't saying nice things agin me all over the place—and in course some of us wouldn't like to see you get a reg'lar good hiding, wouldn't we? Bless you, I knows all about it; but I'm mum, never fear!" Loman was furious.

"The young liar!" he exclaimed. "I did owe him one; I'll pay him when we get back!"

"Hold hard, young gentleman," said Cripps, coolly. "To be sure, he ain't downright sweet on you; but I ain't a-going to have him smashed, mind, all to bits. Well, never mind that. I'll turn back with you, young gentleman, if I may. We're only three miles from Maltby, and maybe you'll honour a poor chap like me by having a look in at the Cockchafer."

Loman did not know how to say "No," much as he disliked and feared his host. He returned with him to Maltby, and there spent an hour in the Cockchafer. He was introduced to several of Mr Cripps's low friends, in whose society he found it easy enough to become low himself. Cripps, by a judicious mixture of flattery and sly threats, managed to keep the boy well in hand, and when at last he rose to go it was with a promise to return again before the holidays were over—"to prevent Cripps having the trouble of calling on him," as that virtuous gentleman significantly put it.

Loman kept his promise, and visited Maltby once or twice, becoming each time more familiar with Cripps and his low friends, who made a great deal of him, and flattered him on all possible occasions, so that the boy presently found himself, as he imagined, quite a young hero at the Cockchafer.

Meanwhile, naturally, his reading fell behindhand. His parents, only too glad to see their boy taking more regular exercise, never suspected or inquired as to the direction of his frequent solitary rides. To them he seemed the same quiet, clever boy they fondly believed him. Little guessed they of the troubles that filled his breast or the toils that were daily enwrapping him!

Thus Loman's holidays came to an end. The farewell was once more said, parents and son parted, and on the first day of an eventful term the boy found himself once more within the walls of Saint Dominic's.

Oliver and Stephen, meanwhile, had been spending a very different sort of holiday at home. There was high feast and revelry when the two boys returned once more to the maternal roof. Stephen for once in a way had the satisfaction of finding himself a most unmistakable hero. He never tired telling of his adventures and discoursing on the whole manner of his life since the day he left home for Saint Dominic's. To his sister he recounted in all the slang phraseology he had at his command, the famous cricket matches in which he had borne a part; and she, though it was exactly like Greek to her, drank in every word with interest. And to his mother he narrated his various fights with Bramble, and the terrific adventures through which he had passed, till the good lady's hair nearly stood on end, and she began to think a public school was a terrible place to send a small boy to.

Oliver, of course, had his stories to tell too, only in a more sober manner.

There was a great scene when, on the first day of the holidays, the elder brother produced his books and announced that he must study at least two hours a day in prospect of the Nightingale Scholarship examination. But every one knew how much depended on his winning that scholarship, and in a few years being able to go to the university, so that the family gave in in the end, and Oliver was allowed his two hours' study, but not a second more, every day. Stephen, meanwhile, taught his sister round-arm bowling, and devoted himself mind and body to the bicycle.

The two brothers, during these holidays, became very great cronies. At school Oliver had seen comparatively little of his young brother, but now they were daily and hourly thrown together, the brotherly instincts in each blossomed wonderfully, and a mutual attachment sprang up which had hardly been there before.

It had been arranged, before breaking-up, that Oliver and Wraysford should spend the last week of the holiday together in rowing down the Thames from Oxford to London.

Great was Stephen's joy and pride when one morning, near the appointed time, Oliver said to him, "Look here, Stee. How would you like to come with Wray and me next week?"

"Like! wouldn't I rather!" shouted the small boy in ecstasy. "Thanks, Noll, old man! I say, it will be a spree." And the youngster became so riotous over the prospect that his elder brother had to threaten not to take him at all, and give him a thrashing into the bargain, before he could be reduced to order.

They were to take a tent with them, and cooking utensils, so as to be quite independent of inns, and each voyager was to contribute his share of provender. Quite a Robinson Crusoe business, even down to the desert island, for on desert islands the boys had declared they intended every night to take up their quarters, and, come hail, snow, or lightning, there to sleep under their waterproof tent.

Mrs Greenfield didn't half like the idea, and became very pathetic on the subject of ague and rheumatic fever. But the boys carried the day by promising faithfully that they would catch neither malady. The looked-for day came at last, and to Oxford they went, where the familiar sight of Wraysford, in boating costume, at the railway station still further elated their high spirits. The boat was ready. The tent, the provender, the blankets, were snugly stowed away on board. The weather was fine, the river was charming, everything promised well; and punctually that Monday afternoon the three adventurers loosed from their moorings and turned the nose of their boat towards London.

I wish I could tell the reader all the events of that wonderful voyage: how they paddled down merrily with the stream; how they found their desert island covered with nettles, which they had to mow down with their oars; how the soup-kettle wouldn't act, and the stew-pan leaked; how grand the potted lobster tasted; how Stephen offered to make tea with muddy water, and how the paraffin oil of their lanterns leaked all over their plum-cake and sandwiches; how Stephen was sent up inland to forage, and came back with wonderful purchases of eggs and milk; how they started off one day leaving their tent behind them, and had to row back in a panic to recover it; how it rained one night, and a puddle formed on the roof of the tent, which presently grew so big that it overflowed and gave Wraysford a shower-bath; how each morning they all took headers into the stream, much to the alarm of the sleepy ducks; how they now and then ran foul of a boat, and now and then were turned off their camping ground by an indignant keeper! It was glorious fun. But it would take a volume to recount all that happened to them.

They were coming near the end of their cruise. They had paddled down past the magnificent woods of Cliveden, and under the pretty bridge of Maidenhead; they had watched the boys bathing at "Athens," and they had rowed through the gloomy shadow of Windsor Castle and on past Eton.

Here the river is broken by a string of islands, which in many parts make the stream narrow; and the river being full of boats and barges, our three adventurers found themselves called upon to exercise more than ordinary precautions in keeping their course. This responsibility became at last so irksome that Oliver said, "I say, can't we get out of this rabble anyhow? Why shouldn't we take the other side of the islands?"

"I don't know. It would be a good deal quieter. I wonder none of the boats do it."

"Let's try, anyhow. We can't be far from the lock, and then the river will be wider. Take us up inside the next island, Stee, and mind you don't foul any one while you're about it."

Stephen did as he was bid. The stream was pretty strong just there, and the two rowers had to pull pretty hard to get round without drifting on to the island.

Once out of the main stream, they were delighted to find the course clear. Indeed, they had the channel all to themselves.

"What a jolly pace the stream is going at!" said Stephen; "why don't you drift, you fellows, instead of pulling like that?"

"Good idea for you, young 'un," said Wraysford, pulling in his oar. Oliver followed his example.

"Keep a look-out ahead," said he to Stephen, "and sing out if any thing's coming."

Stephen said, "All right," but (careless pilot that he was) began pulling on his socks and shoes, which he had dispensed with during the morning.

Thus occupied, and the other two sitting with their backs to the prow, the unnatural pace at which the boat flew along did not for a moment or two become apparent. Suddenly, however, Wraysford started up.

"Get out your oar, Noll—quick!"

"What's the row?" said Oliver, proceeding leisurely to obey the order.

"The weir! Quick, man, quick, or we shall be on to it!"

They had indeed got into the race leading to the weir, and every moment the stream, swelled by recent rains, rushed faster.

"Pull your right—hard!" cried Wraysford, backing water while Oliver flew to his oar.

There was just time, by a tremendous effort, to save themselves; but Oliver's oar was caught under one of the seats, and before he could extricate it the precious opportunity was lost.

No one said a word. Stephen, with pale face, pulled his rudder string; and Wraysford, with his one oar, tried desperately to arrest the headlong progress of the boat.

There was a shout from the bank, and a nearer and louder one from the lock. They became conscious of a great half-open gate on their right, and a rush of footsteps beside them. Then, in far shorter time than it takes to write it, the boat, side on to the weir, lurched and dashed for a moment in the troubled water, and the next instant turned over, and the three boys were struggling in the water.

In an ordinary current such an adventure would have been of little moment, for the boys could swim. But in a torrent like this it was an awful peril. The swift flood sweeps on and sucks under its prey with fearful force. To resist it is impossible—to escape being dashed against its stony bottom is almost as impossible.

Mercifully for Oliver, he did escape this latter peril, and, being cool always in the presence of danger, he offered no resistance to the stream, but struck out hard under the water for as long as his breath would permit.

When at last, exhausted and unable to swim farther, he rose to the surface, he was in calm deep water many yards below the weir. Help was at hand, or he could never have reached the bank. As it was, when at last friendly arms did drag him ashore, he was too exhausted even to utter his brother's name.

Where was Stephen? and where was Wraysford?

Wraysford had been more fortunate even than Oliver in his first capsize. He was swept over the weir, indeed, but into a side eddy which brought him up violently against a projecting branch, to which he clung wildly. Here he would have been safe, and even able to help himself to shore. But at the moment when he began to draw himself up from the water on to the branch, there was something—an arm cast wildly up—in the water beside him. In an instant Wraysford quitted his hold and plunged once more into the rapid. How, he knew not, but he just reached the hapless boy. It was too late to recover the friendly branch. All he could do was to cling to Stephen and trust to reaching calm water safely. Many a bruise the two received in that terrible passage, but the elder boy never once quitted his hold of the younger.

At last—it seemed an age—calm water was reached, providentially near the bank. Still clinging to one another, they were pulled ashore, bruised, stunned, but safe.

Thus ended this famous holiday cruise. The three boys kept their own secret, and talked little about the adventure, even to one another.

In due time the holidays ended, and the Dominicans reassembled once more in their venerable Alma Mater. Need I say there were three within those walls who, whatever they were before, were now friends bound together by a bond the closest of all—a bond which had stood the test of life and death?

Chapter Nineteen.
An old Fire re-kindled.

Saint Dominic's reassembled after the holidays in an amiable frame of mind.

The Guinea-pigs and Tadpoles, as the Doctor had prophesied, had cooled down considerably in spirit during the period, and now returned quietly to work just as if the mighty "strike" had never existed. Stephen's regular fights with Bramble recommenced the very first day, so that everything was quite like old times.

Oliver found that the Fifth, all but one or two, had quite forgotten their suspicions of his bravery which had spoiled the pleasure of his last term, and there seemed every prospect of his getting through this with less risk to his quick temper than before.

As for the Sixth, the Fifth had forgiven them all their offences, and would have been quite prepared, had it been allowed, to live in peace with their seniors, and forget all the dissensions of the Summer term. But it was not allowed, and an event which happened early in the term served to revive all the old animosities between the two head classes.

At Saint Dominic's, for reasons best known to the all-wise beings who presided over its management, the principal examinations and "removes" of the year took place not, as in most schools, at the end of the Midsummer term, but at the beginning of the Autumn term, about Michaelmas; consequently now, with the examinations looming in the distance, everybody who had anything to hope for from hard work settled down to study like mad. Cricket was over for the year, and football had not begun. Except boating there was not much doing out of doors, and for that reason the season was favourable for work. Studies, which used to be bear-gardens now suddenly assumed an appearance of respectability and quiet. Books took the place of boxing-gloves, and pens of fencing-sticks. The disorderly idlers who had been in the habit of invading at will the quarters of the industrious were now given to understand they must "kick-up their heels" elsewhere. *They* might not want to grind, but others did.

The idlers of the Fifth, to whom this warning was addressed on every hand, had nothing for it but to obey, and, feeling themselves greatly ill-used, to retire sadly, to some spot where "they could kick-up a row to themselves."

Casting about them for such a spot, it happened that Braddy and Ricketts one day lit almost by accident on an old empty study, which some years since had been a monitor's room, but was now empty and tenantless.

It at once occurred to these two astute heroes that this would be a magnificent place for boxing-matches. In the other studies one was always banging against the corners of tables, or tripping over fenders, but here there was absolutely nothing, but four bare walls to interfere with anybody.

They called in two more friends—Tom Senior and another—who declared it was a splendid find, and the four thereupon took formal possession of their new territory, and inaugurated the event by a terrific eight-handed match.

Nothing could have been more satisfactory. The room was well out of the way; the studious ones of the Fifth were spared all annoyance, and the riotous ones had an asylum to go to. No one was a bit the worse for the move; every one, on the contrary, found himself decidedly the better.

"Go and kick-up a row in the monitor's room," became quite a common objurgation in the Form, among the diligent; as common, in fact, as "Come along, old man, and have it out in the monitor's room," was among the idlers.

But, as ill-luck would have it, this delightful retreat happened to be situated immediately over the study occupied by Wren of the Sixth. That worthy hero, seated one afternoon over his books, was startled by a terrific noise, followed by a vibration, followed by the rattling of all his tumblers in the cupboard, followed by a dull, heavy thud over his head, which tempted him to believe either that an earthquake was in progress, or that one of the chimney-stacks had fallen on to the roof. When, however, the noise was repeated, and with it were blended laughter and shouts of "Now then, let him have it!"

"Well parried!"

"Bravo, Bully!" and the like, Wren began to change his mind, and laid down his pen. He walked up the stairs to the upper landing, where, at once, the noise guided him to the old monitor's room. Then the truth dawned upon him. He stayed long enough to get a pretty clear idea of who the "new lodgers" were, and then prudently retired without attempting a parley single-handed.

But next morning, when the festive rioters of the Fifth approached once more the scene of their revels, what was their amazement and rage to find the door locked, and the following notice, on a piece of school paper, affixed to the panel—"Monitor's room. This room is closed by direction of the monitors."

You might have knocked them over with a feather, so stupefied were they by this announcement! They stared at the door, they stared at one another, and then they broke out into a tempest of rage.

"The blackguards! what do they mean?" exclaimed Braddy, tearing down the paper and crushing it up in his hands.

"Monitor's room, indeed!" cried Ricketts. "*We'll* let them see whose room it is!"

"Kick open the door, can't you?" said Tom Senior.

They did kick open the door between them. The lock was a weak one, and soon gave way.

Once inside, the evicted ones indulged their triumph by an uproar of more than usual vehemence, longing that it might tempt into their clutches the daring intruders who had presumed to interfere with their possession. No one came. They had their fling undisturbed. But before they quitted their stronghold one of their number, by diligent searching, had found in the lock of a neighbouring study-door a key which would fit theirs. Repairing, therefore, the catch, damaged by their late forcible entry, they calmly locked the door behind them when they went, and affixed to it, in the identical place where the other notice had hung, "Fifth Form. Private study. Not to be entered without permission."

Of course, the news of this interesting adventure soon spread, and for a day or two the diligent as well as the idle on either side looked on with increasing interest for the issue of the contest.

For a while the Fifth had the best of it. They defied the enemy to turn them out, and procured and fixed an additional lock on the door. The Sixth threatened to report the matter to the Doctor, and summoned the invaders for the last time to capitulate. The invaders laughed them to scorn, and protested the room belonged to them, and leave it they would not for all the monitors in the world. The monitors retired, and the Fifth enjoyed their triumph.

But next day the Doctor abruptly entered the Fifth Form room, and said, "There is an unoccupied room at the end of the top landing, which some boys in this class have been making use of to the annoyance of other boys. This room, please remember, is not to be entered in future without my permission."

Checkmate with a vengeance for the Fifth!

This event it was which, trivial in itself, re-kindled once more with redoubled heat the old animosity between the two head Forms at Saint Dominic's. Although the original quarrel had been confined to only half-a-dozen individuals, it became now a party question of intense interest. The Sixth, who were the triumphant party, could afford to treat the matter lightly and smile over it, a demeanour which irritated the already enraged Fifth past description. The two Forms cut one another dead in the passages. The Fifth would gladly have provoked their rivals to blows, but, like sensible men, the Sixth kept the right side of the law, and refused to have anything to do with the challenges daily hurled at them.

As might be expected, the affair did not long remain a secret from the rest of the school. The Fourth Senior, as a body, stood up for the Sixth, and the Third and Second, on the whole, sided with the Fifth. But when it came to the junior school—the Guinea-pigs and Tadpoles—all other partisanship was thrown quite into the shade.

The quarrel was one completely after their own hearts. It had begun in a row, it had gone on in a row, and, if it ever ended, it would end in a row.

A meeting was summoned at the earliest opportunity to take the momentous matter into consideration.

"What I say," said Bramble, "is, it's a jolly good job!"

"What's a jolly good job?" demanded Stephen, who, of course, was red-hot for the Fifth.

"Why, chucking them out! I'm glad to see it, ain't you, Padger?"

"They didn't chuck them out!" roared Paul; "they went and sneaked to the Doctor, that's what they did!"

"I don't care! I say it's a jolly good job! Those who say it's a jolly good job hold up—"

"Shut up your row!" cried Stephen; "you're always sticking yourself up. I say it's a beastly shame, and I hope the Fifth will let them know it!"

"You're a young idiot, that's what you are!" exclaimed Bramble in a rage. "What business have you got at the meeting? Turn him out!"

"I'll turn *you* out!" replied the undaunted Stephen; "I've as much right here as you have. So there!"

"Turn him out, can't you?" roared Bramble. "Bah! who goes and swills ginger-beer down in a public-house in the town, eh?"

This most unexpected turn to the conversation startled Stephen. He turned quite pale as he replied, "*I* did, there! But I didn't go in at the public door. And you've been sneaking!"

"No, I haven't. Padger told me, didn't you, Padger? Padger peeped through the door, and saw you. Oh, my eye! won't I kick-up a shine about it! I'll let out on you, see if I don't. Bah, public-house boy! potboy, yah!"

Stephen's only answer to this was a book, accurately shied at the head of his enemy.

The subsequent proceedings at the meeting were a trifle animated, but otherwise not interesting to the reader. The chief result was that the Guinea-pigs emerged as uncompromising champions for the Fifth, and the Tadpoles equally strong for the Sixth, while Stephen felt decidedly uncomfortable as to the consequences of Bramble's discovery of his secret visits last term to the Cockchafer.

Stephen had in a confidential moment during the holidays told Oliver of these visits, and of his intimacy with Mr Cripps. The elder brother was very angry and astonished when he heard of it. He set before the boy, in no measured terms, the risk he was running by breaking one of the rules of the school; and, more than that, he said Cripps was a blackguard, and demanded of Stephen a promise, there and then, that he would never again enter the Cockchafer under any pretext whatever. Stephen, forced to submit, although not convinced that Cripps was such a wicked man as his brother made out, promised, but reserved to himself mentally the right to see Cripps at least once more at the Lock-House, there to return him the bicycle lantern, which it will be remembered that kind gentleman had lent the boy before the holidays. As to the Cockchafer, he was thoroughly frightened at the thought of having been seen there, and fully determined, even before Bramble's threat, never again to cross its threshold. After all, Stephen knew he had little enough to fear from that small braggadocio; Bramble had neither the wit nor the skill to use his discovery to any advantage. For a day or two he followed his adversary up and down the passages with cries of "Potboy!" till everybody was sick of the sound, and felt heartily glad when, one fine afternoon, Stephen quietly deposited his adversary on his back on the gravel of the playground.

But to return to the feud between Fifth and Sixth.

Things after a little seemed to quiet down once more. The exiled rioters, after a long and disheartening search, found rest for the soles of their feet in Tom Senior's study, which, though not nearly so convenient, afforded them asylum during their pugilistic encounters.

The studious ones settled down once more to their work, and the near approach of the examinations presently absorbed all their attention.

The struggle for the Nightingale Scholarship naturally was regarded with the most intense interest—not because it was the most important examination of the year: it was not. Not because it was worth 50 pounds a year for three years. That to most of the school was a minor consideration. It was as nothing to the fact that of the three candidates for the scholarship one was a Sixth Form boy and two Fifth. If only one of the latter could come out first, the Fifth and their partisans, all the school over, felt that the insult of the past month would be wiped out, and the glory of the Form avenged for ever. And it must be confessed that the Sixth, however much they professed to ignore the rivalry of their juniors, were equally anxious for their own man, and of late Loman had been working hard. He had worked, so it was reported, during the holidays, and now, ever since term had begun, he had remained more or less secluded in his study, or else, with a book under his arm, had taken walks outside.

Of course, the Sixth Form boy would win! Who ever heard of a Fifth boy beating a Sixth? And yet, in Oliver and Wraysford, the Fifth, every one admitted, had two strong men. They would at least make a hard fight for the prize. The Sixth only hoped they would not run their man *too* close, and so make the glory of his certain victory at all doubtful.

Loman was not a favourite even with his own class-fellows, but they could forgive anything now, provided he made sure of the Nightingale.

"He'll be all right!" said Callonby to Wren one day, when the two happened to hit on the topic of the hour; "he's a great deal steadier than he was last term."

"I wish he'd read indoors, then, and not be everlastingly trotting out with his books."

"Oh! I don't know; it's much jollier reading out of doors, if you can do it."

"As long as he *does* read. Well, it will be a regular sell if he comes to grief; the Fifth will be intolerable."

"They're not far short of that now. Hullo!" This exclamation was provoked by the sight of Loman in the playground under their window. He was returning from one of his studious rambles, with his book under his arm, slowly making for the school.

There was nothing in this to astonish the two boys as they looked down. What did astonish them was that he was walking unsteadily, with a queer, stupid look on his face, utterly unlike anything his schoolfellows had ever seen there before. They watched him cross the playground and enter the school-house. Then Wren said, gravely, "It's all up with the Nightingale, at that rate."

"Looks like it," said the other, and walked away. Loman was returning from one of his now frequent visits to the Cockchafer.

Chapter Twenty.
A Crisis.

The eventful day, which at the beginning of the term had seemed an age away, slowly but surely drew near.

This was Saturday. On Monday the examination would be over, and in a week the competitors would know their fates!

Some of my readers may know the queer sensation one sometimes gets at the approach of a long-looked-for and hardly-worked-for examination. For a week or so you have quietly been counting up what you *do* know. Now there breaks upon you an awful picture of what you do *not* know, and with it the absolute conviction that what you do not know is exactly what you ought to know, and what you do know is no use at all. It is too late to do anything. You cannot get up in a day what it would take you a fortnight to go through. And it is not much good, now you are sure it is useless, to go over again what you have done. You begin to feel a sort of despair, which becomes, as the hours close in, positively reckless. What do you care if you do miss? What's the use of bothering any more about it? It cannot be helped; why make yourself miserable? Only, you would give worlds to have the thing all over. Such at least were the sensations which stirred in the breasts of Oliver Greenfield and Horace Wraysford as they sat somewhat dejectedly over their books in Oliver's study that Saturday afternoon.

They had both worked hard since the holidays, generally together, neither concealing from the other what he had read or what he intended to read. Very bad rivals were these two, for though each was intent on winning the scholarship, each felt he would not break his heart if the other beat him, and that, as every one knows, is a most unheard-of piece of toleration. Now, however, each felt he had had enough of it. Oliver in particular was very despondent. He slammed up his books suddenly, and said, "I give it up; it's not a bit of use going on!"

Wraysford pushed back his chair slowly, and said, not very cheeringly, "Upon my word I think you're right, Noll."

"I've a good mind," said Oliver, looking very morose, "to scratch, and leave you and Loman to fight it out."

"Don't be a jackass, Noll," replied Wraysford, half laughing. "That *would* be a sensible thing to do!"

"All very well for you to laugh," said Oliver, his brow clouding. "You know you are well up and are going to win."

"I'm no better up than you are," said the other.

"You know you're going to win," repeated Oliver.

"I only wish I did," said Wraysford, with a sigh.

"Why," pursued Oliver, evidently bent on a melancholy tack, "I assure you, Wray, I've forgotten half even of what I did know. I was going over some of those brutal Roman History dates in bed last night, for instance, and I positively couldn't remember one. Then I tried the map of Greece, but I was still worse there; I couldn't remember where one single place was except Athens and Corinth, and I'm sure I used to be pretty well up in that."

"I expect you were half asleep at the time," suggested his friend.

"No, I wasn't; I couldn't sleep a wink. I say, Wray, *wouldn't* it be jolly if we only knew now what the questions are going to be on Monday?"

"Why don't you go and ask the Doctor?" said Wraysford, laughing; "he'd be delighted to tell you."

"What a humbug you are, Wray! I say, suppose we shut up work now and have a turn on the river. I'm certain it will do us more good than cracking our skulls here."

"Just what I had been thinking. I'm game, and it can't make much difference."

"I suppose Loman is grinding up to the last?"

"I suppose so; I was almost in hopes he wouldn't keep it up."

"Never mind, it will all be over on Monday; that's a comfort! Come along, old man. Suppose we get young Stee to cox us up to the lock and back."

Hue and cry was forthwith made for Stephen, but he was not to be found. He was out, Paul said; at the post, or somewhere.

"Oh, all right; you can come and cox us yourself, youngster," said Wraysford.

"Cox you!" exclaimed Paul; "why, ain't the Nightingale exam coming on, then, on Monday?"

"Of course it is!"

"And you two going out to row! I say, the Sixth will win it if you don't look-out!" said Paul, in a very concerned voice.

It was quite a revelation to the two boys to discover how great was the interest taken by outsiders in the coming event. Paul was in a great state of alarm, and was actually inclined to refuse to aid and abet what he imagined to be a wicked waste of precious opportunity, until, putting his head into Loman's study, he found that the Sixth Form fellow was also not at work.

When Oliver and Wraysford appeared in boating flannels in the playground they created as much sensation as if they had been ghosts.

"You don't mean to say you're going out, you fellows?" exclaimed Ricketts, one of the idle ones of the Fifth.

"Yes, I do," said Wraysford.

"But the Nightingale, I say?"

"That's not till Monday."

"I know; but aren't you grinding for it? I say, don't let them beat you! Hadn't you better work instead of going out?"

Ricketts, by the way, had not done a stroke of work that he could possibly help all the term!

All the other Fifth Form fellows they encountered echoed more or less anxiously the same advice. But the two friends were obdurate. Threats, promises, entreaties, would not put them off their row up the river, and they went on their way, leaving behind them an unusual gloom on the spirits of their dearest friends.

The only person who seemed really glad to see them leaving their work was Bramble. He, with his friend Padger, and a few other irreconcilables, were just returning from a rat-catching expedition, and the sight of the Fifth Form heroes in boating costume filled them with joy.

"Hullo—my eye—hurrah!" shouted Bramble, taking in the situation in a moment. "There they go! I hope they get drowned; don't you, Padger?"

Padger was understood to assent to this benevolent aspiration.

"Go it. *You'll* get the Nightingale! I thought you would! Hope you get drowned, do you hear! Hurrah for the Sixth!"

At this juncture Master Paul gave chase, and for a few moments Bramble and his friends were too much engaged to speak; but at last, when the chase was over, and further reprisals were out of the question, the hero of the Tadpoles summoned up all his remaining powers to yell:

"Yah boo, Nightingale! Hope you get drowned! Yah!" after which he went his way.

The two friends paddled quietly up the river. They talked very little, but both felt relieved to be away from their books. As they went on their spirits rose, greatly to Paul's displeasure. That young gentleman, immoderately jealous for the glory of the Fifth, was content as long as the two rowers remained grave and serious; he could then make himself believe they were engaged in mental exercises favourable to Monday's examination. But as soon as they began to whistle, and chaff him and one another, and talk of their holiday adventures, Paul became displeased, for they could not possibly do this and be inwardly preparing for the examination at the same time.

However, he had to submit as best he could, and gave all his attention to steering them carefully, so that it should be no fault of his, at any rate, if they were prevented from showing up on the critical day.

"This old Shar isn't half such a jolly river as the Thames, is it, Wray?"

"Rather not!" replied Wraysford, resting on his oar; "and yet it's pretty enough in parts."

"Oh, up at the weir?—yes. But I'm out of love with weirs at present. I shudder every time I think of that one up the Thames."

"It wasn't pleasant, certainly," said Wraysford.

"Pleasant! Old man, if you hadn't been there it would have been a good deal worse than unpleasant. Poor Stee!"

"Pull your left, Greenfield senior, or you'll be into the bank!" sung out Paul.

They paddled on again until Gusset Lock came in sight. There were very few boats about; the season was, in fact, at an end, and the river, which a month or two ago had generally swarmed with boats just at this part on Saturday afternoons, looked quite deserted.

"Shall we go through the lock or turn round?" inquired Paul.

"May as well turn, eh, Wray?"

Paul was about to obey the order and turn the boat, when, casting his eyes on the bank, he started suddenly to his feet and exclaimed, pointing towards the lock-house, "Hullo! I say, there's something up there!"

The two others looked round; something more lively than usual was undoubtedly taking place at old Mr Cripps's residence, to judge by the shouts and laughter which proceeded from the group of people assembled near the door.

From where they were the boys in the boat could not see what the nature of the excitement was, and therefore paddled on with a view to satisfy their curiosity.

As they came up to the lock Paul suddenly exclaimed, "That's young Greenfield!"

"What!" said Oliver—"Stephen?"

"Yes, and—what *on earth* are they doing to him?"

The boat being low down under the bank, it was impossible to see what was going on on the tow-path. Oliver, however, having once heard Stephen's name, ordered Paul to put them into the opposite bank quick, where they could land.

While this was being done a shriek from the bank sent the blood suddenly to the faces of the two friends. It was Stephen! They dashed ashore, and in a moment were across the lock and on the spot. The spectacle which met their eyes as they came up was a strange one. The central figure was the luckless Stephen, in the clutches of three or four disreputable fellows, one of whom was Cripps the younger, who, with loud laughter at the boy's struggles and brutal unconcern at his terror, were half dragging, half carrying him towards the water's edge.

Beside them stood Loman, flushed, excited, and laughing loudly. Poor Stephen, very unlike himself, appeared to be utterly cowed and terrified, and uttered shriek upon shriek as his persecutors dragged him along.

"Oh, don't! Please, Cripps! Don't let them, Loman—don't let them drown me!" he shouted.

A laugh was the only answer.

It was at this moment, and just when, to all appearances, the boy was about to be thrown into the water, that Oliver and Wraysford appeared on the scene.

Their appearance was so sudden and unexpected that the fellows, even though they did not know who the two boys were, were momentarily taken aback and dropped their prey.

With a bound Oliver sprang furiously on Cripps, who happened to be nearest him, and before that respectable gentleman knew where he was, had dealt him a blow which sent him staggering back in the utmost alarm and astonishment. Wraysford, no less prompt, tackled one of the other blackguards, while Stephen, now released, and cured of his momentary terror by the appearance of the rescuers, did his share manfully with one of the others.

The contest was short and sharp. A pair of well-trained athletic schoolboys, with a plucky youngster to help them, are a match any day for twice the number of half-tipsy cads. In a minute or two the field was clear of all but Cripps, who appeared, after his short experience, by no means disposed to continue the contest single-handed. As for Loman, he had disappeared.

"What is all this?" demanded Oliver, when at last, breathless and pale with excitement, he could find words.

"Oh, Noll!" cried Stephen, "I'll tell you all about it. But let's get away from here."

"No, I won't go!" shouted Oliver—"not till I know what it all means. You fellow!" added he, walking up to Cripps, "you'd better speak or I'll thrash you!"

Mr Cripps, who had had time to recover somewhat from his first surprise, looked a little inclined to defy his young antagonist, but, thinking better of it, suddenly assumed his usual impudent swagger as he replied, with a laugh, "Come, I say, you *do* do it well, you do! It was a joke—just a joke, young gentleman. You've no occasion to flurry yourself; we wouldn't have hurt a hair of the young gentleman's head. Ask Mr Loman."

"Where's Loman?" demanded Oliver. "Gone," said Stephen. "But I say, Noll, do come away. I'll tell you all about it. Do come."

Cripps laughed. "Don't you swallow all that young swell tells you. He's a nice boy, he is, but—well, he'd better mind what he says, that's all!"

"Do come away!" once more entreated Stephen.

"Yes, do come away," laughed Cripps, mimicking the boy's tones. "When I calls up at the school I'll let them all know what a nice young prig he is, coming down and drinking at my public-house and then turning round on me. Never fear! I*'ll* let them know, my beauties! I'll have a talk with your Doctor and open his eyes for him. Good-bye, you sneaking young—"

"Look here!" said Wraysford, quietly walking up to the blackguard in the midst of this discourse, "if you don't stop instantly you'll be sorry for it."

Cripps stared a moment at the speaker, and at the first he held out. Then, without another word, he turned on his heel into the cottage, leaving the three boys standing in undisputed possession of the tow-path.

"Come on, how, old man!" said Wraysford; "we can't do any good by staying here."

Oliver looked disposed to resist, and cast a glance at the cottage door by which Cripps had just vanished. But he let himself be persuaded eventually, and turned gloomily towards the boat. Here Paul, who had been a witness of the *fracas* on the tow-path, was waiting, ready to steer home, and bursting with curiosity to hear all Stephen had to say.

Greatly to his disgust, Oliver said, peremptorily, "You'll have to walk home, Paul; Stephen will steer."

"Why, you said I might steer."

Oliver was in no humour for an argument, so he gave Paul a light box on his ears and advised him to go home quietly unless he wanted a thrashing, and not say a word to any one about what had occurred.

Paul had nothing for it but sulkily to obey, and walk back. At last the others got on board and put off homeward.

"Now," said Oliver, presently, resting on his oar and bending forward towards Stephen.

"Oh, Noll!" began that unhappy youngster, "I am so very, very sorry! it was all—"

"None of that," angrily interrupted the elder brother. "Just tell me how it came about."

Stephen, quite cowed by his brother's angry manner, told his story shortly and hurriedly.

"Why," he said, "you know I promised you never to go to the Cockchafer again, and I didn't, but I thought I ought to see Cripps and give him back the bicycle-lamp."

"Young muff!" ejaculated his brother.

"So," pursued Stephen, still more falteringly, "I thought I'd come up this afternoon."

"Well, go on, can't you?" said Oliver, losing his temper at the poor boy's evident uneasiness.

"Cripps asked me into the cottage, and there were some fellows there, smoking and drinking and playing cards."

"Was Loman one of them?" put in Wraysford.

"I think so," said poor Stephen, who had evidently started his story in the hope of keeping Loman's name quiet.

"*Think* so, you young cad!" cried Oliver. "Why can't you tell the truth straight out? Was he there or not?"

"Yes, he was. I did mean to tell the truth, Noll, really, only—only there's no need to get Loman in a row."

"Go on," said Oliver.

"They made fun of me because I wouldn't smoke and play with them. You know I promised mother not to play cards, Noll. I didn't mind that, though, but when I wanted to go away they—that is, Cripps—wouldn't let me. I tried to get away, but he stopped me, and they said they'd make me play."

"Who said? Did Loman?" inquired Oliver, again. "Why—yes," said Stephen falteringly, "he and the rest. They held me down in a chair, and made me take hold of the cards, and one of them opened my mouth and shouted beastly words down into it—ugh!"

"Was that Loman?"

"No," said Stephen, relieved to be able to deny it.

"What did he do?" demanded Oliver.

"They all—"

"What did Loman do, I say?" again asked Oliver.

It was no use trying to keep back anything.

"He pulled my ears, but not very hard. Really I expect it was only fun, Noll." This was said quite beseechingly. "I said I thought they were very wicked to be doing what they did; but they only laughed at that, and called me a prig."

"Much better if you'd kept what you thought to yourself," said Wraysford. "Well?"

"Oh, then they did a lot of things to rile me, and knocked me about because I wouldn't drink their stuff, and they swore too."

"Did Loman swear?"

"They all swore, I think," said Stephen; "and then, you know, when I wouldn't do what they wanted they said they'd throw me in the river, and then you fellows turned up."

"Did Loman tell them to throw you in the river?" said Oliver, whose brow had been growing darker and darker.

"Oh, no," exclaimed Stephen, "he didn't, really! I think he was sorry."

"Did he try to prevent it, then?" asked Oliver.

"Well, no; I didn't hear him say—" faltered Stephen; but Oliver shut him up, and turning to Wraysford said, "Wray, I shall thrash Loman."

"All serene," replied Wraysford; "you'd better have it out to-night."

"Oh, Noll!" cried Stephen in great distress; "don't fight, please. It was all my fault, for—"

"Shut up, Stee," said Oliver, quietly, but not unkindly. Then turning to Wraysford, he added, "After tea, then, Wray, in the gymnasium."

"Right you are!" replied his friend.

And then, without another word, the three rowed back to Saint Dominic's.

Chapter Twenty One.
The Fight that did not come off.

On reaching Saint Dominic's the three boys discovered that the news of their afternoon's adventure had arrived there before them. Paul, despite his promise of secrecy, had not been able to refrain from confiding to one or two bosom friends, in strict confidence, his version of the *fracas* on the tow-path. Of course the story became frightfully distorted in its progress from mouth to mouth, but it flew like wildfire through Saint Dominic's all the same.

When Oliver and his friend with Stephen entered the school-house, groups of inquisitive boys eyed them askance and whispered as they went by. It seemed quite a disappointment to not a few that the three did not appear covered with blood, or as pale as sheets, or with broken limbs. No one knew exactly what had happened, but every one knew something had happened, and it would have been much more satisfactory if the heroes of the hour had had something to show for it.

Oliver was in no mood for gratifying the curiosity of anybody, and stalked off to his study in gloomy silence, attended by his chum and the anxious Stephen.

A hurried council of war ensued.

"I must go and challenge Loman at once," said Oliver.

"Let me go," said Wraysford.

"Why?"

"Because most likely if you go you'll have a row in his study. Much better wait and have it out decently in the gymnasium. I'll go and tell him."

Oliver yielded to this advice.

"Look sharp, old man," he said, "that's all."

Wraysford went off on his mission without delay.

He found Loman in his study with his books before him.

"Greenfield senior wants me to say he'll meet you after tea in the gymnasium if you'll come there," said the ambassador.

Loman, who was evidently prepared for the scene, looked up angrily as he replied, "Fight me? What does he want to fight me for, I should like to know!"

"You know as well as I do," said Wraysford.

"I know nothing about it, and what's more I'll have nothing to do with the fellow. Tell him that."

"Then you won't fight?" exclaimed the astounded Wraysford.

"No, I won't to please him. When I've nothing better to do I'll do it;" and with the words his face flushed crimson as he bent it once more over his book.

Wraysford was quite taken aback by this unexpected answer, and hesitated before he turned to go.

"Do you hear what I say?" said Loman. "Don't you see I'm working?"

"Look here," said Wraysford, "I didn't think you were a coward."

"Think what you like. Do you suppose I care? If Greenfield wants so badly to fight me, why didn't he do it last term when I gave him the chance? Get out of my study, and tell him I'll have nothing to do with him or any of your stuck-up Fifth!"

Wraysford stared hard at the speaker and then said, "I suppose you're afraid to fight *me*, either?"

"If you don't clear out of my study I'll report you to the Doctor, that's what I'll do," growled Loman.

There was no use staying, evidently; and Wraysford returned dejectedly to Oliver.

"He won't fight," he announced.

"Not fight!" exclaimed Oliver. "Why ever not?"

"I suppose because he's a coward. He says because he doesn't choose."

"But he *must* fight, Wray. We must make him!"

"You can't. I called him a coward, and that wouldn't make him. You'll have to give it up this time, Noll."

But Oliver wouldn't hear of giving it up so easily. He got up and rushed to Loman's study himself. But it was locked. He knocked, no one answered. He called through the keyhole, but there was no reply. Evidently Loman did not intend to fight, and Oliver returned crestfallen and disappointed to his study.

"It's no go," he said, in answer to his friend's inquiry.

"Oh, well, never mind," said Wraysford. "Even if you could have fought, I dare say it wouldn't have done much good, for he's such a sullen beggar there would have been no making it up afterwards. If I were you I wouldn't bother any more about it. I'll let all the fellows know he refused to fight you!"

"What's the use of that?" said Oliver. "Why tell them anything about it?"

But tell them or not tell them, the fellows knew already. It had oozed out very soon that a fight was coming off, and instantly the whole school was in excitement. For, however little some of them cared about the personal quarrel between Oliver and Loman, a fight between Fifth and Sixth was too great an event to be passed by unheeded.

The Fifth were delighted. They knew their man could beat Loman any day of the week, and however much they had once doubted his courage, now it was known he was the challenger every misgiving on that score was done away with.

"I tell you," said Ricketts to a small knot of his class-fellows, "he could finish him up easily in one round."

"Yes," chimed in another knowing one, "Loman's got such a wretched knack of keeping up his left elbow, that he's not a chance. A child could get in under his guard, I tell you; and as for wind, he's no more wind than an old paper bag!"

"I wish myself it was a closer thing, as long as our man won," said Tom Senior, with a tinge of melancholy in his voice. "It will be such a miserably hollow affair I'm afraid."

"I'm sorry it's not Wren, or Callonby, or one of them," said another of these amiable warriors; "there'd be some pleasure in chawing them up."

At this moment up came Pembury, with a very long face.

"It's no fight after all, you fellows," said he. "Loman funks it!"

"What! he won't fight!" almost shrieked the rest. "It must be wrong."

"Oh, all right, if it's wrong," snarled Pembury. "I tell you there's no fight; you can believe it or not as you like," and off he hobbled, in unusual ill-humour.

This was a sad blow to the Fifth. They saw no comfort anywhere. They flocked to Oliver's study, but he was not there, and Wraysford's door was locked. The news, however, was confirmed by other reporters, and in great grief and profound melancholy the Fifth swallowed their tea, and wondered if any set of fellows were so unlucky as they.

But their rage was as nothing to that of the Guinea-pigs and Tadpoles.

These amiable young animals had of course sniffed the battle from afar very early in the evening, and, as usual, rushed into all sorts of extremes of enthusiasm on the subject. A fight! A fight between Fifth and Sixth! A fight between Greenfield senior and a monitor! Oh, it was too good to be true, a perfect luxury; something to be grateful for, and no mistake!

Of course a meeting was forthwith assembled to gloat over the auspicious event.

Bramble vehemently expressed his conviction that the Sixth Form man would eat up his opponent, and went the length of offering to cut off his own head and Padger's if it turned out otherwise.

Paul and his friends, on the other hand, as vehemently backed the Fifth fellow.

"When's it to come off, I say?" demanded Bramble.

"To-night, I should say, or first thing in the morning."

"Sure to be to-night. My eye! won't Greenfield senior look black and blue after it!"

"No, he won't," cried Paul.

"Turn him out!" shouted Bramble. "No one wants you here; do we, Padger? Get yourself out of the meeting, you sneak!"

"Get yourself out!" retorted Paul.

The usual lively scene ensued, at the end of which the door suddenly opened, and a boy entered.

"Look sharp," he cried: "it's half over by now. They were—"

But what the end of his sentence was to be, history recordeth not. With a simultaneous yell the youngsters rushed headlong from the room, down the passages, out at the door, across the quadrangle, and into the gymnasium. Alas! it was empty. Only the gaunt parallel bars, and idle swings, and melancholy vaulting-horse.

With a yelp of anger the pack cried back, and made once more for the school-house. At the door they met Stephen.

"Where's the fight, young Greenfield?" shouted Bramble.

"Nowhere," replied Stephen.

"What! not coming off?" shrieked the youngsters.

"No," laconically answered Stephen.

"Has your brother funked it again?" demanded Bramble, in his usual conciliatory way.

"He never funked, you young cad!" retorted the young brother.

"Yes, he did, didn't he, Padger? That time, you know, last term. But I say, Greenfield junior, why ever's the fight not coming off?"

"Loman won't fight, that's why," said Stephen; and then, having had quite enough of catechising, turned on his heel and left the indignant youngsters to continue their rush back to the Fourth Junior, there to spend an hour or so in denouncing the caddishness of everybody and to make up by their own conflicts for the shortcomings of others.

Oliver meanwhile had settled down as best he could once more to work, and tried to forget all about the afternoon's adventures. But for a long time they haunted him and disturbed him. Gradually, however, he found himself cooling down under the influence of Greek accents and Roman history.

"After all," said he to Wraysford, "if the fellow is a coward why need I bother? Only I should have rather liked to thrash him for what he did to Stee."

"Never mind—thrash him over the Nightingale instead."

The mention of the Nightingale, however, did not serve to heighten Oliver's spirits at all.

He turned dejectedly to his books, but soon gave up further study.

"You can go on if you like," said he to Wraysford. "I can't. It's no use. I think I shall go to bed."

"What! It's not quite nine yet."

"Is that all it is? Never mind; good-night, old man. I'm glad it will all be over on Monday."

Before Oliver went to bed he had a talk with Stephen in his study. He succeeded in putting pretty vividly before his young brother the position in which he had placed himself by going down to the public-house and associating with a man like Cripps.

"What I advise you is, to make a clean breast of it to the Doctor at once. If he hears of it any other way, you're done for." Oliver certainly had an uncompromising way of putting things.

"Oh, Noll, I never could! I know I couldn't. I say, will you? You can tell him anything you like."

Oliver hesitated a moment, and then said, "All serene; I'll do it. Mind, I must tell him everything, though."

"Oh, yes! I say, do you think I'll be expelled?"

"I hope not. There's no knowing, though."

"Oh, Noll! what *shall* I do?"

"It's your only chance, I tell you. If Cripps comes up and talks about it, or Loman tells, you're sure to be expelled."

"Well," said Stephen, with a gulp, "I suppose you'd better tell him, Noll. Need I come too?"

"No, better not," said Oliver. "I'll go and see if he's in his study now. You go up stairs, and I'll come and tell you what he says."

Stephen crawled dismally away, leaving his brother to fulfil his self-imposed task.

Oliver went straight to the Doctor's study. The door stood half-open, but the Doctor was not there. He entered, and waited inside a couple of minutes, expecting that the head master would return; but no one came. After all, he would have to put off his confession of Stephen's delinquencies till to-morrow; and, half relieved, half disappointed, he quitted the room. As he came out he encountered Simon in the passage.

"Hullo, Greenfield!" said that worthy; "what have you been up to in there?"

"I want the Doctor," said Oliver; "do you know where he is?"

"I saw him go up stairs a minute ago; that is, I mean down stairs, you know," said the lucid poet.

This information was sufficiently vague to determine Oliver not to attempt a wild-goose chase after the Doctor that night, so, bidding a hurried good-night to Simon, he took his way down the passage which led to Stephen's dormitory.

He had not, however, gone many steps when a boy met him. It was Loman. There was a momentary struggle in Oliver's breast. Here was the—very opportunity which an hour or two ago he had so eagerly desired. The whole picture of that afternoon's adventures came up before his mind, and he felt his blood tingle as his eyes caught sight of Stephen's persecutor. Should he pay off the score now?

Loman saw him, and changed colour. He evidently guessed what was passing through his enemy's mind, for a quick flush came to his face and an angry scowl to his brow.

Oliver for one moment slackened pace. Then suddenly there came upon him a vision of Stephen's appealing face as he interceded that afternoon for the boy who had done him such mischief, and that vision settled the thing.

Hurriedly resuming his walk, Oliver passed Loman with averted eyes, and went on his way.

"Well?" said Stephen, in the midst of undressing, as his brother entered the dormitory.

"He wasn't there. I'll see him in the morning," said Oliver. "Good-night, Stee."

"Good-night, Noll, old man! I say, you are a brick to me!" and as the boy spoke there was a tremble in his voice which went straight to his brother's heart.

"You are a brick to me!" A pretty "brick" he had been, letting the youngster drift anywhere—into bad company, into bad ways, without holding out a hand to warn him; and in the end coming to his help only by accident, and serving him by undertaking a task which would quite possibly result in his expulsion from the school.

A brick, indeed! Oliver went off to his own bed that night more dispirited and dissatisfied with himself than he had ever felt before. And all through his dreams his brother's troubled face looked up at him, and the trembling voice repeated, again and again, "You are a brick to me—a brick to me!"

Chapter Twenty Two.
The Nightingale Examination.

The next morning early, before breakfast, Oliver joined the Doctor in his study, and made a clean breast to him there and then of Stephen's delinquencies. He had evidently taken the right step in doing so, for, hearing it all thus frankly confessed by the elder brother, Dr Senior was disposed to take a much more lenient view of the case than he would had the information come to him through any other channel.

But at its best the offence was a grave one, and Oliver more than once felt anxious at the sight of the head master's long face during the narrative. However, when it was all over his fears were at once dispelled by the doctor saying, "Well, Greenfield, you've done a very proper thing in telling me all this; it is a straightforward as well as a brotherly act. Your brother seems to have been very foolish, but I have no doubt he has got a lesson. You had better send him to me after morning service."

And so, much relieved, Oliver went off and reported to the grateful Stephen the success of his mission, and the two boys went off to the school chapel together a good deal more happy than they had been the previous day.

"I say," said Stephen, as they went along, "I suppose you didn't say anything about Loman, did you?"

"Of course not! he's no concern of mine," said Oliver, rather tartly. "But look here, young 'un, I'm not going to let you fag any more for him, or have anything to do with him."

"All right!" said Stephen, who had no desire to continue his acquaintance with his late "proprietor."

"But the captain will row me, won't he?"

"If he does I'll make that square. You can fag for Wraysford if you like, though, he wants a fellow."

"Oh, all right!" cried Stephen, delighted, "that'll be jolly! I like old Wray."

"Very kind of you," said a voice close by.

It was Wraysford himself, who had come in for this very genuine compliment.

"Hullo! I say, look here, Wraysford," said the beaming Stephen, "I'm going to cut Loman and fag for you. Isn't it jolly?"

"Depends on whether I have you. I don't want any Guinea-pigs in my study, mind."

Stephen's face fell. For even such a privilege as fagging for Wraysford he could not afford to sever the sacred ties which held him to the fellowship of the Guinea-pigs. "I really wouldn't kick-up shines," said he, imploringly.

"You'd be a queer Guinea-pig if you didn't!" was the flattering answer. "And how many times a week would you go on strike, eh?"

"Oh!" said Stephen, "I'll never go on strike again; I don't like it."

The two friends laughed at this ingenuous admission, and then Wraysford said, "Well, I'll have you; but mind, I'm awfully particular, and knock my fags about tremendously, don't I, Noll?"

"I don't mind that," said the delighted Stephen. "Besides, you've not had a fag to knock about!"

At that moment, however, the bell for morning chapel cut short all further talk for the present. Stephen obeyed its summons for once in a subdued and thankful frame of mind. Too often had those weekly services been to him occasions of mere empty form, when with his head full of school worries or school fun he had scarcely heard, much less heeded, what was said.

To-day, however, it was different. Stephen was a sobered boy. He had passed through perils and temptations from which, if he had escaped, it had been through no merit of his own. Things might have been far different. His life had been saved, so had his peace of mind, and now even the consequences of old transgressions had been lightened for him. What had he done to deserve all this?

This was the question which the boy humbly asked himself as he entered the chapel that morning, and the Doctor's sermon fitted well with his altered frame of mind.

It was a sermon such as he had often heard before in that chapel; the words struck him now with a new force which almost startled him. "Forgetting those things which are behind—reaching forth unto those things which are before,"—this was the Doctor's text, and in the few simple words in which he urged his hearers to lay the past, with all its burdens, and disappointments, and shame, upon Him in whom alone forgiveness is to be found, Stephen drank in new courage and hope for the future, and in the thankfulness and penitence of his heart resolved to commit his way more honestly than ever to the best of all keeping, compared with which even a brother's love is powerless.

Before the morning was over Stephen duly went to the Doctor, who talked to him very seriously. I need not repeat the talk here. Stephen was very penitent, and had the good sense to say as little as possible; but when it was all over he thanked the Doctor gratefully, and promised he should never have to talk to him for bad conduct again.

"You must thank your brother for my not dealing a great deal more severely with the case," said Dr Senior; "and I am quite ready to believe it will not occur again. Now, good-bye."

And off Stephen went, the happiest boy alive, determined more than ever to respect the Doctor's authority, and prove himself a model boy.

Sunday afternoon at Saint Dominic's was usually spent by the boys in fine weather, in strolling about in the gardens, or rambling into the woods by the banks of the Shar.

This afternoon, however, was somewhat overcast, and a good many of the boys consequently preferred staying indoors to running the risk of spoiling their best hats in a shower. Among those who kept the house was Oliver, who, in reply to Wraysford's invitation to go out, pleaded that he was not in the humour.

This indeed was the case, for, now that Stephen's affairs were settled, the dread of the approaching Nightingale examination came back over him like a nightmare, and made him quite miserable. The nearer the hour of trial came the more convinced did Oliver become that he stood no chance whatever of winning, and with that conviction all the bright hopes of a university course, and the prospects of after-success, seemed extinguished.

Of course it was very ridiculous of him to worry himself into such a state, but then, reader, he had been working just a little too hard, and it was hardly his fault if he was ridiculous.

Wraysford, though by no means in high spirits, kept his head a good deal better, and tried to enjoy his walk and forget all about books, as if nothing at all was going to happen to-morrow. As for Loman, he was not visible from morning till night, and a good many guessed, and guessed correctly, that he was at work, even on Sunday.

The small boys, not so much though, I fear, out of reverence for the day as for partisanship of the Fifth, were very indignant on the subject, and held a small full-dress meeting after tea, to protest against one of the candidates taking such an unfair advantage over the others.

"He ought to be expelled!" exclaimed Paul.

"All very well," said Bramble. "Greenfield senior's cramming too, he's been in all the afternoon."

"He's not cramming, he's got a headache!" said Stephen.

"Oh, yes, I dare say, don't you, Padger? Got a headache—that's a nice excuse for copying out of cribs on a Sunday."

"He doesn't use cribs, and I tell you he's not working!" said Stephen, indignantly.

"Shut up, do you hear, or you'll get turned out, Potboy!"

This was too much for Stephen, who left the assembly in disgust, after threatening to take an early opportunity on the next day of giving his adversary "one for himself," a threat which we may as well say at once here he did not fail to carry out with his wonted energy.

The long Sunday ended at last—a Sunday spoiled to many of the boys of Saint Dominic's by distracting thoughts and cares—a day which many impatiently wished over, and which some wished would never give place to the morrow.

But that morrow came at last, and with it rose Oliver, strengthened and hopeful once more for the trial that lay before him. He was early at Wraysford's study, whom he found only just out of bed.

"Look alive, old man. What do you say to a dip in the river before breakfast? We've got plenty of time, and it will wash off the cobwebs before the exam."

"All serene," said Wraysford, not very cheerily, though. "Anything's better than doing nothing."

"Why, Wray, I thought you weren't going to let yourself get down about it?"

"I thought you weren't going to let yourself get up—why, you're quite festive this morning."

"Well, you see, a fellow can't do better than his best, and so as I have done my best I don't mean to punish myself by getting in the blues."

"Pity you didn't make that resolution yesterday. You were awfully glum, you know, then; and now I've got my turn, you see."

"Oh, never mind, a plunge in the Shar will set you all right."

"Stee," said he, addressing his younger brother, who at that moment entered proudly in his new capacity as Wraysford's fag, "mind you have breakfast ready sharp by eight, do you hear? the best you can get out of Wray's cupboard. Come along, old boy."

And so they went down to the river, Oliver in unusually good spirits, and Wraysford most unusually depressed and nervous. The bathe was not a great success, for Wraysford evidently did not enjoy it.

"What's wrong, old man?" said Oliver, as they walked back, "aren't you well?"

"I'm all right," said Wraysford.

"But you're out of spirits. It's odd that I was in dumps and you were in good spirits up to the fatal day, and now things are just reversed. But, I say, you mustn't get down, you know, or it'll tell against you at the exam."

"It strikes me every answer I give will tell against me. All I hope is that you get the scholarship."

"I mean to try, just like you and Loman."

And so they went into breakfast, which was a solemn meal, and despite Stephen's care in hunting up delicacies, not very well partaken of.

It seemed ages before the nine o'clock bell summoned them down to the Fifth Form room.

Here, however, the sympathy and encouragement of their class-fellows amply served to pass the time till the examination began.

"Well, you fellows," cried Pembury, as the two entered, "do you feel like winning?"

"Not more than usual," said Oliver. "How do you feel?"

"Oh, particularly cheerful, for I've nothing to do all day, I find. I'm not in for the Nightingale, or for the Mathematical Medal, or for the English Literature. Simon's in for that, you know, so there's no chance for any one."

Simon smiled very blandly at this side compliment.

"So you fellows," continued Tony, "may command my services from morning to night if you like."

"Loman was grinding hard all yesterday," said Braddy. "I'm afraid he'll be rather a hot one to beat."

"But we *must* beat him, mind, you fellows," said Ricketts, calmly, comprehending the whole class in his "we."

"Why, Wray," said another, "how jolly blue you look! Don't go and funk it, old man, or it's all UP."

"Who's going to funk it?" said Oliver, impatiently, on his friend's behalf. "I tell you Wray will most likely win."

"Well, as long as one of you does," said Tom Senior, with noble impartiality, "we don't care which; do we, Braddy?"

"Of course not."

So, then, all this sympathy and encouragement were not for the two boys at all, but for their Form. They might just as well have been two carefully trained racehorses starting on a race with heavy odds upon them.

The Doctor's entry, however, put an end to any further talk, and, as usual, a dead silence ensued after the boys had taken their seats.

The Doctor looked a little uneasy. Doubtless he was impressed, too, by the importance of the occasion. He proceeded to call over the lists of candidates for the different examinations in a fidgety manner, very unlike his usual self, and then turning abruptly to the class, said:

"The Mathematical Medal candidates will remain here for examination. The English Literature and Nightingale Scholarship candidates will be examined in the Sixth Form room. Boys not in for either of these examinations may go to their studies till the twelve o'clock bell rings. Before you disperse, however,"—and here the Doctor grew still more fidgety—"I want to mention one matter which I have already mentioned in the Sixth. I mention it not because I suspect any boy here of a dishonourable act, but because—the matter being a mystery—I feel I must not neglect the most remote opportunity of clearing it up."

What on earth was coming? It was as good as a ghost story, every one was so spellbound and mystified.

"On Saturday evening I had occasion to leave my study for rather less than five minutes, shortly after nine o'clock. I had been engaged in getting together the various papers of questions for to-day's examinations, and left them lying on the corner of the table. On returning to my study—I had not been absent five minutes—I found that one of the papers—one of the Nightingale Scholarship papers, which I had only just copied out, was missing. If I were not perfectly sure the full number was there before I left the room, I should conclude I was mistaken, but of that I am sure. I just wish to ask this one question here, which I have already asked in the Sixth. Does any boy present know anything about the missing paper?"

You might have heard a pin drop as the Doctor paused for a reply.

"No? I expected not; I am quite satisfied. You can disperse, boys, to your various places."

"What a fellow the Doctor is for speeches, Wray," said Oliver, as he and his friend made their way to the Sixth Form room.

"Yes. But that's a very queer thing about the paper, though."

"Oh, he's certain to have mislaid it somewhere. It's a queer thing saying anything about it; for it looks uncommonly as if he suspected some one."

"So it does. Oh, horrors! here we are at the torture-chamber! I wish it was all over!"

They entered the Sixth Form room, which was regularly cleared for action. One long desk was allotted to the three Nightingale candidates, two others to the English Literature boys, and another to the competitors in a Sixth Form Greek verse contest.

Loman was already in his place, waiting with flushed face for the ordeal to begin. The two friends took their seats without vouchsafing any notice of their rival, and an uncomfortable two minutes ensued, during which it seemed as if the Doctor were never to arrive.

He did arrive at last, however, bringing with him the examination papers for the various classes.

"Boys for the Greek verse prize come forward."

Wren, Raleigh, Winter, and Callonby advanced, and received each one his paper.

"Boys for the Nightingale Scholarship come forward."

The three competitors obeyed the summons, and to each was handed a paper.

It was not in human nature to forbear glancing hurriedly at the momentous questions, as each walked slowly back to his seat. The effect of that momentary glance was very different on the three boys. Wraysford's face slightly lengthened, Loman's grew suddenly aghast, Oliver's betrayed no emotion whatever.

"Boys for the English Literature prize come forward."

These duly advanced and were furnished, and then silence reigned in the room, broken only by the rapid scratching of pens and the solemn tick of the clock on the wall.

Reader, you doubtless know the horrors of an examination-room as well as I do. You know what it is to sit biting the end of your pen, and glaring at the ruthless question in front of you. You know what it is to dash nervously from question to question, answering a bit of this and a bit of that, but lacking the patience to work steadily down the list. And you have experienced doubtless the aggravation of hearing the pen of the man on your right flying along the paper with a hideous squeak, never stopping for a moment to give you a chance. And knowing all this, there is no need for me to describe the vicissitudes of this particular day of ordeal at Saint Dominic's.

The work went steadily on from morning to afternoon. More than one anxious face darted now and then nervous glances up at the clock, as the hour of closing approached.

Loman was one of them. He was evidently in difficulties, and the Fifth Form fellows, who looked round occasionally from their English Literature papers, were elated to see their own men writing steadily and hard, while the Sixth man looked all aground. There was one boy, however, who had no time for such observations. That was Simon. He had got hold of a question which was after his own heart, and demanded every second of his attention—"Describe, in not more than twelve lines of blank verse, the natural beauties of the River Shar." Here was a chance for the *Dominican* poet!

"The Shar is a very beautiful stream,
Of the Ouse a tributary;
Up at Gusset Weir it's prettiest, I ween,
Because there the birds sing so merry."

These four lines the poet styled, "Canto One." Cantos 2, 3, and 4 were much of the same excellence, and altogether the effusion was in one of Simon's happiest moods. Alas! as another poet said, "Art is long, time is fleeting." The clock pointed to three long before the bard had penned his fifth canto; and sadly and regretfully he and his fellow-candidates gathered together and handed in their papers, for better or worse.

Among the last to finish up was Oliver, who had been working hammer and tongs during the whole examination.

"How did you get on?" said Wraysford, as they walked back to the Fifth.

"Middling, not so bad as I feared; how did you?"

"Not very grand, I'm afraid; but better than I expected," said Wraysford. "But I say, did you see how gravelled Loman seemed? I fancy he didn't do very much."

"So I thought; but I hadn't time to watch him much."

In the Fifth there was a crowd of questioners, eager to ascertain how their champions had fared; and great was their delight to learn that neither was utterly cast down at his own efforts.

"You fellows are regular bricks if you get it!" cried Ricketts.

"It'll be the best thing that has happened for the Fifth for a long time."

"Oh, I say," said Simon, suddenly, addressing Oliver in a peculiarly knowing tone, "wasn't it funny, that about the Doctor losing the paper? Just the very time I met you coming out of his study, you know, on Saturday evening. But of course I won't say anything. Only wasn't it funny?"

What had come over Oliver, that he suddenly turned crimson, and without a single word struck the speaker angrily with his open hand on the forehead?

Was he mad? or could it possibly be that—

Before the assembled Fifth could recover from their astonishment or conjecture as to the motive for this sudden exhibition of feeling, he turned abruptly to the door and quitted the room.

Chapter Twenty Three.
A Turn of the Tide.

An earthquake could hardly have produced a greater shock than Oliver's strange conduct produced on the Fifth Form at Saint Dominic's. For a moment or two they remained almost stupefied with astonishment, and then rose a sudden clamour of tongues on every hand.

"What can he mean?" exclaimed one.

"Mean! It's easy enough to see what he means," said another, "the hypocrite!"

"I should never have thought Greenfield senior went in for that sort of thing!"

"Went in for what sort of thing?" cried Wraysford, with pale face and in a perfect tremble.

"Why—cheating!" replied the other.

"You're a liar to say so!" shouted Wraysford, walking rapidly up to the speaker.

The other boys, however, intervened, and held the indignant Wraysford back.

"I tell you you're a liar to say so!" again he exclaimed. "He's not a cheat, I tell you; he never cheated. You're a pack of liars, all of you!"

"I say, draw it mild, Wray, you know," interposed Pembury. "You needn't include me in your compliments."

Wraysford glared at him a moment and then coloured slightly.

"*You* don't call Oliver a cheat?" he said, inquiringly.

"I shouldn't till I was cock-sure of the fact," replied the cautious editor of the *Dominican*.

"Do you mean to say you aren't sure?" said Wraysford.

Pembury vouchsafed no answer, but whistled to himself.

"All I can say is," said Bullinger, who was one of Wraysford's chums, "it looks uncommonly ugly, if what Simon says is true."

"I don't believe a word that ass says."

"Oh, but," began Simon, with a most aggravating cheerfulness, "I assure you I'm not telling a lie, Wraysford. I'm sorry I said anything about it. I never thought there would be a row about it. I promise I'll not mention it to anybody."

"You blockhead! who cares for your promises? I don't believe you."

"Well, I know I met Greenfield senior coming out of the Doctor's study on Saturday evening, about five minutes past nine. I'm positive of that," said Simon.

"And I suppose he had the paper in his hand?" sneered Wraysford, looking very miserable.

"No; I expect he'd put it in his pocket, you know, at least, that is, I would have."

This candid admission on the part of the ingenious poet was too much for the gravity of one or two of the Fifth. Wraysford, however, was in no laughing mood, and went off to his study in great perturbation.

He could not for a moment believe that his friend could be guilty of such a dishonourable act as stealing an examination paper, and his impulse was to go at once to Oliver's study and get the suspicions of the Fifth laid there and then. But the fear of seeming in the least degree to join in those suspicions kept him back. He tried to laugh the thing to scorn inwardly, and called himself a villain and a traitor twenty times for admitting even the shadow of a doubt into his own mind. Yet, as Wraysford sat that afternoon and brooded over his friend's new trouble, he became more and more uncomfortable.

When on a former occasion the fellows had called in question Oliver's courage, he had felt so sure, so very sure the suspicion was a groundless one, that he had never taken it seriously to heart. But somehow this affair was quite different. What possible object would Simon, for instance, have for telling a deliberate lie? and if it had been a lie, why should Oliver have betrayed such confusion on hearing it?

These were questions which, try all he would, Wraysford could not get out of his mind.

When Stephen presently came in, cheery as ever, and eager to hear how the examination had gone off, the elder boy felt an awkwardness in talking to him which he had never experienced before. As for Stephen, he put down the short, embarrassed answers he received to Wraysford's own uneasiness as to the result of the examination. Little guessed the boy what was passing in the other's mind!

There was just one hope Wraysford clung to. That was that Oliver should come out anywhere but first in the result. If Loman, or Wraysford himself, were to win, no one would be able to say his friend had profited by a dishonourable act; indeed, it would be as good as proof he had not taken the paper.

And yet Wraysford felt quite sick as he called to mind the unflagging manner in which Oliver had worked at his paper that morning, covering sheet upon sheet with his answers, and scarcely drawing in until time was up. It didn't look like losing, this.

He threw himself back in his chair in sheer misery. "I would sooner have done the thing myself," groaned he to himself, "than Oliver." Then suddenly he added, "But it's not true! I'm certain of it! He couldn't do it! I'll never believe it of him!"

Poor Wraysford! It was easier to say the generous words than feel them.

Pembury looked in presently with a face far more serious and overcast than he usually wore.

"I say, Wray," said he, in troubled tones, "I'm regularly floored by all this. Do you believe it?"

"No, I don't," replied Wraysford, but so sadly and hesitatingly that had he at once confessed he did, he could not have expressed his meaning more plainly.

"I'd give anything to be sure it was all false," said Pembury, "and so would a lot of the fellows. As for that fool Simon—"

"Bah!" exclaimed Wraysford, fiercely, "the fellow ought to be kicked round the school."

"He's getting on that way already, I fancy," said Pembury. "I was saying I'd think nothing at all about it if what he says was the only thing to go by, but—well, you saw what a state Greenfield got into about it?"

"Maybe he was just in a sudden rage with the fellow for thinking of such a thing," said Wraysford.

"It looked like something more than rage," said Pembury, dismally, "something a good deal more."

Wraysford said nothing, but fidgeted in his chair. A long silence followed, each busy with his own thoughts and both yearning for any sign of hope. "I don't see what good it could have done him if he did take the paper. He'd have no time to cram it up yesterday. He was out with you, wasn't he, all the afternoon?"

"No," said Wraysford, not looking up, "he had a headache and stayed in."

Pembury gave a low whistle of dismay.

"I say, Wray," said he, presently, "it really does look bad, don't you think so yourself?"

"I don't know what to think," said Wraysford, with a groan; "I'm quite bewildered."

"It's no use pretending not to see what's as plain as daylight," said Pembury, as he turned and hobbled away.

The Fifth meanwhile had been holding a sort of court-martial on the affair.

Simon was made to repeat his story once more, and stuck to it too, in spite of all the browbeating he got.

"What makes you so sure of the exact time?" asked one of his inquisitors.

"Oh, because, you know, I wanted to get off a letter by the post, and thought I was in time till I saw the clock opposite the Doctor's study said five minutes past."

"Did Greenfield say anything to you when he saw you?" some one else asked.

"Oh, yes, he asked me if I knew where the Doctor was."

"Did you tell him?"

"Oh, yes, I said he'd gone down to the hall or somewhere."

"And did Greenfield go after him?"

"Oh, no, you know, he went off the other way as quick as he could," said Simon, in a voice as though he would say, "How can you ask such an absurd question?"

"Did you ask him what he wanted in the study?"

"Oh, yes; but of course he didn't tell me—not likely. But I say, I suppose we're sure to win the Nightingale now, aren't we? Mind, I'm not going to tell anybody, because, of course, it's a secret."

"Shut up, you miserable blockhead, unless you want to be kicked!" shouted Bullinger. "No one wants to know what you're going to do. You've done mischief enough already."

"Oh, well, I didn't mean, you know," said the poet; "all I said was I met him coming—"

"Shut up, do you hear? or you'll catch it!" once more exclaimed Bullinger.

The wretched Simon gave up further attempts to explain himself. Still what he had said, in his blundering way, had been quite enough.

The thing was beyond a doubt; and as the Fifth sat there in judgment, a sense of shame and humiliation came over them, to which many of them were unused.

"I know this," said Ricketts, giving utterance to what was passing in the minds of nearly all his class-fellows, "I'd sooner have lost the scholarship twenty times over than win it like this."

"Precious fine glory it will be if we do get it!" said Braddy.

"Unless Wray wins," suggested Ricketts.

"No such luck as that, I'm afraid," said Bullinger. "That's just the worst of it. He's not only disgraced us, but he's swindled his best friend. It's a blackguard shame!" added he, fiercely.

"At any rate, Loman is out of it, from what I hear; he got regularly stuck in the exam."

"I tell you," said Ricketts, "I'd sooner have had Loman take the scholarship and our two men nowhere at all, than this."

There was nothing more than this to be said, assuredly, to prove the disgust of the Fifth at the conduct of their class-fellow.

"I suppose Greenfield will have the grace to confess it, now it's all come out," said Ricketts.

"If he doesn't I fancy we can promise him a pretty hot time of it among us," said Braddy.

One or two laughed at this, but to most of those present the matter was past a joke.

For it must be said of the Dominicans—and I think it may be said of a good many English public schoolboys besides—that, however foolish they may have been in other respects, however riotous, however jealous of one another, however well satisfied with themselves, a point of honour was a point which they all took seriously to heart. They could forgive a schoolfellow for doing a disobedient act sometimes, or perhaps even a vicious act, but a cowardly or dishonourable action was a thing which nothing would

106

excuse, and which they felt not only a disgrace to the boy perpetrating it, but a disgrace put upon themselves.

Had Oliver been the most popular boy in the school it would have been all the same. As it was, he was a long way from being the most popular. He never took any pains to win the good opinion of his fellows. When, by means of some achievement in which he excelled, he had contrived (as in the case of the cricket match last term) to bring glory on his school and to make himself a hero in the eyes of Saint Dominic's, he had been wont to take the applause bestowed on him with the utmost indifference, which some might even construe into contempt. And in precisely the same spirit would he take the displeasure which he now and then managed to incur.

Boys don't like this. It irritates them to see their praise or blame made little of; and for this reason, if for no other, Oliver would hardly have been a favourite.

But there was another reason. Now that the Fifth found their faith in Greenfield senior rudely dashed to the ground, they were not slow to recall the unpleasant incidents of last term, when, by refusing to thrash Loman, he had discredited the whole Form, and laid himself under the suspicion of cowardice.

Most of the fellows had at the time of the Nightingale examination either forgotten, or forgiven, or repented of their suspicions, and, indeed, by his challenge to Loman the previous Saturday Oliver had been considered quite to have redeemed his reputation in this respect. But now it all came up again. A fellow who could do a cowardly deed at one time could do a mean one at another. If one was natural to his character, so was the other, and in fact one explained the other. He was mean when he showed himself a coward last term. He was a coward when he did a mean act this term.

What wonder, in these circumstances, if the Fifth felt sore, very sore indeed, on the subject of Oliver Greenfield?

To every one's relief, he did not put in an appearance again that day. He kept his study, and Paul brought down word at prayer time that he had a headache and had gone to bed.

At this the Fifth smiled grimly and said nothing.

Next morning, however, Oliver turned up as usual in his place. He looked pale, but otherwise unconcerned, and those who looked-for traces of shame and self-abasement in his face were sorely disappointed.

He surely must have known or guessed the resolution the Fifth had come to with regard to him; but from his unabashed manner he was evidently determined not to take it for granted till the hint should be given pretty clearly.

On Ricketts, whose desk was next to that of Oliver, fell the task of first giving this hint.

"How did you get on yesterday in the English Literature?" asked Oliver.

Ricketts' only answer was to turn his back and begin to talk to his other neighbour.

Those who were watching this incident noticed a sudden flush on Oliver's cheek as he stared for an instant at his late friend. Then with an effort he seemed to recover himself.

He did not, however, attempt any further conversation either with Ricketts or his other neighbour, Braddy, who in a most marked manner had moved as far as possible away from him. On the contrary, he coolly availed himself of the extra room on the desk and busied himself silently with the lessons for the day.

But he now and then looked furtively up in the direction of Wraysford, who was seated at an opposite desk. The eyes of the two friends met now and then, and when they did each seemed greatly embarrassed. For Wraysford, after a night's heart-searching, had come to the determination not, after all, to cut his friend; and yet he found it impossible to feel and behave towards him as formerly. He tried very hard indeed not to appear constrained, but the more he tried the more embarrassed he felt. After class he purposely walked across the room to meet his old chum.

"How are you?" he said, in a forced tone and manner utterly unlike his old self.

It was a ridiculous and feeble remark to make, and it would have been far better had he said nothing. Oliver stared at him for a moment in a perplexed way, and then, without answering the question, walked somewhere else.

Wraysford was quite conscious of his own mistake; still it hurt him sorely that his well-meant effort, which had cost him so much, should be thus summarily thrust aside without a word. For the first time in his life he felt a sense of resentment against his old friend, the beginning of a gap which was destined to become wider as time went on.

The only person in the room who did meet Oliver on natural ground was the poetic Simon. To him Oliver walked up and said, quietly, "I beg your pardon for hitting you yesterday."

"Oh," said Simon, with a giggle. "Oh, it's all right, Greenfield, you know; I never meant to let it out. It'll soon get hushed up; I don't intend to let it go a bit farther."

The poet was too much carried away by the enthusiasm of his own magnanimity to observe that he was in imminent risk, during the delivery of this speech, of another blow a good deal more startling than that of yesterday. When he concluded, he found Oliver had left him to himself and hurriedly quitted the room.

Chapter Twenty Four.
The Result of the Examination.

The adventures of the morning did not certainly tend to make the Fifth think better of Oliver Greenfield.

Had he appeared before them humble and penitent, there were some who even then might have tried to forgive him and forget what was done. But instead of that he was evidently determined to brazen the thing out, and had begun by snubbing the very fellows whom he had so deeply injured.

Wraysford felt specially hurt. It had cost him a good deal to put on a friendly air and speak as if nothing had happened; and to find himself scorned for his pains and actually avoided by the friend who had wronged him was too much. But even that would not have been so bad, had not Oliver immediately gone and made up to Simon before all the class.

Wraysford did not remain to join in the chorus of indignation in which the others indulged after morning school was over. He left them and strolled out dismally into the playground.

He must do something! He must know one way or the other what to think of Oliver. Even now he would gladly believe that it was all a dream, and that nothing had come between him and his old friend. But the more he pondered it the more convinced he became it was anything but a dream.

He wandered unconsciously beyond the playground towards the woods on the side of the Shar, where he and Oliver had walked so often in the old days.

The old days! It was but yesterday that they had last walked there. Yet what an age ago it seemed! and how impossible that the old days should ever come back again.

He had not got far into the wood when he heard what seemed to him familiar footsteps ahead of him. Yesterday he would have shouted and whistled and called on the fellow to hold hard. But now he had no such inclination. His impulse was to turn round and go back.

"And yet," thought he, "why should *I go* back? If it is Oliver, what have *I* to feel ashamed of?"

And so he advanced. The boy in front of him was walking slowly, and Wraysford soon came in view of him. As he expected, it was Oliver.

At the sight of his old friend, wandering here solitary and listless, all Wraysford's old affection came suddenly back. At least he would make one more effort. So he quickened his pace. Oliver turned and saw him coming. But he did not wait. He walked on slowly as before, apparently indifferent to the approach of anybody.

This was a damper certainly to Wraysford. At least Oliver might have guessed why his friend was coming after him.

It was desperately hard to know how to begin a conversation. Oliver trudged on, sullen and silent, in anything but an encouraging manner. Still, Wraysford, now his mind was made up, was not to be put from his purpose.

"Noll, old man," he began, in as much of his old tone and manner as he could assume.

"Well?" said Oliver, not looking up.

"Aren't we to be friends still?"

The question cost the speaker a hard effort, and evidently went home. Oliver stopped short in his walk, and looking full in his old friend's face, said, "Why do you ask?"

"Because I'm afraid we are not friends at this moment."

"And whose fault is that?" said Oliver, scornfully.

The question stung Wraysford as much as it amazed him. Was he, then, of all the fellows in the school, to have an explanation thus demanded of him from one who had done him the most grievous personal wrong one schoolboy well could do to another?

His face flushed as he replied slowly, "Your fault, Greenfield; how can you ask?"

Oliver gave a short laugh very like contempt, and then turned suddenly on his heel, leaving Wraysford smarting with indignation, and finally convinced that between his old friend and himself there was a gulf which now it would be hard indeed to bridge over.

He returned moodily to the school. Stephen was busy in his study getting tea.

"Hullo, Wray," he shouted, as the elder boy entered; "don't you wish it was this time to-morrow? I do, I'm mad to hear the result!"

"Are you?" said Wraysford.

"Yes, and so are you, you old humbug. Noll says he thinks he did pretty well, and that you answered well too. I say, what a joke if it's a dead heat, and you both get bracketed first."

"Cut away now," said Wraysford, as coolly as he could, "and don't make such a row."

There was something unusual in his tone which surprised the small boy. He put it down, however, to worry about the examination, and quietly withdrew as commanded.

The next day came at last. Two days ago, in the Fifth Form, at any rate, it would have been uphill work for any master to attempt to conduct morning class in the face of all the eagerness and enthusiasm with which the result of the examinations would have been looked-for. Now, however, there was all the suspense, indeed, but it was the suspense of dread rather than triumph.

"Never mind," said Ricketts to Pembury, after the two had been talking over the affair for the twentieth time. "Never mind; and there's just this, Tony, if Wray is only second, it will be a splendid win for the Fifth all the same."

"I see nothing splendid in the whole concern," said Pembury. And that was the general feeling.

Oliver entered and took his accustomed seat in silence. No one spoke to him, many moved away from him, and nearly all favoured him with a long and unfriendly stare.

All these things he took unmoved. He sat coolly waiting for class to begin, and when it did begin, any one would have supposed he was the only comfortable and easy-minded fellow in the room. The lesson dragged on languidly that morning. Most of the boys seemed to regard it as something inflicted on them to pass the time rather than as a serious effort of instruction. The clock crawled slowly on from ten to eleven, and from eleven to half-past, and every one was glad when at last Mr Jellicott closed his book. Then followed an interval of suspense. The Doctor was due with the results, and was even now announcing them in the Sixth. What ages it seemed before his footsteps sounded in the passage outside the Fifth!

At last he entered, and a hush fell over the class. One or two glanced quickly up, as though they hoped to read their fate in the head master's face. Others waited, too anxious to stir or look up. Others groaned inwardly with a sort of prophetic foresight of what was to come.

The Doctor walked up to the desk and unfolded his paper.

Wraysford looked furtively across the room to where his old friend sat. There was a flush in Oliver's face as he followed the Doctor with his eyes; he was breathing hard, Wraysford could see, and the corners of his mouth were working with more than ordinary nervousness.

"Alas!" thought Wraysford, "I don't envy him his thoughts!"

The Doctor began to speak.

"The following are the results of the various examinations held on Monday. English Literature—maximum number of marks 100. 1st, Bullinger, 72 marks; 2nd, West, 68; 3rd, Maybury, 51; 4th, Simon, 23. I'm afraid, Simon, you were a little too venturesome entering for an examination like this. Your paper was a very poor performance."

Simon groaned and gulped down his astonishment.

"I say," whispered he to Oliver, who sat in front of him, "I know it's a mistake: you know I wrote five cantos about the Shar—good too. He's lost that. I say, had I better tell him?"

Oliver vouchsafing no reply, the unfortunate poet merely replied to the head master's remarks, "Yes, sir," and then subsided, more convinced than ever that Saint Dominic's was not worthy of him.

"The Mathematical Medal—maximum number of marks 80. 1st, Heath, 65; 2nd, Price, 54; 3rd, Roberts, 53. Heath's answers, I may say, were very good, and the examiners have specially commended him."

Heath being a Sixth Form man, this information was absolutely without interest to the Fifth, who wondered why the Doctor should put himself out of the way to announce it.

"The Nightingale Scholarship."

Ah, now! There was a quick stir, and then a deeper silence than ever as the Doctor slowly read out, "The maximum number of marks possible, 120. First, Greenfield, Fifth Form, 112 marks. And I must say I and the examiners are astonished as well as highly gratified with this really brilliant performance. Greenfield, I congratulate you as well as your class-fellows on your success. It does you the very greatest credit!"

A dead silence followed this eulogium. Those who watched Oliver saw his face first glow, then turn pale, as the Doctor spoke. He kept his eyes steadily fixed on the paper in the head master's hand, as if waiting for what was to follow.

The Doctor went on, "Second, Wraysford, Fifth Form, 97 marks, also a creditable performance."

One or two near Wraysford clapped him warmly on the back, and throughout the class generally there was a show of satisfaction at this result, in strange contrast with the manner in which the announcement of Oliver's success had been received.

Still, every one was too eager to hear the third and final announcement to disturb the proceedings by any demonstration just now.

"Loman, Sixth Form—" and here the Doctor paused, and knitted his brows.

"Loman, Sixth Form, 70 marks!"

This finally brought down the house. Scarcely was the Doctor's back turned, when a general clamour rose on every hand. He, good man, set it down to applause of the winners, but every one else knew it meant triumph over the vanquished.

"Bravo, Wray! old man. Hurrah for the Fifth!" shouted Bullinger.

"Ninety-seven to seventy. Splendid, old fellow!" cried another.

"I was certain you'd win," said another.

"I have not won," said Wraysford, drily, and evidently not liking these marked congratulations; "I'm second."

"So you are, I quite forgot," said Ricketts: then turning to Oliver, he added, mockingly, "Allow me to congratulate you, Greenfield, on your really brilliant success. 112 marks out of 120! You could hardly have done better if you had seen the paper a day or two before the exam! Your class, I assure you, are very proud of you."

A general sneer of contempt followed this speech, in the midst of which Oliver, after darting one angry glance at the speaker, deliberately quitted the room.

This proceeding greatly irritated the Fifth, who had hoped at least to make their class-fellow smart while they had the opportunity. They greeted his departure now with a general chorus of hissing, and revenged themselves in his absence by making the most of Wraysford.

"Surely the fellow won't be allowed to take the scholarship after this?" said Ricketts. "The Doctor must see through it all."

"It's very queer if he doesn't," said Bullinger.

"The scholarship belongs to Wray," said Braddy, "and I mean to say it's a blackguard shame if he doesn't get it!"

"It's downright robbery, that's what it is!" said another; "the fellow ought to be kicked out of the school!"

"I vote some one tells the Doctor," said Braddy.

"Suppose you go and tell him now, yourself," said Pembury, with a sarcastic smile; "you could do it capitally. What do you say?"

Braddy coloured. Pembury was always snubbing him.

"I don't want to tell tales," he said. "What I mean is, Wraysford ought not to be cheated out of his scholarship."

"It's a lucky thing Wray has got you to set things right for him," snarled Pembury, amid a general titter.

Braddy subsided at this, and left his tormentor master of the situation.

"There's no use our saying or doing anything," said that worthy. "We shall probably only make things worse. It's sure to come out in time, and till then we must grin and bear it."

"All very well," said some one, "but Greenfield will be grinning too."

"I fancy not," said Pembury. "I'm not a particular angel myself, but I've a notion if I had cheated a schoolfellow I should be a trifle off my grinning form; I don't know."

This modest confession caused some amusement, and helped a good deal to restore the class to a better humour.

"After all, I don't envy the fellow his feelings this minute," continued Pembury, following up his advantage.

"And I envy his prospects in the Fifth still less," said Ricketts.

"If you take my advice," said Pembury, "you'll leave him pretty much to himself. Greenfield is a sort of fellow it's not easy to score off; and some of you would only make fools of yourselves if you tried to do it."

Wraysford had stood by during this conversation, torn by conflicting emotions. He was undoubtedly bitterly disappointed to have missed the scholarship; but that was as nothing to the knowledge that it was his friend, his own familiar friend, who had turned against him and thus grievously wronged him. Yet with all his sense of injury he could hardly stand by and listen to all the bitter talk about Oliver in his absence without a sense of shame. Two days ago he would have flared up at the first word, and given the rash speaker something to remember. Now it was his misery to stand by and hear his old chum abused and despised, and to feel that he deserved every word that was spoken of him!

If he could only have found one word to say on his behalf!

But he could not, and so left the room as soon as it was possible to escape, and retired disconsolately to his own study.

As for the Fifth, Pembury's advice prevailed with them. There were a few who were still disposed to take their revenge on Oliver in a more marked manner than by merely cutting him; but a dread of the tongue of the editor of the *Dominican*, as well as a conviction of the uselessness of such procedure, constrained them to give way and fall in with the general resolution.

One boy only was intractable. That was Simon. It was not in the poet's nature to agree to cut anybody. When the class dispersed he took it into his gifted head to march direct to Oliver's study. Oliver was there, writing a letter.

"Oh, I say, you know," began Simon, nervously, but smiling most affably, "all the fellows are going to cut you, you know, Greenfield. About that paper, you know, the time I met you coming out of the Doctor's study. But *I* won't cut you, you know. We'll hush it all up, you know, Greenfield; upon my word we will. But the fellows think—"

"That will do!" said Oliver, angrily.

"Oh, but you know, Greenfield—"

"Look here, if you don't get out of my study," said Oliver, rising to his feet, "I'll—"

Before he could finish his sentence the poet, who after all was one of the best-intentioned jackasses in Saint Dominic's, had vanished.

Chapter Twenty Five.
Loman in Luck.

While we have been talking of Oliver and Wraysford, and of the manner in which the results of the Nightingale examination affected them and the class to which they belonged, the reader will hardly have forgotten that there was another whose interest in that result was fully as serious and fully as painful.

Loman had been counting on gaining the scholarship to a dead certainty. From the moment when it occurred to him he would be able to free himself of his money difficulties with Cripps by winning it, he had dismissed, or seemed to dismiss, all further anxiety from his mind. He never doubted that he in the Sixth could easily beat the two boys in the Fifth; and though, as we have seen, he now and then felt a sneaking misgiving on the subject, it never seriously disturbed his confidence.

Now, however, he was utterly floored. He did not need to wait for the announcement of the results to be certain he had not won, for he had known his fate the moment his eyes glanced down the questions on the paper on the morning of examination.

At his last interview with Cripps that memorable Saturday afternoon, he had promised confidently to call at the Cockchafer next Thursday with the news of the result, as a further guarantee for the payment of the thirty pounds, never doubting what that result would be. How was he to face this interview now?

He could never tell Cripps straight out that he had been beaten in the examination; that would be the same thing as telling him to go at once to the Doctor or his father with the document which the boy had signed, and expose the whole affair. And it would be no use making a poor mouth to the landlord of the Cockchafer and begging to be forgiven the debt; Loman knew enough by this time to feel convinced of the folly of that. What was to be done?

"I shall have to humbug the fellow some way," said Loman to himself, as he sat in his study the afternoon after the announcement of the result. And then followed an oath.

Loman had been going from bad to worse the last month. Ever since he had begun, during the holidays, regularly to frequent the Cockchafer, and to discover that it was his interest to make himself agreeable to the man he disliked and feared, the boy's vicious instincts had developed strangely. Company which before would have offended him, he now found—especially when it flattered him—congenial, and words and acts from which in former days he would have shrunk now came naturally.

"I shall have to humbug the fellow somehow," said he; "I only wish I knew how;" and then Loman set himself deliberately to invent a lie for Mr Cripps.

A charming afternoon's occupation this for a boy of seventeen!

He sat and pondered for an hour or more, sometimes fancying he had hit upon the object of his search, and sometimes finding himself quite off the tack. Had Cripps only known what care and diligence was being bestowed on him that afternoon he would assuredly have been highly flattered.

At length he seemed to come to a satisfactory decision, and, naturally exhausted by such severe mental exertion, Loman quitted his study and sought in the playground the fresh air and diversion he so much needed. One of the first boys he met there was Simon. "Hullo, Loman!" said that amiable genius, "would you have believed it?"

"Believed what?" said Loman.

"Oh! you know, I thought you knew, about the Nightingale, you know. I say, how jolly low you came out!"

"Look here! you'd better hold your row!" said Loman, surlily, "unless you want a hiding."

"Oh; it's not that, you know. What I meant was about Greenfield senior. Isn't that a go?"

"What about him? Why can't you talk like an ordinary person, and not like a howling jackass?"

"Why, you know," said Simon, off whom all such pretty side compliments as these were wont to roll like water off a duck's back—"why, you know, about that paper?"

"What paper?" said Loman, impatiently. "The one that was stolen out of the Doctor's study, you know. Isn't that a go? But we're going to hush it up. Honour bright!"

Loman's face at that moment was anything but encouraging. Somehow, this roundabout way of the poet's seemed particularly aggravating to him, for he turned quite pale with rage, and, seizing the unhappy bard by the throat, said, with an oath, "What do you mean, you miserable beast? What about the paper?"

"Oh!" said Simon, not at all put about by this rough handling—"why, don't you know? *we* know who took it, we do; but we're all going to—"

But at this point Simon's speech was interrupted, for the very good reason that Loman's grip on his throat became so very tight that the wretched poet nearly turned black in the face.

With another oath the Sixth Form boy exclaimed, "Who took it?"

"Why—don't you know?—oh!—oh, I say, mind my throat!—haven't you heard?—why, Greenfield senior, you know!"

Loman let go his man suddenly and stared at him.

"Greenfield senior?" he exclaimed in amazement.

"Yes; would you have thought it? None of us would—we're all going to hush it up, you know, honour bright we are."

"Who told you he took it?"

"Why, you know, I saw him;" and here Simon giggled jubilantly, to mark what astonishment his disclosure was causing.

"*You* saw him take it?" asked Loman, astounded.

"Yes; that is, I saw him coming out of the Doctor's study with it."

"You did?"

"Yes; that is, of course he must have had it; and he says so himself."

"What, Greenfield says he took the paper?" exclaimed Loman, in utter astonishment.

"Yes; that is, he doesn't say he didn't; and all the fellows are going to cut him dead, but we mean to hush it up if we can."

"Hush yourself up, that's what you'd better do," said Loman, turning his back unceremoniously on his informant, and proceeding, full of this strange news, on his solitary walk. What was in his mind as he went along I cannot tell you. I fancy it was hardly sorrow at the thought that a schoolfellow could stoop to a mean, dishonest action, nor, I think, was it indignation on Wraysford's or his own account.

Indeed, the few boys who passed Loman that afternoon were struck with the cheerfulness of his appearance. Considering he had been miserably beaten in the scholarship examination, this show of satisfaction was all the more remarkable.

"The fellow seems quite proud of himself," said Callonby to Wren as they passed him.

"He's the only fellow who is, if that's so," said Wren.

Loman stopped and spoke to them as they came up.

"Hullo! you fellows," said he, in as free and easy a manner as one fellow can assume to others who he knows dislike him, "I wanted to see you. Which way are you going?—back to the school?"

"Wren and I are going a stroll together," said Callonby, coldly; "good-bye."

"Half a minute," said Loman. "I suppose you heard the results of the Nightingale read out."

"Considering I was sitting on the same form with you when they were, I suppose I did," said Wren.

"That's all right," said Loman, evidently determined not to notice the snubbing bestowed on him. "Mine wasn't a very loud score, was it? Seventy! I was surprised it was as much!"

The two Sixth boys looked at him inquiringly.

"The fact is, I never tried to answer," said Loman, "and for a very good reason. I suppose you know."

"No—what?" asked they.

"Haven't you heard? I thought it was all over the school. You heard about the Doctor missing a paper?"

"Yes; what about it? Was it found, or lost, or what?"

"No one owned to having taken it, that's certain."

"I should hope not. Not the sort of thing any fellow here would do."

"That's just what I should have thought," said Loman. "But the fact is, some one did take it—you can guess who—and you don't suppose I was going to be fool enough to take any trouble over my answers when I knew one of the other fellows had had the paper in his pocket a day and a half before the exam." And here Loman laughed.

"Do you mean to say Greenfield stole it?" exclaimed both the friends at once, in utter astonishment.

"I mean to say you're not far wrong. But you'd better ask some of the Fifth. It's all come out, I hear, there."

"And you knew of it before the exam?"

"I guessed it; or you may be sure I'd have taken a little more trouble over my answers. It wasn't much use as it was."

Loman had the satisfaction of seeing the two Sixth boys depart in amazement, and the still greater satisfaction of seeing them a little later in confidential conference with Simon, from whom he guessed pretty correctly they would be sure to get a full "all-round" narrative of the whole affair.

"I'm all right with the Sixth, anyhow," muttered he to himself. "I only wish I was as right with that blackguard Cripps."

"That blackguard Cripps" had, next afternoon, the peculiar pleasure of welcoming his young friend and patron under the hospitable roof of the Cockchafer. As usual, he was as surprised as he was delighted at the honour done him, and could not imagine for the life of him to what he was indebted for so charming a condescension. In other words, he left Loman to open the business as best he could.

"I promised to come and tell you about the exam, didn't I?"

"Eh? Oh, yes, to be sure. That was last Saturday. Upon my word, I'd quite forgotten."

Of course Loman knew this was false; but he had to look pleasant and answer, "Well, you see, my memory was better than yours."

"Right you are, young captain. And what about this here fifty-pound dicky-bird you've been after?"

"The Nightingale?" said Loman. "Oh, it's all right, of course; but the fact is, I forgot when I promised you the money now, that of course they—"

"Oh, come now, none of your gammon," said Mr Cripps, angrily; "a promise is a promise, and I expect young swells as makes them to keep them, mind that."

"Oh, of course I'll keep them, Cripps. What I was saying was that they don't pay you the money till the beginning of each year."

Loman omitted to mention, as he had omitted to mention all along, that young gentlemen who win scholarships do not, as a rule, have the money they win put into their hands to do as they like with. But this was a trifling slip of the memory, of course!

"I don't care when they pay you your money! All I know is I must have mine now, my young dandy. Next week the time's up."

"But, Cripps, how *can* I pay you unless I've got the money?"

"No, no; I've had enough of that, young gentleman. This time I'm a-going to have my way, or the governor shall know all about it,—you see!"

"Oh, don't say that!" said Loman. "Wait a little longer and it will be all right, it really will."

"Not a bit of it. That's what you said three months ago," replied Cripps.

"I won't ask you again," pleaded the boy; "just this time, Cripps."

"Why, you ought to be ashamed of yourself, that you ought," exclaimed the virtuous landlord of the Cockchafer, "a keeping a honest man out of his money!"

"Oh, but I'm certain to have it then—that is, next to certain."

"Oh! then what you're telling me about this here Nightingale of yours is a lie, is it?" said the 'cute Mr Cripps. "You ain't got it at all, ain't you?"

Loman could have bitten his tongue off for making such a blunder.

"A lie? No; that is—Why, Cripps, the fact is—" he stammered, becoming suddenly very red.

"Well, drive on," said Cripps, enjoying the boy's confusion, and proud of his own sharpness.

"The fact is—I was going to tell you, Cripps, I was really; there's been something wrong about this exam. One of the fellows stole one of the papers, and so got the scholarship unfairly."

"And I can make a pretty good guess," said Mr Cripps, with a grin, "which of the fellows that gentleman was."

"No, it wasn't me, Cripps, really," said Loman, pale and quite humble in the presence of his creditor; "it was one of the others—Greenfield in the Fifth; the fellow, you know, who struck you on Saturday."

"What, him?" exclaimed Cripps, astonished for once in a way. "That bloke? Why, he looked a honest sort of chap, he did, though I *do* owe him one."

"Oh," said Loman, following up this temporary advantage, "he's a regular swindler, is Greenfield. He stole the paper, you know, and so won the scholarship, of course. I was certain of it, if it hadn't been for that. I mean to have a row made about it, and there's certain to be another exam, so that I'm sure of the money if you'll only wait."

"And how long do you want me to wait, I'd like to know?" said Cripps.

"Oh, till after Christmas, please, at any rate. It'll be all right then, I'll answer for that."

"You'll answer for a lot of things, it strikes me, young gentleman," said Cripps, "before you've done."

There were signs of relenting in this speech which the boy was quick to take advantage of.

"*Do* wait till then!" he said, beseechingly.

Cripps pretended to meditate.

"I don't see how I can. I'm a poor man, got my rent to pay and all that. Look here, young gentleman, I must have 10 pounds down, if I'm to wait."

"Ten pounds! I haven't as much in the world!" exclaimed Loman. "I can give you five pounds, though," he added. "I've just got a note from home to-day."

"Five's no use," said Cripps, contemptuously, "wouldn't pay not the interest. You'll have to make it a tenner, young gentleman."

"Don't say that, Cripps, I'd gladly do it if I could; I'd pay you every farthing, and so I will if you only wait."

"That's just the way with you young swells. You get your own ways, and leave other people to get theirs best way they can. Where's your five-pound?"

Loman promptly produced this, and Cripps as promptly pocketed it, adding, "Well, I suppose I'll have to give in. How long do you say—two months?"

"Three," said Loman. "Oh, thanks, Cripps, I really *will* pay up then."

"You'd better, because, mind you, if you don't, I shall walk straight to the governor. Don't make any mistake about that."

"Oh, yes, so you may," said the wretched Loman, willing to promise anything in his eagerness.

Finally it was settled. Cripps was to wait three months longer; and Loman, although knowing perfectly well that there was absolutely less chance then of having the money than there had been now, felt a weight temporarily taken off his mind, and was all gratitude.

Of course, he stayed a while as usual and tasted Mr Cripps's beer, and of course he met again not a few of his new friends—sharpers, most of them, of Cripps's own stamp, or green young gentlemen of the town, like Loman himself. From one of the latter Loman had the extraordinary "good luck" that afternoon to win three pounds over a wager, a sum which he at once handed over to Cripps in the most virtuous way, in further liquidation of his debt.

Indeed, as he left the place, and wandered slowly back to Saint Dominic's, he felt quite encouraged.

"There's eight pounds of it paid right off," said he to himself; "and before Christmas something is sure to turn up. Besides, I'm sure to get some more money from home between now and then. Oh, it'll be all right!"

So saying he tried to dismiss the matter from his mind and think of pleasanter subjects, such, for instance, as Oliver's crime, and his own clever use of it to delude the Sixth.

Things altogether were looking up with Loman. Cheating, lying, and gambling looked as if they would pay after all!

Chapter Twenty Six.
At Coventry.

Were you ever at Coventry, reader? I don't mean the quaint old Warwickshire city, but that other place where from morning till night you are shunned and avoided by everybody? Where friends with whom you were once on the most intimate terms now pass you without a word, or look another way as you go by? Where, whichever way you go, you find yourself alone? Where every one you speak to is deaf, every one you appear before is blind, every one you go near has business somewhere else? Where you will be left undisturbed in your study for a week, to fag for yourself, study by yourself, disport yourself with yourself? Where in the playground you will be as solitary as if you were in the desert, in school you will be a class by yourself, and even in church on Sundays you will feel hopelessly out in the cold among your fellow-worshippers?

If you have ever been to such a place, you can imagine Oliver Greenfield's experiences during this Christmas term at Saint Dominic's.

When the gentlemen of the Fifth Form had once made up their minds to anything, they generally carried it through with great heartiness, and certainly they never succeeded better in any undertaking than in this of "leaving Oliver to himself."

The only drawback to their success was that the proceeding appeared to have little or no effect on the *very* person on whose behalf it was undertaken. Not that Oliver could be *quite* insensible of the honours paid him. He could not—they were too marked for that. And without doubt they were as unpleasant as they were unmistakable. But, for any sign of unhappiness he displayed, the whole affair might have been a matter of supreme indifference to him. Indeed, it looked quite as much as if Greenfield had sent the Fifth to Coventry as the Fifth Greenfield. If they determined none of them to speak to him, he was equally determined none of them should have the chance; and if it was part of their scheme to leave him as much as possible to himself, they had little trouble in doing it, for he, except when inevitable, never came near them.

Of course this was dreadfully irritating to the Fifth! The moral revenge they had promised themselves on the disgracer of their class never seemed to come off. The wind was taken out of their sails at every turn. The object of their aversion was certainly not reduced to humility or penitence by their conduct; on the contrary, one or two of them felt decidedly inclined to be ashamed of themselves and feel foolish when they met their victim.

Oliver always had been a queer fellow, and he now came out in a queerer light than ever.

Having once seen how the wind lay, and what he had to expect from the Fifth, he altered the course of his life to suit the new circumstances with the greatest coolness. Instead of going up the river in a pair-oar or a four, he now went up in a sculling boat or a canoe, and seemed to enjoy himself quite as much. Instead of doing his work with Wraysford evening after evening, he now did it undisturbed by himself, and, to judge by his progress in class, more successfully than ever. Instead of practising with the fifteens at football, he went in for a regular course of practice in the gymnasium, and devoted himself with remarkable success to the horizontal bar and the high jump. Instead of casting in his lot in class with a jovial though somewhat distracting set, he now kept his mind free for his studies, and earned the frequent commendation of the Doctor and Mr Jellicott.

Now, reader, I ask you, if you had been one of the Fifth of Saint Dominic's would not all this have been very riling? Here was a fellow convicted of a shameful piece of deceit, caught, one might say, in the very act, and by his own conduct as good as admitting it. Here was a fellow, I say, whom every sensible boy ought to avoid, not only showing himself utterly indifferent to the aversion of his class-fellows, but positively thriving and triumphing before their very faces! Was it any wonder if they felt very sore, and increasingly sore on the subject of Oliver Greenfield?

One boy, of course, stuck to the exile through thick and thin. If Oliver had murdered all Saint Dominic's with slow poison, Stephen would have stuck to him to the end, and he stuck to him now. He, at least, never once admitted that his brother was guilty. When slowly he first discovered what were the suspicions of the Fifth, and what was the common talk of the school about Oliver, the small boy's indignation was past description. He rushed to his brother.

"Do you hear the lies the fellows are telling about you, Noll?"

"Yes," said Oliver.

"Why don't you stop it, and tell them?"

"What's the use? I've told them once. If they don't choose to believe it, they needn't."

Any other boy would, of course, have taken this as clear evidence of the elder brother's guilt; but it only strengthened the small boy's indignation.

"*I'll* let them know, if *you* won't!" and forthwith he went and proceeded to make himself a perfect nuisance in the school. He began with Wraysford.

"I say, Wray," he demanded, "do you hear all the lies the fellows are telling about Noll?"

"Don't make a row now," said Wraysford, shortly. "I'm busy." But Stephen had no notion of being put down.

"The fellows say he stole an exam paper, the blackguards! I'd like to punch all their heads, and I will too!"

"Clear out of my study, now," said Wraysford, sharply.

Stephen stared at him a moment. Then his face grew pale as he grasped the meaning of it all.

"I say, Wray, surely *you* don't believe it?" he cried.

"Go away now," was Wraysford's only answer.

But this did not suit Stephen, his blood was up, and he meant to have it out.

"Surely *you* don't believe it?" he repeated, disregarding the impatience of the other; "*you* aren't a blackguard, like the rest?"

"Do you hear what I tell you?" said Wraysford.

"No, and I don't mean to!" retorted the irate Stephen. "If you were anything of a friend you'd stand up for Oliver. You're a beast, Wraysford, that's what you are!" continued he, in a passion. "You're a blackguard! you're a liar! I could kill you!"

And the poor boy, wild with rage and misery, actually flung himself blindly upon his brother's old friend—the saviour of his own life.

Wraysford was not angry. There was more of pity in his face than anger as he took the small boy by the arm and led him to the door. Stephen no longer resisted. After giving vent to the first flood of his anger, misery got the upper hand of him, and he longed to go anywhere to hide it. He could have endured to know that Oliver was suspected by a good many of the fellows, but to find Wraysford among them was a cruel blow.

But in due time his indignation again came to the fore, and he ventured on another crusade. This time it was to Pembury. He knew before he went he had little enough to expect from the sharp-tongued editor of the *Dominican*, so he went hoping little.

To his surprise, however, Pembury was kinder than usual. He told him plainly that he did suspect Oliver, and explained why, and advised Stephen, if he were wise, to say as little about Oliver as possible at present. The young champion was quite cowed by this unexpected reception. He did his best to fly in a rage and be defiant, but it was no use, and he retired woefully discomfited from the interview.

Others to whom he applied, when once again his anger got the better of his wretchedness, met him with taunts, others with contempt, others with positive unkindness; and after a week Stephen gave it up and retired in dudgeon to the territory of the Guinea-pigs and Tadpoles, determined that there at least he would, at the edge of the knuckle, if needs be, compel a faction to declare for his brother.

In this undertaking, I need hardly say, he was eminently successful. There were those among the Guinea-pigs and Tadpoles who were ready to declare for anybody or anything as long as there was a chance of a row on the head of it. Already the question of Greenfield senior had been occupying their magnificent minds. When the story first fell suddenly into their midst, it was so surprising that, like the frogs and the log in the fable, they were inclined to be a little shy of it. But, gradually becoming accustomed to it, and looking carefully into it from all sides, it seemed somehow to contain the promise of a jolly row, and their hearts warmed to it proportionally. No one quite liked to start the thing at first, for fear doubtless of not doing it full justice, but it only wanted a spark to kindle the whole lower school on the question of Greenfield senior. Stephen it was who supplied the spark.

He entered the Fourth Junior room one day, after one of the unsuccessful crusades of which we have spoken, utterly cast down and out of humour. He flung his cap on to the peg, and himself on to his seat, in an unusually agitated manner, and then, to the astonishment of everybody, broke out into tears!

This was a rare and glorious opportunity, of course, for Bramble.

"Beastly young blub-baby!" exclaimed that doughty hero, "you're always blubbing! I never knew such a fellow to blub, did you, Padger?"

Padger said it was worse than the baby at home, and the two thereupon started a mocking caterwaul on their own account, in which not a few of their nearest and dearest friends joined.

This performance had the effect of restoring Stephen's composure. Hastily dashing away his tears, he flew with unwonted wrath at his enemy. Bramble, however, managed to get behind Padger and the rest, and thus fortified shouted out, "Yah, boo, howling young sucking pig! go home to your mammy, or your great big cheat of a blackguard thief of a caddish big brother! Do you hear? Who stole the exam paper? Eh, Padger? Yah, boo, pack of sneaking Guinea-pigs!"

This last objurgation, which was quite unnecessary to the beauty or force of the speech, gave rise to a huge tumult.

The Guinea-pigs present took it up as a direct challenge to themselves, and it decided them instantly to declare in favour of Stephen and his big brother. Paul led the attack.

"Shut up, you young cad, will you?" said he; "you know well enough *you* stole the paper."

Of course no one, not even Paul himself, attached any meaning to such an absurd accusation, but it came conveniently to hand.

This declaration of war was promptly taken up on all sides, and for a short period the Fourth Junior had a rather dusty appearance. When at length a little order was restored, a lively discussion on the crime of Greenfield senior ensued. The Tadpoles to a man believed in it, and gave it as their candid opinion that the fellow ought to be hung. "Yes, and expelled too!" added a few of the more truculent.

The Guinea-pigs, on the other hand, whatever they thought, protested vehemently that Greenfield senior was the most virtuous, heroic, saintly, and jolly fellow in all Saint Dominic's, and denounced the Tadpoles and all the rest of the school as the most brutal ruffians in Christendom.

"They ought all to be expelled, every one of them," said one; "all except Greenfield senior, and I hope they will be."

"All I know is," said Paul, "I'll let them have a bit of my mind, some of them."

"So will I," said another.

"You haven't got any to give 'em a bit of," squealed Bramble, "so now!"

"All right, I'll give 'em a bit of *you* then," retorted Paul.

"You wouldn't get any of them to touch him with a pair of tongs," added another.

This was too much for Bramble, and another brief period of dust ensued. Then, comparative quiet once more prevailing, Paul said, "I tell you what, *I* mean to stick to Greenfield senior."

"So do I," said another youth, with his face all over ink. "I mean *to fag* for him."

"So do I!" shouted another.

"So do I!" shouted another.

And a general chorus of assent hailed the idea.

"We'll all fag for him, I vote, eh, Stee?" said Paul, "the whole lot of us! My eye, that'll be prime! Won't the others just about look black and blue!"

It was a magnificent idea! And no sooner conceived than executed.

There was a great rush of Guinea-pigs to Oliver's study. He was not there. So much the better. They would give him a delightful surprise!

So they proceeded straightway to empty his cupboards and drawers, to polish up his cups, to unfold his clothes and fold them again, to take down his books and put them up again, to upset his ink and mop it up with one of his handkerchiefs, to make his tea and spill it on the floor, to dirty his collars with their inky hands, to clean his boots with his hat-brush, and many other thoughtful and friendly acts calculated to make the heart of their hero glad.

In the midst of their orgies, Wraysford and Pembury passed the door, and stopped to look in, wondering what on earth the tumult was about. But they were greeted with such a storm of yells and hisses that they passed on, a little uneasy in their minds as to whether or no hydrophobia had broken out in Saint Dominic's.

After them a detachment of Tadpoles, headed by Bramble appeared on the scene, for the purpose of mocking. But, whatever their purpose may have been, it was abandoned for more active opposition when Paul presently emptied a tumblerful of lukewarm tea in the face of Master Bramble.

A notable battle was fought on the threshold of Greenfield senior's study, in which many were wounded on both sides, and in the midst of which Oliver arrived on the scene, kicking right and left, and causing a general rout.

How their hero appreciated the attentions his admirers had paid him during his absence the Guinea-pigs did not remain or return to ascertain. They took for granted he was grateful, and bashfully kept out of the way of his thanks for a whole day.

After that their enthusiasm returned, but this time it found a new vent. They decided that, although they would all fag for him to the end of his days, they would not for a season, at any rate, solicit jobs from him, but rather encourage him by their sympathy and applause at a more respectful distance.

So they took to cheering him in the playground, and following him down the passages. And this not being enough, they further relieved themselves by hooting (at a respectful distance also) the chiefs of the senior school, whose opinions on the question of Greenfield senior were known not to agree with their own.

If Oliver was not grateful for all this moral support in his trouble, he must have been a villain indeed of the deepest dye. He never said in so many words he was grateful; but then the Guinea-pigs remembered that feelings are often too deep and too many for words, and so took for granted the thanks which their consciences told them they deserved.

Meanwhile a fresh number of the *Dominican* was in progress, and rapidly nearing the hour of publication.

Chapter Twenty Seven.

The "Dominican" on the Situation.

The examination at the beginning of the term had seriously interfered with the prospects of the *Dominican*. Pembury knew well enough it was no good trying to get anything out of the diligent section of his class-fellows at such a time; and he knew equally well that a number contributed entirely by the idlers of the Fifth would neither be creditable to the paper nor appreciated by any one outside.

So like a prudent man he held back patiently till the examinations were over, and then pounced down on his men with redoubled importunity.

"Look here," said he one day to Ricketts, "when are you going to let me have that paper of yours?"

"What paper do you mean?" demanded Ricketts.

"Why for the *Dominican*, of course; you don't suppose I want one of your cast-off exam papers, do you?"

"Oh, I can't do anything for the *Dominican* this time," said Ricketts.

"Yes, you can, and yes, you will," coolly replied Anthony.

"Who says I will?" demanded Ricketts, inclined to be angry.

"It sounds as if *I* do," replied the editor. "Why of course you'll do something for it, Rick?"

"I'd be glad enough, but really I'm not in the humour," said Ricketts.

"Why ever not?" demanded Tony.

"Why, the fact is," said Ricketts, "I fancy the Fifth is not exactly looking up at present, and we've nothing particular to be proud of. If you take my advice you'll keep the *Dominican* quiet for a bit."

"My dear fellow, that's the very thing we mustn't do. Don't you see, you old duffer you, that if we shut up shop and retire into private life, everybody will be thinking we daren't hold up our heads? I mean to hold up my head, for one," added Tony, proudly, "if there were a thousand Greenfields in the class; and I mean to make you hold up yours too, old man. It'll be time enough to do the hang-dog business when we all turn knaves; but till we do, we've as good a right to be known at Saint Dominic's as anybody else. So none of your humbug, Rick. We'll get out an extra good *Dominican*, and let the fellows see we're alive and kicking."

This speech had the required effect. It not only won over Ricketts, but most of the other leading spirits of the Fifth, who had been similarly holding back.

Tony was not the fellow to let an advantage go by. Having once got his men into a becoming frame of mind, he kept them well in hand and worked them up into something like the old enthusiasm on the subject of the *Dominican*.

Every one was determined the present number should be an out-and-out good one, and laboured and racked his brains accordingly.

But somehow or other the fellows had never found it so hard, first to get inspirations, and then to put them down on paper, as they did at present. Every one thought he had something very fine and very clever to say if he could only find expression for it. The amount of brain-cudgelling that went on over this *Dominican* was simply awful. Wraysford gave it up in disgust. Ricketts, Bullinger, Tom Senior, and others stumbled through their tasks, and could only turn out lame productions at the best. Even Pembury's lucubrations lacked a good deal of their wonted dash and spirit. The cloud which was hanging over the Fifth seemed to have overshadowed its genius for a while.

Still Pembury kept his men at it and gave them no peace till their productions, such as they were, were safe in his hands. One boy only was equal to the emergency; that I need hardly say was Simon. He was indeed more eloquent than ever. He offered Pembury a poem of forty verses, entitled, "An Elegy on the Wick of a Candle that had just been blown out," to begin with, and volunteered to supplement this contribution with one or two smaller pieces, such as, "My Little Lark," or "An Adventure outside the Dormitory Door," or "Mind Mewsings."

Pembury prudently accepted all, and said he would insert what he thought fit, an assurance which delighted Simon, who immediately sat down and wrote some more "pieces," in case at the last moment there might be room for them too. But, in spite even of these valuable contributions, the *Dominican* fell flat. There were a few good things in it here and there, but it was far below its ordinary form; and not a few of the writers repented sorely that ever they had put pen to paper to help produce it.

The chief amusement of the paper was contained in a "New Code of Regulations for the Better Management of Guinea-pigs and Tadpoles," from the editor's pen. It began thus:

"A society has lately been started at Saint Dominic's for the preservation and management of Guinea-pigs and Tadpoles. The following are some of the rules to be observed:—

"Any one owning a Guinea-pig or Tadpole is to be responsible for washing it with soap and hot water at least twice a day.

"Any one owning a Guinea-pig or Tadpole is to supply the rest of the school with cotton wool and scent.

"No Guinea-pig or Tadpole is on any account to use hair oil or grease which has not been sanctioned by a joint committee of the Fifth, Sixth, and masters.

"During the approaching winter, every one possessing a Guinea-pig or Tadpole shall be at liberty, providing it is regularly washed, to use it as a warming-pan for his own bed."

The small tribe of furious juniors who as usual had crowded round the paper on the morning of publication to get "first read," broke forth at this point into a howl of exasperation.

"They won't! I'll see they won't use me as a warming-pan, won't you, Padger? The brutes! I'll bite their horrid cold feet if they stick them against me, that's what I'll do."

"I'll keep a pin to stick into them," said another.

"I'll get some leeches and put on their legs," shouted another.

"I'll tell you what," said Stephen, changing the subject, "it's cool cheek of them calling us 'it,' as if we were things."

"So they have," exclaimed Paul; "oh, I say, that's too much; I'll let them know *I'm* not a thing."

"Yes, you are a thing, isn't he, Padger? A regular *it*," exclaimed the vindictive Bramble. "Yah, boo, old '*its*,' both of you."

"Hold hard," said some one, just as the usual hostilities were about to commence. "Listen to this." And he read the next "regulation":—

"Immediate steps are to be taken to pickle a Tadpole as a specimen for the school museum. The following is a recipe for this. Take the ugliest, dirtiest, noisiest, and most ignorant specimen that can be found. Lift it carefully with a pair of tongs into a bath full of vinegar. Close the lid and let it remain there to soak for a week. At the end of that time lift it out and scrape it well all over with a sharp substance, to get off the first coating of grime. Soak again for another week and scrape again, and so on till the ninth or tenth coating is removed. After that the creature will appear thinner than when it began. Hang it up to dry in a clean place, and be sure no other Guinea-pigs or Tadpoles come near it. Then put it in a clean gown, and quickly, before it can get at the ink, put it in a large glass bottle and fasten down the stopper. Label it, 'Specimen of a curious reptile formerly found at Saint Dominic's. Now happily extinct.'"

"There you are," said Paul, when, after much blundering and sticking at words, this remarkable paragraph had been read through. "There you are, Bramble, my boy; what do you think of that?" Bramble had no difficulty in intimating what he thought of it in pretty strong language, and for some little time the further reading of the *Dominican* was suspended.

When, however, the row was over, the group had been joined by several of the elder boys, who appeared to appreciate Simon's poem, "An Adventure outside the Dormitory Door." It was called an "epick," and began thus. The reader must be contented with quite a short extract:—

"Outside the Dormitory door
I walked me slow upon the floor
And just outside the Doctor's study
A youth I met all in a hurry;
His name perhaps I had better not tell
But like a snail retire into my shell."

This last simile had evidently particularly delighted the poet. So much so, that he brought it in at the close of every succeeding verse. The "epick" went on, of course, to unravel the threads of the "adventure," and to intimate pretty plainly who "the youth" referred to was. To any one not interested in the poet or his epic the production was a dull one, and the moral at the end was not quite clear even to the most intellectual.

"Now I must say farewell; yet stay, methinks
How many many youths do sit on brinks.
Oh joy to feel the soft breeze sigh
And in the shady grove to wipe the eye,
It makes me feel a man I know full well,
But like a snail I'll now retire within my shell."

These were the only articles in the *Dominican* that afforded any amusement. The remainder of the paper, made up of the usual articles sneering at the Sixth and crowing over the school generally, were very tame. The result of the Nightingale Scholarship was announced as follows:—

"The examination for the Nightingale Scholarship was held on the 1st October. The scholarship was lost by Loman of the Sixth by 70 marks to 97. A good performance on the whole."

This manner of announcing the unfortunate result was ingenious, and did Tony credit. For, whether his object was to annoy the Sixth or to shield the Fifth, he succeeded amply in both. There were some, however, in the Fifth who were by no means content that Greenfield should be let off so easily in the *Dominican*, and these read with interest the following "Notes from Coventry," contributed by Bullinger. Anthony had accepted and inserted them against his better judgment.

"If the fellow is at Coventry, why not let him stay there?" he said to Bullinger. "The best thing we can possibly do is to let him alone."

"I don't see it," said Bullinger. "Everybody will think we are trying to shield him if we keep so quiet. Anyhow, here's my paper. You can put it in or not, which you like. I'm not going to write anything else."

Pembury took the paper and put it in. The reader may like to hear a few of the "Notes from Coventry."

"The quaint old city of Coventry has lately been visited by a 'gentleman' from Saint Dominic's, who appears so charmed with all he has seen and heard that it is expected he will remain there for some considerable time.

"The object of his visit is of a private nature, possibly for the purpose of scientific research, for which absolute quiet is necessary. His experiments are chiefly directed to the making or taking of examination papers, and on his return we may look for valuable discoveries. Meanwhile he sees very little company. The society in which he most delights is that of certain Guinea-pigs, between whom and himself a special bond of sympathy appears to exist. It is a touching sight to see him taking his daily walks in company with these singular animals; who, be it said, seem to be the only creatures able to appreciate his character. Curiously enough, since he left us, Saint Dominic's has not collapsed; indeed, it is a singular fact that now he is away it is no longer considered necessary for every fellow to lock his study-door when he goes out, and keep the key." And so on.

Miserable stuff indeed, as Stephen thought, but quite stinging enough to wound him over and over again as he saw the sneers and heard the laughs with which the reading of the extract was greeted. Everybody evidently was against his brother, and, with a deep disgust and fury at his heart, he left them to laugh by themselves and returned to Oliver's study.

He found his brother in what were now his usual cheerful spirits. For after the first week or so of his being sent to Coventry, Oliver, in his own study at least, kept up a cheerful appearance.

"Hullo, Stee," said he as the young brother entered. "You're just in time. Here's a letter from mother."

"Is there? How jolly! Read it out, Noll."

So Oliver read it out. It was an ordinary, kind, motherly epistle, such as thousands of schoolboys get every week of the school year. All about home, and what is going on, how the dogs are, where sister Mary has been to, how the boiler burst last week, which apple-tree bore most, and so on; every scrap of news that could be scraped up from the four winds of heaven was in that letter.

And to the two brothers, far away, and lonely even among their schoolfellows, it came like a breath of fresh air that morning.

"I have been so proud," went on Mrs Greenfield towards the end of the letter, "ever since I heard of dear Oliver's success in winning the scholarship. Not so much for the value of it, though that is pretty considerable, but because I am so sure he deserves it."

"Hear, hear!" put in Stephen.

"Poor Mr Wraysford! I hope he is not very much disappointed. How nice it would have been if there had been two scholarships, and each could have had one! I suppose the Fifth is making quite a hero of Oliver. I know one foolish old woman who would like to be with her boys this moment to share their triumph."

Oliver laughed bitterly.

"That *would* be a treat for her!"

Stephen, very red in the face, was too furious for words, so Oliver went on:

"And if, instead of triumph, they should ever be in trouble or sorrow, still more would I love to be with them, to share it. But most of all do I trust and pray they may both make a constant friend of the Saviour, who wants us all to cast our burdens on Him, and follow the example He has left us in all things."

There was a silence for some moments after this home message fell on the brothers' ears. The hearts of both were full—too full for words—but I think, had the widow-mother far away been able to divine the secret thoughts of her boys, hope would have mingled with all her pity and all her solicitude on their account.

But the old trouble, for the present at any rate, was destined to swamp all other emotions.

Oliver continued reading: "Christmas will not be so very long now in coming. We must have a real snug, old-fashioned time of it here. Uncle Henry has promised to come, and your cousins. It would be nice if you could persuade Mr Wraysford to come here then. I am so anxious to see him again. Tell him from me I reckon on him to be one of our party if he can possibly manage it."

"Baa!" exclaimed Stephen. "The beast! I'll let her know what sort of blackguard the fellow is!"

"Easy all, young 'un," said Oliver.

"I shan't easy all, Noll!" exclaimed the boy; "he *is* a blackguard, you know he is, and I hate him."

"I think he's a fool just now," said Oliver, "but—well, he fished you out of the Thames, Stee; you oughtn't to call him a blackguard."

"I wish he'd left me in the Thames," said Stephen, nearly breaking down. "I've been miserable enough this term for half a dozen."

Oliver looked hard and long at his young brother. It never seemed to have occurred to him before how deeply the boy took the trouble of his elder brother to heart.

Now if Oliver had really been innocent, the natural thing would have been—wouldn't it?—for him to be quite cut up at this exhibition of feeling, and fall on his brother's neck and protest once more that he never did or would or could do such a thing as that he was suspected of. But instead of this, the hardened villain turned quite cross when he saw his brother at the point of tears, and exclaimed, hurriedly, "Don't make a young fool of yourself, Stee, whatever you do. It won't do a bit of good."

"But, Noll, old man," pleaded the boy, "why ever don't you—"

"Because I don't choose, and it would be no use if I did," retorted the other.

"But the fellows all suspect you!"

"I can't help that, if they do. Come now, Stee, we've had enough of this. It'll all come right some day, you see, and meanwhile what do you say to a turn in the gymnasium?"

"Well, but," persisted Stephen, not half satisfied, "you surely aren't going to give mother's message to Wraysford? *I* don't want him home at Christmas."

"No one asked you if you did, you young duffer. But I don't think, all the same, I shall give it just yet."

They were walking down the big passage arm-in-arm in the direction of the gymnasium, and as Oliver spoke these last words the subject of their conversation appeared advancing towards them.

Who could have believed that those three friends who only a month or two ago were quoted all over Saint Dominic's as inseparables could ever meet and pass one another as these three met and passed one another now?

Wraysford coloured as he caught sight of his old ally, and looked another way. Oliver, more composed, kept his eyes fixed straight ahead, and appeared to be completely unconscious of the presence of any one but Stephen, who hung on to his arm, snorting and fuming and inwardly raging like a young tiger held in by the chain from his prey.

An odd meeting indeed, and a miserable one; yet to none of the three so miserable as to the injured Wraysford, who ever since the day of the Nightingale examination had not known a happy hour at Saint Dominic's.

Chapter Twenty Eight.
Mr Cripps at Saint Dominic's.

Oliver Greenfield's banishment from civilised society, however much it may have gratified the virtuous young gentlemen of the Fifth, was regarded by a small section of fellows in the Sixth with unmitigated disgust. These fellows were the leading spirits of the Saint Dominic Football Club, which was just about to open proceedings for the season. To them the loss of the best half-back in the school was a desperate calamity.

They raged and raved over the matter with all the fury of disappointed enthusiasts. *They* didn't care a bit, it almost seemed, whether the fellow was a cheat or not. All they knew was, he was the quickest half-back and the safest drop-kick the school had, and here was the match with Landfield coming on, and, lo and behold! their man was in Coventry, forsooth, and not to be had out for love or money. Thus baulked, the Sixth Form athletes could afford to wax very virtuous and philanthropic on the subject of Coventry generally.

"The Doctor ought to put a stop to it," said Stansfield, who this year occupied the proud position of captain of the fifteen.

"Why, we've not got a single man worth twopence behind the scrimmage!"

This was gratifying for Loman, one of the council of war, who usually played quarter or half-back in the matches.

"I don't see why we shouldn't get him to play if he *is* at Coventry," said Callonby; "*we* didn't send him there."

"All very well," said the captain; "if we got him we should lose Ricketts, and Bullinger, and Tom Senior, and Braddy, which would come to about the same thing."

"And I shouldn't play either," said Loman, "if Greenfield played."

Stansfield shrugged his shoulders and looked vicious.

"All child's play!" said he. "They think it's very grand and a fine spectacle and all that. But they ought to have more consideration for the credit of the school."

"It's not much to the credit of the school," said Loman, "to have a fellow like him in the fifteen."

"It's less credit to have a pack of louts who tumble head over heels every time they try to pick up a ball, and funk a charge twice out of every thrice!" retorted Stansfield, who was one of the peppery order. "Greenfield's worth any half-dozen of you, I tell you."

"Better get him to play Landfield by himself," growled Loman, who generally got the worst of it in discussions like this.

"It's a plaguey nuisance, that's what it is," said Stansfield; "we are sure to get licked. Who's to play half-back instead of him, I'd like to know?"

"Forrester, in the Fourth, plays a very good half-back," said Callonby; "he's tremendously quick on his feet."

"Yes, but he can't kick. I've a good mind to put Wraysford in the place. And yet he's such a rattling steady 'back' I don't like to move him."

"Wraysford told me yesterday," said Wren, "he wasn't going to play."

"What!" exclaimed Stansfield, starting up as if he had been shot. "Wraysford not going to play!"

"So he said," replied Wren.

"Oh, this is a drop too much! Why ever not?"

"I don't know. He's been awfully down in the mouth lately; whether it is about the Nightingale, or—"

The captain gave a howl of rage.

"I wish that miserable brute of a Nightingale had been scragged, that I do! Everything's stopped for the Nightingale! Who cares a button about the thing, I'd like to know? Wraysford can get dozens more of them after the football season's over. Why, the Doctor gave out another scholarship to be gone in for directly after Christmas, only to-day. Can't he go in for that?"

"So he will, I expect," said Wren; "but I don't fancy he'll play, all the same, on Saturday."

Stansfield groaned. "There go my two best men," he said; "we may as well shut up shop and go in for croquet."

A powerful deputation waited on Wraysford that same evening to try to prevail upon him to play in the fifteen. They had hard work to do it. He said he was out of form, and didn't feel in the humour, and was certain they could get on well enough without him.

"Oh, no, we can't," said Stansfield. "I say, Wraysford," he added, bluntly, "I expect it's this Nightingale affair's at the bottom of all this nonsense. Can't you possibly patch it up, at any rate till after Saturday? I'd give my head to get you and Greenfield in the team."

"Do play, Wraysford," put in Callonby. "Don't let the school be beaten just because you've got a row on with another fellow."

"It's not that at all," said Wraysford, feeling and looking very uncomfortable. "It's nothing to do with that. It's just that I'm not in the humour. I'd really rather not."

"Oh, look here," cried Stansfield; "that won't wash. Come to oblige me, there's a good fellow."

In the end Wraysford gave in, and the captain went off half consoled to complete his preparations, and inveigh in his odd moments against all Nightingales and Coventrys, and examinations, and all such enemies and stumbling-blocks to the glorious old English sport of football.

Loman looked forward to the coming match with quite good spirits. Indeed, it was a long time since he had felt or appeared so light-hearted.

That very day he had received a most unexpected present in the shape of a five-pound note from an aunt, which sum he had promptly and virtuously put into an envelope and sent down to Mr Cripps in further liquidation of his "little bill." Was ever such luck? And next week the usual remittance from home would be due; there would be another three or four pounds paid off. Loman felt quite touched at the thought of his own honesty and solvency. If only everybody in the world paid their debts as he did, what a happy state of things it would be for the country!

So, as I said, Loman looked forward to the football match in quite good spirits, just as a man who has been working hard and anxiously for eleven long months looks forward to his well-earned summer holiday. Things were looking up with him, and no mistake.

And then, just like his luck, the Doctor had that same day made the announcement, already referred to, of another scholarship to be competed for directly after Christmas. It was for Sixth form boys under seventeen, and he meant to go in for it! True, this scholarship was only for twenty pounds for a single year, but that was something. As far as he could see, Wraysford, who would get his move up at Christmas, would be the only man in against him, if he did go in, and he fancied he could beat Wraysford. For in the Nightingale exam he had not really tried his best, but this time he would and astonish everybody. Greenfield would scarcely go in for this exam, even if he got his move up; it was safe to conclude his recent exploit would suffice him in the way of exams, for some time to come.

And then, what could be more opportune than its coming off just after Christmas, at the precise time when Cripps would be looking for a final settlement of his account, or whatever little of it remained still to pay! Oh, dear! oh, dear! What a thing it is to be straight and honest! Everything prospers with a man when he goes in for being honest! Why, Loman was positively being bathed in luck at the present time!

The Saturday came at last. Stansfield had drilled his men as well as he could during the interval, and devoutly hoped that he had got a respectable team to cope with the Landfield fellows. If he could only have been sure of his half-back he would have been quite happy; and never a practice passed without his growling louder than ever at the disgraceful custom of sending useful behind-scrimmage men to Coventry. At the last moment he decided to give the responsible post to Loman, rather than move forward Wraysford from his position at "back"; and Loman's usual place at quarter-back was filled up by young Forrester of the Fourth, greatly to that young gentleman's trepidation and to the exultation of the Fourth Senior as a body, who felt terrifically puffed up to have one of their men actually in the first fifteen.

Some of my readers may perhaps know from actual experience what are the numerous and serious anxieties which always beset the captain of the football fifteen. If the fellow is worth his salt he knows to a nicety where he is strong and where he is weak; he knows, if the wind blows one way, which is the best quarter-back to put on the left and which on the right. He knows which of his "bulldogs" he can safely put into the middle of the scrimmage, and which are most useful in the second tier. He knows when to call "Kick!" to a man and when to call "Run!" and no man knows better when to throw the ball far out from touch, or when to nurse it along close to the line. It is all very well for outsiders to talk of football everlastingly as a *game*. My dear, good people, football is a science if ever there was a science; the more you know of it the more you will find that out.

This piece of lecturing is thrown in here for the purpose of observing that Stansfield was a model football captain. However worried and worrying and crabby he was in his ordinary clothes, in his football togs and on the field of battle he was the coolest, quickest, readiest, and cunningest general you could desire. He said no more than he could help, and never scolded his men while play was going on, and, best of all, worked like a horse himself in the thick of the fight, and looked to every one else to do the same.

Yet on this Saturday all the captain's prowess and generalship could not win the match for Saint Dominic's against Landfield.

The match began evenly, and for the first half of the time the game was one long succession of scrimmages in the middle of the ground, from which the ball hardly ever escaped, and when it did, escaped only to be driven back next moment into the "mush."

"It'll do at this rate!" thinks Stansfield to himself. "As long as they keep it among the forwards we shan't hurt."

Alas! one might almost have declared some tell-tale evil spirit had heard the boast and carried it to the ear of the enemy, for next moment half-time was called, the sides changed over, and with them the Landfielders completely reversed their tactics.

The game was no longer locked up in a scrimmage in the middle of the ground. It became looser all along the line; the ball began to slip through the struggling feet into the hands of those behind, who sent it shooting over the heads of the forwards into more open ground. The quarter-backs and half-backs on either side ran and got round the scrimmages; and when at last they were collared, took to ending up with an expiring drop-kick, which sent the ball far in the direction of the coveted goals.

Nothing could have happened worse for Saint Dominic's, for the strain fell upon them just at their weakest point. Stansfield groaned as he saw chance after chance missed behind his scrimmages. Young Forrester played pluckily and hard at quarter-back, and shirked nothing; but he could not kick, and his short runs were consequently of little use. Callonby, of course, did good work, but Loman, the half-back, was woefully unsteady.

"What a jackass I was to put the fellow there!" said Stansfield to himself.

And yet Loman, as a rule, was a good player, with plenty of dash and not a little courage. It was odd that to-day he should be showing such specially bad form.

There goes the ball again, clean over the forwards' heads, straight for him! He is going to catch it and run! No; he is not! He is going to take a flying kick! No, he is not; he is going to make his mark! No, he is not; he is going to dribble it through! Now if there is one thing fatal to football it is indecision. If you wobble about, so to speak, between half a dozen opinions, you may just as well sit down on the ground where you are and let the ball go to Jericho. Loman gets flurried completely, and ends by giving the ball a miserable side-kick into touch—to the extreme horror of everybody and the unmitigated disgust of the peppery Stansfield.

Yet had the captain and his men known the cause of all this—had they been aware that that flash, half-tipsy cad of a fellow who, with half a dozen of his "pals," was watching the match with a critical air, there at the ropes was the landlord of the Cockchafer himself, the holder of Loman's "little bill" for 30 pounds, they would perhaps have understood and forgiven their comrade's clumsiness. But they did not.

Whatever had brought Cripps there? A thousand possibilities flashed through Loman's mind as he caught sight of his unwelcome acquaintance in the middle of the match. Was he come to make a row about his money before all the school? or had anything fresh turned up, or what? And why on earth did he bring those other cads with him, all of whom Loman recognised as pot-house celebrities of his own acquaintance? No wonder if the boy lost his head and became flurried!

He felt miserable every time the ball flew over to Cripps's side of the ground. There was a possibility the landlord of the Cockchafer had only come up out of curiosity, and, if so, might not have recognised his young friend among the players. But this delusion was soon dispelled.

The ball went again into touch—this time close to the spot occupied by the unwelcome group, and was about to be thrown out.

Stansfield signalled to Loman. "Go up nearer the line: close up."

Loman obeyed, and as he did so there fell on his ears, in familiar tones, the noisy greeting, "What cheer, Nightingale? What cheer, my hearty? Stick to your man; eh, let him have it, Mr Loman! Two to one in half-sovereigns on Mr Loman."

A laugh greeted this encouraging appeal, in the midst of which Loman, knowing full well every one had heard every word, became completely disconcerted, and let the ball go through his fingers as if it had been quicksilver.

This was too much for Stansfield's patience.

"Go up forward, for goodness' sake," he exclaimed, "if you must play the fool! I'll go half-back myself."

Loman obeyed like a lamb, only too glad to lose himself in the scrimmages and escape observation.

The match went on—worse and worse for Saint Dominic's. Despite Stansfield's gallant efforts at half-back (where he had never played before), despite Wraysford's steady play in goal, the ball worked up nearer and nearer the Dominican lines.

The Landfield men were quick enough to see the weak point of their enemies, and make use of the discovery. They played fast and loose, giving the ball not a moment's peace, and above all avoiding scrimmages. The Saint Dominic's forwards were thus made practically useless, and the brunt of the encounter fell on the four or five players behind, and they were not equal to it.

The calamity comes at last. One of the Landfield men gets hold of the ball, and runs down hard along the touch-line. Forrester is the quarter-back that side, and gallant as the Fourth Form boy is, his big opponent runs over him as a mastiff runs over a terrier.

Stansfield, anticipating this, is ready himself at half-back, and it will go hard with him indeed if he does not collar his man. Alas! just as the Landfielder comes to close quarters, and the Saint Dominic's captain grips him round the waist, the ball flies neatly back into the hands of another of the enemy, who, amid the shouts of his own men and the crowd, makes off with it like fury, with a clear field before him, and only Wraysford between him and the Dominican goal.

"Look-out behind there!"

No need of such a caution to a "back" like Wraysford. He is looking out, and has been looking out ever since the match began.

But if he had the eyes of an Argus, and the legs of an Atlas, he could not prevent that goal. For the Landfield man has no notion of coming to close quarters; he is their crack drop-kick, and would be an ass indeed if he did not employ his talent with such a chance as this. He only runs a short way. Then he slackens pace. Wraysford rushes forward in front, the pursuing host rush on behind, but every one sees how it will be. The fellow takes a deliberate drop-kick at the goal, and up flies the ball as true as a rocket, clean over the posts, as certain a goal as Saint Dominic's ever lost! It was no use crying over spilt milk, and for the rest of the game Stansfield relaxed no efforts to stay the tide of defeat. And he succeeded too, for though the ball remained dangerously near the school goal, and once or twice slipped behind, the enemy were unable to make any addition to their score before "Time" was called.

When the match was over, Loman tried his best to slip away unobserved by his respectable town acquaintances; but they were far too polite to allow him.

"Well," cried Mr Cripps, coolly joining the boy as he walked with the other players back to the school—"well, you *do* do it, you do. Bless me! I call that proper sport, I do. What do you put on the game, bobs or sovereigns, eh? Never mind, I and my pals we wanted a dander, so we thought we'd look you up, eh? You know Tommy Granger here? I heard him saying as we came along he wondered what you'd stand to drink after it all."

All Loman could do was to stand still as soon as this talk began, and trust his schoolfellows would walk on, and so miss all Mr Cripps's disgusting familiarities.

"I say," whispered he, in an agitated voice, "for goodness' sake go away, Cripps! I shall get into an awful row if you don't."

"Oh, all serene, my young bantam," replied Cripps, aloud, and still in the hearing of not a few of the boys. "I'll go if you want it so particular as all that. *I* can tear myself away. Only mind you come and give us a look up soon, young gentleman, for I and my pals ain't seen you for a good while now, and was afraid something was up. Ta! ta! Good-day, young gentlemen all. By-bye, my young Nightingales."

Loman's feelings can be more easily imagined than expressed when Cripps, saying these words, held out his hand familiarly to be shaken. The boy did shake it, as one would shake hands with a wolf, and then, utterly ashamed and disgraced, he made his way among his wondering schoolfellows up to the school.

Was this his luck, after all? A monitor known to be the companion and familiar friend of the disreputable cad at the Cockchafer! The boy who, if not liked, had yet passed among most of his schoolfellows as a steady, well-conducted fellow, now suddenly shown up before the whole school like this!

Loman went his way to his study, feeling that the mask was pretty nearly off his face at last, and that Saint Dominic's knew him almost as he really was. Yet did they know all?

As Loman passed Greenfield's study he stopped and peeped in at the door. The owner was sitting in his armchair, with his feet upon the mantelpiece, laughing over a volume of *Pickwick* till the tears came. And yet the crime Oliver was suspected of was theft and lying? Was it not strange—must it not have struck Loman as strange, in all his misery, that any one under such a cloud as Greenfield could think of laughing, while *he*, under a cloud surely no greater, felt the most miserable boy alive!

Chapter Twenty Nine.
A queer Prize-Day.

The long Christmas term crawled slowly on unsatisfactorily to everybody. It was unsatisfactory to Loman, who, after the football match, discovered that what little popularity or influence he ever had was finally gone. It was unsatisfactory to Wraysford, who, not knowing whether to be ashamed of himself or wroth with his old friend, settled down to be miserable for the rest of the term. It was unsatisfactory to the Fifth, who felt the luck was against them, and that the cloud overhead seemed to have stuck there for good. It was unsatisfactory to Stephen, who raged and fretted twenty times a day on his brother's behalf, and got no nearer putting him right than when he began. And undoubtedly it must have been unsatisfactory to Oliver, a banished man, forgetting almost the use of tongue and ears, and, except his brother, not being able to reckon on a single friend at Saint Dominic's outside the glorious community of the Guinea-pigs.

In fact, the only section in the school to whom the term was satisfactory, was these last-named young gentlemen and their sworn foes, the Tadpoles.

Now, at last, they had a clear issue before them—Greenfield senior, was he a hero or was he a blackguard? There was no mistaking sides there. There was no unpleasant possibility of having to make common cause and proclaim an armistice. No! on the question of Greenfield senior, Guinea-pigs and Tadpoles had something to fight about from morning till night, and therefore *they*, at any rate, were happy!

"Jellicott," said Dr Senior one day, as the masters met for five minutes' talk in the head master's study, "Greenfield in the Fifth is not well, I'm afraid. I never see him out in the playground."

"Really?" said Mr Jellicott. "I'm so rarely out there that I haven't noticed. I believe, however, he is quite well."

"I hope he is not overworking," said the Doctor. "He has done so very well this term that it would be a pity if he spoiled his chance by knocking himself up."

"Greenfield senior," put in Mr Rastle, "appears to be unpopular just at present; at least, so I gather from what I have heard. I don't know what crime he has committed, but the tribunal of his class have been very severe on him, I fancy."

The Doctor laughed.

"Boys will be boys! Well, it's a relief if that's the solution of the mystery, for I was afraid he was ill. We have no right to interfere with these boyish freaks, as long as they are not mischievous. But you might keep your eye on the little comedy, Jellicott. It would be a pity for it to go too far."

Mr Jellicott did keep his eye on the little comedy, and came to the conclusion that, whatever Greenfield had done, he was being pretty severely paid out. He reported as much to the Doctor, who, however, still deprecated interference.

"We might only make things worse," said he, "by meddling. Things like this always right themselves far better than an outsider can right them. Besides, as Greenfield will get his move up after Christmas, he will be less dependent on the good graces of his present class-fellows."

And so the matter ended for the present, as far as the masters were concerned. The reader will, perhaps, feel very indignant, and declare the Doctor was neglecting his duty in treating so serious a matter so lightly. He ought (some one says) to have investigated the whole affair from beginning to end, and made sure what was the reason of the Fifth's displeasure and of Oliver's disgrace. In fact, when one comes to think of it, it is a marvel how the Doctor had not long ago guessed who took the lost examination paper, and treated the criminal accordingly.

Christmas prize-day was always a great event at Saint Dominic's. For, as all the examinations had been held at the beginning of the term, all the rewards were naturally distributed at the end of it.

Fellows who were leaving made on these occasions their last appearance before their old companions. Fellows who had earned their removes figured now for the last time as members of their old classes; and fellows who had distinguished themselves during the last year generally were patted on the back by the masters and cheered by their schoolfellows, and made much of by their sisters, and cousins, and aunts.

For ladies turned up at the Christmas prize-day at Saint Dominic's; ladies, and big brothers, and old boys, and the school governors, with the noble Earl at their head to give away the prizes. It was a great occasion. The school was decorated with flags and evergreens; Sunday togs were the order of the day; the Doctor wore his scarlet hood, and the masters their best gowns. The lecture-theatre was quite gay with red-baize carpet and unwonted cushions, and the pyramid of gorgeously-bound books awaiting the hour of distribution on the centre table.

Prize-day, too, was the object of all sorts of preparations long before the eventful date came round. Ten days at least before it arrived the Guinea-pigs and Tadpoles were wont secretly to buy pumice-stone for their finger ends, and used one by one to disappear casually into Maltby and come back with their hair cut. Then the Fourth Senior, who were for ever getting up testimonials to their master (they gave him a testimonial on an average twice every term), were very busy collecting contributions and discussing whether Mr Brand would prefer an ormolu mustard-pot, or a steel watch-chain, or an antimacassar. The musical set at the school, too, were busy rehearsing part songs for the evening's festivities, and the dramatic set were terribly immersed for a fortnight beforehand in the preparations for a grand charade.

Altogether the end of the Christmas term at Saint Dominic's was a busy time, and the present year was certainly no exception to the rule. Greatly to the relief of Stephen and Oliver, Mrs Greenfield found herself unable at the last moment to come down and take part in the proceedings of the eventful day. As long as the boys had expected her to come they had looked forward to prize-day with something like horror, but now that that danger was passed, Oliver recovered his old unconcern, and Stephen relapsed once more into his attitude of terror-in-chief to his big brother, snapping and snarling at any one who dared so much as to mention the name of Greenfield senior in his hearing.

Well, the day came at last, fully as grand an occasion as any one expected. The noble Earl turned up half an hour early, and spent the interval in patting the greasy heads of all the Guinea-pigs and Tadpoles he came across. The mothers and sisters swarmed up and down the staircases and in and out the studies, escorted proudly by their dear Johnnys and precious Bobs. The red robes of the Doctor flashed down the corridor, and in the lecture-theatre there was such a rustling of silk gowns and waving of feather bonnets, and gleaming of white collars and sparkling patent-leather boots, as must have fairly astonished that sombre place. Every one was there—every fellow nearly had got a mother or somebody to show off to. Even Bramble turned up with a magnificent grandmother, greatly to the envy of friend and foe, and would have been the proudest Tadpole alive if the dear good old lady had not insisted on taking her descendant's *hand* instead of his arm, and trotting him about instead of letting him trot her. Oliver and Stephen alone had no kith and kin to see them on this proud day.

In due time the lecture-theatre filled up, crowded from floor to ceiling. The noble Earl walked in amid terrific cheers and took his seat. The Doctor walked in after him, amid cheers almost as terrific, and after him the ordinary procession of governors, masters, and examiners; and when they were all seated prize-day had begun.

For up steps Mr Raleigh, the captain of the school, on to the raised daïs, whence, after bowing profoundly to the noble Earl and everybody, he delivers a neat speech in honour of a good old soul who lived three or four centuries ago, and left behind him the parcel of ground on which Saint Dominic's now stands, and a hatful of money besides, to found the school. Raleigh having said his say (and how proud the smallest boys are of the captain's whiskers as they listen!), up steps Wren and commences a similar harangue in Greek. The small boys, of course, cheer this even more than the English. Then up gets Mr Winter and spins off a Latin speech, but this does not go down so well, for the juniors know a *little* Latin, and so are a good deal more critical over that than over the Greek. The French and German speeches however, restore them to good humour, and then the speeches are done.

Then comes the noble Earl. He is an old, old man, and his voice is weak and wavering, and scarcely any one hears a word he says. Yet how they cheer him, those youngsters! They watch the back of his head, and when it bobs then they know the end of a sentence has come, and they let out accordingly.

"My dearie," says Bramble's grandmother, "don't stamp so. The poor old gentleman can't hear his own voice."

"That's no matter," says "my dearie," pounding away with his feet. "If we keep it up the old boy may give us an extra week's holiday."

The old lady subsided at this, in a resigned way; and certainly when the good old nobleman did reach his final bob, his merry, jovial face looked particularly promising for the extra week. And now the Doctor advances to the table with the prize list in his hand. The prize boys are marshalled in the background, in the order in which their names appear, and Bramble tries hard to look as if nothing but his duty to his grandmother would have kept him from forming one of that favoured band himself.

The prize list is arranged backwards way; that is, the small boys come on first and the great events last.

It is a treat to see the little mites of the First, Second, and Third Junior trot up to get their prizes. They look so pleased, and they blush so, and look so wistfully up to where their relatives are sitting, that it is quite pathetic, and the good old Earl has a vigorous wipe of his spectacles before he calls up the Fourth Junior.

"General proficiency," reads the Doctor from his list—"Watson." No one knows Watson; he is quite an obscure member of the glorious community, and so he trots in and out again without much excitement. In fact, all the best prizes of the Form go without much applause, but when the Doctor summons "Paul" to advance and receive "the second arithmetic prize," there rises a shout enough to bring down the house.

"Bravo, Guinea-pigs!" shouts one small voice up somewhere near the ceiling, whereat there is a mighty laugh and cheer, and Bramble turns crimson in the face, and tells his grandmother gloomily, "That fellow Paul is a beast!"

But the youth's face brightens when the next name is called: "Third arithmetic—Padger."

Then doth Bramble the Tadpole stand in his seat and cheer till he is hoarse, and till his grandmother pulleth him by the tail of his jacket. The hero Padger, perspiring very much in the face, but otherwise composed, takes the homage of his chief and the third arithmetic prize with becoming humility, and clears off the arena as fast as he conveniently can.

Surely the Fourth Junior have come to an end now! No! there is one more prize.

"First Latin—Greenfield junior."

This time there was a louder cheer than ever, for Stephen is a popular boy outside his own class. Oliver joins in the cheer, and Pembury and Wraysford and one or two others, and of course the Guinea-pigs, go in a lump for him. It is quite a minute before the noble Earl can get hold of the words of presentation; and when at last Stephen is dispatched, the Doctor turns round and says, "If you boys will make a *little* less noise I dare say we shall get through the list quite as satisfactorily, and possibly a little more quickly."

"Hear, hear!" says one of the governors, and nod, nod goes the noble Earl's head.

The consequence of this is that the prizes to the First, Second, Third, and Fourth Senior are presented amid something very much like silence, which, however, grows less and less solemn as the proceedings go on. The last Fourth Senior boy to be called is the hero Forrester, who is now fully constituted a member of the first football fifteen. He gets a vehement cheer at all costs, mingled with shouts of "Well kicked, sir!"

"Hack it through!" and the like, which clearly show that the sympathy of Saint Dominic's is quite as much with the exploits accomplished by the young hero's feet as by those of his head.

Now for the Fifth! If the Doctor expects the company is to remain solemn during the next quarter of an hour he knows nothing at all about the school over which he presides.

"Fifth Form—(cheers)—French—(cheers)—Pembury—(terrific applause, during which Tony walks in demurely on his crutches and receives his well-merited award). English history—(applause)—Pembury."

Once more enter Tony on his crutches to receive another prize.

"Bravo, Tony!"

"Hurrah for the *Dominican*!"

"Well done, Editor!" rise from various parts of the hall, in the midst of which Pembury retires positively for the last time.

"First Greek prize—Wraysford."

Wraysford advances gravely and slowly. The instant he appears there arises a cheer—the mightiest of any yet. Everybody cheers, and when they have done cheering they stamp, and when they have done stamping they clap. Wraysford stands disconcerted and flushed with the demonstration, at a loss whether to smile or frown. He knows the meaning of that cheer as well as anybody, and it grates on his ear unpleasantly as he listens. What ages it seems before it is done, and the noble Earl at last holds out the book and says, "I have great pleasure, Wraysford, in handing you this prize. Your schoolfellows are all proud of you; I feel sure you deserve their good opinion. I wish you success, Wraysford;" and so saying, the good old gentleman bobs affably, and Wraysford, amid another tempest of applause, bows too, and takes off his prize.

"The next name," says the Doctor, referring to his list, "is that of the winner of the Nightingale Scholarship—(sensation)—and I may tell your lordship that the boy is, in the opinion of his examiners and myself, one of the most promising boys for his age that Saint Dominic's has known. The examiners report that his answers to the questions on the paper deserve the greatest credit. I will say only this before his face: Nightingale Scholarship—Greenfield senior."

A solemn silence marks the close of the Doctor's speech, in the midst of which Oliver, with pale face, but otherwise unmoved, advances to where the noble Earl stands. A few of the strangers greet his appearance with a clapping of hands, but the sound falls strangely on the silence all round.

The noble Earl, who is evidently ready with a neat little speech which shall sum the applause that never comes, is disconcerted at this unwonted stillness. You might hear a pin fall as the old gentleman, in dumb show, places the certificate into the boy's hand and tries to get at the words which the silence has scared away.

Oliver waits no longer than he can help. With a bow, he takes the parchment and turns to quit the scene.

It is at this moment, that somewhere or other in the hall, there rises a faint, almost whispered, hiss. Slight as it is, it falls with startling effect upon the dead silence which reigns. Then, like the first whisper of a storm, it suddenly grows and swells and rushes, angrily and witheringly, about the head of the wretched Oliver. Then as suddenly it dies away into silence, and the presentation of the Nightingale Scholarship is at an end.

The visitors, the committee, the ladies, the noble Earl, look about them in blank astonishment and misery. The Doctor's face flushes up mightily as he glares for one instant around him, and then drops his head over the prize list.

The only thing there is for him to do he does. He calls on the next name as composedly as he can, and proceeds with the business of the day.

But the magic has suddenly gone out of prize-day, and no coaxing can bring it back. The Fifth, and after them the Sixth, advance and receive their rewards amidst the listless indifference of the audience, and uncheered by the faintest spark of enthusiasm. No one takes the trouble to cheer anybody. Even Raleigh, the captain, comes in and out almost unheeded; and when at last the final name is reached, it is a relief to every one.

The rest of the day drags heavily—it is no use trying to get up the steam. The visitors are out of humour, and the noble Earl leaves early. The musical feast provided by the glee club is a failure altogether. A few only come to it, and nothing interferes with music like a poor audience.

As to the charade, it is abandoned at the last moment.

Then a great many mothers and aunts make the discovery that there is an evening train from Maltby; and having made it, act upon it; and the tide of emigration sets out forthwith.

Among the first to depart is Wraysford.

As he appears at the school door, trunk in hand, waiting for the school omnibus (which vehicle, by the way, is having a busy time of it), Pembury hobbles up, similarly equipped for the road.

"You off by this train?" says the latter to Wraysford.

"Yes; are you?"

"I may as well. I can get home by nine; and my people won't be in a great rage if I turn up earlier than they expect."

"Well, we may as well get a fly as wait for the wretched omnibus," says Wraysford. "Come along; there are flies at the corner of Hall Street."

Out walked the two, saying good-bye to one or two on the road. At the drive gate two boys are standing waiting for the omnibus. Wraysford and Pembury are upon them before they observe that these are Oliver and his brother.

What is to be done? There is no escaping them—they must pass; yet both of them, somehow, would at that moment—they couldn't tell why—have dropped into the earth.

Oliver looks up as they approach.

Now or never! Wraysford feels he must say something!

"Good-bye, Greenfield," he says. "I hope—"

Oliver quietly takes Stephen's arm and turns on his heel.

Wraysford stares after him for a moment, and then slowly goes on his way, breathing hard.

"I wonder," said Pembury, after a long silence—"I wonder, Wray, if it's possible we are wrong about that fellow?"

Wraysford says nothing.

"He doesn't act like a guilty person. Just fancy, Wray,"—and here Tony pulls up short, in a state of perturbation—"just fancy if you and I and the rest have been making fools of ourselves all the term!"

Ah! my Fifth Form heroes, just fancy!

Chapter Thirty.
A new Turn of the Tide.

The three weeks of Christmas holiday darted past only too rapidly for most of the boys at Saint Dominic's. Holidays have a miserable knack of sliding along. The first few days seem delightfully long. Then, after the first week, the middle all of a sudden becomes painfully near. And the middle once passed, they simply tear, and bolt, and rush pitilessly on to the end, when, lo and behold! your time is up before you well knew it had begun.

So it happened with most of the boys. With one or two, however, the holiday dragged heavily, and one of these was Master Thomas Senior. This forlorn youth, no longer now rollicking Tom of the Fifth, but the meek and mild, and withal sulky, hopeful of the Reverend Thomas Senior, D.D., of Saint Dominic's, watched the last of his chums go off with anything but glee. He was doomed to three weeks' kicking of his heels in the empty halls and playgrounds of Saint Dominic's, with nothing to do and no one to do it with. For the boy's mother was ill, which kept the whole family at home, and Tom's baby brother, vivacious youth as he was, was hardly of a companionable age yet.

As to the Doctor (Tom, by the way, even in the bosom of his family, always thought and talked of his father as the "Doctor")—as for the Doctor, well, Tom was inclined to shirk the risk of more *tête-à-têtes* than he could possibly help with so formidable a personage, even though he *was* his own parent.

But try all he could, Tom was let in for it once, when he found himself face to face one day at dinner with the Doctor, and no third person to help him out.

The occasion was quite early in the holidays, and was indeed about the first opportunity the father had had since breaking-up for anything like a conversation with his affable son.

Tom's conversational powers were never very brilliant, and when in the subduing presence of his father they always dwindled down to nothing. It was, therefore, somewhat difficult, under the circumstances, to keep the talk going, but the Doctor did his best. Tom answered in monosyllables, and looked fearfully sheepish, and found his best policy was always to keep his mouth full, and so have the excuse of good manners on his side for his silence.

"Tom," said the Doctor, presently, steering round to a subject which it had been for some time in his mind to question his son about, "that was an extraordinary demonstration on prize-day, when Greenfield senior came up to get his scholarship."

"It wasn't me," said Tom, colouring up.

"My dear boy, I never supposed it was," said the Doctor, laughing. "But it surprised me very much, as well as pained me."

"I couldn't help it," again said Tom.

"Of course you couldn't, Tom. But I am sorry to find Greenfield is so unpopular in the school."

The Doctor did not care to put a direct question to Tom on the matter that was perplexing him. He hoped to draw him out by more indirect means. But he was mistaken if he ever expected it, for Tom, with the perversity of a fellow who *will* take everything that is said as a rebuke to himself, showed no inclination to follow the lead. The Doctor had, therefore, to ask outright.

"What dreadful crime has he committed, Tom, to be treated so severely?"

"I don't want to treat him severely," said Tom. "Tom," said the Doctor, half angrily, "you are very foolish. I was not referring to you particularly, but to the whole school."

Tom sulked at this more than ever. *He* wasn't going to be called foolish. The Doctor, however, tried once more.

"What has he done to offend you all? Has he missed a catch at cricket, or a kick at football? I hope, whatever it is—"

"It isn't me!" once more growled Tom, heartily wishing the meal was over.

The Doctor gave it up as a bad job. There was no use trying to get a rise out of Tom. If that ingenuous youth had been trying to shield his Form, he could not have done it better. As it was, he was only stupidly trying to shield himself, and letting his dread of his "Doctor" father get the better of his common sense and good manners.

Luckily for Tom, a friend wrote to invite him to spend the last week of the holidays in London, an invitation which that youth, as well as his parent for him, thankfully accepted. Indeed, during the holidays Mrs Senior became so ill that the poor Doctor had no thoughts to spare for anybody or anything but her and her hope of recovery. He watched her night and day through all the vicissitudes of her fever, and when at last the crisis was over, and the doctors said she would recover, they said also that unless Dr Senior wanted to have an illness himself he must go away and get perfect rest and change for a week or two at the very least.

The consequence of all this was that Saint Dominic's had to reassemble after the Christmas holidays without the Doctor.

To some of the boys this was sorrowful news; others regarded the circumstance with indifference, while one section there was who received the intelligence with positive joy.

Strange that that section should contain in it two such opposites as Loman of the Sixth and Bramble of the Fourth Junior.

Loman, despite his "run of luck," had spent an uneasy holiday. He had been in constant terror of seeing Cripps every time he ventured outside his house; and he had been in still more terror of Cripps calling up at Saint Dominic's and telling the Doctor all about him directly after the holidays. For now Loman's time was up. Though he had in one way and another paid off all his debt to the landlord of the Cockchafer but eight pounds, still he knew Cripps could make himself quite as unpleasant about eight pounds as about thirty pounds, and probably would.

But as long as the Doctor was away it didn't matter so much. And, besides, the examination for the exhibition would of course be postponed, which meant so much longer time for preparation—which meant so much better chance for Loman of winning it. For, when he tried, he could work hard and effectively.

So Loman was very glad to hear the Doctor was away ill. So was Bramble!

That youth (who, by the way, had during the holidays quite recovered from the sobering effect of his grandmother's visit to the school) was always on a look-out for escaping the eye of the constituted authorities. He hardly ever saw the Doctor from one month's end to another; but somehow, to know he was away—to know any one was away who ought to be there to look after him—was a glorious opportunity! He launched at once into a series of revolutionary exploits on the strength of it. He organised mutinies ten times a day, and had all the specifications drawn up for blowing up Saint Dominic's with paraffin oil. There was nothing, in short, Bramble would not venture while the Doctor was away; and there is no knowing how far he might have carried his bloodthirsty conspiracies into effect had not Mr Rastle caught him one day with a saw, sawing the legs off the writing-master's stool, and given him such a chastisement, bodily and mental, as induced him for a brief season to retire from public life, and devote all his spare time to copying out an imposition.

On the first morning after reassembling, Mr Jellicott, the master in charge of Saint Dominic's, summoned the Fourth, Fifth, and Sixth to meet him in the lecture-theatre, and there announced to them the reason of the head master's absence.

"In consequence of this," said Mr Jellicott, "the removes gained last term will not be put into force for a week or two, till the head master returns; but, meanwhile, Dr Senior is anxious that the work of the school should go on as usual. We shall, therefore, resume studies to-morrow; and on Monday next the examination for the Waterston Exhibition will be held, as arranged. The three boys—Loman, Greenfield senior, and Wraysford—entered for this will be excused ordinary lessons till after the examination."

Greenfield senior! Then Oliver *was* in for it after all! The announcement amazed Wraysford as much as it did Loman and every one else. It had never entered their minds that he would go in for it. Hadn't he got the Nightingale? and wasn't that enough for one half-year? And didn't every one know *how* he had got it, and how could the fellow now have the assurance to put in for another examination?

Oliver always had been a queer fellow, and this move struck every one as queerer than ever.

But to Wraysford and one or two others it occurred in a different light. If Oliver had really won the Nightingale in the manner every one suspected, he would hardly now boldly enter for another examination, in which he might possibly not succeed, and so prove those suspicions to be true. For the subjects were almost exactly the same as those examined in for the Nightingale, and unless Oliver did as well here as he did there—and that was *remarkably* well—it would be open for anybody to say, "Of course—he couldn't steal the paper this time, that's why!"

Wraysford, as he thought over it, became more and more uneasy and ashamed of himself. One moment he persuaded himself Oliver was a hypocrite, and the next that he was innocent. "At any rate," said he to himself, "this examination will settle it."

In due time the examination day came, and once more the three rivals heard their names called upon to come forward and occupy that memorable front desk in the Sixth Form room.

This time at any rate there had been no chance for any one to take an unfair advantage, for the Doctor's papers did not reach Saint Dominic's till the morning of the examination. Indeed, Mr Jellicott was opening the envelope which contained them when the boys entered the room.

Any one closely observing the three boys as they glanced each down his paper would once more have been struck by the strange contrast in their faces. Oliver's, as his eyes glanced rapidly down the page, was composed and immovable; Wraysford's, as he looked first at his paper and then hurriedly at Oliver and Loman, was perplexed and troubled; Loman's was blank and pale and desponding.

But of the three, the happiest that morning was Wraysford—not that he was sure of success, not that his conscience was clear of all reproach, but because, as he sat there, working hard himself and hearing some one's pen on his left flying with familiar sound quickly over the paper, he felt at last absolutely sure that he had misjudged his friend, and equally resolved that, come what would of it, and humiliating as the confession would be, he would, before that day ended, be reconciled to Oliver Greenfield. What mattered it to him, then, who won the exhibition? Loman might win it for all *he* cared, as long as he won back his friend.

However, Loman at that moment did not look much like winning anything. If he had been in difficulties in the former examination, he was utterly stranded now. He tried first one question, then another, but no inspiration seemed to come; and at last, after dashing off a few lines at random, he laid down his pen, and, burying his face in his hands, gave himself up to his own wretched thoughts. He must see Cripps soon; he must go to him or Cripps would come up to Saint Dominic's, and then—

Well, Loman did not do much execution that morning, and was thankful when presently Mr Jellicott said, "Time will be up in five minutes, boys."

The announcement was anything but welcome to the other two competitors, both of whom were writing, hammer and tongs, as though their lives depended on it. Loman looked round at them and groaned as he looked. Why should they be doing so well and he be doing so ill?

"Look at those two beggars!" said Callonby to Stansfield, in a whisper, pointing to Wraysford and Oliver. "There's a neck-and-neck race for you!"

So it was. Now Oliver seemed to be getting over the ground quicker, and now Wraysford. Now Wraysford lost a good second by looking up at the clock; now Greenfield made a bad shot with his pen at the inkpot, and had to dip again, which threw him back half a second at least.

Unconscious of the interest and amusement they were exciting among the sporting section of the Sixth, they kept the pace up to the finish, and when at last Mr Jellicott said, "Cease writing and bring up your papers," both groaned simultaneously, as much as to say, "A second or two more would have done it."

The examination was over, but the event of that memorable day was still to take place.

Five minutes later Oliver, who had retired alone, as usual, to his study, there to announce to the anxious Stephen how he had fared in the examination, caught the sudden sound of an old familiar footstep outside his door, which sent the blood to his cheeks with strange emotion. Stephen heard it, and knew it too.

"There's that beast Wraysford," he said, at the very instant that Wraysford, not waiting to knock, flung open the door and entered.

There was no need for him to announce his errand. It was written on his face as he advanced with outstretched hand to his old friend.

"Noll, old man," was all he could say, as their eyes met, "the youngster's right—I *am* a beast!"

At the first word—the first friendly word spoken to him for months—Oliver started to his feet like one electrified; and before the sentence was over his hand was tightly grasping the hand of his friend, and Stephen had disappeared from the scene. It is no business of ours to pry into that happy study for the next quarter of an hour. If we did the reader would very likely be disappointed, or perhaps wearied, or perhaps convinced that these two were as great fools in the manner of their making up as they had been in the manner of their falling out.

Oh! the happiness of that precious quarter of an hour, when the veil that has divided two faithful friends is suddenly dashed aside, and they rush one to the other, calling themselves every imaginable bad name in the dictionary, insisting to the verge of quarrelling that it was all their fault, and no fault at all of the other, far too rapturous to talk ordinary common sense, and far too forgetful of everything to remember that they are saying the same thing over and over again every few minutes.

"The falling out of faithful friends"—as the old copybooks say in elegant Virgilian Latin—"renewing is of love." And so it was with Oliver and Wraysford.

Why, they were twice the friends they were before! Twice! Fifty times! And they laughed and talked and made fools of themselves for a whole half-hour over the discovery, and might have done so for an hour, had not Stephen, who had patiently remained outside for a reasonable time, now returned to join in the celebration.

"Stee, you young beggar," said Wraysford, as the boy entered, "if you don't have my tea piping hot to-night, and fresh herrings for three done to a regular turn, I'll flay you alive, my boy. And now, if you're good, you may come and kick me!"

Stephen, overflowing with joy, and quite rickety with emotion, flew at his old friend, and, instead of kicking him, caught hold of his arm, and turning to his brother, cried, "Oh, Noll! *isn't* this prime? Why, here's old Wray—"

"That beast Wraysford," suggested the owner of the title; "do give a fellow his proper name, young 'un."

This little interruption put Stephen off his speech; and the three, locking the study-door, settled down to talk rationally, or, at any rate, as rationally as they could, over affairs.

"You see," said Wraysford, "I can't imagine now what possessed me to make such a fool of myself."

"Now you needn't begin at that again," said Oliver. "If I hadn't cut up so at that jackass Simon, when he began about my being in the Doctor's study that evening, it would never have happened."

"Bah! any one might have known the fellow was telling lies."

"But he wasn't telling lies," said Oliver. "I *was* in the Doctor's study all alone that evening, and at the very time the paper went too. That's just the queer thing about it."

"You were?" exclaimed both the boys, for this was news even to Stephen.

"Yes, of course I was. Don't you know I went to see him about Stephen, and that row he had up at the Lock?"

"Oh, yes," said Stephen, "I remember. I was in a regular blue funk that evening."

"Well, the Doctor wasn't there. I hung about a few minutes for him, and then, as he didn't turn up, I left, and met that old booby just as I was coming out of the door."

"And he's gone and told everybody he saw you coming out with the paper in your pocket."

Oliver laughed loud at this.

"Upon my word, the fellow must have sharp eyes if he could do that! Well, I was so disgusted when he came up after the examination, and began to insinuate that I knew all about the missing paper, that—Well, you know how I distinguished myself."

"It would have served him right if you'd throttled him," observed Wraysford. "But I say, Noll," added he more gravely, "why on earth, old man, didn't you say all this then? What a lot of unpleasantness it would have saved."

"What!" exclaimed Oliver, suddenly firing up, "do you suppose, when the fellows all chose to believe that miserable idiot's story, I was going to stir a finger or bother myself a snap about what they thought? Bah! I'm not angry now, Wray; but, upon my word, when I think of that time—"

"What a pack of curs we all were," said Wraysford, almost as angry as his friend.

"Hear, hear!" put in Stephen, an observation which had the effect of making the whole thing ridiculous and so restoring both the friends to their composure.

"But, Noll, I say, old man," said Wraysford, presently, "of course you didn't intend it, but if you meant to make every one believe you did it, you couldn't have gone on better than you did. I'm certain not half the fellows would have believed Simon if you hadn't—"

"Made such an ass of myself," said Oliver, laughing. "Of course I can see now how it would all work in beautifully against me, and I'm certain I've myself to thank for the whole business."

"Now, don't say that. Nothing can excuse the way all of us treated you, poor old boy. But, thank goodness, it's all right now. I'll let them know—"

"Now, Wray, that's just what I won't have you do. You must not say a word to them about it, or, seriously, I'll be in a great rage. If they can't think well of me of their own accord, I won't have them do it for anybody else's, so there."

"But, Noll, old man—"

"Upon my word, Wray, I mean what I say. Not a word to anybody."

"Do you mean to say you intend to live at Coventry all your life?"

"It's not Coventry now, is it, Stee, old boy?" said Oliver, with a bright smile. "And now, Wray," said he, "I want to know how you got on in the exam to-day. You were going ahead furiously, it seemed to me."

"Yes, but wasn't doing much good, I'm afraid. How have you done?"

"Pretty well; but I hadn't time to touch the last question."

"I knew, as soon as I saw you were entered for the exam," said Wraysford, "we had all been taking you up wrong. I can guess now why you went in for it."

"Well, it struck me it might be a way of putting myself right with the fellows if I won; but I'm half afraid I won't win, and then their highnesses will be doubly sure of my villainy!"

"I know you will win," said Wraysford.

"If I do I shall feel an awful blackguard, for you would have been certain of it."

"I'm not so very sure. However, I think I could have beaten Loman."

"He seemed out of it, quite. Do you know I think that fellow is going to the dogs altogether?"

"Pity," said Wraysford, "if he is, but it does look like it."

Chapter Thirty One.
Loman in Luck again.

It certainly did look as if Loman was going to the dogs. And any one able to see and know all that was going on in his mind would have found out that he was a good deal nearer "the dogs" even than he seemed.

On the evening after the examination he received a note from Cripps—brought up in a most barefaced way by one of the potboys at the Cockchafer—requesting the pleasure of Mr Loman's company at that pleasant spot *immediately*, to talk over business!

"Why didn't he send it by post?" demanded Loman, angrily, of the disreputable messenger. "Don't you know if you were seen up here there'd be a row?"

"Dunno so much about that, but the governor, he says he's dead on the job this time, he says, and if you don't show up sharp with the stumpy, he says he'll give you a call himself and wake you up, he says—"

"Tell him I'll come, and go off quick," said Loman, hurriedly.

"Beg pardon, mister," said the potboy, with a leer, and touching his cap, "anything allowed for this here little job—carrying up the letter?"

"I'll allow you a kick if you don't go!" exclaimed the wretched Loman, furiously.

"Oh, very good," said the boy, making a long nose. "Wait till the governor walks up. We'll see who'll kick then!"

And so saying the amiable and respectable youth departed.

"Hullo!" said Wren, coming up just at this moment, "who's your friend, Loman? He looks a nice sort of boy!"

Wren was now captain and head monitor at Saint Dominic's—far too blunt and honest ever to be an object of anything but dislike and uneasiness to Loman. Now the uneasiness was the more prominent of the two. Loman replied, confused and reddening, "Oh, that boy? Why—oh, he's a shop-boy from the town, come up about an order—you know—for a hat-box."

"I don't know. Do you mean Morris's boy?"

"Ye—yes. A new boy of Morris's."

"Well, whoever he is, he's a precious cheeky specimen. Why didn't you kick him?"

"Eh? Kick him? Yes, I was just going to," began Loman, scarcely knowing what he said, "when—"

"When I turned up? Well, I shouldn't have interfered. By the way, Loman, I suppose you've given up going to that public now? What's the fellow's name?"

"Cripps," said Loman. "Oh, I never go near the place now."

"That's a good job. It was awkward enough his turning up as he did last term, and all a chance the Doctor didn't hear of it, I can tell you. Anyhow, now I'm captain, that sort of thing will have to drop, mind."

"Oh, I assure you I've never been near the place since," said Loman, meekly, anxious if possible to keep the new captain in humour, much as he disliked him.

"I'm glad of it," said Wren, coldly.

Just at that moment a third personage arrived on the scene. This was Simon, who approached, not noticing Wren, and crying out with his usual gush, "Hullo, Loman, I say. I saw Cripps to-day. He was asking after you. He says you've not been down since last Sat—Hullo, Wren!"

And here the poet caught sight of the captain.

"So *you've* been down to the Cockchafer, have you?" inquired Wren.

"Well. Oh, don't tell, Wren, I say. I don't often go. Ask Loman if I do. He's always there, and could easily tell if I went. Do I go often, Loman? Besides, I've given it up now!"

"Quick work," observed Wren, drily, "if you were down there this morning."

"Well," said Simon, shifting his ground slightly, "I didn't think there could be any harm, as Loman goes. *He's* a monitor. And then I don't owe Cripps money, do I, Loman? Or play cards and bet, like you, do I? Oh, look here, Wren, do let us off this time. Don't

143

report me, there's a good fellow. I promise I won't do it again! Oh, I say, Loman, beg us off. I never let out on you—not even when you got—"

Wren, who had allowed this burst of eloquence to proceed thus far, here turned sharply on his heel, and left the two companions in wrong in possession of the field.

Next morning, when Loman got up, he found the following note on his table:

"Wraysford takes your place as monitor. The Doctor will be told you have 'resigned.'—C.W."

Loman crushed the paper angrily in his hand, and muttered a curse as he flung it into the fire. He felt little enough gratitude to Wren for describing him merely as resigned, and not, as was actually the case, dismissed. Yet, even in his wretchedness, there was an atom of relief in knowing that at least a shred of his good old name remained.

Poor shred indeed! but better than nothing.

Every one treated him as usual—except Wren, who cut him contemptuously. The Sixth, ever since the exposure at the football match last term, had lost any respect they ever had for their comrade, and many had wondered how it was he was still allowed to remain a monitor. Every one now supposed he had taken "the better part of valour" in resigning, and, as it mattered very little to any one what he did, and still less what he thought, they witnessed his deposition from the post of honour with profound indifference.

Poor Loman! Some righteous reader will be shocked at my pitying such a foolish, miserable failure of a fellow as this Edward Loman; and yet he was to be pitied, wasn't he? He hadn't been naturally a vicious boy, or a cowardly boy, or a stupid boy, but he had become all three; and as he sat and brooded over his hard luck, as he called it, that morning, his mind was filled with mingled misery and fear and malice towards every one and everything, and he felt well-nigh desperate.

His interview with Cripps came off that afternoon. The landlord of the Cockchafer, as the reader may have gathered, had changed his tone pretty considerably the last few days, and Loman found it out now.

"Well?" said he, gloomily, as the boy entered.

"Well?" said Loman, not knowing how to begin.

"I suppose you've got my money?" said Cripps.

"No, Cripps, I haven't," said the boy.

"All right," said Cripps; "that's quite enough for me;" and, to Loman's astonishment and terror, he walked away without another word, and left the unhappy boy to stay or go as he pleased.

Loman could not go, leaving things thus. He must see Cripps again, if it was only to know the worst. So he stayed in the bar for the landlord's return. Cripps took no notice of him, but went on with his ordinary pursuits, smiling to himself in a way which perfectly terrified his victim. Loman had never seen Cripps like this before.

"Cripps," he said, after half an hour's waiting—"Cripps, I want to speak to you."

"You may want," was the surly reply. "I've done with you, young gentleman."

"Oh, Cripps, don't talk like that! I do mean to pay you, every farthing, but—"

"Yes, you're very good at meaning, you are," said the other. "Anyhow, it don't much matter to me *now*."

"What *do* you mean, Cripps? Oh, do give me a little more time! A week—only a week longer."

"Aren't you done?" was the only reply; "aren't you going home?"

"Will you, Cripps? Have pity on me! I'm so miserable!"

Cripps only whistled pleasantly to himself.

144

Loman, almost frantic, made one last effort.

"Give us just a week more," he entreated.

No answer.

"Do speak, Cripps; say you will; please do!"

Cripps only laughed and went on whistling.

"Oh, what shall I do, what *shall* I do?" cried the wretched boy. "I shall be ruined if you don't have some pity—"

"Look here," said Cripps, curtly, "you'd better stop that noise here, my lad. You can go; do you hear? Look alive."

It was no use staying further. Loman went What anguish he endured for the next twenty-four hours no one knows. What plans he turned in his head, what wild schemes, what despair, what terrors filled him, only he himself could tell. Every moment he expected the fatal vision of Cripps at Saint Dominic's, and with it his own certain disgrace and ruin, and, as time went on, his perturbation became so great that he really felt ill with it.

But Cripps did not come that day or the next. The next day was one of mighty excitement in Saint Dominic's. The result of the examination for the Waterston Exhibition was announced.

Had any other three boys but those actually taking part been the competitors, few outsiders would have felt much interest in the result of an ordinary examination confined to Sixth Form boys. But on this occasion, as we have seen, the general curiosity was aroused. No one expected much of Loman. The school had discovered pretty well by this time that he was an impostor, and their chief surprise had been that he should venture into the list against two such good men as Oliver and Wraysford.

But which of those two was to win? That was the question. Every one but a few had been positive it would be Wraysford, whom they looked upon as the lawful winner of the Nightingale last term, and whom, they were convinced, Oliver was unable to beat by fair means. And yet to these it had been a great astonishment to hear that Oliver had entered for the examination. Unless he was certain of winning he would only do himself harm by it, and confirm the suspicions against him. And yet, if he should win after all—if he was able fairly to beat Wraysford—why should he have gone to the trouble last term of stealing the examination paper and making himself the most unpopular boy in all Saint Dominic's?

These questions sorely exercised the school, and made them await eagerly the announcement of the result.

The news came at last.

"I have just received," said Mr Jellicott that morning, when the Fifth and Sixth were assembled together in the lecture-theatre—"I have just received from the examiners the report on the Waterston examination. The result is as follows: First—Greenfield, 108 marks; second—Wraysford, 96 marks; third—Loman, 20 marks."

Here Mr Jellicott was interrupted by a laugh and a muttered "Bravo, Loman! very good!" in what sounded to the knowing something like Pembury's voice. The master looked up and frowned angrily, and then proceeded: "The examiners add an expression of their very high approval of Greenfield's answers. The highest marks obtainable were 120, and, considering he left the last question untouched—doubtless for want of time—they feel that he has passed with very great distinction, and fully in accordance with their expectations of the winner of the Nightingale Scholarship last term. We will now proceed to the usual lessons."

This announcement made the strangest impression on all present. No one attempted any demonstration, but while Mr Jellicott was speaking many perplexed and troubled faces turned to where Oliver, by the side of his friend Wraysford, was sitting. Wraysford's face was beaming as he clapped his friend on the back. Oliver looked as unconcerned and indifferent as ever. The fellow *was* a puzzle, certainly.

As soon as lesson was over, the Fifth retired to its own quarters in a perturbed state of mind, there to ponder over what had happened. Oliver spared them the embarrassment of his society as usual, and Wraysford was not there either. So the Fifth were left pretty much to their own devices and the guidance of some lesser lights.

"Isn't it queer?" said Ricketts. "Whoever would have thought of it turning out like this?"

"One could understand it," said Braddy, "if there had been any chance of his repeating the dodge of last term. But he couldn't have done that."

"I don't know," said another; "he may have been up to some other dodge. Perhaps he copied off Wraysford."

"Hardly likely," said Bullinger, "up on the front desk just under Jellicott's nose."

"Well, I can't make it out at all," said Ricketts.

"Nor can I," said Bullinger.

All this while Pembury had not spoken, but he now turned to Simon, and said, "What do *you* think, Simon? Did you see Greenfield stealing the examination paper this time, eh?"

"Oh, no, not this time," promptly replied the poet; "last term it was, you know. I didn't see him this time."

"Oh, you didn't even see him with it in his pocket? Now, be very careful. Are you sure he didn't have it in his pocket a day before the exam?"

"Why," said Simon, laughing at Pembury's innocence, "how could I see what was in a fellow's pocket, Pembury, you silly! I can't tell what's in your pocket."

"Oh, can't you? I thought you could, upon my honour. I thought you saw the paper in Greenfield's pocket last term."

"So I did. That is—"

Here the wretched poet was interrupted by a general laugh, in the midst of which he modestly retired to the background, and left the Fifth to solve the riddle in hand by themselves.

"Suppose," began Pembury, after a pause—"suppose, when Braddy's done playing the fool, if such a time ever comes—"

Here Braddy collapsed entirely. He would sooner be sat upon by Dr Senior himself than by Pembury.

"Suppose," once more began Pembury, amid dead silence—"suppose, instead of Greenfield senior being a thief and liar, I and all of you have been fools and worse for the last six months? Wouldn't that be funny, you fellows?"

"Why, whatever do you mean?" demanded Tom Senior.

"Why, you don't suppose I mean anything, do you?" retorted the cross-grained Tony. "What's the use of saying what you mean—"

"But do you really—" began Bullinger.

"I say, suppose I and you, Bullinger, and one or two others here who ought to have known better, have been making fools of ourselves, wouldn't that be funny?"

There was a pause, till Simon, plucking up heart, replied, "Very funny!"

The gravity even of Pembury broke down at this, and the present conference of the Fifth ended without arriving at any nearer conclusion on the question which was perplexing it.

Meanwhile, Oliver and Wraysford were in their study, talking over the event of the day.

"I was certain how it would be, old boy," said Wraysford, genuinely delighted. "I wonder what the Fifth will say now? Bah! it doesn't become me to say too much, though, for I was as bad as any of them myself."

"No, you weren't, old boy; you never really believed it. But I say, Wray, I don't intend to take this exhibition. You must have it."

"I!" exclaimed Wraysford. "Not a bit of me. You won it."

"But I never meant to go in for it, and wouldn't have if it had not been for the Fifth. After all, it's only twenty pounds. Do take it, old man. I've got the Nightingale, you know."

"What does that matter? I wouldn't have this for anything. The fellows tried to make me think *I* was the real winner of the Nightingale, and I was idiot enough half to believe it. But I think I've had a lesson."

"But, Wray—"

"Not a word, my dear fellow; I won't hear of it."

"Very well, then; I shall shy the money when I get it into the nearest fish-pond."

"All serene," said Wraysford, laughing; "I hope the fish will relish it."

At that moment there was a knock at the door.

"Come in," said Oliver.

The door opened, and, to the astonishment of the two boys, Loman entered.

Was it peace, or war, or what? Loman's miserable face and strange manner quickly answered the question.

"Oh, Greenfield," he said, "excuse me. I want to speak to you;" and here he glanced at Wraysford, who rose to go.

"Stay where you are, Wray," said Oliver. "What is it, Loman?"

Loman, quite cowed, hardly knew how to go on.

"I was glad to hear you got the Waterston," he said. "I—I thought you would."

What was the fellow at?

After a long pause, which seemed to drive Loman almost to despair, he said, "You'll wonder what I have come here for. I know we've not been friends. But—but, Greenfield, I'm in awful trouble."

"What is it?" again asked Oliver.

"Why, the fact is," said Loman, gaining courage, as he found neither Oliver nor Wraysford disposed to resent his visit—"the fact is, Greenfield, I'm in debt. I've been very foolish, you know, betting and all that. I say, Greenfield, *could* you possibly—would you lend me—eight pounds? I don't know why I ask you, but unless I can pay the money to-day, I shall—"

"What!" exclaimed Oliver, "eight pounds to pay your bets?"

"Oh, no, not all bets. I've been swindled too—by Cripps. You know Cripps."

And here Loman, utterly miserable, threw himself down on a chair and looked beseechingly at the two friends.

"I could pay you back in a month or so," he went on; "or at any rate before Easter. Do lend it me, please, Greenfield. I don't know where else to go and ask, and I shall get into such an awful row if I can't pay. Will you?"

Oliver looked at Wraysford; Wraysford looked at Oliver; and then both looked at Loman. The sight of the wretched boy there entreating money of the very fellow who had least reason in all Saint Dominic's to like him, was strange indeed.

"Wray," said Oliver, abruptly, after another pause, during which he had evidently made up his mind, "have you any money about you?"

"I've three pounds," said Wraysford, taking out his purse.

Oliver went to his desk and took from it a five-pound note which was there, his savings for the last year. This, with Wraysford's three sovereigns, he handed without a word to Loman. Then, not waiting to hear the thanks which the wretched boy tried to utter, he took Wraysford's arm and walked out of the study.

Chapter Thirty Two.
The "Dominican" comes round.

The Fifth were a good while coming round on the question of Greenfield senior. But the delay was more on account of pride than because they still considered their old class-fellow a knave. They had taken up such a grand position last term, and talked so magnificently about honour, and morality, and the credit of the school, that it was a sad come-down now to have to admit they had all been wrong, and still more that they had all been fools. And yet, after what had happened, they could no longer retain their suspicions of Oliver Greenfield.

A few of the better sort, like Pembury and Bullinger, had the courage, at whatever cost, to act up to their convictions, and declared at once that they had been wrong, and were ashamed of it.

The next step was to approach Oliver, and that was more difficult, for he was such a queer fellow there was no knowing where to have him. However, Pembury's wit helped him over the difficulty as usual.

He was hobbling down the passage one morning when he suddenly encountered Oliver and Wraysford, arm-in-arm, approaching him. If at any time in his life Pembury did feel uncomfortable and awkward he felt it now. If he let Oliver go by this time without making it up somehow, the chance might never come again; but how to set about it, that was the difficulty, and every half-second brought the two nearer. Twenty different ideas flashed through his mind. He was not the sort of fellow to go to any one and eat humble-pie straight off. That was far too tame a proceeding. No, there was only one way he could think of, and he would chance that.

"Noll, old man," said he, in the old familiar tones, "you've got a spare arm. May I take it?"

Oliver stopped short and looked at him for an instant in astonishment. Next moment, with a hearty "Rather!" he slipped his arm into that of the happy Pembury, and the three went on their way rejoicing, a sight and a moral for all Saint Dominic's.

That was the whole of Anthony Pembury's making up. As for Bullinger, he wrote his man a letter, worded in beautiful English, in the most elegant handwriting and punctuated to a nicety, setting forth his contrition, and his hope that Greenfield would henceforth reckon him among his friends—"Yours very sincerely, H. Bullinger." This literary effort he carefully dispatched by a Guinea-pig to its destination, and awaited a reply with the utmost impatience. The reply was laconic, but highly satisfactory. It was a verbal one, given by Oliver himself in class that afternoon, who volunteered the information to the delighted Bullinger that it was a "jolly day."

It was indeed a jolly day to that contrite youth. He never believed it would all be got over so easily. He had dreaded all sorts of scenes and lectures and humiliations, but here he was, by a single word, passed back straight into friendship, and no questions asked.

The sight of Oliver surrounded by these three friends, of whom it would have been hard to say which was the happiest, made a deep impression on the rest of the Fifth, and certainly did not tend to make them feel more comfortable as to what they ought to do in a similar direction.

"It's all very well," said Ricketts, when the question was being canvassed for the hundredth time among his immediate friends. "I dare say they are all right, but it makes it jolly uncomfortable for us."

"They oughtn't to have given in in this way without letting the rest of us know first," said Braddy. "Just see what a corner it puts us in."

"All I can say is," said Tom Senior, "I'll be better satisfied when I know who *did* collar that paper if Greenfield didn't."

"Oh, but," said Simon, seeing a chance, "I can assure you I saw him when he took it. I was going—"

"Shut up, you great booby!" cried Ricketts; "who asked *you* anything about it?"

Simon modestly retired hereupon, and Braddy took up the talk.

"Yes, who did take the paper? that's it. Greenfield must have done it. Why, he as good as admitted it last term."

"Well, then, it's very queer those fellows making up to him," said Ricketts. "It's no use our trying to send the fellow to Coventry when the others don't back us up."

"Wraysford always was daft about Greenfield," said Tom Senior, "but I am astonished at Pembury and Bullinger."

"All I can say is," said Braddy, "Greenfield will have to ask me before I have anything to do with him."

"And do you know," said Ricketts, "I heard to-day he is down to play in the match against the County."

"Is he?" exclaimed Braddy in excitement; "very well, then. *I* shall not play if he does. That's all about that."

Ricketts laughed.

"Awfully sorry, old man, but you're not in the fifteen this time."

Braddy's face was a picture at this moment—he turned red and blue and white in his astonishment.

"What!" he exclaimed, as soon as he could find words. "I'm not in the team!"

"You'll see the list on the notice board; you'd better go and look."

Off went the wretched Braddy to be convinced of his fate.

"You're in the team, Ricketts, I see," said Tom Senior. "Shall *you* play if Greenfield does?"

"Don't know," said Ricketts. "A fellow doesn't get a chance to play against the County every day. It's precious awkward."

"So it is; that's just where we began, too," said Tom, philosophically. And, as a matter of fact, whenever these young gentlemen of the Fifth started the subject of Greenfield senior among themselves, they always found themselves in the end at the identical place from which they had set out.

Nor were they the only boys at Saint Dominic's in this dilemma. The Guinea-pigs and Tadpoles were equally taken aback by the new aspect of affairs. These young gentlemen had looked upon Oliver's "row" with his class as a peculiar mercy designed specially for their benefit. They had hardly known such a happy time as that during which the row had lasted. Did they want a pretext for a battle? Greenfield senior was a glorious bone of contention. Did they want an object for an indignation meeting? What better object could they have than Greenfield senior? Did they want an excuse generally for laziness, disobedience, and tumult? Greenfield senior served for this too. Indeed, the name of the Fifth Form Martyr had passed into a household word among the lower school, either of glory or reproach, and round it the small fry rallied, as round an old flag of battle.

But now, both friend and foe were aghast. To the Guinea-pigs half the charm of their position had been that they were Greenfield senior's sole champions in all Saint Dominic's. While every one else avoided him, they stuck to him, week-days and Sundays. Now, however, they discovered, with something like consternation, that they no longer had the field to themselves.

The sight of Greenfield senior walking down the passage one day, arm-in-arm with Wraysford, and the next day with one arm in Wraysford's and the other in Pembury's, and the day after between Pembury and Bullinger, with Wraysford and Stephen in the rear, struck bewilderment and bitter jealousy to their hearts.

They had come out into the passage to cheer, but they went away silently and sadly, feeling that their very occupation was departed.

Bramble, always quick to see a chance, took advantage as usual of this panic.

"Hullo, I say, Guinea-pigs, you can shut up shop now, you know. We're going to let off Greenfield senior this time, ain't we, Padger? Jolly fellow, Greenfield senior."

This was abominable! To have their hero and idol thus calmly taken out of their hands and appropriated by a set of sneaking Tadpoles was more than human patience could endure!

"Bah! A lot he'll care for *your* letting him off!" exclaimed Paul, in dire contempt. "He wouldn't touch you with a shovel."

"Oh, yes, he would, though, wouldn't he, Padger? And what do you think, Guinea-pigs? *we're going to get Greenfield senior to take the chair at one of our meetings*!"

Bramble came out with the last triumphant announcement with a positive shout, which made the hearts of his adversaries turn cold. In vain they laughed the idea to scorn; in vain they argued that if for the last six months he had never said a word even to the Guinea-pigs, he would hardly now come and take up with the Tadpoles. Bramble and Padger insisted on their story.

"Now, you fellows," concluded Bramble, at the end of another oration; "those who say three cheers for Greenfield senior hold up—"

The infuriated Paul here hurled the cap of a brother Guinea-pig, who was standing near him, full at the face of the speaker, who thereupon, altering the current of his observations, descended from his form and "went for" his opponent.

From that day a keener war raged round the head of Greenfield senior than ever. Not of attack and defence of his character, but of rivalry as to whom should be accounted his foremost champions.

It was at this critical period in the history of Saint Dominic's that a new number of the *Dominican* came out. Pembury had been compelled to write it nearly all himself, for, in the present state of divided feeling in the Fifth, he found it harder than ever to get contributions.

Even those of his own way of thinking, Oliver, Wraysford, and Bullinger, begged to be let off, and, indeed, the two former ingeniously pleaded that, as they were now really Sixth Form fellows (though remaining in their old class till the Doctor came home), they had no right to have a hand in the Fifth Form magazine. And their conscientious scruples on this ground were so strong that no persuasions of Anthony's could shake them. So the unlucky editor had finally, as on a previous occasion, to retire into private life for a season, and get the whole thing out himself, with only the aid of a few inches of "Sonits" from Simon.

But "what man has done man can do," and this time the editor's efforts were crowned with no less success than on the former occasion.

The *Dominican* certainly did not seem to have lost its novelty, to judge by the crowd which once more assembled outside the classic portals of the Fifth, to peruse the contents of the now familiar big oak frame.

"School News" was the first item of Tony's bill of fare.

After announcing in appropriate terms the Doctor's illness, and "universal hope of seeing him back in all his former vigour" (one or two boys whistled low as they read this, and thought the editor might at least have been content to "speak for himself"), Anthony went on to announce the various school events which had happened since the publication of the last number. Christmas prize-day of course came in for a good share of the description, and contained a touch-off for everybody.

"The Guinea-pigs and Tadpoles," said the *Dominican*, "looked quite unearthly in their cleanliness. It was commonly reported that one or two of them had washed their faces twice in one week. But this is hardly credible. It is, however, a fact that Bramble was shut up in his study for half an hour with his grandmother and a basin of hot water, and that the conclusion come to from the yells and shrieks which proceeded from the torture-chamber that evening, and the appearance of the dear child next day, is that he undoubtedly underwent one scrubbing this term."

Bramble's face turned so purple at the reading of this that it was impossible to say whether or not any traces of the scouring still remained. He favoured Paul, who stood in front of him, with a furious kick, which that young gentleman, always punctual in his obligations, promptly repaid, and the two combatants somehow managed to miss a good deal of what immediately followed.

After describing the other incidents of prize-day, the *Dominican* went on as follows:

"But the event of the day was the presentation of the Nightingale Scholarship, which will be sufficiently fresh in our readers' memories to need no comment here, save this one word—that the only Dominican who behaved himself like a gentleman during that remarkable scene was the winner of the scholarship himself!"

This was coming round with a vengeance! The Fifth had half expected it, and now they felt more uncomfortable than ever.

Nor did the succeeding paragraphs leave them much chance of recovery.

"The Waterston Exhibition, our readers will be glad to hear, has been won—and won brilliantly—by Oliver Greenfield, now of the Sixth. No fellow in Saint Dominic's deserves the honour better."

Then, as if his penitence were not yet complete, Pembury went on boldly farther on:

"Speaking of Greenfield senior, it is time some of us who have been doing him injustice for a whole term did what little we could to make amends now. So here goes. Take notice, all of you, that we, the undersigned, are heartily ashamed of our conduct to Greenfield senior, and desire all Saint Dominic's to know it. Signed, A. Pembury, H. Wraysford, T. Bullinger."

The effect of this manifesto was curious. Pembury himself had been unable to prophesy how it would be taken. The boys in front of the board, as they heard it read out, couldn't tell exactly whether to laugh or be serious over the paragraph. Most, however, did the latter, and hurried on to the next sentence:

"The following are also ashamed of themselves, but don't like to say so. The *Dominican* means to give them a leg up:—Tom Senior, G. Ricketts, R. Braddy, and the rest of the Fifth, except Simon, who never was or could be ashamed of himself while he lived to write such pathetic, soul-stirring lines as the following 'Sonits:'"

(It was a great relief to one or two who stood by that Pembury had thus cunningly gone on from grave to gay, and left no pause after the very awkward paragraph about the Fifth.)

  Sonit A.

To the *Dominican*.

I cannot write as I would like all in a noisy room
There's such a noise of mortal boys who sometimes go and come
Oh I will to the woods away all in the lonely shade
Where I no more of being disturbed need not to be afraid.

  Sonit B.

  To Dr Senior.

Dear Doctor I am very grieved to hear that you are not well
Oh cruel fate and yet methinks one cannot always tell
Things are so catching nowadays I wonder if I ever
Shall like unto the Doctor be by catching a low fever.

  Sonit C.

  To O— G—.

Oh Greenfield melancholy wite hear me once before I go
'Tis sad to see the blossoms all in autumn time fall low
Canst thou recall that night in September when in the passage fair
I met you all so unexpectedly and you didn't seem to care
Oh may my hair turn white and me become a soreing lark
Before the memory of that day shines out in life's last spark.

(Wite, possibly wight.)
  This was beautiful. Saint Dominic's was beginning to appreciate poetry at last! Simon was positively delirious with triumph when, after the burst of laughter (he called it applause) which greeted the reading of this gem, some one cried out—

"Oh, I say! read that last one again, some one!" And then, amid redoubled hilarity, the whole effusion was encored.

  The poet promptly sought out his enthusiastic admirer.

  "Oh! I say," said he, "would you like a copy of it?"

  "Eh—oh, rather!" was the reply.

  "Very good. You won't mind if I put a few more verses in, will you? Pembury had to cut some out."

  "My dear fellow, I shan't be happy unless I get at least twenty pages."

So off went the delighted Simon to work at this self-imposed task, and caring little about the rest of the *Dominican*.

But some of that was worth reading, too. Tony's leading article, for instance, was an important document. It was headed "Gone Up," and began, "Alas! our occupation's gone! No longer will the *Dominican* be able to bring its sledge-hammer down on high places and walk into the Sixth. For two of our men, O Fifth!—Greenfield and Wraysford—have joined the classic ranks of those who eat toffee in the top form, and play 'odds and evens' under the highest desks of Saint Dominic's. We must be careful now, or we shall catch it. And yet we ought to congratulate the Sixth! At last they have got intelligence and high principle, and two good men behind a scrimmage among them; and more are coming! There's some hope for the Sixth yet, and we would not grudge even our two best men for such a good object as regenerating the top form of Saint Dominic's," and so on—not very flattering to the Sixth, or very comfortable for its two newest members, who, however, had prudently retired from the scene long ago, as soon as the first references to Oliver had been read out.

Then came "Notes from Coventry, continued," which were very brief. "Since our last, the population of Coventry has undergone a change. The former inhabitant has walked out with flying colours, and the place is empty. Who wants to go?"

Then came one or two odd paragraphs; one of them was:—

"By the way, the *Dominican* wants to know why Loman is no longer a monitor? Do his engagements with friends in Maltby prevent his giving the necessary time to this duty? or are the Sixth beginning to see that if they want order in the school they must have fellows who have at least a little influence to do it? They have done well in appointing Wraysford. But why is Loman resigned? Who can tell? It's a riddle. A prize for the best answer in our next."

The finishing stroke, however, was Pembury's "Notes and Queries from Down Below," supposed to be of special interest to the Fourth Junior. The first was as follows:—

"Lessons.—Padger the Tadpole writes to ask, 'How do you do lessons?' The answer is a simple one, Padger. If you are a member of the Fourth Junior, as we have a vague idea you are, the way of 'doing' lessons there is as follows: Sit at a desk full of old cherry-stones, orange-peel, and dusty sherbet, and put your elbows on it. Then with your pen scatter as much ink as you conveniently can over your own collar and face, and everybody else, without unduly exerting yourself. After that kick your right and left neighbours; then carefully rub your hands in the dust and pass them several times over your countenance, all the while making the most hideous and abominable howls and shrieks you can invent. And then your lessons are 'done.'"

This paragraph so grievously incensed the honourable community at which it was directed, that for the first time for some months Guinea-pigs and Tadpoles made common cause to protest against the base insinuations it contained.

The "meeting" in the Fourth Junior that afternoon lasted, on and off, from half-past four to half-past eight. Among the speakers were Bramble, Paul, and Stephen; while Padger, Walker, and Rook did very good execution with their fists. About half-past seven the dust was so dense that it was impossible to see across the room; but those who knew reported that there was another row on about Greenfield senior, and that Paul and Padger were having their twenty-seventh round! Anyhow, the Guinea-pigs and Tadpoles missed the rest of the *Dominican*, which, however, only contained one other paragraph of special interest:

"To-morrow week the football match of the season, School against County, will be played in the Saint Dominic's meadow. We are glad to say the School team will be a crack one, including this time Greenfield senior, and excluding one or two of the 'incompetents' of last term. The following is the school fifteen:—Stansfield (football captain), Brown, Winter, Callonby, Duncan, Ricketts, T. Senior, Henderson, Carter, and Watkins, forwards; Wren (school captain) and Forrester (iv.), quarter-back; Greenfield and Bullinger, half-back; and Wraysford, back. With a team like this the school ought to give a good account of itself against our visitors."

This announcement was interesting in more than one respect. Greenfield *was* in the team, Loman was *not*.

Chapter Thirty Three.
A startling Discovery.

It is now time to return to Loman, whom we left two chapters ago, with his usual luck, standing in Greenfield's study with the 8 pounds in his hand which was finally to clear him of all his troubles, set him once for all on his feet again, and take such a weight off his mind as ought to leave him the lightest-hearted boy in all Saint Dominic's.

He stood there for a minute or two after Oliver and Wraysford had left the room, too bewildered to collect his thoughts or realise one-half of his good fortune, for he had come to Oliver in his extremity as a desperate chance, fully expecting an angry rebuff—or, at best, a chilling snub. But to get through the interview like this, and find the money in his hand within three minutes of his entering the room—why, it quite took his breath away.

Oliver Greenfield *was* a queer, unaccountable fellow, and no mistake!

Yet, strange to say, when Loman did come to himself he did not burst out into a rapture of delight and gratitude. On the contrary, he suddenly felt himself growing to such a pitch of misery and low spirits as even in the worst of his troubles he had never experienced. He repented bitterly of ever bringing himself to come and ask such a favour of his worst enemy, and, stranger than all, he felt his dislike for Greenfield increased rather than swept away by this abrupt, startling piece of generosity. Strange the whims that seize us! Loman would almost have been happier in his old suspense about Cripps than to feel he owed such a debt to such a creditor.

However, the thought of Cripps, his other creditor, flashed suddenly through his mind at that moment, so, closing his hand over the money, he turned moodily and left the room.

At any rate, he would get clear of Cripps now he had the chance.

As soon as ever morning school was over he took his hat and traversed once more the familiar road between Saint Dominic's and the Cockchafer. "Is Cripps at home?" he inquired of the potboy.

"Yas," said the boy. "Who wants him?"

"I do, you young blockhead!"

"You do? Oh, all right! I'll tell him, mister. Don't you collar no mugs while I'm gone, mind!"

The very potboys despised and ridiculed him!

Loman waited patiently for a quarter of an hour, when the boy returned.

"Oh!" said he, "the governor can't see you, he says. He's a-smoking his pipe, he says, and he ain't a-goin' to put himself about, he says, for the likes of you. That's what he says! Ti ridde tol rol ro!" and here the youth indulged in a spitefully cheerful carol as he resumed the polishing of the mugs.

"Look here!" said Loman, miserable and half frightened, "tell him I *must* see him; I've got some money for him, tell him."

"No! have you?" said the boy. "Well, wait till I've done this here job—I'm dead on this here job, I am! You can keep, you can."

This was too much even for the dispirited and cowed Loman. He caught the impudent boy a box on the ear, which resounded all over the Cockchafer, and sent him howling and yelling to his master.

Cripps appeared at last in a fury. What, he demanded, with half a dozen oaths, did Loman mean by coming there and assaulting him and his assistants? "What do you mean, you thieving jackanapes, you! Get out of my shop, do you hear? or I'll get some one in who will help you out! *I'll* teach you to come here and make yourself at home, you lying—"

"Now, Cripps," began Loman.

"Hold your noise! do you hear?" said Cripps, savagely.

"I'm very sorry, Cripps," said the wretched boy; "I didn't mean to hurt him, but he—"

"Oh! you won't go, won't you? Very good! we'll see if we can make you;" and Cripps departed from the bar, leaving his young "patron" in anything but a comfortable frame of mind.

For once in a way, however, Loman was roused, and would not go. The boy— miserable specimen as he was—had some courage in him, and when once goaded up to the proper pitch it came out. If he went, he argued to himself, Cripps would certainly come up to Saint Dominic's after him. If he waited till the police or some of the roughs came and ejected him he could not be much worse off; and there was a chance that, by remaining, he might still be able to pacify his evil genius.

So he stayed. Another quarter of an hour passed; no one came to turn him out. A few customers came into the bar and were served by the sulky potboy, but there was no sign of Cripps.

"Go and tell your master I'm here still, and want to see him particularly," said Loman, presently, to the boy.

The boy looked up and scowled and rubbed his ear, but somehow that timely blow of Loman's had wrought wonders with his spirit, for he quietly went off and did as he was bid.

In a few minutes he came back and delivered the laconic message, "You're got to wait."

This was satisfactory as far as it went. Loman did wait, simmering inwardly all the time, and not wholly losing his desperation before once again Cripps appeared and beckoned him inside.

"Here's the rest of the money," said Loman, hurriedly. "You can give me back the bill now, Cripps."

Cripps took up the money, counted it and pocketed it, and then turned on his victim with an impudent smile.

"Give me the bill," repeated Loman, suddenly turning pale with the dreadful misgiving that after all he had not got rid of the blackguard.

"What do you want the bill for?" asked Cripps, laughing.

"Want it for? Why, Cripps—" and here Loman stopped short.

"Fire away," said Cripps.

"I've paid you all I owe," said Loman, trembling.

"What if you have?"

"Then give me back that bill!"

Cripps only laughed—a laugh which drove the boy frantic. The villain was going to play him false after all. He had got the money, every farthing of it, and now he was going to retain the bill which contained Loman's promise to pay the whole amount! Poor Loman, he was no match in cunning for this rogue. Who would believe him that he had paid, when Cripps was still able to produce the promise signed with his own name to do so?

Bitterly did the boy repent the day when first, by a yielding to deceit, he had put himself in the power of such a villain!

He was too confounded and panic-struck to attempt either argument or persuasion. He felt himself ruined, and muttering, in a voice which trembled with misery, "I must tell father all about it," he turned to go.

Oh, Loman! Why have you left such a resolve till now? Why, like that other prodigal, have you waited till everything else has failed, till your own resources and cunning have been exhausted to the last dregs, before you turn and say this!

The boy uttered the words involuntarily, not intending that they should be heard. Little he thought Cripps or any one would heed them. But Cripps did heed them. His quick ear caught the words, and they *had* a meaning for him; for he might be able to cheat and browbeat and swindle a boy, but when it came to dealing no longer with the boy, but with the boy's father, Cripps was sharp enough to know that was a very different matter. He had relied on the boy's fears of exposure and his dread of his father's anger to carry his extortions to the utmost limit with confidence. But now he had gone a step too far. When, in his desperation, the boy naturally turned to the very being he had all along most carefully kept ignorant of his proceedings, it was time for Cripps to pull up.

He stopped Loman as he was going away, with a laugh, as he said, in his old tones, "Steady there, young gentleman, what a hurry you are in! A man can't have a little bit of fun, just to see how you like it, but there you go, and give it all up, and go and get yourself into a regular perspiration! Tell the governor, indeed! You don't suppose I'd let you get yourself into such a mess as all that, do you? No, no. You shall have the bill, my man, never fear."

"Oh, thank you, Cripps, thank you!" cried Loman, in a sudden convulsion of gratitude and relief.

"'Pon my word, I might take offence, that I might, at your wanting the paper. As if *I'd* ever take advantage of a young gentleman like you! No, no; honesty's the best policy for us poor folks as well as for you nobs. No one can say I defrauded any one."

"Oh, no, of course not," cried Loman, enthusiastically. "I should like to see any one who did!"

Mr Cripps, smiling sweetly and modestly, went to his cupboard, and after a good deal of fumbling and search, produced the little slip of blue paper he was looking for.

"Is that it?" cried the excited Loman.

"Looks like it," said Cripps, unfolding it and reading out, with his back to the boy, "'Three months after date I promise to pay George Cripps thirty-five pounds, value received. Signed, E. Loman.' That's about it, eh, young gentleman? Well, blessed if I ain't a soft-hearted chap after the doing you've given me over this here business. Look here; here goes."

And so saying, Mr Cripps first tore the paper up into little bits, and then threw the whole into the fire before the eyes of the delighted Loman.

"Thanks, Cripps, thanks," said the boy. "I am so glad everything's settled now, and I am so sorry to have kept you waiting so long."

"Oh, well, as long as it's been an obligement to you, I don't so much care," said the virtuous Cripps. "And now you've done with me I suppose you'll cut me dead, eh, young gentleman? Just the way. You stick to us as long as you can get anything out of us, and then we're nobodies."

And here Mr Cripps looked very dejected.

"Oh, no," said Loman, "I don't mean to cut you, Cripps. I shall come down now and then—really I will—when I can manage it. Good-bye now."

And he held out his hand.

Foolish and wicked as Loman was, there was still left in him some of that boyish generosity which makes one ready to forget injuries and quick to acknowledge a good turn. Loman forgot for a moment all the hideous past, with its suspense and humiliations and miseries, and remembered only that Cripps had torn up the bill and allowed him to clear off accounts once for all at the hated Cockchafer. Alas! he had forgotten, too, about telling all to his father!

"Good-day, young gentleman," said Cripps, with a pensive face which made the boy quite sorry to see.

He shook hands cordially and gratefully, and departed lighter in heart than he had felt for some time.

But as he returned to Saint Dominic's the thought of Oliver, and of his debt to him, returned, and turned again all his satisfaction into vexation. He wished he had the money that moment to fling back into the fellow's face!

I don't pretend to explain this whim of Loman's. It may have been his conscience which prompted it. For a mean person nearly always detests an honest one, and the more open and generous the one is, the meaner the other feels in his own heart by contrast.

However, for some days Loman had not the painful reminder of his debt often before his eyes; for as long as the Doctor was absent Oliver remained in the Fifth.

At length, however, the head master returned, restored and well, and immediately the "removes" were put into force, and Oliver and Wraysford found themselves duly installed on the lowest bench of the Sixth—the only other occupant of which was Loman. The two friends, however, held very little intercourse with their new class-fellow, and Oliver never once referred to the eight pounds; and, like every one and everything else, Loman grew accustomed to the idea of being his rival's debtor, and, as the days went on, ceased to be greatly troubled by the fact at all.

But an event happened one day, shortly after the Doctor's return, which gave every one something else to think about besides loans and debtors.

It was the morning of the day fixed for the great football match against the County, and every one, even the Sixth and Fifth, chafed somewhat at the two hours appointed on such a day for so mundane an occupation as lessons.

Who could think of lessons when any minute the County men might turn up? Who could be bothered with dactyls and spondees when goal-posts and touch-lines were far more to the point? And who could be expected to fix his mind on hexameters and elegiacs when the height of human perfection lay in a straight drop-kick or a fast double past the enemy's half-backs? However, the Doctor had made up his mind Latin verses should get their share of attention that morning, and the two head forms were compelled to submit as best they could.

Now, on this occasion, the Doctor was specially interested in the subject in hand, and waxed more than usually eloquent over the comparative beauties of Horace and Virgil and Ovid, and went into the minutest details about their metres. Over one line which contained what seemed to be a false quantity he really became excited.

"It is a most remarkable thing, and I am really pleased we have fallen on the passage," said he, "that this identical mistake, if it is a mistake, occurs in a line of Juvenal; it is in the—dear me, I have forgotten how it begins! Has any one here a Juvenal?"

"I have one in my study, sir," said Loman. (Juvenal had been one of the Latin subjects for the Nightingale.)

"Ah! Would you fetch it, Loman, please? I think I know precisely where the line occurs."

Loman rose and went for the book, which he found upon his bookcase, enjoying a dignified and dusty repose on the top shelf. Carefully brushing off the dust, so as to give the volume a rather less unused look, he returned with it to the class-room, and handed it to the Doctor.

"Thank you, Loman. Now, it is in the Fourth—no, the Fifth Satire," said he, turning over the pages. "Let me see—yes, not far from—ah!"

This last exclamation was uttered in a voice which made every boy in the room look suddenly up and fix his eyes on the Doctor. It was evidently something more than an exclamation of recognition on finding the desired passage. There was too much surprise and too much pain in the word for that.

Was the Doctor ill? He closed the book and sat back in his chair in a sort of bewilderment. Then suddenly, and with an evident effort, recovering himself, he let his eyes once more rest on the closed Juvenal.

"Loman," he said, "will you come and find the passage for me? Turn to the Fifth Satire."

Loman obeyed, much wondering, notwithstanding, why the Doctor should ask him, of all people, to come up and turn to the passage.

He advanced to the head master's desk and took up the Juvenal.

"The Fifth Satire," repeated the Doctor, keeping his eyes on the book.

Certainly the Doctor was very queer this morning. One would suppose his life depended on the discovery of that unlucky line, so keenly he watched Loman as he turned over the pages.

Was the book bewitched? Loman, as he held it, suddenly turned deadly white, and closed it quickly, as if between the leaves there lay a scorpion! Then again, seeing the Doctor's eye fixed on him, he opened it, and, with faltering voice, began to read the line.

"That will do. Hand me the book, Loman."

The Doctor's voice, as he uttered these words, was strangely solemn.

Loman hurriedly took a paper from between the leaves and handed the book to the Doctor.

"Hand me that paper, Loman!"

Loman hesitated.

"Obey me, Loman!"

Loman looked once at the Doctor, and once at the Juvenal; then, with a groan, he flung the paper down on to the desk.

The Doctor took it up.

"This paper," said he, slowly, and in an agitated voice—"this paper is the missing paper of questions for the Nightingale Scholarship last term. Loman, remain here, please. The other boys may go."

Chapter Thirty Four.
The Match against the County.

The boys, astounded and bewildered by this unexpected revelation, slowly rose to obey the Doctor's order, leaving Loman alone with the head master.

The boy was ashy pale as Dr Senior turned to him and said, solemnly—

"How do you account for this, Loman?"

Loman lowered his eyes and made no reply.

"Answer me please, Loman. Can you account for this?"

"No."

"Did you ever see this paper before?"

"No."

"Do you know how it came into your Juvenal?"

"No."

"Did you know anything at all about the lost paper?"

"No."

The Doctor looked long and searchingly at him as he said once more—

"Loman, are you sure you are telling me the truth? You know nothing whatever about the paper—never saw it before this moment?"

"No."

"You knew the paper had been missed off my desk?"

"Yes."

"Had you the least reason for believing any boy took it?"

Loman hesitated.

"I would rather not say," he said at last.

"You must please answer me frankly, Loman. Had you any reason, I ask, for believing any boy took the paper?"

"Must I say?" asked Loman.

"Yes—you must."

"Well, then, I did fancy some one had taken it."

"Who?"

"Greenfield senior," said Loman, flushing quickly as he said the name.

"And what made you suspect Greenfield senior?"

"All the boys suspected him."

"That is not an answer, Loman. Why?"

"Because, for one thing," said Loman, sullenly, "he was seen coming out of your study that evening."

"And why else?"

"Because he came out so high in the exam."

"And for these reasons you suspected Greenfield of taking the paper? Why did you not mention the matter to me?"

Loman did his best to look virtuous.

"I did not wish to get any one into trouble."

"And you preferred to let an affair like this go on without taking any steps to have it cleared up? Did Greenfield deny the charge?"

"No."

"Did he admit it?"

"Very nearly. He wouldn't speak to any one for months."

"And you really believe that Greenfield took the paper?"

Loman looked up at the Doctor for a moment and answered, "Yes."

"Did you lend him your Juvenal at any time?"

"Not that I remember."

"Do you suppose he put the paper in the book?"

"I couldn't say; but I don't see who else could."

"That will do, Loman; you can go. Kindly leave the paper and the Juvenal with me."

Loman turned to go, but the Doctor stopped him with one more question.

"You know, I suppose, that the questions which you actually had set for the Nightingale examination were quite different from those on the paper?"

"Yes," said Loman. "I mean—that is," he added, stammering, and taking up the paper in question. "I see by this paper they were quite different."

"Yes; you can go now, Loman."

There was something so solemn and hard in the head master's voice as he dismissed the boy that Loman felt very uncomfortable as he slowly departed to his own study.

He, at any rate, was in no humour for enjoying the big football match which was just beginning.

And it must be confessed the event of the morning had had the effect of disconcerting a good many more than himself. Stansfield had quite hard work going round among his troops and rousing them once more to the proper pitch of enthusiasm.

"What—whatever does it matter," he said, "if the fellow did take it? *You* didn't take it, Winter, or you, Wren; and what on earth's the use of getting down in the mouth, and perhaps losing the match, because of it? We're always having our football spoiled by something or other," he added with a groan. "I'll tell you what it is, let's only lick these fellows this afternoon, and then I'll howl and groan and do anything you like, for a week."

There was no resisting such a generous offer. The fellows made up their minds to forget everything else that afternoon but the County, and so to play that the County should have some difficulty in soon forgetting them.

"Fire away, you fellows, and peel!" cried Stansfield, as Oliver and Wraysford sauntered past.

They fired away. But while dressing they exchanged a few words on the forbidden subject.

"Did you ever expect it would be brought home to Loman like this, Noll?" asked Wray.

"No, I didn't. And yet in a way—"

"Eh? What do you say?"

"Why, Wray, you remember me saying that evening, after I left the study, the only fellow I met in the passage besides Simon was Loman?"

"Yes; so you did."

"He was going towards the Doctor's study," said Oliver.

"Hum! I remember now you said so."

"And yet," continued Oliver, plunging into his jersey—"and yet I can't see how, if he did take the paper, he didn't do better in the exam. He came out so very low."

"Yes, that's queer, unless he took a fit of repentance all of a sudden, and didn't look at it."

"Then it's queer he didn't destroy it, instead of sticking it in his Juvenal."

"Well, I suppose the Doctor will clear it up, now he's on the scent."

"I suppose so," said Oliver; "but, I say, old man," he added, "of course there's no need for us to say anything about it to anybody. The poor beggar doesn't want *our* help to get him into trouble."

"No, indeed. I'd be as glad, quite, if it were found to be another wrong scent, after all," said Wraysford. "The fellow's in a bad enough way as it is."

"Are you nearly ready, you two?" thundered Stansfield at the door.

"Just ready!" they exclaimed; and in another minute they, too, had dismissed from their minds everything but Saint Dominic's versus County, as they trotted off to join the rest of their comrades on the field of battle.

And, indeed, for the next two hours there was no opportunity, even, had they desired it, for any one to think of anything but this momentous struggle.

For three years running the County had beaten the schoolboys, each time worse than before, until at last the latter had got to be afraid the others would begin to think them foemen not worthy of their steel. This year they hardly dared hope a better fate than before, for the enemy were down in force. Yet the boys had determined to die hard, and at least give their adversaries all the trouble they could before their goal should fall; and of this they were all the more sanguine, because their team was the very best the school could muster, and not a man among them but knew his business, and could be depended on to do it too.

Bad luck! Of course, just when it's not wanted there's a breeze got up, blowing right down the field, and in the very teeth of the schoolboys, who have lost the toss, and have to play from the oak-tree end for the first half of the game!

"It's always the way," growls Ricketts. "They'll simply eat us up while they've got the chance, you see!"

"No they won't," says Stansfield, bound to take a cheerful view of things. "We're strong in backs. It's not like last match, when Greenfield wasn't playing, and Loman was there to make such a mess of it."

"Well, it's a comfort, that, anyhow."

"Of course it is," says the captain. "What you fellows have got to do is to keep the ball in close, and nurse it along all the while, or else run—but you'd better let the quarter-backs do that."

This sage advice is not thrown away on the worthies who lead the van for Saint Dominic's, and an opportunity for putting it into practice occurs the moment the game begins. For the School has to kick-off, and to kick-off against that wind is a hopeless business. Stansfield does not attempt anything like a big kick, but just drives the ball hard and low on to the legs of the County forwards, sending his own men close after it, so that a scrimmage is formed almost at the very spot where the ball grounds.

"Now, School, sit on it! Do you hear?" calls out the captain; and certainly it looks as if that unhappy ball were never destined to see the light again. The enemy's forwards cannot get it out from among the feet of the School forwards, try all they will, until, by sheer weight, they simply force it through. And then, when it does go through, there is young Forrester of the Fourth ready for it, and next moment it is back in its old place in the middle of the "mush." In due time, out it comes again—this time on Wren's side—and once again, after a short run, there it is again, on almost the identical spot of earth where it has undergone its last two poundings.

"Played up, Dominies!" cries out Stansfield, cheerily. "Stick to it now!"

Stick to it they do, with the wind fresh on their faces, and the County fellows charging and plunging and shoving like fury upon them.

Ah! there goes the ball, out at the County end for a wonder. The spectators cheer loudly for the schoolboys. Little they know! It had much better have stayed there among their feet than roll out into the open. The County quarter-back has it in his hands in a twinkling, and in another twinkling he has lifted it with a drop-kick high into the air, all along the wind, which carries it, amid cheers and shouts, right up to the boundary of the School goal.

So much for cutting through the scrimmage!

Wraysford, the Dominican "back," is ready for it when it drops, and, without touching-down, runs out with it. He is a cautious fellow, is Wraysford, and does not often try this game. But the ball has far outstripped the enemy's forwards, and so he has a pretty open field. But not for long. In a *few* seconds the County is upon him, and he and the ball are no longer visible. Then follow a lot more scrimmages, with similar results. It is awfully slow for the spectators, but Stansfield rejoices over it, and the County men chafe.

"Can't you let it out there? Play looser, and let it through," says their captain.

Loose it is.

"That's better!" says the County captain, as presently the ball comes out with a bound full into the quarter-back's hands, who holds it, and, to the horror of the boys, makes his mark before he can be collared.

The scrimmage has been near up to the Dominican goal—within a kick—and now, as the schoolboys look round first at the goal and then at the County man with the ball, the distance looks painfully small. And even if it were greater, this wind would do the business.

The County man takes plenty of room back from his mark, up to which the School forwards stand ready for one desperate rush the moment the ball touches the ground. Alas, it is no go! They have a knowing hand and a quick foot to deal with. Before they can cover the few yards which divide them, the ball is dropped beautifully, and flies, straight as an arrow, over the cross-bar, amid the tremendous cheers of the County men and their friends.

"Never mind!" says Stansfield, as his men walk out once more to the fray, "they shan't get another before half-time!"

Won't they? Such is the perversity of that creature people call Luck, and such is the hatred it has for anything like a boast, that two minutes—only two minutes—after the words are out of the captain's mouth another Dominican goal has fallen.

For Stansfield in kicking off gets his foot too much under the ball, which consequently rises against the wind and presents an easy catch to any one who comes out to take it. A County forward sees his chance. Rushing up, he catches the ball, and instantaneously, so it seems, drop-kicks it, a tremendous kick clean over the School goal, before even the players have all taken up their places after the last catastrophe.

This is dreadful! worse than ever! Never in their worst days had such a thing happened. For once in a way Stansfield's hopefulness deserts him, and he feels the School is in for an out-and-out hiding.

The captain would like extremely to blow some one up, if he only knew whom. It is so aggravating sometimes to have no one to blow-up. Nothing relieves the feelings so, does it?

However, Stansfield has to bottle up his feelings, and, behold! once more he and his men are in battle array.

This time it's steady all again, and the ball is kept well out of sight. It can't even slip out behind now, as before; for the School quarter-backs are up to that dodge, and ready to pounce upon it before it can be lifted or sent flying. Indeed, the only chance the wretched ball has of seeing daylight is—

Hullo! half-time!

The announcement falls on joyful ears among the Dominicans. They have worked hard and patiently against heavy odds; and they feel they really deserve this respite.

Now, at last, if the wind wouldn't change for them, they have changed over to the wind, which blows no longer in their faces, but gratefully on to their backs.

The kick-off is a positive luxury under such circumstances; Stansfield needn't be afraid of skying the ball now, and he isn't. It shoots up with a prodigious swoop and soars right away to touch-line, so that the County's "back" is the first of their men to go into action. He brings the ball back deftly and prettily, slipping in and out among his own men, who get beside him as a sort of bodyguard, ready at any moment to carry on the ball. It is ludicrous to see Ricketts and Winter and Callonby flounder about after him. The fellow is like an eel. One moment you have him, the next he's away; now you're sure of him, now he's out of all reach. Ah! Stansfield's got him at last! No he hasn't; but Winter has—No, Winter has lost him; and—just look—he's past all the School forwards, no one can say how.

Young Forrester tackles him gamely—but young Forrester is no hand at eel-catching; in fact, the eel catches Forrester, and leaves him gracefully on his back. Past the quarter-backs! The man has a charmed life!

Ah! Greenfield has got him at last. Yes, Mr Eel, you may wriggle as hard as you like, but you'd hardly find your way out of that grip without leave!

Altogether this is a fine run, and makes the School see that even with the wind they are not going to have it all their own way. However, they warm up wonderfully after this.

Steady is still the word (what grand play we should get if it were always the word at football, you schoolboys! You may kick and run and scrimmage splendidly, but you are not steady—but this is digression). Steady is still the word, and *every* minute Saint Dominic's pulls better together. The forwards work like one man, and, lighter weight though they are, command the scrimmages by reason of their good "packing."

Wren and young Forrester, the quarter-backs, are "dead on" the ball the moment it peeps out from the scrimmage; and behind them at half-back Oliver and Bullinger are not missing a chance. If they did, Wraysford is behind them, a prince of "backs."

Oh, for a chance to put this fine machinery into motion! Time is flying, and the umpire is already fidgeting with his watch. Oh, for one chance! And while we speak here it comes. A County man has just darted up along the touch-line half the length of the field. Wren goes out to meet him, and behind Wren—too close behind—advances Oliver. The County man thinks twice before delivering himself up into the clutches of one of these heroes, and ends his run with a kick, which, Oliver being not in his place, Wraysford runs forward to take. Now Wraysford has hardly had a run this afternoon. He means to have one now! And he does have one. He takes the ball flying, gives one hurried look round, and then makes right for the thick of the fray. Who backs him up? Greenfield for one, and all the rest of Saint Dominic's for the other.

"Stick close!" he says to Oliver, as he flies past. Oliver wants no bidding. He follows his man like a shadow. In and out among the forwards, and round about past the quarter-backs; and when at last Wraysford is borne down by a combined force of half and three-quarter-backs, Greenfield is there to take the ball on.

"Look-out there!" cries the County captain, "mark that man." The County does mark that man, and they have the painful task of marking him pass one half-back and floor another before he is arrested.

"I'm here!" cries Wraysford's voice at that moment; and next instant the ball is again hurrying on towards the County goal in Wraysford's arms, Greenfield once more being in close attendance.

And now the County backs come into action, and the first of them collars Wraysford. But it is Oliver who collars the ball, and amid the shouts, and howls, and cheers of players and spectators rushes it still onward. The second "back" is the County's only remaining hope, nor surely will he fail. He rushes at Oliver. Oliver rushes at him. Wraysford, once more on his feet, rushes on them both.

"Look-out for the ball there!" is the panic cry of the County. Ay, look indeed! Oliver is down, but Wraysford has it, and walks with it merrily over the County's goal-line, and deposits it on the ground in the exact centre of the posts.

"There never was such a rush-up, or such a pretty piece of double play," say the knowing ones among the onlookers; and when a minute later the ball is brought out, and Stansfield kicks it beautifully over the goal, every one says that it is one of the best-earned goals that old meadow has ever seen kicked, and that Saint Dominic's, though beaten, has nothing in that day's performance to be ashamed of.

Chapter Thirty Five.
A vocal, instrumental, and dramatic Entertainment in the Fourth Junior.

Now among those who were present to witness the famous "rush-up" of Greenfield senior and Wraysford, which ended in the fall of the County goal, was one boy who showed very little enthusiasm over the achievement, or very little delight at the glory which the school thereby derived.

Loman, who, unable to sit in his study, and not knowing what else to do, had wandered almost instinctively to the meadow, found himself on this particular afternoon one of the most miserable boys in Saint Dominic's.

Two years ago, when he first entered the school, he was popular with his fellows and voted an acquisition on the cricket-ground and football-field whenever the youth of Saint Dominic's strove in emulation against their rivals. He could remember a time when fellows strolled arm-in-arm with him down to the matches; when the small boys looked quite meek in his presence, and the masters gave a friendly nod in answer to his salutes. That was when he was quite new at Saint Dominic's; but how changed now! This afternoon, for instance, as he stood looking on, he had the cheerful knowledge that not a boy in all that assembly cared two straws about him. Why wasn't *he* playing in the match? Why did the fellows, as they came near him, look straight in front of them, or go round to avoid him? Why did the Guinea-pigs and Tadpoles strut about and crack their vulgar jokes right under his very nose, as if he was nobody? Alas, Loman! something's been wrong with you for the last year or thereabouts; and if we don't all know the cause, we can see the effect. For it is a fact, you *are* nobody in the eyes of Saint Dominic's at the present time.

However, he was destined to become a somebody pretty soon; and, indeed, as soon as the football match was over, and the supper after it was disposed of, and the Guinea-pigs and Tadpoles (who, you know, had selected this same afternoon *for their* great football match) had ceased their rows in slumber, every one's mind, at least the mind of every one in the two head forms, turned naturally to the strange and mysterious event of the morning. What various conclusions they came to it is not for me to set down here. They probably came to as good a conclusion as the reader has done, and waited impatiently to have the whole thing cleared up.

And it looked as if the Doctor were about to do this next morning, for he summoned together the Fifth and Sixth, and thus solemnly addressed them:—

"Before we begin the lesson for the day, boys, I wish to refer to an incident that happened here yesterday morning, which must be fresh in your memories. I mean the accidental discovery of the lost examination paper for the Nightingale Scholarship. I hope you will not draw hasty conclusions from what then occurred. The boy in whose book the paper was found is present here, and has assured me on his honour he never saw the paper before, and is quite ignorant how it came into his book. That is so, Loman?"

"Yes, sir," replied Loman.

"When a boy makes a statement to me on his honour, I accept it as such," said the Doctor, very gravely, and looking hard at the boy. "I accept it as such—"

Loman sat motionless with his eyes on the desk before him.

"But," went on the Doctor, turning again to the boys, "before I dismiss the subject I must do justice to one among you who I find, much to my pain, has been an object of suspicion in connection with this same lost paper. Greenfield senior, I have no hesitation in saying, is perfectly clear of any such imputation as that you put upon him. I may say in his presence I believe him to be incapable of a fraudulent and mean act; and further than that, you boys will be interested to hear that the questions which he answered so brilliantly in that examination were not the questions which appeared on the lost paper at all, but an entirely new set, which for my own satisfaction I drew up on the morning of examination itself."

This announcement *did* interest every one—the Fifth particularly, who felt their own humiliation now fourfold as they looked at Oliver, and thought of what their conduct to him had been.

It interested Oliver and Wraysford as much as any one, but for a different reason. Supposing Loman had taken the paper—this was the reflection which darted through both their minds—supposing Loman *had* taken the paper and worked up the answers from it, might not the sudden change of questions described by the Doctor account for the low place he had taken in the exam?

Altogether the Doctor's speech left things (except as concerned Oliver) not much more satisfactory than before. The natural impulse of everybody was to suspect Loman. But, then, six months ago the natural impulse had been equally as strong to suspect Oliver, and—well, that had somehow turned out a bad "spec," and so might this.

So Saint Dominic's really didn't know what to think, and settled down to the work of the term in an uneasy frame of mind, wishing something would turn up, to end the wretched affair of the lost paper definitely one way or another.

Of course the report of the new state of affairs soon penetrated down to the lower school, and the Guinea-pigs and Tadpoles at any rate were not slow in making up *their* minds on the burning question.

They turned out in a body and hooted Loman up and down the passages with as much, if not more, glee than some of them had lately hooted Oliver. "Yah, boo! Who stole the exam paper?—there! old Loman." Such were the cries which presently became familiar in the school, until one day Mr Rastle dropped down on some twenty of the "howlers," and set them each twelve propositions of Euclid to learn by heart, and two hours a-piece in the detention-room, there to meditate over their evil ways.

The quiet of the lower school during the next week was something delicious.

The tyrannical proceeding on the part of Mr Rastle provoked bitter indignation, of course, in the breasts of the culprits. Why weren't they to be allowed to express their feelings? And if Rastle did want to "pot" them, why should he give them Euclid to learn, when he knew perfectly well Euclid was the very thing not one of them *could* learn by heart? And if he did want to detain them, why *ever* should he fix on the identical week in which the grand "Vocal, Instrumental, and Dramatic Entertainment" of the Fourth Junior was due to come off.

It was an abominable piece of spite, that was a fact; and Mr Rastle was solemnly condemned one evening in the dormitory to be blown up with dynamite at the first convenient opportunity. Meanwhile, come what would, the "Vocal, Instrumental, and Dramatic Entertainment" *should* come off, if it cost every man Jack of the "entertainers" his head.

Stephen, who by this time was a person of authority in his class, was appointed president of the "V. I. and D. Society." The manner of his election to this honourable office had been peculiar, but emphatic. He had been proposed by Paul and seconded by himself in a short but elegant speech, in which he asserted he would only serve if his appointment was unanimous. It *was* unanimous, for directly after this magnanimous statement he and Paul and a few others proceeded summarily to eject Bramble, Padger, and others who showed signs of opposition; and then, locking the door, proceeded to an immediate vote, which, amid loud Guinea-pig cheers, was declared to be unanimous, one contumacious Tadpole, who had escaped notice, having his hands held down by his sides during the ceremony. As soon as the doors were open, Bramble, who had meanwhile collected a large muster of adherents, rushed in, and, turning out all the Guinea-pigs, had himself elected treasurer, and Padger honorary secretary. These exciting appointments having been made, the meeting was "thrown open," a programme was drawn up, and the preparations were in a very forward state when the sad interruption occasioned by Mr Rastle's brutal conduct took place. But if Mr Rastle thought he was going to extinguish the "Vocal, Instrumental, and Dramatic Entertainment" he was woefully mistaken.

As soon as ever, by superhuman exertions, Bramble and a few others of the "potted" ones had struggled through their Euclid, and served their term of detention, an evening was fixed upon for the great event to come off.

Immediately a question arose. Should the public be admitted?

"Rather!" exclaimed Bramble, the treasurer, "five bob each."

"Masters half price," suggested Padger.

"Greenfield senior free!" shouted the loyal Paul.

"Bah! do you think Greenfield senior would come to hear you spout, you young muff!" roared the amiable Bramble.

"I know what he would come for," retorted Paul, "and I'd come with him too. Guess!"

"Shan't guess. Shall I, Padger?"

"May as well," suggested Padger.

"He'd come," cried Paul, not waiting for the Tadpole to guess—"he'd come a mile to see you hung. So would I—there!"

It was some time before the meeting got back to the subject of admitting the public. But it was finally agreed that, though the public were not to be invited, the door should be left open, and any one ("presenting his card," young Bilbury suggested) might come in, with the exception of Loman, Mr Rastle, Tom Braddy, and the school cat.

For the next few days the Guinea-pigs and Tadpoles were busy, learning their parts, practising their songs, arranging all the details of their dramatic performance, and so on; and Mr Rastle had to "pot" one or two more of them, and detain one or two others, before he could get anything like the ordinary work of the class done. All this the young vocal, instrumental, and dramatic enthusiasts bore patiently, devoting so many extra ounces of dynamite to Mr Rastle's promised blow-up for each offence.

At last the festival day arrived. Stephen, on whom, somehow, all the work had devolved, while the talking and discussion of knotty points had fallen on his two brother officers, looked quite pale and anxious on the eventful morning.

"Well, young 'un," said Oliver, "I suppose Wray and I are to be allowed to come and see the fun to-night."

"Yes," said Stephen, with considerable misgivings about the "fun."

"All serene; we'll be there, won't we, Wray? Not the first Guinea-pig kick-up we've been witness to, either."

"Do you think Pembury will come?" asked Stephen, nervously.

"Oh, rather. He'll have to report it in the next *Dominican*. I'll see he comes."

"Oh, I think he needn't mind," said Stephen, with a queer shyness; "I could write out a report for him."

"Oh, I dare say; a nice report that would be. No, Tony must be there. He wouldn't miss it for a five-pound note."

Stephen retired to report these rather alarming prospects of an audience to his comrades.

"Talking of five-pound notes," said Wraysford, after he had gone, "does Loman ever mean to pay up that 8 pounds?"

"I don't know; it doesn't look like it," said Oliver. "The fact is, he came to me yesterday to borrow another pound for something or another. He said Cripps had been up to the school and tried to make out that there was another owing, and had threatened, unless he got it, at once to speak to the head master."

"Did you lend it him?" said Wraysford. "It's a regular swindle."

"I hadn't got it to lend. I told him I was sure the fellow was a thief, and advised him to tell the Doctor."

"What did he say?"

"Oh, he got in an awful state, and said he would get into no end of a row, and wouldn't for the world have the Doctor know a word of it."

"I don't like it at all," said Wraysford. "Don't you have more to do than you can help with that business, Noll, old man."

"But the poor beggar seems regularly at his wits' end."

"Never mind; you'll do him and yourself no good by lending him money."

"Well, I haven't done so, for a very good reason, as I tell you. But I'm sorry for him. I do believe he can't see that he's being fleeced. He made me promise not to utter a word of it to the Doctor, so I really don't know how to help him."

"It's my impression he's good reason to be afraid of the Doctor just now," said Wraysford. "That Nightingale business has yet to be cleared up."

The two friends pursued this disagreeable topic no farther, but agreed, for all Loman wasn't a nice boy, and for all they had neither of them much cause to love him, they would see the next day if they could not do something to help him in his difficulty. Meanwhile they gave themselves over to the pure and refined enjoyment of the "Vocal, Instrumental, and Dramatic Entertainment."

At seven that evening, after tea, the Fourth Junior room became a centre of attraction to all Saint Dominic's. Fellows from the Sixth and Fifth, always ready for novelty in the way of amusement, looked in to see the sport. The Fourth Senior grandly condescended to witness the vulgar exploits of their juniors, and the other classes were most of them represented by one or more spectators.

The programme had been carefully got up. Stephen took the chair solemnly at the appointed hour, and with a great deal of stammering announced that the proceedings were now about to commence, and then sat down. An awful pause ensued. At first it was borne with interest, then with impatience; then, when Stephen began to whisper to Paul, and Paul began to signal to Bramble, and Bramble gesticulated in dumb show at Padger, and all four whispered together, and finally looked very gravely in an opposite direction to the audience, then they began to be amused.

"Oh," said Stephen, very red, turning round abruptly after this awkward pause had continued for a minute or two—"oh, that was wrong; he doesn't begin, and the other fellow's away. Look here, Bramble, do your thing now."

"No, I can't," whispered Bramble in an audible voice. "I've forgotten the first line."

"Something about a kid asleep," suggested Padger, also audibly.

"Oh, yes," said Bramble, starting up and blushing very red as he began.

"'Lines on Seeing my Wife and Two Children Asleep'—Hood."

This modest announcement of his subject was overwhelming in itself, and was greeted with such yells of laughter that the poor elocutionist found it utterly impossible to go on. He tried once or twice, but never got beyond the first half line.

"And has the earth—" and here he stuck, but in answer to the cheers began again, looking round for Padger to help.

"And has the earth—(Go it, Padger, give a fellow a leg up, can't you?)"

"I can't find the place," said Padger, very hot and flurried, and whipping over the pages of a book with his moist thumb.

"And has the earth—(Look in the index, you lout! Oh, won't I give it to you afterwards!)" once more began the wretched Bramble. He got no farther. Even had he remembered the words his voice could never have risen above the laughter, which continued as long as he remained on his feet.

He retired at length in dudgeon, and Stephen called on Paul for a song. This went off better, only everybody stamped the time with his feet, so that the singer could neither be heard for the row nor seen for the dust. After that followed another "reading." This time the subject was a humorous one—"Ben Battle," by T. Hood. Every one, by the way, chose Hood. It was the only poetry-book to be had in the Fourth Junior. The reading progressed satisfactorily for the first two lines—indeed, until a joke occurred, and here the reader was so overcome with the humour of the thing that he broke into a laugh, and every time he tried to begin the next line he laughed before he could get it out, until at last it got to be quite as monotonous as watching the hyena at the Zoological Gardens. Finally he did get through the line, but in a voice so weak, wavering by reason of his efforts not to laugh, that the effect was more ludicrous than ever. He could get no farther, however. For the recollection of the joke that had passed, and the anticipation of the one that was coming, fairly doubled him up, and he let the book drop out of his hands in the middle of one of his convulsions.

The next performance was an "instrumental" one, which bade fair to be a great success. Four of the boys had learned to whistle "Home, Sweet Home" in parts, and were now about to ravish the audience with this time-honoured melody. They stood meekly side by side in a straight line facing the audience, waiting for the leader to begin, and screwing their mouths up into the proper shape. Just as the signal was given, and each had taken a long breath and was in the act of letting out, some lout in the audience laughed! The result may be imagined. The first note, which was to have been so beautiful, sounded just like the letting off of steam from four leaky safety-valves, and no effort could recover the melody. The more they tried the more they laughed. The more they laughed the more the audience roared. There they stood, with faces of mingled agony and mirth, frantically trying to get the sound out; but it never came, and they finally had to retire, leaving the audience to imagine what the effect of "Home, Sweet Home" might have been had they only got at it.

However, as the "dramatic" performance came next, the audience were comforted. The modest subject chosen was *Hamlet*.

Stephen, who was combining the duties of master of the ceremonies with those of president, rose and said to the company, "All turn round, and don't look till I tell you."

Of course every one pretended to turn round, and of course everybody looked as hard as he could. And they saw Bramble hop up on a chair and lower the gas, to represent night. And they saw Paul and Padger stick up two or three forms on end, to represent a castle. And they saw two other boys walk majestically on to the platform in ulsters and billycock hats, and their trousers turned up, and sticks in their hands to represent soldiers.

"Now you can turn round," cried Stephen.

They did turn round, just at the very moment when Bramble, attempting to lower the gas still further, turned it right out. The effect was remarkable. No one and nothing was visible, but out of the black darkness came the following singular dialogue:—

"*Who's there?*"

"Have you got a lucifer about you, any of you?"

"*Nay, answer me. Stand and unfold yourself.*"

"Don't be a fool (in agitated accents); you're shoving me off the platform."

"Why don't you light up?"

"*Long live the king.*"

"Ah, here's one. What's become of the chair?"

Next moment, amid great applause, the gas was re-lit, and the thrilling tragedy proceeded.

It went on all right till the ghost enters, and here another calamity occurred. Padger was acting ghost, dressed up in a long sheet, and with flour on his face. Being rather late in coming on, he did so at a very unghostlike pace, and in the hurry tripped up on the bottom of his sheet, falling flop on the platform, which, being none of the cleanest, left an impression of dust on his face and garment, which greatly added to the horror of his appearance. He recovered the perpendicular with the help of two soldiers and a few friends, and was about to proceed with his part, when the door suddenly opened and Mr Rastle appeared.

He had evidently not come to see the show—indeed he hardly seemed aware that a show was going on. His face was grave, and his voice agitated, as he said—

"Has any one here seen Loman?"

No one had seen him since breakfast that morning.

"Is Greenfield senior here?"

"Yes, sir," answered Oliver.

"Will you come with me to the Doctor at once, please?"

Oliver was out in the passage in a moment, and hurrying with the master to Dr Senior's study.

"I'm afraid," said Mr Rastle, as they went—"I'm afraid something has happened to Loman!"

Chapter Thirty Six.
Missing.

Slowly Oliver followed Mr Rastle to the Doctor's study with strange forebodings at heart.

What the "something that must have happened to Loman" could be, he could not conjecture; but the recollection of his unhappy schoolfellow's troubles and of his difficulties, and—worse still—of his dishonesty (for Oliver had no doubt in his mind that Loman had taken the examination paper), all came to his mind now with terrifying force.

Oliver had never been fond of Loman, as the reader knows, but somehow there are times when one forgets whether one is fond of another person or not, and Oliver felt as if he would give anything now to be sure—

Here he was at the Doctor's study.

Dr Senior was standing at the fireplace with a very grave look, holding a letter in his hand.

"Greenfield," said he, the moment the boy entered, "when did you see Loman last?"

"Last night, sir, after preparation."

"He was not in his class this morning?"

"No, sir—he sent down word he had a headache."

"You saw him last night—where?"

"In my study."

The Doctor paused uncomfortably, and Mr Rastle put in a question.

"Are you and Loman great friends?"

"No, we are not friends."

"Does he often come to your study?"

"No, sir. Very rarely."

"May I ask, Greenfield," said the Doctor, "why he was in your study last night?"

This was getting close quarters for Oliver, who, however, had made up his mind he must, if put to it, say all he knew.

"He came to—to ask me about something."

"Yes, what?"

"He made me promise not to tell any one."

"Greenfield," said the Doctor, seriously, "Loman has disappeared from Saint Dominic's. Why, I cannot say. If you know of anything which will account for this proceeding, you owe it to yourself, to me, and to your schoolfellow, who may yet be recovered, to speak plainly now."

The Doctor's voice, which had been stern when he began to speak, betrayed his emotion before the sentence was ended, and Oliver surrendered without further demur.

"He came to borrow some money," he replied.

"Yes," said the Doctor.

Oliver had nothing for it but to narrate all he knew of Loman's recent money difficulties, of his connection with Cripps, and of his own and Wraysford's share in helping him out of his straits.

The Doctor heard all he had to say, putting in a question here and there, whenever by the boy's manner there seemed to be anything kept in the background which wanted some coaxing to bring out.

"And he wanted to borrow more money yesterday, then?"

"Yes, sir. He said Cripps had found there was another sovereign owing, and had threatened to expose Loman before you and the whole school unless he got it at once. But I fancy that must only have been an excuse."

"Yes. And did you lend him the pound?"

"I hadn't got it to lend," replied Oliver, "the last lot had completely cleared me out."

"There is one other question I want to ask you, Greenfield," said the Doctor, fidgeting with the paper in his hand. "How long do you suppose this has been going on?"

"I don't know, sir—but should think for some time."

"What makes you think so?"

"Because," replied Oliver—and there was no help for it—"because at the time I spoke to you about the scrape my young brother got into at the lock, last autumn, Loman was very thick with Cripps."

"Indeed? That was just before the Nightingale examination, was it not?"

"Yes, sir," said Oliver, beginning to feel the ground very uncomfortable all round. Here he was telling tales right and left, and no help for it. Surely the Doctor was carrying it a little too far.

"Do you suppose Loman was in debt at that time?"

"I have no idea," replied the boy, wondering whatever that had to do with Loman's disappearance now.

"You wonder why I ask this question," said the Doctor, apparently reading the boy's thoughts. "This letter will explain. I will read it to you, as you may be able to throw some light on it. I received it just now. It is from Cripps."

"Hon. Sir,—I take the liberty of informing you that one of your young gents, which his name is Mister Loman, is a prig. He's been a regular down at my shop this twelve month, and never paid a farthing for his liquor. More than that, he's been a-drawing money from me up to thirty-five pounds, which I've got his promissory note due last Micklemas. He said he was a-going to get a Nightingale or something then that would pay it all off, and I was flat enough to believe him. If that ain't enough, he's a-been and played me nicely over a rod I sold him. I might have persecuted him over that job but I didn't. He cracked it to rights, and then tries to pass it back on me for same as when he got it, and if I hadn't a-been a bit sharper nor some folk I should have been clean done. This is to tell you I ain't a-going to stand it no longer, and if I don't get my money there'll be a rumpus up at the school which won't be pleasant for none of you. So the shortest cut is to send on the money sharp to your humble servant, Ben Cripps.

"P.S.—I've wrote and told the young swell I've put you on the job."

"It is evident," said Mr Rastle, "this letter has something to do with Loman's disappearance."

"Yes," said Oliver, "he was awfully frightened of you or his father getting to know about it all, sir."

"Foolish boy!" said the Doctor, with a half groan.

What little could be done at that late hour was done. Strict inquiries were made on all hands as to when and where the missing boy was last seen, and it was ascertained that he must have left Saint Dominic's that morning during early class time, when every one supposed him ill in bed with a headache.

But where had he gone, and with what object? A telegram was sent to his father, and the reply came back that the boy had not gone home, and that Mr Loman was on his way to Saint Dominic's. At the Maltby railway station no one had seen or heard anything of him.

Meanwhile, Mr Rastle had gone down to the Cockchafer to see Cripps. The landlord was not at home, but, said the potboy, was most likely "up along with the old 'un at the lock-'us." From which Mr Rastle gathered there was a chance of seeing Mr Cripps junior at the residence of Mr Cripps senior, at Gusset Lock-house, and thither he accordingly went. Mr Cripps junior was there, sweetly smoking, and particularly amiable.

In answer to Mr Rastle's inquiries, he made no secret of his belief that the boy had run away for fear of exposure.

"You see, Mister," said he, "I don't like a-getting young folk into trouble, but when it comes to robbing a man downright, why, I considers it my dooty to give your governor the tip and let him know."

Mr Rastle had no opinion to offer on this question of morals. What he wanted to know was whether Cripps had seen the boy that day, or had the slightest idea what had become of him.

Mr Cripps laughed at the idea.

"Not likely," he said, "he'd tell me where he was a-goin' to, when he'd got thirty-five-pound of mine in his pocket, the young thief. All I can say is, he'd better not show up again in a hurry till that little bill's squared up." And here Mr Cripps relapsed into quite a state of righteous indignation.

"Wait till he do come back, I says," he repeated. "I'll be on him, mister, no error. I'll let the folks know the kind of young gents you turn out up at your school, so I will."

Mr Rastle took no notice of all this. He admitted to himself that this man had some reason for being disagreeable, if Loman had really absconded with such a debt as he represented.

"Thirty-five pounds," continued Cripps, becoming quite sentimental over his wrongs, "and if you won't believe me, look at this. This here bit of paper's all I've got in return for my money—all I've got!"

And so saying he took from his pocket and exhibited to Mr Rastle the very promissory note, signed by Loman, which he had pretended to tear up and burn the last time that unhappy boy was at the Cockchafer.

Had Mr Rastle known as much as the reader knows he would not have wasted more time over Mr Cripps. He would have seen that, whatever had happened to the boy, Mr Cripps's purpose was to make money by it. But he did not know all, and looked at the bill with mingled astonishment and sorrow as an important piece of evidence.

"He really owed you this?" he asked.

"He did so—every brass farthing, which I've waited ever since Michaelmas for it, mister. But I ain't a-going to wait no longer. I must have my money slap down, I let you know, or somebody shall hear of it."

"But he has paid you something?" said Mr Rastle, remembering Oliver's account of the loan of eight pounds.

"Has he?" exclaimed Cripps, satirically. "Oh, that's all right, only I ain't seen it, that's all."

"Do you mean he hasn't paid you anything?" demanded Mr Rastle, becoming impatient with his jocular manner.

"Of course, as you says so, it ain't for me to say the contrairy; but if you hadn't told me, I should have said he ain't paid me one brass farthing, so now."

"Dear me, dear me!" exclaimed Mr Rastle. Of course, if that was so, Loman must have borrowed the eight pounds from Oliver on false pretences, and kept it for his own use.

"I tell you what," broke in Mr Cripps, in the midst of this meditation, "I don't want to do nothing unpleasant to you, or the governor, or anybody. What I say is, you'd better see this little bill put square among you, and then the thing can be kept quiet, do you see? It would be awkward for you to have a regular shindy about it, my man, but that's what it'll come to if I don't get my money."

This declaration Mr Cripps delivered in a solemn voice which was his nearest approach to earnestness. But he was mistaken in expecting Mr Rastle to be much affected or overawed by it. On the contrary, it gave that gentleman a new insight into his acquaintance's character, which decided him that a prolongation of this interview would neither be pleasant nor profitable.

So Mr Rastle abruptly turned and went, much to the regret of Cripps, who had not half spoken his mind yet.

Returning to the school, the master reported all he had to say, which was not much. There an anxious night was spent by the masters and the one or two boys who were in their confidence in the matter.

The half hope that Loman might return of his own accord before night was quickly dispelled. Bed-time came, and no signs of him. Later his father arrived, anxious and excited, and was closeted for some time with the Doctor.

Meanwhile everything that could be done at that time of night was done. The Maltby newspapers were communicated with, and the police. Unpleasant as it was, the masters decided the right thing to do was to make the matter known at once, and not damage the chance of the boy's discovery by any attempt to keep his disappearance quiet.

At dawn next day an organised search was begun, and inquiries were started in every direction. Mr Cripps, among others, once more received the honour of a visit, this time from Mr Loman himself, who, greatly to the astonishment of the worthy landlord, called for his son's promissory note, which, being produced, he paid without a word. Cripps was fairly taken aback by this unexpected piece of business, and even a trifle disconcerted. It never suited him to be quite square with anybody, and now that Mr Loman had paid every farthing that could be claimed against his son, he did not like the look of Mr Loman at all, and he liked it less before the interview ended. For Mr Loman (who, by the way, was a barrister by profession) put his man that morning through a cross-examination which it wanted all his wits to get over creditably. As it was, he was once or twice driven completely into a corner, and had to acknowledge, for the sake of telling one lie, that the last twenty statements he had made had been lies too. Still Mr Loman kept at him. Now he wanted to know exactly how often his son had visited the Cockchafer? When he was there last? When the time before that? What he had done during his visits? Had he played cards? With whom? With Cripps? Had he lost? Had Cripps won? Had Cripps gone on letting him run up a score and lose money, even though he got no payment? Why had Cripps done so? Where had he expected to get payment from in the end?

Altogether it was hot quarters for Cripps that morning, and once or twice he struck completely, and putting himself on his dignity, declared "he wasn't a-going to be questioned and brow-beated as if he was a common pickpocket!" which objection Mr Loman quietly silenced by saying "Very well," and turning to go, a movement which so terrified the worthy publican that he caved in at once, and submitted to further questions.

Mr Loman then followed up his advantage by finding out all he could about the companions whom his son had been in the habit of meeting on the occasion of his visits to the Cockchafer. What were their names, occupations, addresses, and so on? Cripps, if any one had told him twenty-four hours ago that he would be meekly divulging all this information to any one in his own house, would have scoffed at the idea. But there was something about Mr Loman's voice, and Mr Loman's eye, and Mr Loman's note-book, which was too much for the publican, and he submitted like a lamb.

In due time the ordeal was over, and Mr Loman said he would now go and call upon these young gentlemen, and see what they had to say, and that Mr Cripps would most likely hear from him again.

Altogether the landlord of the Cockchafer had hardly ever passed such an uncomfortable morning.

Meanwhile the other searchers, among whom were Oliver and Wraysford, were busy.

For a whole day there came no news of the missing boy. No one could be met who had seen him or heard of him. Neither in Maltby nor up the river, nor in the country roads round, could any tidings of him be found. Towards evening those who remained anxiously behind began to entertain fresh fears. Had the boy been merely running away, some one would surely have seen him or heard of him. Had anything worse happened to him?

Mr Loman and the police-inspector paid a hurried visit to the boathouse. Had the boy been there? No, no one had been there for two days. They followed the paths through the woods, asking at every cottage and stopping every passer-by. But no, no one knew anything. No boat had passed through the lock, no passenger on foot had gone past it.

The night came, and with it most of the searchers returned, dejected and worn-out.

The school was strangely silent. Not a sound could be heard in the passages or class-rooms. Nothing but the heavy rain, which now began to fall dismally upon the roof and windows of the old school-house.

Boys who heard it shuddered, and their minds went out into the dark wet night after their lost schoolfellow, wherever he might be.

Where was he now? they wondered, and how was he faring?

"Has Greenfield returned?" asked the Doctor, as about ten o'clock the masters and Mr Loman met for the mockery of supper in the head master's study.

"No," said Mr Jellicott. "I have just been inquiring. He has not returned."

"Strange," said the Doctor; "which direction did he take?"

"Up towards Grandham," said Wraysford; "we went together as far as the cross roads, and then I went off on the Dallingford road and back by the river."

"He ought to be back now," said the Doctor, looking concerned.

"There is no railway or coach from Grandham," suggested Mr Rastle; "he would have to walk back most likely."

"And in this rain!" said the Doctor.

"Perhaps," said Wraysford, "he may have heard something."

It was a cheery suggestion. If it could but be true!

"He would have telegraphed," said Mr Loman.

"There is no telegraph office there," said the Doctor; "the Grandham people have to come here or to Dallingford to telegraph."

They waited an hour, but Oliver did not return.

The night became more and more stormy. The bleak February wind whistled among the chimneys, and the hard rain beat pitilessly at the windows and on the gravel walk outside.

The Doctor rose and pulled up the blind and looked out. It was a dreary prospect. The rain had turned to sleet, and the wind was growing fast to a gale. The trees round the house creaked and groaned beneath it.

"It is a dreadful night," said the Doctor. "Those two poor boys!"

No one else said anything. The storm grew fiercer and fiercer. Boys in their dormitories sit up in bed and listened to the roar of the wind as it howled round the house. And that silent party in the Doctor's study never once thought of seeking rest. Midnight came; but no Oliver, no Loman—and the storm as furious as ever.

Presently there came a soft knock at the door, which made every one start suddenly as the door opened.

It was Stephen in his night-shirt. He, like every one else, had been awakened by the storm. Oliver was the monitor of his dormitory; and now for the first time the boy missed his elder brother. Where was Oliver? he asked. No one could say. He had been out all day, and no one had seen him since he got back.

This was enough for Stephen. With bounding heart and quivering lips he sprang from his bed and hurried down stairs. There was a light in the Doctor's study; and there he went.

The boy's alarm and terror on hearing that his brother had not returned was piteous to see. He begged to be allowed to go and look for him, and only the Doctor's authoritative command could put him from this purpose. But nothing would induce him to return to bed; so Wraysford fetched him an ulster to keep out the cold.

The night wore on, by inches; and the storm raged outside with unabated wildness.

More than once the impulse had seized Wraysford to sally out at all risks and look for his friend. But what *could* one do in a night like this, with a blinding sleet full in one's face, and a wind which mocked all attempts at progress or shouting!

No, there was nothing for it but to sit patiently and await daylight.

One, two, three o'clock came, and still nothing but the storm. Stephen crouched closer up beside Wraysford, and the elder boy, as he put his arm round the younger, could feel how his chest heaved, and how his teeth chattered.

"You're cold, old boy," said he, kindly.

"No, I'm not, Wray," said the boy, with a gulp; "but don't talk, Wray, I—"

The next instant Stephen, with a sudden cry, had bounded to his feet and rushed to the window.

"Some one called!" he cried.

Chapter Thirty Seven.
Found!

The little company of watchers sprang to their feet with one accord and listened, as Stephen wildly flung up the window. The storm burst into the room as he did so, with all its vehemence, drenching those who stood near, and deafening every one with its roar. But no other sound could be heard. Stephen, heedless of the weather, stood motionless with his head out of the window, listening. Alas! it must have been a false hope after all— a brother's fancy.

"A mistake, I fear," said Dr Senior. "Greenfield, I think you had better close the window. It will be daylight in—"

He had not time to finish his sentence, for with a sudden exclamation and a shout of, "There it is again; come, Wray!" the boy had leapt from the low window, half clad as he was, into the garden.

For Wraysford to follow him was the work of an instant. Mr Rastle and Roach the porter did the same, while the others went hurriedly out into the passage to the hall door. Close as they were to one another, Wraysford lost sight of Stephen for a moment in the blinding sleet which dashed full in their faces. But he heard him shouting a few yards off, and was at his side the same moment.

"No use shouting," said he, "against the wind."

"I *must* shout!" exclaimed Stephen, calling out once more.

"Where—what did you hear?" asked Wraysford.

"Some one shouting. I'm positive of it!" said the boy, plunging forward.

"Stand still, and listen again," said Wraysford; "we may be going all wrong."

It was all he could do to keep the younger boy still for a few seconds. What ages those seconds seemed!

A voice somewhere? No, only Mr Rastle and Roach coming up behind.

"Well?" inquired the master, breathlessly.

"Hush!" said Stephen, turning his head to the wind to listen.

What a wind it was! Surely it would beat any voice to shreds!

"We may as well go on," said the boy, impatiently.

"Wait a second or two longer," said Wraysford.

Scarcely had he spoken when, joyous sound! there came on the wind from somewhere what sounded like a feeble shout!

In an instant all four bounded forward and were once more lost in the storm.

But they had hope, and every moment, a night like this, was precious. They groped down the garden walk, and towards the meadow, shouting as they went. Then presently they halted again and listened.

Yes there was the call again, and nearer. Thank Heaven! they were on the right track. On they went once more. Another shout! Nearer still!

Oh, for a lull in the tempest, that they might give one shout back!

"Try," said Mr Rastle, "they may hear it. Here, Roach, come and shout—one, two, three, and a—"

What a shout it was! The wind got hold of it as if it had been a sparrow's twitter, and tossed it mockingly over their heads and far away behind them, who knows where?

"It's no go," said Wraysford. "Hullo, here's the meadow ditch. Hadn't we better follow it up and down? Stephen and I will take the left."

Once more, as they turned, a shout!

"Oh, be quick!" cried Stephen. "Where does it come from? Come, Wray, quick!"

They might as well have tried to fly as run against that wind; but they crawled rapidly forward.

Suddenly, close at their side, rose the shout again. With a bound the two boys were over the ditch, and in another moment a fourfold shout proclaimed that the wanderers were found!

Oliver and Loman were crouching under a tree, the former without coat or waistcoat, which he had thrown round the shivering and now senseless form of his companion.

It was no time for words, either of joy or explanation; time enough for that when every one was safe indoors. Mr Rastle and Roach between them carried Loman, while Oliver, in scarcely better plight, was helped along by his brother and friend.

"Is it far?" he asked, faintly.

"No, old man; that light there is Saint Dominic's."

"Is it? I didn't know that when I shouted; I thought we were miles away."

"Oh, no! Hold up, old boy; we're just there."

And so this strange procession returned before the wind to Saint Dominic's, and when, a few minutes later, watchers and rescuers and rescued all gathered in the Doctor's study, Oliver, as well as Loman, was insensible.

It was some days before the true story of that terrible night could be told, and then Oliver only told it briefly.

Late in the afternoon, as he was about to turn back, he said, he heard from a farmer's boy that he had seen a stranger that morning asleep under a hedge about a mile off. Vague as this information was, it decided Oliver at once to go forward, which he did. As might have been expected, there was no trace of the "stranger" at the hedge, and no amount of searching along it could discover any clue. Still, he did not like to turn back while a chance remained. He went on towards Grandham, inquiring of everybody and looking everywhere.

At last—it was getting dusk—he entered a field across which ran a footpath which led direct to Grandham Green. He was half way across, wondering if he could by any chance find a cart or vehicle of any kind to drive him back to Saint Dominic's, when at the other side of the field he suddenly caught sight of a figure getting up from under the hedge and moving quickly away. He instantly and instinctively gave chase. The other, seeing he was discovered, began to run too. It was Loman. Oliver called to him to stop, but he paid no heed. He continued to run as long as he could, and then, like a hunted animal, turned at bay.

Oliver told very few all that had passed when finally he did come up with the wanderer. His first impression, judging from the unhappy boy's strange and excited manner, was that he had gone out of his mind. He appeared reckless and desperate at first, and determined to resist all attempts to bring him back. He would sooner die than go back to Saint Dominic's, he said. What right had Oliver to interfere with him and dog him in this way? He had a right to go where he chose, and no one should stop him. Oliver let him talk on, not attempting to reply, and avoiding all appearance of using force to detain him.

This wise policy had its effect. In time the poor fellow, who was really suffering more from hunger and fatigue (he had not had a morsel of food since the afternoon before) than from anything else, quieted down, and gave up further resistance. Oliver told him, in as few words as he could, of the distress which his disappearance had caused at Saint Dominic's and to his parents, and besought him to return quietly, promising forgiveness for the past, and undertaking that all would be made right if he would only come home.

Loman listened to all doggedly. "You're humbugging me!" he said. "You know I stole that paper?"

"Oh, don't talk of that!" cried Oliver. "Do come back!"

"You know—can't you get me something to eat?"

As he said this he sunk down with a groan upon the grass. Oliver started wildly to rush to the nearest cottage. As he did so, however, a doubt crossed his mind, and he said, "You'll promise to wait here, will you?"

"Oh, yes! be quick."

Oliver flew on the wings of the wind towards the village. There was a cottage a few hundred yards away. As he neared it, he cast one look back. The wretched boy was on his feet, hurrying away in an opposite direction.

Another chase ensued, though only a short one. For Loman was in no condition to hold out long. Oliver half led, half dragged him to Grandham, where at last he procured food, which the unhappy fugitive devoured ravenously. Then followed another talk, far more satisfactory than the last. Restored once more in body and mind, Loman consented without further demur to accompany Oliver back to Saint Dominic's, but not before he had unburdened his mind of all that was on it.

Oliver implored him not to do it now, to wait till he got back, and then to tell all to his father, not to him. But the poor penitent was not to be put off. Until he had confessed all he would not stir a foot back to the school.

Then Oliver heard all that sad story with which the reader is now familiar. How that first act of fraud about the rod had been the beginning of all this misery. How Cripps had used his advantage to drive the boy from one wickedness and folly to another—from deceit to gambling, from gambling to debt, from debt to more deceit, and so on. How drinking, low company, and vicious habits had followed. How all the while he was trying to keep up appearances at the school, though he saw that he was gradually becoming an object of dislike to his fellows. How he had staked everything—his whole hope of getting free from Cripps—on the result of the Nightingale examination; and how, when the critical moment came, he yielded to the tempter and stole the paper.

"And you can fancy how punished I was when, after all, the Doctor missed the paper and altered the questions, Greenfield. I was so taken aback that I didn't even answer as well as I could. And then I lost the paper I had stolen—couldn't find it anywhere, and for weeks I was in constant terror lest it should turn up. Then I saw the fellows were all suspecting you to be the thief, and you know how meanly I took advantage of that to hide my own guilt. Oh, Greenfield, what a wretch, what a miserable wretch I have been!"

"Poor fellow!" said Oliver, with true sympathy. "But, I say, do let's be going back, it's getting late, and looks as if it might rain."

"I *must* tell you the rest, Greenfield, please. You're the only fellow I can tell it to. Somehow I think if I'd had a friend like you all the last year I shouldn't have gone wrong as I have. How I used to envy you and Wraysford, always together, and telling one another your troubles! Well, of course, after the Nightingale exam, things were worse than ever. I'd given Cripps a bill, you know, a promise to pay in September. I don't know anything about bills, but he made me sign it. Of course I couldn't pay when it came due, and had to make all sorts of excuses and tell all sorts of lies to get him to give me more time; as if I was more likely to pay later on than then! But, somehow, if I could only get the thing off my mind for the present, I felt that was all I cared about. He gave in at last, and I was able to pay it off bit by bit. But I was in constant terror all that term of his coming up to Saint Dominic's. You know he did come once, at the football match against Landfield, and I thought I was done for."

Here Loman paused a moment, and Oliver, seeing that he was determined to tell his story to the end, waited patiently till he continued.

"Then there was that Waterston exam. I fancied I might get that if I worked. Ass that I was to think, after all my wasted time and sin, I had any chance against you or Wraysford! I tried to work, but soon gave it up, and went on going down to the Cockchafer instead, to keep Cripps in good humour, till I was quite a regular there. You know what a fearful hash I made of the exam. I could answer nothing. That very day Cripps had sent up to threaten to tell the Doctor everything unless I paid what I still owed. I had paid off all the bill but eight pounds. I had got some of it from home, and some of it by gambling; I'd paid off all but eight pounds. You know, Greenfield, who lent me that."

"I'm thankful we were able to do it," said Oliver.

"If you'd known how I hated you and despised myself over that eight pounds you would hardly have been glad. Everything was hateful. I took the money down to Cripps and paid it him. He pretended at first that he wouldn't take it; and then when he did, and I asked him to give me back my promissory note, he laughed at me. I nearly went mad, Greenfield, at the thought of not being clear after all. At length he did make believe to give in, and produced what I thought was the bill, and tore it up in my presence. I couldn't see it, but he read it out aloud, and I had no doubt it was actually the thing. I was so grateful I actually felt happy. But then came the discovery of that miserable exam paper. I must have left it in my Juvenal last September, and forgotten all about it. I was certain the Doctor knew quite well I was the thief, but I denied it and tried feebly to put it on you. Then everybody cut me; but I hoped still all might blow over in time. But every day it became harder to bear; I should have had to confess at last, I believe. Then came

Cripps's final villainy. He had never destroyed my bill after all, but now calmly claimed the whole amount."

"The scoundrel!" exclaimed Oliver, indignantly.

"I had no receipts to show what I had paid, and of course was at his mercy. This last move really drove me half crazy. I daren't tell any one about it. I was too desperate to think of anything but running away and hiding somewhere. I had no money. I came to you with a lie to try to borrow a pound, so that I might go somewhere by train. You couldn't do it, and so I had to walk, and—and—oh! Greenfield, what shall I do? what will become of me?"

"My dear fellow," said Oliver, laying his hand on the unhappy boy's arm, "we'll go back together, and I can promise you you'll find nothing but kindness and forgiveness when you get back. If I wasn't sure of that, I wouldn't urge you to come. There! I wish you could have seen your poor father's face last night."

Loman held out no longer; and, indeed, it was high time to think of moving, for the afternoon was closing in and rain was already beginning to fall.

Loman was in no condition for walking, nor, indeed, was Oliver, who had been on his feet since early morning. A farmer's cart was with some difficulty found, which happened to be going a good part of the distance, and in this the two boys late that afternoon ensconced themselves. They talked little at first, and presently not at all. Each had his own thoughts, and they were serious enough to occupy them for a much longer journey.

Night fell presently, soon after they had started, and with it the rain and wind came heavily. There was little enough protection for these two worn-out ones in an empty open cart, but what they could get from an old wrap and some boards they secured.

As the storm grew worse this poor shelter became quite useless, and the two boys suffered all the horrors of a bitter exposure.

Loman, who had got a cough already, was the first to show distress, and he soon became so cold and numbed that Oliver grew alarmed. They would be better walking than sitting still in that jolting cart a night like this.

So, much against their own inclination and the advice of the carman, who characterised the proceedings as "tomfoolery," they alighted, and attempted to take the short cut across the fields to Saint Dominic's.

Short cut, indeed! It was indeed a sarcastic name for the road those two boys took that terrible night. Oliver could never recollect all that happened those few hours. He was conscious of the tremendous storm, of the hopeless losing of their way, and of Loman's relapse into a state of half-unconsciousness, in the midst of which he constantly begged to be allowed to lie down and sleep.

To prevent this was Oliver's principal occupation during that fearful time. More than once he was forced into a hand-to-hand struggle to keep his companion from his purpose. To let him lie down and sleep on such a night would be, he knew, to leave him to certain death. At any cost he must be kept moving. At last the storm fairly vanquished them. Even Oliver began to grow half-hearted in his determination. He took off his own coat and waistcoat and pat them on his comrade, who by this time was stupid with cold and exhaustion. A few minutes longer and both might have given themselves up, when suddenly there flickered a light before them. All Oliver could do was to shout. He had no power left to drag Loman farther, and leave him he would not. He shouted, and the reader knows who heard that shout, and what the answer was.

Such was Oliver's story, and it needed little amplification. If it had, the only boy who could have added to it was in no position to do so. For four weeks after that night

Loman lay ill with rheumatic fever, so ill that more than once those who watched him despaired of his recovery. But he did recover, and left Saint Dominic's a convalescent, and, better still, truly penitent, looking away from self and his own poor efforts to Him, the World's Great Burden Bearer, whose blood "cleanseth us from all sin."

His schoolfellows saw him no more; did not know, indeed, when he left them. Only one of them shook hands with him at the door of the old school as he went. That boy was Oliver Greenfield.

Chapter Thirty Eight.
Good-Bye to Saint Dominic's.

And now, reader, we are at the end of our story, and there only remain the usual "last words" before we say good-bye.

Saint Dominic's flourishes still, and only last season beat the County by five wickets! The captain on that occasion was a fellow called Stephen Greenfield, who carried his bat for forty-eight in the first innings. He is a big fellow, is the captain, and has got a moustache. Though he is the oldest boy at Saint Dominic's, every one talks of him as "Greenfield junior." He is vastly popular, and fellows say there never was such a good Sixth at the school since the days of his brother, Greenfield senior, five years ago. The captain is an object of special awe among the youngsters of the Fourth Junior, who positively quake in their shoes whenever his manly form appears in the upper corridor.

These youngsters, by the way, are still the liveliest section of Saint Dominic's. The names Guinea-pig and Tadpole have died out, and left behind them only the Buttercups and Daisies, who, however, are as fierce rivals and as inky scamps as even their predecessors were. There is a lout of a fellow in the Fourth Senior called Bramble, who is extremely "down" on these juveniles, always snubbing them, and, along with one Padger, a friend of his, plotting to get them into trouble. But somehow they are not much afraid of Bramble, whereat Bramble is particularly furious, and summons Padger to a "meeting" about once a week in his study, there to take counsel against these irreverent Buttercups and Daisies.

About the only other fellow the reader will recollect is Paul, now in the Sixth, a steady-going sort of fellow, who, by the way, has just won the Nightingale Scholarship, greatly to the delight of his particular friend the captain.

Last year the Fifth tried to revive an old institution of their Form, in the shape of a newspaper entitled the *Dominican*, directed chiefly against the members of the Sixth. But somehow the undertaking did not come off. The *Dominican* was a very mild affair for one thing, and there was nothing amusing about it for another thing, and there was a good deal offensive about it for another thing; and for another thing, the captain ordered it to be taken down off the wall on the first day of its appearance, and announced that if he had any more of this nonsense he would thrash one or two whose names he mentioned, and knock one or two others out of the first eleven.

The *Dominican* has not appeared since.

The big cricket match against the County I spoke of just now was a famous event for more reasons than one. The chief reason, of course, was the glorious victory of the old school; but another reason, almost as notable, was the strange muster of old boys who turned up to witness the exploits of the "youngsters."

There was Tom Braddy, for instance, smoking a big cigar the size of a pencil-case, looking the picture of a snob. And with him a vacant-looking young man with a great crop of whiskers on his puffy cheeks. His name was Simon. The great idea of these two worthies seemed to be to do the grand before their posterity. They were convinced in their own minds that in this they were completely successful, but no one else saw it.

Boys took a good deal more interest in a lame gentleman present, who was cracking jokes with everybody, and hobbling about from one old crony to another in a manner that was perfectly frisky. Every one seemed to like Mr Pembury, and not a *few* to be afraid of him. Perhaps that was because he was the editor of a well-known paper of the day, and every one likes to be on good terms with an editor.

Then there were a batch of fellows whose names we need hardly enumerate, who had run over from Oxford, or Cambridge, or London for the day, and who got into clusters between the innings and talked and laughed a great deal over old times, when "Bully did this," and "Rick did that," and so on. A nice lot of fellows they looked on the whole, and one or two, so people said, were doing well.

But among these *the* lions of the day were two friends who strolled about arm-in-arm, and appeared far more at home in Saint Dominic's even than the boys themselves. One of them was the big brother of the captain—a terrible fellow by all accounts. He rowed in the boat of his 'Varsity the last year he was at Cambridge, and since then he has been called to the bar, and no one knows what else! People say Oliver Greenfield is a rising man; if so, we may hear of him again. At any rate in the eyes of the admiring youngsters of Saint Dominic's he was a great man already.

So was his friend Wraysford, a fellow of his college, and a "coach" for industrious undergraduates. He does not look like a tutor, certainly, to judge by his jovial face and the capers he persisted in cutting with some of his old comrades of years ago. But he is one, and Saint Dominic's Junior eyed him askance shyly, and thought him rather more learned and formidable a person than the old Doctor himself.

No one enjoyed themselves on that day more than these two, who prowled about and visited every nook and cranny of the old place—studies, passages, class-rooms, Fourth Junior and all.

The match is over, the jubilations of victory have subsided, and one by one the visitors depart. Among the last to leave are Oliver and Wraysford; they have stayed to dine with the Doctor, and when at last they do turn their backs on the old school it is getting late.

Stephen accompanies them down to the station. On the way they pass the well-known Cockchafer. The old board is still there, but a new name is upon it.

"Hullo! what's become of Cripps?" asked Wraysford.

"Oh! he's gone," said Stephen. "Didn't you know?"

"No! When was that?"

"The very time you and Noll went up to Cambridge. The magistrates took away his licence for allowing gambling to go on at his house. He stuck on at the lock-house for some time, and then disappeared suddenly. They said he was wanted for some bit of swindling or other. Anyhow, he's gone."

"And a very good riddance too," says Oliver.

"So it is," replies Stephen. "By the way, Noll, what's the last news of Loman?"

"Oh, I meant to tell you. He's coming home; I had a letter from him a week or two ago. He says the four or five years' farming and knocking about in Australia have pulled him together quite; you know how ill he was when he went out?"

"So he was," says Wraysford.

"He's coming home to be near his father and mother. He's been reading law, he says, out in the backwoods, and means to go into his father's office."

"I'm glad he's coming home," says Wraysford. "Poor fellow! I wonder when he'll come to this old place again."

A silence follows, and Oliver says, "When he does, I tell you what: we must all make up a jolly party and come down together and help him through with it."

"Well, old man!" said Stephen, taking his brother's arm, "if it hadn't been for you, he—"

"Hullo, I say! there's the train coming!" breaks out Oliver. "Look alive, you fellows, or we shall be late!"

The End.

Printed in Great Britain
by Amazon